CW01067228

A GHOST FOR A CLUE

IMMORTOLOGY, BOOK 1

C.L.R. DRAECO

AMARANTH PUBLISHING

Copyright © 2020 Amaranth Publishing

Written by C.L.R. Draeco

Cover Art by Vincent Trinidad

All rights reserved.

www.clrdraeco.com

To A, N, and R
Thank you for believing

1

AN EMPTY CHAIR

Yesterday, no one had given that empty chair a thought. Now, everyone who entered the room regarded it like some quiet stranger dressed in black. The ergonomic piece of furniture received respectful nods and solemn shakes of the head. One had given it an uncertain glance and made sure to steer clear of it.

Yesterday, the person who'd always sat in that chair had cracked about a half dozen dirty jokes to get himself through another workday. Now, he was in a morgue. Dead at thirty-six.

2032. *And a person can still die from a car crash. Bloody hell.*

I stared at the empty chair next to me, still in disbelief.

"Hey, Bram," came a husky greeting from behind me. It was Sienna, our senior technician, the aroma of her hot mug of coffee trailing her as she breezed by.

I nodded back a greeting.

She settled down at her workstation two seats away from mine, her vivid-green hair the closest thing we had to nature in our gray-carpeted space. Her clothes, as usual, were the color of asphalt. She took a sip from her steaming cup and stared at the empty chair between us.

For a couple of minutes, that's how it stayed, with us facing but not minding each other, our thoughts lost in what death had stolen from us—or so I thought, until the sound of Sienna's chuckle, muffled by her mug, cut into the silence.

"It's just going to be like this between us from now on, isn't it?" she said, her amusement lighting up her big brown eyes.

"What?"

"With Franco gone, you and I. We'll have nothing to talk about."

My brow knotted. Was that her way of saying she was going to miss him? I shrugged, unsure of how to console her. "There's always work."

"Well, yeah." She flashed her confident, fresh-faced smile. "That's what we're here for."

I nodded. No other response came to mind.

She kept her eyes on me. Was she waiting for me to pick up the conversation? Or was she thinking of what else to say?

Jesus. Death was something people just weren't taught how to deal with. I broke eye contact and went back to staring at Franco's abandoned chair.

"You know what I'll miss most about him?" she asked.

"His being alive?"

She laughed. More than my comment deserved, I thought. "His silly pranks. You remember that time when he left really late just to set up the security guards? It was close to Halloween . . ."

I put on a smile and pretended to be interested as she recounted whatever it was. I didn't feel like reminiscing happy times right now, so I picked up the coffee mug from my desk and cradled it in my hands. I just wanted to sit quietly and lick my wounds without letting others know how much it hurt to have lost a good friend. A confidante. Someone who believed even broken dreams could be mended.

"Oh, god," she said and wiped the corner of her eye with her fingers. "Death can't ever come slow enough."

She was crying but still smiling. *I should've known.* A person could be bleeding without showing an open wound. Even though I'd always hidden my own wounds, I'd ended up scarred anyway.

Twist ties tightened around my tongue, so I got up, towering over the cubicle walls, and scanned the entire fluorescent-lit workstation. The hum of life went on despite the loss of a friend. Later tonight, we would all get together and give mournful pause; meanwhile, there were robots to be designed, prototypes to be tested, enhancements to be made. Everything was as busy today as it had been yesterday—but much quieter.

Francis Omkareshwar, the man whom we called Franco, was gone.

One thing he should have done last night was linger another minute to crack one last joke. Or maybe taken the elevator instead of the stairs. Whatever the case, coincidence had brought him at the worst time to some intersection where it had all ended—the aftermath marked by a flurry of posts, texts, and calls asking how and why and who or what was to blame.

It was death by coincidence. The only way it could have happened despite autonomous cars, robotic traffic cops, and every conceivable safety measure out there. A person could plan as much as he wanted to, but at the end of the day—

I sighed and sank back into my seat. It was like getting a warning that I was running out of time—but I didn't know what to do about it.

Sienna was right. *Death can't come slow enough.* I glanced at her; she was still sipping her coffee and staring at Franco's chair.

From the corner of my eye, I detected a lone, dark figure by the doorway. I turned to find our boss, Dave, standing there with arms crossed as he looked at the same piece of furniture. He rubbed a knuckle over his thick black mustache. "It's just like him to think it's funny to leave me with a bunch of losers like you."

Sienna made a quirky face at me, swiveled her seat towards her monitor, and got to work.

I smiled. I hadn't realized how friendly she was. Maybe

because Franco's rowdy sense of humor had always been blocking the view.

"Morrison, come with me," Dave barked.

My smile shriveled up, and my jaw muscles tightened as I trailed him towards the corridor. *Did I miss a deadline? Submit the wrong thing? Misunderstand his instructions?* Jesus. As spotless as I kept my employee record—and as much as I liked Dave—I feared a reprimand each time he called me in. Simple reflex, I assumed, because—well, I wanted to keep that record spotless.

Dave strode into the semiorganized mess that was his office. Despite the white walls and bright lights, the place seemed a lot darker after he faced me with a worried scowl.

"Tomorrow's when you fly out to JSC to present your designs?"

"To Dr. Grant, yeah." Bugger. *Is this about me working after hours without clearance?* "I didn't mean to stay so late the past few nights."

"What?"

"I've been fixing some of my designs. I know I should have asked you, but—"

Dave flicked aside my explanation like it was some annoying fly. "Take a seat." He settled down behind his almost-neat desk; one side was where he worked while the other held a mound of everything he still didn't have time for. "Didn't you just turn thirty?"

"Uh . . . yeah?" My tone had a *Why'd you ask?* built into it.

"But you've already applied to the astronaut corps three times and been rejected three times, then a couple of weeks ago, you applied again?" There was an unmistakable *Are you nuts?* built into that one.

I shrugged. "Anderson got in on his sixteenth try."

"You know that's not going to happen for you. So it's a better use of your time to focus on being the best robotics engineer and computer scientist out there."

"Don't forget mathematician." I rubbed an eyelid, like what he'd said was nothing more than dust in my eye.

He leveled his gaze at me. "And with all that under your belt, why keep knocking on a door that you know can't open for you?"

To let them know I'm still standing there, waiting. I leaned back and distanced myself from what he'd just said. The chair's leatherette upholstery squeaked. "Since when does NASA do this?"

"Do what?"

"Tell someone not to shoot for the stars."

"After that someone's overshot the goddamned stars. Plain and simple: You're too tall to be an astronaut. And NASA isn't ever going to shift that height limit, so—"

"You can't say that for sure. There's no equation you can use to predict that."

Dave paused before he grimaced, as though my argument were a slow-burn hot pepper. "Blasted math majors. You think you can plug everything into a formula."

"Because you can." It was a fact that always gave me comfort.

"Well, there's an equation out there—with budget cuts, logistics, and politics factored in—that's keeping you from realizing your dream."

"Time's also a factor." I'd gotten good at dodging every bullet aimed at shooting that dream down. "And after next year's Mars mission, there are bound to be others. So I'll wait. Things can change."

Dave scratched the space between his brows as he stared at me like a tired mechanic trying to change a flat tire whose lug nuts refused to budge. "Why don't you just change the goal, Morrison?"

One of my hidden scars began to throb. "Why are you telling me this?"

"Because it's been brought to my attention that you're reading too much into this presentation you've been asked to make."

"Brought to your atte—" I narrowed my eyes. "By whom?"

"It doesn't matter. The point is, your trip to Houston is about your robotic physiotherapist design. It's got nothing to do with your application. Have you rehearsed it?"

"My application?"

"Your goddamned presentation," Dave snarled. If he'd had an aneurysm, it would have burst right then. "Keep your eye on the ball. I want that design approved, and I don't want you winging it like you always do. So I'm asking again. Have you practiced your deck?"

I'd passed exams without studying much. I remembered facts without trying that hard. I got to work on time without waking up too early. "All right. Fine. I'll rehearse."

He narrowed his eyes. He knew me too well. "If you get this through, I'm giving you Project Husserl."

I jerked at the suggestion. "Husserl? Isn't that your baby?"

He stuck his pointer finger out at me like Uncle Sam recruiting for his army. "I'm telling you—you're no Shakespeare, no Michael Jordan, and you're no Hollywood heartthrob either. But when it comes to problems, you solve them. So don't you screw up tomorrow. I need Dr. Grant to push for your designs."

It sounded like praise. But I guessed he had to dampen it by telling me everything I wasn't. At least he didn't say I was no Warren Buffet—which I wasn't either. "I've got this, chief. I won't let you down."

"You'd better not. I'm scared you'll make a fool of yourself when you meet him. You'll probably fall over your own feet begging to get a chance to fly out there."

"I'm not going to beg—but I'm not quitting the dream either." I swallowed, suddenly reminded I'd lost one of my most ardent supporters. "I still think I've got better chances of getting it than dying in a car crash."

2

ALL THE WAY TO HOUSTON

MY FRIENDS, MY BOSS, AND EVEN MY NOT-SO-CLOSE FRIENDS HAD TOLD me not to read anything into it. *But why have me fly all the way to Houston from Langley Research Center, Virginia?* No one flew over a thousand miles to make a slide presentation anymore. There had to be more to this trip than just . . . that.

I tried not to get my hopes up, but there was no stopping it from rising as I sat alone in my autonomous cab. I'd chosen one of the front seats from among six captain chairs arranged in two comfortable rows. The panoramic windshield was moderately tinted. Swiping on the touchscreen dashboard, I turned it completely transparent.

An old surge of excitement hit me as my ride approached the long-and-low rectangular sign of the *Lyndon B. Johnson Space Center*. It glinted and gleamed at me like polished platinum against chrome with a proud spark of cerulean. I took a deep breath, let a moment pass, and managed to see it as it really was—plain block letters of dark gray on lighter gray with a blue NASA logo tucked at the corner. No grand, arching gateway. No colorful pennants. But when I'd first laid eyes on that sign as a kid over two decades ago, it had thrilled me more than Disneyland's entranceway.

I thought I'd grown to hate coming here almost as much as I loved it. The home of the astronaut corps. The home I'd been denied, three times over—and counting. I slid forward in my seat and craned my neck as I imagined the grand displays inside the structures with the same kid-like wonder I'd always had. Unlike Disneyland, this place wasn't made up of fantasy. Yet it had remained mine. A fantasy, out of reach.

As the cab neared Building One, I collapsed back into my seat and sighed. I'd been labeled a bunch of things—from stubborn to ridiculous to delusional—because I refused to let go of the dream. But what else could I be—after being told I couldn't be something even before I ever tried?

"You have arrived," said my driverless taxi. "We hope you had a pleasant ride."

With all my anxiety balled up into a knot in my belly, I made my way towards my official destination: The office of Dr. Rubin Grant.

I paused at the doorway of the physician and veteran astronaut, prepared to make a simple presentation that I knew from start to finish and back again. *This has nothing to do with my application. This has nothing to do with my application.* I had to convince myself before walking through the door. But my hands remained so goddamn sweaty. Maybe the fact that Grant was nothing less than the director of the Johnson Space Center had something to do with it.

Jesus Christ. I think part of me was terrified that Dave was right; at some point during the presentation, I just might lose it, kneel, and beg for a chance to at least go through training.

Armed with nothing but a laptop bag and a tightened gut, I wiped my palms against the side of my pants and stepped into the room. A tufted leather sofa to my right and two matching armchairs gave the place the faint smell of rich leather. Defining the area was a slightly worn Persian carpet, and scattered around were select, antique conversation pieces, most likely from the director's personal collection. The office was an oasis of the past amidst a place that helped shape the future.

At the far end of the room, behind an imposing desk of solid wood, sat the director, facing his computer monitor, his broad shoulders declaring his dominance even from a distance.

"Good morning, sir."

"Yes, good morning. Come in." The director stood up and hobbled over.

I stifled my surprise at seeing the man limping and using a cane. Tall, black, and with a commanding presence, Grant had been dubbed The Doberman in his youth. But now, in his early seventies with a bald head, salt-and-pepper beard, and leaning on a cane, he looked like a guard dog who no longer growled.

"Anterior knee pain," Grant said, as though apologizing for letting an admirer down with his crippled stance. "Comes and goes. I can't believe it's still a medical mystery in this day and age."

Though I stood a few inches taller, I felt no less intimidated.

"Please, have a seat." Grant sank into an armchair and triple-tapped the corner of what seemed like a regular coffee table made of solid hardwood and activated the monitor on its surface. For a moment, what looked like my personnel file flashed onscreen. I glimpsed my ID picture where I looked more cleanshaven than I normally was, my short brown hair neater than it usually was, and my eyes probably a little bluer than they really were.

Grant swiped the screen and flicked through old files of robot designs, which I'd come here to explain. "You've got interesting schematics for this initiative here. Tell me about this . . . 'Petey' and how you came to think of it."

I recited my well-rehearsed pitch. "Petey's the nickname I gave a physical therapist robot for astronauts hibernating in zero gravity. I know that scientists are fiddling with the genes that could allow humans to hibernate for long-distance space travel. And I learned that physical therapy on comatose patients prevents contractures and bone deformity. So I put two and two together and thought of Petey."

Grant nodded. "Hypo-metabolic torpor induced through a chemical trigger. So far, our most viable option."

I proceeded with my presentation—flawless, in my opinion—and silently thanked Dave as it came to its end.

Grant squinted at the monitor as though still making up his mind. "I'd like to take your designs forward."

"Wow. That's great." It was hard to sound enthusiastic, especially since my heart was quickly sinking. Everyone had been right all along. This meeting had nothing to do with my application. "Is it for the Mars mission?"

"Before we go any further . . ." The doctor picked up a cliPad—a digital, A4-sized clipboard—and handed it to me. "I'll need to get your signature for an NDA."

As an employee of NASA, I'd already signed a confidentiality agreement, but the director of JSC was no doubt about to lead me deeper into the rabbit hole. I scanned through the document, my anxiety rising, and signed, barely breathing.

"Very well. Now, allow me to tell you about a little-known project called Pangaea." Grant leaned back, and it seemed as though all the strain caused by his knee pain disappeared. "Decades before you were born, in anticipation of Apollo's last manned missions in the seventies, NASA had braced for the future by teaming up with the world's greatest powers, richest nations, and quite a number of, shall we say, prosperous individuals and private corporations. It's for a bold, magnificent, and utterly mad endeavor involving a fleet of self-sustaining starships that will set sail for the nearest inhabitable planet."

Sweet Jesus. "I'd heard rumors about something like this being kept under wraps, but—"

"At this point, rumors are as far as we want this to get. Technology is one thing best kept secret until it's ready for the world. And vice versa."

I blew out my cheeks and nodded. "So you'd want me to

finalize Petey for the mission? It would be an incredible honor, sir."

"Yes, yes. But I had you come here to talk about something else." He paused as his eyes narrowed in the slightest, as though what he was about to say was bound to scare me away.

Oh crap. *He's going to tell me to forget about applying.* I warned myself not to kneel and beg.

"You are one among thousands of individuals we are inviting to be part of Starfleet Pangaea. Many are called but few will accept —and even fewer will pass the final screening."

My breathing stopped for a moment, and I coughed to force my lungs back into their normal rhythm. "Excuse me, but . . . are you sure you have the right person?"

Grant's eyes twinkled in mild amusement as he flicked back to my file. "Bram Morrison. Born in Australia to an Aussie father and an English mother. Moved to America in 2007. Homeschooled in your early years." He cocked a brow. "Explains that trace of an accent. Single. No siblings. Do I have the right individual in my office?"

"Yes, but there must have been a mistake—"

"You've applied to be an astronaut four times?"

"And been rejected three times, so far, always for the same reason." I swallowed and thought back to that time when reality had come crashing down on me. "At sixteen, I hit six feet five and went past NASA's height limit. I thought my future was over, but . . ." I sighed. ". . . eventually, I decided on being the best robotics engineer I could be so I could still get a piece of me out there."

"But you never gave up." He raised his brow. "Is it because you can't take no for an answer? Or because you're used to getting what you want?"

"I'm just not one to give up on dreams, sir. My parents got bowled over by it, actually." I paused and grinned at the memory of me, sometime in grade school, asking my parents to draw up a step-by-step plan to make sure I'd get to be an astronaut someday. "They got worried the dream would pass, so every year, on my birthday—when they were still alive—they had me renew a promise not to let go of it. As the years went by, my conviction just grew stronger that it's where I could make a difference."

He nodded appreciatively. "What kind of difference?"

"I just know there's something waiting to be discovered. There's just so much space!" I chuckled, feeling like I was a kid again explaining myself to my mom and dad. "I have this picture in my head, like I'm a miner, drifting into a massive, dark cave looking for precious nuggets. And those stars—those gems that I see sparkling from down here—are nothing compared to what they'd look like out there." I stared in awe at the man. "And you've been there. You've seen what I can only dream about."

"And you'd like to go on a treasure hunt yourself."

"All my life," I said, almost in a whisper, and held my breath.

Grant gave a subtle shake of his head and said the very words I dreaded to hear. "NASA hasn't changed its height limit."

The knot in my belly constricted so tightly I was on the verge of throwing up.

But the director gave me the kind of hopeful smile a father gives to encourage a son. "This offer isn't from NASA. It's from Isaiah." At least, that's what I thought he'd said.

"I'm sorry. Isaiah who?"

"ISEA. The International Space Exploration Alliance. NASA is but one member. And for Pangaea, the height limit is two meters. That nudges you in by a hair."

My heart pounded so hard Grant probably saw my chest thudding. I kept expecting the door to burst open with someone rushing in shouting, "There's been a mistake!" But the room remained utterly quiet—yet I couldn't hear my own thoughts.

So this was what shock felt like.

"I, uh, suppose most people would pinch themselves at this point."

"Surprisingly, no. Most think up a polite way to decline. But you . . ." Grant gave a subtle nod, his brown-black eyes gleaming. "You think you're living a dream."

I blinked. It was the only movement I was capable of at the moment, besides breathing.

Grant turned towards the side table holding an antique brass model of the solar system, lustrous metal balls representing the planets and their moons. "You see this time-worn contraption over here? It's a fully functioning orrery." He spun the device and pointed at a tiny globe the color of turquoise. "That little fellow is our planet. Earth. Beautiful, hmm?"

"Absolutely." I huffed out a breath and focused my attention.

"Tell me, how would you feel about leaving Earth for good?"

For good? The words were like two metal doors slamming shut in front of me. I stared at the orrery as it slowly spun to a stop.

"Pangaea is a convoy of starships—sleeper ships wherein you get to spread the seed of humanity on another world. To illustrate the distance . . ." He pointed at the blue planet on the contraption. "If this is where we are, then we're aiming to take you about two buildings away from here." Grant held up a solitary finger. "It's a one-way voyage. You understand the implications?"

I gritted my teeth, feeling I'd just been tricked with some sleight of mind by the director himself. "I couldn't believe . . ." I swabbed a hand over my mouth. ". . . you didn't think to lead with that?"

He bowed his head slightly and flashed that fatherly smile again, which managed to earn the senior gentleman a measure of forgiveness. "It's a lesson I learned about persuasion. You can sometimes get to the big 'yes' by taking baby steps."

I shook my head. *How the bloody hell does one baby-step his way to never coming back to Earth?*

"Your records say you're single. Does that also mean you have no children?"

"None."

"Any relatives, wards—anyone depending on you for financial support or guardianship?"

"No." I had to clear my throat, which had gone dry. "None."

"Are you in a relationship?"

"I . . . wouldn't say that."

"Nothing serious, then?"

The image of a woman with long black hair and striking almond eyes appeared inside my mind—then the vision disappeared like a long-ago dream I'd failed to chase. "No, I wouldn't say it's serious." I scratched a nonexistent itch on my chin.

Grant nodded. "It's best if no one's pulling at your heartstrings. You'll be surprised how far into space those strings can pull." The esteemed man then went on to explain the demands and rigor of the mission that was aimed for a tiny dot in the constellation Ophiuchus. How the convoy would be launched in three batches of three ships at a time with a gap of nine years before the departure of the next triad, and each new batch was to be made up of faster ships with more advanced technology. "As for the crew, we're working our way through a list from around the globe. But we'll stop once we arrive at 333 yeses, to be further trimmed down to a final ninety-nine. Three sets of thirty-three."

"Why the magic numbers?" I asked, though I already suspected the answer.

He leaned back and smiled, seemingly glad I had asked. "The official reason is a combination of ergonomics and economics. But the truth comes down to the fact that the top decision-makers are founding members of Deltoton. That about says it all."

Just as I thought. For those in-the-know, the number three was akin to Deltoton's fingerprint. I was a member of the online society —and the top dogs were pioneers? Cool.

"Now, let's not get bogged down by these inputs at the moment," Grant said. "This talk is preliminary for you to answer the simple, basic question: Can you detach yourself from all things Earth? Permanently."

I swallowed. Hard. I had long visualized, yearned, ached for this moment, but despite my countless imaginings, I had never—not once—pictured myself leaving Earth *for good*.

"Does the mission accept couples?" I blurted out.

Grant's brows shot up. "We actually prefer couples. Both parties passing our criteria, of course."

"I see." I didn't even know how that question slipped past me.

Grant peered closer at my face. "Seems that 'nothing serious' is more serious than you'd care to admit."

I managed a polite smile. I did say I wasn't one to give up on dreams.

"So tell me. Is this still a proposition you might be tempted to accept?"

"It might be." Simply saying the words made me queasy. "An extremely shaky and tentative might."

"Fair enough. I consider that a sane answer. I'm required to give you sixty days to mull this over. Pangaea is designed to be space-efficient. It has no room for regrets."

"I understand."

"Indeed, I hope you do. If your happiness lies amidst a global population hooked on cinematic superheroes, sports, and sugar— who enjoy vacationing in underwater cities or subterranean parks and gardens, then say no. If you love to hear applause or enjoy making money to afford every extravagance, say no. It means saying goodbye to sights you've taken for granted, like a neighbor's lawn or a crowded street. Never again immersing in Earth's ancient ruins, Eastern cultures, and European wonders. The price is steep. And, I must say, it's foolhardy for anyone to think Earth— and all its loves and luxuries—can be easily left behind."

He reached into his breast pocket, pulled out two white envelopes, and laid one of them on the table. "This is the form rejection letter from NASA in response to your latest application. You won't have to receive this should you choose to accept ISEA's offer."

He placed the other envelope next to it. "This is an acceptance letter for you to be counted among the candidates for Mission Pangaea—which will be ready for you to sign when the time comes, should you choose it."

I stared at the two letters, each spelling out a different future for me in black and white. Both holding at bay a distinct version of pain.

Grant slid the envelopes aside, tucked them out of sight underneath the cliPad, then rose from his seat with ease. I, on the other hand, carried a heavier burden as I came to my feet.

"We'll meet again in two months," Grant said. "Should you decide to decline before then, just let me know. Meanwhile, live life. Explore the ties that bind you here. Family. Friends. Plans and dreams. And ask yourself if you can bring yourself to leave them all . . . for good."

3
DID I MISS A CALL?

She stood in a shaft of moonlight at the end of a long, dark hall. But somehow, even at that distance, I could see her almond eyes sparkle in striking blue-violet as she smiled. I wished I could touch her. Hold her. Be with her.

The twist ties around my tongue loosened and fell away as I walked towards her. "I have so much to tell you."

"Do you really know what you want to tell me?" Her voice reverberated as though the universe itself had spoken. Then half her face began to glow like starlight, turning into a constellation that merged with an endless night sky. I reached out, afraid she'd disappear.

"Be with me," I said, and like magic, she rose and floated towards my outreached—Bloody hell. Was that my iHub ringing?

Crap.

With a jolt, I opened my eyes. By then, there was nothing but the faint drone of central heating—and a tightness in my chest weighed down by a strong throb of dread. No one had ever woken me up with good news that couldn't wait till morning.

I rubbed a hand over my eyes and squinted into the shadows trying to sense where my best buddy was, but I couldn't see a thing. He was somewhere in my bedroom watching over me. Probably sitting on the floor with his head retracted into the rest of his body.

"Hey, Diddit. Wake up," I rasped, my throat still not quite awake.

A row of lights blinked on around his cubed girth as he roused himself from sleep mode. A smaller cube emerged from his flat top displaying a pleasant robotic face, its neon blue eyes an exaggerated reflection of mine.

"What's up, mate?" asked my mechanized best friend with an outbacker's twang. The vintage LED sound visualizer, representing Diddit's mouth, oscillated color bars with his words.

"Did I miss a call?"

"Yes, thirty-three days ago, and you returned it half an hour later."

"Weird." I shook my head, still pretty sure I'd been nudged awake by the *Star Base* movie theme. "I guess I must've been dream—"

My iHub wristband cut me short with exactly that ringtone, the glow of its display blinking a dull green where it lay on my nightstand. I checked the caller ID.

There was no number. No name. Nothing.

The nape of my neck prickled as I placed the tiny receiver into my ear. "Hello?"

"Hey, Bram." Static hissed and sizzled. "Something weird just happened. I have no idea where I am."

My breath got sucked out of me. The words had sputtered their way through a bad connection, but there was no mistaking Franco's voice. Or was I just groggy?

I pressed on my earpiece to hear better. "Who is this?"

"I've been . . . Can't get through . . . I'm on my way." I barely heard the rest. "If this is it—*Carpe diem*, bro."

"Bloody hell." I leaned closer to my iHub and its pinprick of a mic. "Whoever you are, this isn't funny."

Only the crackle of white noise answered, and then the line

went silent. I checked the wristband display, and it said: Call Ended. The glow of my iHub dimmed as it went out, and I pulled the receiver out of my ear, tossed the iHub onto my nightstand, and slumped back into bed. *What a bloody tasteless prank.*

Maybe I could still pick up that dream from where it had left off. I breathed deeply and pictured her long black hair. Her smiling eyes. Porcelain skin. His bushy black eyebrows and bearded chin —What the hell?! I tossed in bed and thrust a fist into my pillow, hoping to smash away the unsettling vision of Franco.

Minutes went by, and the more I tried to relax, the more strain I felt in my shoulders.

Damn it. *Who the hell would do a thing like that?*

"Diddit, turn my lamp on."

As the warm white light slowly increased in intensity to just the right level, my gaze landed back on my iHub on the bedside table. "Can you trace where that last call came from?"

"Sorry, mate. No number registered."

"But . . . I did get a call, right?" I couldn't have been *that* groggy.

"Yes, and it lasted fifteen seconds."

I huffed a befuddled breath. "Call the telecom company. Try customer service or something." I put on my earpiece just as some stranger's friendly voice came on the line.

"Hello, mate. I just got a crank call a while ago. Could you please trace the number and block it for me?"

"Sure. I can walk you through the steps on how to block it on your device—"

"Sorry, but the number didn't register on my iHub. A glitch of some kind."

"No problem," said the chap who sounded remarkably cheery despite the ghoulish hour. "Could you tell me the exact time you received the call?"

"Hang on," I said and clicked on my iHub to check the phone log. "It came at 3:03 a.m."

A few seconds ticked by. "I'm very sorry, but it seems that

glitch wasn't on your device. It may have been . . . from the caller's end? Our records show you did receive a call at that time, but there's no data available as to its origin."

"What do you mean?"

"It's untraceable, so I'm afraid I can't do anything at the moment to block it."

Bloody what? "Is it . . . How do you explain it then?"

"I'm sorry, but—not knowing any other details—I can't."

4

SOME TECHNOLOGICAL MISHAP

THE BLACK SCREEN OF MY COMPUTER MONITOR WAS FILLED WITH coding for advanced robotics, but none of it registered. Scanning through the stream of multi-colored commands at least gave the appearance I was working. The image of two white envelopes, side-by-side, filled my mind, and I'd given myself this entire day to choose between them. One contained a dream. The other a nightmare. But it was hard to tell which was which.

Sienna, with her shock of green hair and all-black garb, began to tap away on her keyboard from two seats away. My computer stared at me, waiting for me to follow her lead, but the mood of the daily grind failed to grip me—especially with the eerie vibe I was getting from the empty chair next to me.

Instead of going for the computer keyboard, my fingers dawdled over my iHub.

That phone call from Franco must have been some technical mishap. A signal relaying switch of a glitch that had caused some crazy fluke of a digital delay. Or it could have been my iHub. I stared at the wristband technology, which combined an Apple watch, an iPhone, and a miniaturized foldout monitor of the MacBook. It was an ambitious hunk of a runt still bound to have bugs. Those were the only explanations I could think of. Logical ones, at least.

I rechecked the iHub's log but found no new or delayed or unseen notification that could also help explain the glitch. I shook my head and tried to focus on the work I was ignoring, right when Sienna let out a little laugh. "Franco is such a funny guy, Bram." She sat smiling at her computer screen.

"Was, Sienna."

"What?" She turned to me with misty eyes.

"He *was* a funny guy."

She shook her head. "But I'm chatting with him right now."

"Say again?" Did she have some other friend named Franco I didn't know about?

Her face grew taut, seemingly suddenly guarded. "Didn't you get a . . . note or something?"

A tiny jolt crawled up my scalp. "What note?"

"Nothing. I was just going through our old chats." She turned away, quickly changing her computer display with a click of her mouse.

I narrowed my eyes. So what was that about? I waited for her to say something more, but she kept her eyes riveted to the screen, her hand on her mouse, as if looking my way again was bound to be a big mistake. *Should I tell her I got a phone call?*

"Sienna, is everything all right?"

She turned to me with a crinkle on her brow. "Yes, I'm fine. What about you? Are you doing okay?" She wiped a tear away, her fingernails a vivid green that matched her hair.

"Still getting over the shock myself." I cracked my knuckles as I figured out how to explain what happened. "Listen, I did get . . . something. But . . . I don't know." I glanced uneasily at Franco's chair between us. "I think I got a call."

Her eyes grew wide. "From Franco?"

It took some effort to nod. "Early this morning."

"Are you serious?"

I swallowed in response.

"Oh, my god." Her voice quivered. "How did you feel . . . hearing his voice?"

"I don't know." I raked a hand over my scalp. "Shocked. Confused." Probably the same way I felt now.

"Gosh, I can't imagine." A tear fell down her cheek. "I've never gotten one."

"Gotten what?"

"A VN call."

"VN?"

"Virtual Nexus." She looked at me like some long-lost-friend who assumed I recognized her.

I shrugged, completely clueless.

"It's an app that creates an afterlife surrogate so that—" Her mouth hung open for a second, and in that suspended moment, I saw the subtle shift from amazement to amusement in her eyes. "Oh, my god. Let me get this straight. You don't know about VN? So you thought the call was . . . real?" She laughed, I think harder than she should've, bringing fresh tears of a different kind to her eyes.

I scowled, wishing so hard I could give some clever excuse, but my tongue stayed paralyzed.

"Face it, Bram. You've been punked from beyond the grave." She snorted. "I'm sorry, but I just can't help picturing how you must've . . . Oh, my god." She burst out laughing again and tried plugging up her tear ducts with her fingertips until she could collect herself. "Oh, I will so miss his sense of humor." She turned to Franco's empty chair with a fond smile for someone no longer there.

Something acrid rose up my throat. It was probably what people called the bitter truth: This was Franco's version of goodbye. His idea of a last laugh together. I almost teared up myself. "I can't believe he thought I'd find this funny."

"You know Franco. He's allergic to sadness."

"So you were in on the joke all along." I sighed like a deflating balloon.

"No. I just got an email and clicked on the link. That's how I ended up in his VN chatroom. Remember the note I asked about? I thought you didn't get one, and I didn't want you to feel bad if you didn't. Turns out, he actually considered you special enough for a call. That costs extra."

I grunted. "Sounds like Virtual Nonsense to me."

Her expression quickly softened to that of a friend who actually seemed like she cared. "Hey, don't be a poor sport. Franco did it because he likes you."

"Liked," I corrected, then swiveled my seat to continue the conversation with someone who never considered anyone's ignorance funny—Google—who, when asked to define VN, coughed up 556,000 results in 0.03 seconds. Virtual Nexus, it explained, was a proprietary online service that enabled people to chat with a digital proxy of someone who had died, put together from an authorized archive of data the person had provided and accumulated like email, texts, social media posts, and chats.

But that didn't explain the other "phantom call" I'd gotten. I could have sworn I'd woken up to the sound of the phone ringing, and yet the logs showed I'd only received one call last night. What kind of tech did VN have that masked calls just to freak people out? And how could that be legal?

I checked my inbox and found a message from Virtual Nexus. I was about to click on it when—

"Carpe diem, bro," Sienna said.

I winced. "Stop it, Sienna. The joke's on me. Now drop it."

"What are you talking about?" She gestured at her monitor. "I just asked Franco if he had any last words for you, and that's his answer."

I shrugged it aside. "It's the same message he sent over the phone."

"You know why he said that, right?"

"It's an app, Sienna. It's not him."

"It's your many failed attempts to get into the Astronaut Candidate Program."

Oh, Jesus.

"I'm only saying this because I think it's what's best for you. Look . . ." She got up, grabbed her coffee mug, and thumped it down on my desk. "It's a matter of looking at your glass as half full instead of half empty. You're working at NASA. What does that even mean to you?"

I glanced at her mug. It was half empty.

Folding my arms, I leaned back and concluded she was the likeliest suspect to have talked to Dave about me making a fool of myself in Houston.

"Franco's message was for you to seize the day. Live for the here and now." She leaned closer. "So why don't you join me and the guys later? Let's toast to new beginnings, instead of sitting and waiting for the impossible to happen."

My gaze darted to my own coffee mug and found it empty. *I could never raise a toast to giving up on a dream.*

"No," I said, easing my computer chair backward. "I'm not here to sit and wait. I'm filing for a leave of absence."

Sienna straightened up. "You're going on leave? How long?"

I took a breath and committed to the decision. "Sixty days."

5

THE POWER OF NOSTALGIA

I WASN'T A BETTING MAN, YET HERE I WAS, PLACING ALL MY CHIPS ON the slimmest of hopes. I'd flown over two thousand miles to gamble the next two months of my life in the place I used to call home.

I got myself a fresh haircut and a clean shave, changed my shirt three times, stared at myself in the mirror, slipped on a dark blazer, and told myself this was as good as it could get. Hoping the power of nostalgia could up my chances, I headed for the old-Hollywood inspired restaurant she and I had considered our favorite when we were kids. The place had the same cream-colored walls, same arched alcoves decorated with blockbuster posters, and a movie soundtrack playing softly over the speakers. It did have one major addition: Robotic waiters that looked like nothing more than digital placards on wheels. Far cry from state-of-the-art, but that was fine, considering I planned to remind her of our past.

I chose a cozy corner table with a semi-circular banquette seat and a vintage poster of *Shrek* hanging right next to it. *I can't believe I got sixty days off!* Even though all I needed were sixty seconds. I simply had to say, "Hey, there. How would you like to leave all your Earthly joys, plans, and ambitions and travel with me to some distant planet—and probably die before we get there?"

The room suddenly felt warm, and I slipped out of my jacket. I was early. And anxious. Hoping to *carpe* in one *diem* the shreds of a relationship tattered by time and distance.

Diddit's way of bolstering my hopes had been to provide me with stats. "There have been approximately 450 hours of voice calls and 190 hours of holocalls between you and Torula in the past ten years." So all in all, he concluded, our friendship was solid and secure.

I sighed over that conclusion. Friendship. Yeah.

Somehow, I knew she'd arrived before I turned to look. She walked in wearing a dark jacket over low-rider jeans and boots. Clad in drab brown and black, she still sparkled. Some chaps glanced at her discreetly as she walked by, and I tried to ease my nerves by combing my hair with my fingers.

"It's great to see you," Torula said. Her dark eyes, with their tinge of blue-violet, were far more penetrating in person; I had to catch my breath.

"Hey, Spore," I said, calling her by the nickname I'd given her —a nickname only I ever got to call her. I wanted to reach out and hug her, but she had her hand on the strap of her shoulder bag across her torso. It read like a "Keep Distance" sign. I leaned in to buss her on the cheek just as she turned her head in the same direction, and we almost touched lips.

She laughed. So did I. She looked as nervous as I was.

I sat down to cover up my unease, then realized she was still standing, getting out of her coat. I shot back up and moved behind her to take her jacket. Her subtle fragrance brought to mind a pastel sunrise with a cooling, soothing mist. Before I knew it, the coat had slipped through my fingers, falling to the floor. "Sorry," I said, picking it up and giving it a hearty shake as she sat down.

After that fumbling-fool of a hello, I laid her jacket down next to mine and slid into our semi-circular nook, taking a deep breath and swabbing a hand over my mouth. If I had intended to remind her of how things used to be, then that was the only way our greeting could have gone. She had once said we were a couple of social klutzes, lucky to have found each other in the same school. I had eagerly agreed, willing to accept anything that meant there was something that we shared.

She tilted her head as she looked at me with a subtle smile. Her black hair—which, like her almond eyes, hinted at her father's Asian descent—fell in a provocative swirl down one side. "I can't believe you're really here," she said.

"It's about time, I know. You look great."

She shrugged. "This is just me. Every day."

"Exactly."

She flicked a lock of hair off her forehead and averted her gaze —a tell of a gesture that let me know when she was uneasy. It was probably best to skip the next flattering statement then. This was the girl who, when chosen to play Sleeping Beauty back in middle school, had insisted on being a stagehand. Otherwise, I would've demanded to be the prince. It could've ended up an unforgettable match: The school's prettiest tomboy with that year's tallest dork.

I sat back and watched her. She seemed oblivious—her elbows on the table, hands clasped as she glanced around.

"I'm not!" she said, looking at me suddenly.

"Not what?" I asked baffled.

"Ignoring you."

"I didn't say anything."

She gestured with one hand. "I missed this place. I was just being nostalgic for a few seconds, not the least bit ignoring you."

"Like I said, I didn't say anything." I leaned back into my seat and wondered what it was she'd heard.

Slowly, Torula turned to look at the table next to ours. I followed her gaze towards a senior couple who sat munching their dinner—eyes fixed on their plates, faces on the verge of scowling, both ignoring the other.

Did she mistake the old man's voice for mine? I winced inwardly and cleared my throat.

She leaned closer and whispered, "Promise me we won't end up like that."

I froze for a second. Did she mean not to end up a grumpy old pair? Or ignoring each other? Or both?

"I promise . . . never to order food that I'll enjoy more than your company," I said.

She laughed, and that eased up the tightness in my chest.

"So what brings you here," she asked, her eyes still sparkling with amusement, "so far away from work?"

"Not that far away, really. I'm working on something offsite." Talking about Project Husserl—the assignment Dave had given me to work on remotely—could get her thinking about space travel. "They want to improve on a system for incapacitated astronauts to activate medic robots in case the automatic switches failed. The triggering mechanism being considered is voice control, but given the cacophony of an emergency . . ." Bugger. Project Husserl was all about survival and danger. What I needed was her thinking of the awesomeness of outer space. "Well, I guess that's a poor choice of topic."

"No, it's great, really. I find it a defying."

"Uhm, defying what?"

She chuckled.

"No." I scratched my forehead. "I really didn't get what you said." It was conversations with her, like this, back in grade school, that had gotten me out of YouTube and into reading.

"Oh! It's *edifying*. I get exposed to a whole new world just listening to you talk about what you do. It's . . . transporting."

I smiled and pictured ISEA doing exactly that to me—with her —on Pangaea. Where we would grow old together. As a couple. And never ignore each other.

A robotic waiter approached the table, hi-definition images of their bestselling dishes serving as its face. "Hi, there! Ready to order?" it said in the default, friendly female voice many midrange restaurants across America selected.

"No. Just give us a minute." I blindly browsed through the

menu. Here I was, on a dinner date, in no mood to eat, and lost over what to say. Jesus. If Dave saw me now, he'd facepalm over my not having rehearsed a thing.

"Will you be in town for long?" Torula asked, pressing a button on the waiter, telling it how much time we needed before it should come back.

"Uh, yeah." If only I had a button Torula could press telling me how much time I needed to ask what I'd come here to ask. "Long enough, I guess."

"For what?"

Simple question. Hard to answer. "I'm here to . . . consider an offer."

Her lips parted in surprise. "So you're checking it out? Here? Is it at Ames?"

"No, it's not . . . here."

She narrowed her eyes. "Not here in California? Or not here in the States?"

Shite. I can't just jump into it like this. Dr. Grant had said something about persuasion. *Get to the big "yes" through baby steps.* I guess that meant I shouldn't let it all out tonight.

Her iHub began beeping, and she glanced at the caller ID. "Oh, no. I'm sorry, I have to take this."

"No worries."

She clicked on her wristband and spoke in a low tone into it.

Well, that was a welcome interruption. I needed to backpedal this conversation before it got too close to the edge of Earth's atmosphere.

She glanced my way with an apologetic smile, and I concluded that long-distance holocalls—3D-like as they were—had never managed to cast her eyes in full, vivid color. When we were kids, she had picked apart her features and declared them all "unspectacular." I'd told her purple eyes definitely qualified as spectacular, but she dismissed it as an abnormality. A rare mutation she couldn't even pass on to her "progeny," which was her way of saying kids.

"Sorry about that," she said, ending her call. "It was Mom."

Oh, gawd. I winced, suspecting something was up. "Did you tell her you were meeting me tonight?"

"No. I just said you were back in town."

I nodded, having a good idea what was going on. Her mother was no supporter of monogamy and had raised her four children, fathered by four different men, all on her own. And here I was, no doubt, in her opinion, a mistake her daughter was about to make.

"Anyway," Torula said, "you were saying? About the new job?"

"Uhm, nothing. We can talk about it later. Have you decided what to order yet?"

"Bram, this isn't the first mind-numbing offer you've received. Is it from some company in Korea again? Or Dubai?"

I gritted my teeth, unable to fill the following dead air with anything.

Her shoulders drooped as she let out a breath. "Does this mean you flew all this way just to tell me you're leaving the country? Giving up the dream?"

"Giving up? No! I've held on all this time despite the—"

"*Held* on? Past tense? So you've accepted?"

"No, not . . . yet."

"Good. I mean, NASA's where you belong."

That was exactly what she'd said so many years ago when I found out I'd gone past the astronaut height limit, and from thousands of miles away, she had helped keep me together—and the dream alive.

She leaned back, visibly relaxing, as though I were some attempted-escapee she'd managed to detain. "Don't be dazzled by the offers," she said. "Your dream far outshines the money."

"I agree." I let out a chuckle. "But really? Coming from the highest-paid botanist in California?"

She crinkled her brow. "Don't deflect. And don't exaggerate."

"Who's exaggerating?" Though I admit, I was deflecting. "I think every scientist where you work is overpaid."

Her eyes bored into mine. "If your job offer is from overseas, why are you here?"

"Hi, there!"

I jumped at the artificial waiter's sudden reappearance.

"Ready to order?"

I swabbed my brow even though I wasn't sweating.

"Are you feeling all right?" Torula asked.

"Yeah. Why?"

"You just lost a good friend. It might have sent you into a quarter-life crisis, and that's why you're considering this offer."

"There's no crisis."

"I'm assuming you cried for him?"

I shrugged, getting a sudden sense of sadness that she and Franco never got a chance to meet.

"Did you?" she asked.

"Did I what?"

"Cry for him."

Was she serious about that question? "Not as much as I did when he made me laugh."

"Hmm . . ." She pursed her lips, her gaze wandering sideward as I tried to figure out the point behind the question—but couldn't.

I gestured at the waiting waiter. "Come on, let's order."

"No," Torula said. "I'm sorry, Bram. I can't stay."

"What? Whuh—why?"

She bit her lower lip before answering. "Mom's waiting at my apartment lobby with my little brother. She didn't confirm she was coming over, so I—"

"No worries. I can drive over to your place and—"

"No. I mean . . ." She glanced about as if her answer were some bee buzzing about her head. "Mom and I rarely get to see each other, you know?"

I sat slack-jawed for a moment. "We haven't been together in sixteen years."

She swallowed, then flicked the hair off her brow. What could her mother possibly have told her? All the sparkle was gone from her eyes, and it looked like my chances of rekindling any warmth in them this evening had been snuffed out.

I sighed. "Fine."

As soon as I said it, she slid out of her seat and grabbed her stuff, all too eagerly. "Thank you so much for understanding."

Do I? I stood up befuddled, having possibly overlooked a powerful reason why she would want to stay bound to life on Earth.

Her family. Her closest of ties. Something I had lost long ago.

What were the chances Torula would give that up for me? For good.

6

AN OVERPAID BOTANIST

(TORULA)

BRAM WAS RIGHT. I WAS AN OVERPAID BOTANIST. AND DELIRIOUSLY happy with my job. In fact, I should have been the one paying the Green Manor for letting me work here.

I approached the wax begonia enclosed in its glass dome, looking radiant as it flaunted scarlet petals around bright yellow anthers. "How are you feeling today, Michel?"

"Fantastique," came the begonia's reply in its haughty, male voice. Its pot vibrated lightly, making the entire plant quiver.

I placed a checkmark next to its botanical name, *Begonia x semperflorens-cultorum*, on my cliPad and smiled with satisfaction. Every day, I entered this lush botanical laboratory and talked to my plants—and taught them all to talk right back. *Who needs to get paid to do that?*

Of course, it was all with the help of the Verdabulary program, recorded spiels, and well-concealed speakers, but the effect was breathtaking.

From the wooden platform at the center of my nursery came the highly recognizable click-clack of high heels. I glanced at my iHub; I was supposed to go to Starr's nursery in a few minutes, so why was she here?

"Have you seen my phone, honey?" she asked, answering my question with her trademark pet name for anyone she considered likable. Which, for her, was almost everyone.

"It's right there, next to Bram's jacket."

Starr picked up her mobile in its sparkling case covered with rhinestones, beads, and pearls. Given her bangled wrist and colorful fashion, no chunky iHub could possibly match her sense of style. It didn't matter she was somewhat on the heavy side and a forty-something widow and mother of three; she was every bit glamorous.

She raised a perfectly plucked brow on her beautifully made-up face framed by nicely highlighted strawberry-blonde hair. "Bram was here?"

"No." I climbed the steps to join her on the workstation platform. Me in my Henley shirt, camos, and a haphazard ponytail. "I picked up his jacket by mistake. Now I'm obligated to see him again to return it."

"Obligated? Since when did you not want to see him?"

"Ever since I realized he's leaving for a job overseas." *And making a horribly wrong choice.* "Why reconnect with someone on a stopover to Dubai or Korea or Vanuatu, for all I care. I don't see the point in a protracted goodbye."

"Why? You're scared you'll cry?" she teased with a wink.

That little quip, touching on something I'd shared with her about my past with Bram, almost made me wince. I pulled out the barb before she could tell it stung. "I used my mom's call as an excuse to abort dinner."

"You took a call on a date? That's not very nice." She crinkled her nose.

"It was Mom. She had an early morning doctor's appointment near my place, so she came to sleep over with my baby brother and —" *Why am I bothering to defend myself?* I waved a dismissive hand. "It's not important. We can go now."

"You are such a KJ." Starr tossed the jacket at me.

I caught it deftly before it hit me in the face. The whoosh of

Bram's barely perceptible but unmistakable scent coursed through me like exhilaration at the brink of a roller coaster drop. Outwardly, I made sure to look unaffected and tossed the garment back on my chair and asked, "I'm a knee jerk?"

"A killjoy! What's so wrong with reconnecting? I like him."

"You do, do you?" I glanced at the tiny gold crucifix she wore every day around her neck. "He's an atheist."

"Oh, how ironic. You seem like a match made in nerd heaven."

I frowned. "We're friends. He doesn't think of me that way."

She arched a brow and pursed her glossy lips, but I refused to read the taunt that flashed in her eyes. I marched down the steps, out of the greenhouse, and away from any more frivolous discussions about a man who'd only visited me twice in sixteen years—both times to say goodbye.

I led Starr past my collection of specimen plants, each one in its glass cloche—bell-shaped enclosures that made my conservatory look like a jewelry store with the late afternoon sun glinting off the transparent domes.

"See you later, guys," I hollered.

"Buh-bye!"

"Au revoir."

"Tata!"

"G'day, Torula."

"See yah!"

It was a chorus of farewells from my garden that talked in a rich mixture of accents, personalities, and temperaments—and my heart swelled with immeasurable pride. It had been a long, awkward climb from being the introverted kid, who felt more at home talking to plants than to people, to becoming the scientist leading the project that got plants to talk right back. I couldn't imagine leaving the Green Manor to work anywhere else in the world.

We took a short, brisk walk to Starr's nursery. Much larger than mine, it was divided into plots, each about the size of two pickup trucks, holding a variety of shrubs. I never could get used to the shift in atmosphere. Entangled amongst the branches and leaves were electrified wires and rods, metallic plates, magnets, and other paraphernalia Starr used in her experiments. She'd insisted there was order in the mess, even though it always looked like a mad scientist had gone berserk in there.

Today, she was going to test if a jolt of electricity in addition to magnetite in the soil was going to yield larger papaya fruit. Poor papayas. Unless, of course, electricity was a pleasant treat for them.

I walked past a dense cluster of plants, and the hair on my nape stood on end just before I got the shivers.

How peculiar. I'd had the exact same feeling last night after I'd woken up to find my baby brother in my bedroom sleep-walking at three a.m.

I moved a little closer to the bed of plants, and the tingling rose to my scalp.

"I'll set things up for the *Carica papaya* while you get the VeggieVolt ready," Starr called out.

"Right. I'm on it." I shook off the eerie sensation and hustled across stone paths to the central platform of her greenhouse and settled down at the console. After I clicked on the VeggieVolt icon on her computer screen, it seemed to start up, but then it stalled.

"I don't believe it. I called I.T. to reinstall this, and they said they'd get it done."

"They did," Starr said. "They sent someone this morning."

I stared at the frozen screen. "Well, it's just hanging here like a dead program on a noose. I'm restarting everything." I leaned back and resigned myself to the wait; as I sat there, my mind on idle, my eyes staring blindly at nothing, the hair on my arms stood on end.

This is so weird. Was I coming down with something? With the computer back on, I clicked on the VeggieVolt and brushed the odd feeling aside.

"Please don't ignore me," said a man, close to my ear.

I gasped and turned, expecting Bram to be right next to me—but no one was there.

"Did you hear that?" I asked Starr.

"Hear what?"

It was the same phrase I'd heard last night at the restaurant, but I thought . . . it was probably—"Nothing," I said, flustered, and quickly clicked on a program icon, navigating to the library of plants. Okay, Carica, Carica. *There you go!* I found the name and pressed enter.

A soothing woman's voice issued through the computer speakers declaring, "I am a *Ficus Carica*."

"What in heaven's name?" Starr cried. "My garden can't talk. What have you done?"

"I don't know." I checked the computer display and realized I'd clicked the Verdabulary icon out of habit. "Wait a minute." I frowned at Starr. "Why do you have my Verdabulary in your system?"

"I don't."

"Yes, you do." A quick flashback instantly told me what might have happened. "Oh, no. The I.T. guy must've gotten things mixed up because *I* made the call about *your* software."

"How ya going, Torula?" It was the friendly male voice of my eucalyptus plant, which I suddenly realized sounded a lot like Bram.

"Will you shut that program down?" Starr cried. "It's giving me goose bumps."

"Right. Sorry." I glanced at Starr and—froze.

What? Is. That?

There—just beyond arm's reach from Starr—stood a badly smudged illusion of a man. Floating. Distorted. Misshapen. But somehow, recognizably . . . though vaguely, human. I slowly rose to my feet and gaped at the bewildering sight. Its features were blurry. No mouth. No nose. With a shadowy smear beneath its brow. Though the silhouette of its torso and arms were discernible, there was nothing but mist beneath its hips.

This couldn't possibly be . . . a ghost?

The image slowly turned as it hovered, and a pair of golden eyes gleamed at me. A dark hole for a mouth gaped open on the specter's face. "Cool burn," said the Verdabulary.

Starr screamed and ran down the pathway.

The image held out a sprig of blue flowers, and then, it vanished. Starr rushed past me, heading out of the nursery, and only then did I realize the oddest thing about the whole experience. I wasn't afraid.

7

WHAT DID WE SEE?

(TORULA)

Six times in three hours. That was how many times Starr and I had tried to make it reappear. That illusion. That anomaly. That mystery.

I stepped out of the elevator and trudged down the corridor to my apartment. I hadn't realized how tired I was until simply walking to my door seemed beyond me.

What did we see? Why couldn't we reproduce it?

Maybe the temperature had dipped too low. Or the humidity had gone too high. Or quite likely, time of day had been a major factor. Having had no other way to control that last aspect, we had packed up and agreed to try again at dusk tomorrow.

I pushed open my apartment door and found some lights already on. *Mom's still here?* The sweet scent of potpourri came to embrace me as I walked in. "I'm home," I said under my breath, sending the greeting to my pots of fern, philodendron, and dracaena sitting next to windows filtered by lace. All the tiredness lifted from me as I imagined the day when I could bring the Verdabulary technology home so they could all greet me right back, and I smiled.

Amidst my pastel-colored collection of flea market finds—an

assemblage of vintage and shabby chic furniture—was my mother seated on the floor in a lotus position, meditating. Her long auburn hair fell in a bohemian twist down one shoulder. An aromatherapy candle glimmered nearby.

"Is everything all right?" I asked.

Mom opened one eye and peered at me. "Do I look anxious to you?" She closed both eyes again. "The reason one sits in the shape of a triangle is for stability and balance. It lets you sit strong like a mountain so your mind can be open like the sky." She rose from the floor with the grace of a ballerina, her taut and slender frame clad in loose, cream-colored pants and a white halter top. My mind sent out a quiet wish that I had enough of her genes to look that good when I too neared sixty.

"Do you literally watch your grass grow?" she asked. "I can't imagine a reason for any botanist to do overtime."

"Do you need to go for another checkup tomorrow?" I asked.

"No."

"Then why are you still here? What did the doctor say?"

"Sorry, I can't tell you," she said as she slipped on her classy leather sandals. "Doctor-patient confidentiality."

"Mom, you're the patient."

"But I'm also a doctor."

I looked at her askance. "What happened at your check-up?"

"My doctor peeved me, that's what happened." Mom's voice remained calm even as she expressed aggravation. "He says I'm healthier than most women half my age, but that I should learn to accept the inescapable."

"Does he mean old age?"

Mom cringed, though with her poise, it looked more like she had just closed her eyes to smell the herb-scented air. "I will not be a lemming to be led down that path just because no one has yet found a way to turn back."

I chuckled. As far as I knew, only a legal inquisition could pry the real age out of Dr. Triana Jackson. "So everything's all right, then?"

"Of course. I've never been ill a day in my life." She quickly reconsidered. "Well . . . excluding that time when I died."

"When you *nearly* died, Mom." I glanced at the guestroom. The door was ajar. "Is Truth in there?"

"Yes, sleeping."

I moved towards the bedroom, wanting to kiss my little brother goodnight.

"Truth told me he saw a stranger in your bedroom last night," Mom said, stopping me in my tracks.

Oh, so that's what this is about? Because Bram was in town, she wanted to scrutinize my sex life? "Truth was sleepwalking, Mom."

"Are you sure?"

I raised a brow. "Am I sure he was dreaming, or that I wasn't hiding a man in my closet?"

"I believe in ghosts, you know. So you can tell me anything."

A sudden chill coursed through me. "That's quite a leap, Mom."

"Did your brother wake you up in the middle of the night or not?"

"Yes, he did."

"Did he not point out your visitor to you?"

The haze lifted from my bleary recollection. Truth had pointed at a blank wall and giggled, then kept staring at the same spot as I carried him out of my room. But the explanation had seemed obvious. "He's just three, Mom. He's only beginning to distinguish between dreams and waking life."

"Was he also dreaming when he told you he needed to pee?"

"Well, no, but . . ."

"He had to be awake to recount it. Sleepwalkers don't remember what they do. Did you not talk to him, and he talked back? Did he look at you and answer quickly? Did his eyes focus?"

Yes, to all. But the last thing I wanted was to fan my mother's eccentric flames. "Mom, I didn't have a visitor, imaginary or otherwise, all right? I'm . . . going to get a drink." I took a detour to my kitchen.

A ghost? I snorted. Truth had been dreaming with his eyes wide open. That was that. *I doubt he even remembers it now.* And the entire reason Starr and I had been trying to reproduce the anomaly *we'd* seen was to find the more logical explanation.

After a refreshing drink of water, and with my equanimity restored, I walked back along the dimly lit corridor. But an eerie sensation told me there was something not quite familiar there just when a featherlike touch brushed against my arm. I gasped and lurched away from a wispy figure in white . . . then winced when I got a better look at my mom's ivory-white pashmina dangling from a coat hook.

"Oh, Bloody Mary." *Simply talking with Mom has gotten me spooked over a scarf.* Yet I had watched calmly as some human-like silhouette materialized right next to my friend. Maybe because my subconscious had instantly known better, that it was definitely *not* a ghost.

I huffed away my anxiety and headed back towards the guestroom. Truth, so pudgy and perfectly adorable, stood by the door in his powder-blue pajamas as Mom stroked his puffy blonde hair.

"He heard your voice," she said. "Now he insists you tuck him back in bed."

I smiled, holding out my arms, and he rushed over to embrace me. We laughed as I hugged him tight and relished the lingering scent of babyhood in his hair as I carried him. I deposited him back in bed and tucked in his teddy bear next to him.

"Where's your friend?" he asked, his Rs sounding more like Ws.

"My friend?" I hoped he was asking about one of my old stuffed toys.

"In your room. I saw him."

I swallowed and forced out a smile. "Can you describe . . . my friend?"

"He was watching you. I think I scared him."

I managed a chuckle. "Well, of course you did." I poked his little button nose. "You're my superhero."

"He went into your broken wall. Is he still there?"

"I don't have a—" All my walls were immaculate. Did he just say it disappeared into a wall? The hair on my nape stood on end. "You should go back to sleep. And this time . . ." I ran my hand gently over his eyes to shut them. "Sleep tight and dream sweet dreams." I kissed him goodnight and kept a made-up smile on my face until I turned off his light.

I walked out of the room and jumped at the sight of my mother standing there.

"If you agree he's seen a ghost, you must tell me," she said. "Otherwise, he could be hallucinating, and I'll have to address it clinically."

Mass hallucination. *Does that explain what Starr and I saw too? Was that phenomenon even real?*

I walked towards my living room, away from Truth's earshot. "You think it might be a symptom?"

"Only if what he saw was irrefutably all in his head. Was it?"

Not wanting to confirm or deny, I didn't say anything, which to my mother, a psychiatrist, was tantamount to saying everything. I paused and raised my right hand as if to pledge a solemn oath. "I promise, if I see anything that scares me, I'll be at your doorstep within the hour."

"Oh goodness, no," she said, crossing her arms with a taunting smile. "You'll be knocking every other day."

"What's that supposed to mean?"

"You're scared of greatness, sweetheart, but would never admit it."

I gaped at the remark. "What sort of diagnosis—"

"You're scared of the spotlight but feel trapped because your very chemistry attracts it. You believe you have what it takes to succeed but also fear that maybe you don't. You want to change the world but are afraid you don't know how."

"Those aren't fears, Mom. Those are just . . . doubts."

"Then, are you afraid of the metaphysical, or do you just doubt it? Ghosts are real. It's not your fault, so don't be ashamed of it."

"I'm not a—" I paused, then bit my lip, unable to deny it. "Okay. All right. Enlighten me. How can ghosts be possible?"

Her eyes glowed like that of someone who'd swum to Atlantis and back, certain it was real. "I existed—conscious and alive— even when my brain showed no electrical activity. I saw what my parents were doing while they were waiting outside the ER. I heard their conversation with my sisters over the phone while I was on the operating table. Isn't that proof enough? Even devoid of a functioning body and brain, the psyche could sense its surroundings, gather memories, and hold itself intact. The mind doesn't come to an end until it decides it's over."

I shook my head and noticed the still-glimmering aromatherapy candle on the coffee table. "Death isn't a decision, Mom." I walked over towards the table.

"People working in hospitals observe it all the time—patients lingering at death's door choose to cross over when it's least stressful for their loved ones. Or they wait for one last person to say goodbye. They decide on the best time to leave their body."

Death by sheer will? I scoffed at the thought. "You can't just decide to stop your heart."

"That's because you've come to equate life with a heartbeat."

"I'm a botanist." I blew out the candle. "I don't deal with heartbeats."

Mom stared at the faint tendril of smoke that coiled upwards to nothingness. "Anything extinguished leaves behind a residue."

"I agree." I nodded. "That's why every life extinguished leaves behind a dead body."

"All right then." Mom took a seat on my tapestry-covered settee. "Let's look at life and death in terms of compost. Even after we go back to the Earth as fertilizer, bones can stay intact for thousands of years. But does anyone know how long it takes to decompose the stuff that makes up our soul?" She gestured towards the candle, its smoke, its glow, its warmth all gone, though its scent still hung in the air.

"Assuming there's such a thing as a soul." I flicked the hair off my brow.

She clasped her hands and clipped her ankles, like a merciful queen deciding what to do with one of her stubborn subjects. "Do you know why children below the age of five see ghosts far more frequently than adults do?"

"Probably the same reason they have more imaginary friends. They're kids."

The sparkle of wisdom beyond mine shone in Mom's eyes, and I braced for the assault of her science. "The brain is the only body organ left incomplete at birth. At three, Truth's brain is still being sculpted. Dendrites still being formed, synapses chipped. Electrical impulses are being tossed about his head, still unrestrained by the bindings of myelin. That means a toddler's brain contains hundreds of trillions more synapses—wantonly communicating—endowing it with capabilities it will eventually lose."

"Okay." I shrugged. "So you're saying it's possible little children can see things we don't. The same way eagles can see farther, and deer can see better at night. That doesn't mean what they're seeing are ghosts."

She glanced down the hall towards the room where Truth was sleeping. "Very young children speak of having past-life memories, talking to the dead, or even seeing the future. By five, they'd have all their basic neurons in place. But genetics, epigenetics, and life in general will continue to sculpt their brains until one day, in puberty, they'd have been shaped like the rest of us, desensitized to all stimuli classified as irrelevant by the brain."

I gnawed on my lower lip as I searched for all the loopholes in her explanation.

"For all you know," she said, "there really is a ghost walking around here right now."

No, Mom. It's just your silk pashmina.

"If ghosts were dangerous and ought to be feared," she continued, "evolution would have allowed us to sense them easily. But no. The brain learns rather early that they're useless sensory information. Isn't that a plausible argument as to why he sees the ghost, and we don't?"

I kneaded my temple, summoning some genie of science to give me an erudite response, but all I could say was, "Mom, you're an MD. I'm a PhD. He's three. I rest my case."

"And you've strengthened mine." The gracious queen-mother smiled even as she sighed. "At his tender age, Truth's brain is still dependent on eidetic memory. A photographic ability to remember things that most children eventually lose. Right now, his brain is like a sponge—a naked receiver of information rather than a sensitized sieve attuned to logic. So when he sees a man standing by his sister's bed, he'd say he saw a man standing by his sister's bed." She pursed her lips. "Grownups, on the other hand, would come up with an explanation like a hallucination or an optical illusion— or liken it to something only deer or eagles can see."

I crossed my arms, it being my only other means of defense. "Considering I'm a grownup, I guess I'm excused for proposing it's a hallucination?"

She gave the subtlest shake of her head. "I know—as both a doctor and mother—that what your brother experienced last night was something external. And just like those with hyperthymesia, synesthesia, and tetrachromacy, your brother may have a little-known capacity most people find bizarre. So have you yourself seen or sensed anything unusual around here?"

"No." If she hadn't included those last two words, I would have said yes.

Mom narrowed her eyes. "You know what he's talking about, don't you?"

I couldn't stop myself from swallowing.

"What are you afraid of?" she asked.

"Nothing, I'm just—"

"Scared people will laugh at you? For considering something utterly absurd."

I suppose . . . yes. I tilted my head. "Isn't it?"

She raised a brow. "Don't assume that something that seems supernatural isn't worth any reasonable person's time. If no one had ever figured out the answers, we'd still think rainbows, thunder, and lightning are heavenly signs of how the gods feel."

"Believing in gods sounds sublime." I shuddered inwardly, suddenly dreading how our efforts could lead Starr and me to uncover the absurd. "Believing the dead come back to haunt the living just sounds downright ludicrous."

"It sounds ludicrous because you chose to put it that way. If it's so unreasonable to think our consciousness lingers even after a person dies, then medical science should be ashamed of itself for working on technology to revive a dead brain." She rose from her seat and headed towards the hallway. "Perfectly reasonable things can seem like a joke. People used to laugh at one headstrong doctor who insisted on handwashing in clinics because of 'cadaverous particles' that nobody could see. He lost his job because of his assertions and eventually had a nervous breakdown. But now that we know what germs are, half the world walks around with hand-sanitizers in their bags." She paused at the guestroom doorway, like a diva about to make a grand exit. "That ought to tell you it's not all that ludicrous to believe in things that you can't see."

She disappeared into the room, and I sat frozen until I let my gaze slowly make its way towards my bedroom door that gaped wide open. Could it be welcoming some cadaverous guest that nobody could see?

What am I thinking? I pulled my hair back and away from my face, prodding myself to think straight. I needed to discuss this with someone perfectly logical and objective—yet someone I could trust not to laugh.

Only one person came to mind.

8

KING OF THE STARS

Two days went by before Torula could find time for us to meet again. Two entire days that proved to me she and I had one thing very much in common: Our work had turned into our lives.

This time, I chose a much better restaurant. Quieter. Fancier. Pricier.

She walked in with back straight, chin high, clutching a shoulder bag and a jacket. She turned towards me, and my gaze shifted to the front of her button-down shirt left hanging open over a tank top that dipped low enough for me to have to will myself to keep my eyes on her face.

"Here's your jacket," she said, handing it to me. "Sorry for the mistake."

"No worries." I kept my eyes averted, pushing her chair in as she sat down. "How was your day?" I asked and settled across the table from her.

"Oh, kind of average," she said with a shrug. "Until we tried to electrocute a papaya."

I paused, realizing it wasn't a joke—but I laughed anyway. The fact that she was serious made it funnier. And more fascinating.

With that quick exchange, I hoped the ice was broken, at least for the evening. Soon, a waitperson—a human servitor who was among the reasons this place was extravagant—approached our table. As Torula placed her order, I moved aside a vase that obscured my perfect view of her. She caught me staring and used two fingers to push a floating candle away from her and closer to the center of the table, making its ivory glow dance across the crystal.

She seemed far more at ease than the first time we'd met up. She gestured more as she talked, mostly about work, her best friend Starr, and quite a lot about this new Verdabulary software she had.

Verdabulary. Clever name. She'd come up with it and was proud of it. So was I.

I leaned back and enjoyed her buoyant mood. Better I bided my time than have her suddenly close up in shock over my news. She was like one of those sensitive plants we had played with as children. Touch a frond, and the leaves curled up, and if one tried to coax it open, the tighter it folded and the longer one would have to wait before it unfurled.

My mind wandered back to the day when she had first shown me the trailing plant. "It's a *Mimosa pudica*," she had said. "It's also known as Sensitive Plant. Touch-Me-Not. Or a Shy Plant."

"You're serious about becoming a botanist, aren't you?"

"And you're serious about becoming an astronaut, aren't you?"

"Yeah, I wanna be king of the stars!"

Her eyes had twinkled so brightly then, as she looked at me and shared in my dream, that I blurted out, "Maybe you can be my queen."

At the age of thirteen, I barely had a clue what I was feeling—but on an impulse, I had pulled her close, the way I'd seen some superhero do it in a movie, and in that longest moment, I felt her heart beating against mine. Her breath against my lips. And I kissed her.

She shoved me away and said, "You're so cheesy! I smell a rat." Blushing, she dashed home to her mother.

With my heart slightly bruised, but also thrilled, I had learned an irony that day: To keep her close, I had to stay at the right distance.

"People don't comprehend the torture they put plants through," the grown-up Torula said, wrenching me back to the here and now.

"What torture?" I asked, hoping she hadn't noticed I'd drifted off.

"They're often treated like decorations that grow, just a notch above inanimate objects because they can't walk or speak." She tilted her head at me. "How would you define something to be alive?"

I shrugged. "I imagine there's an equation out there that defines it."

"Biologists have a list of criteria, actually."

"A list? Your definition of life is a list?"

"More like a sum of distinguishing phenomena."

"A *sum*. That's more like it." I grinned.

"Only you would reduce life to a numeric entity." Her lips curled into a smile. "Sometimes, I think that's the only reason you want to walk in space. So you could glimpse that cosmic blackboard on which the universal chalk sticks."

Finally, an opening! "A walk in space. Is that . . ." I cleared my throat. "Is that something you've ever thought about?"

She shook her head. "Can you imagine being uprooted from your natural habitat and forced to survive in a contained environment, away from sunshine and completely dependent on artificial sources of food, energy, and water?"

I winced. "That's what you think of space travel?"

"No. It's what life is like as a potted plant, particularly one that's kept indoors."

I cracked my knuckles, having had enough talk about vegetables. "Besides the Verdabulary—what's the most interesting thing that's happened to you lately?"

"At work?"

"Anywhere. Is there anyone you're seeing?" My heart thudded at the question.

She smiled teasingly. "Yes, there is. And I'd like to see it again soon."

"It?" An image of Shrek flashed in my mind. "Exactly how ugly is he?"

She laughed, but I found it impossible to share in her mirth.

"Starr and I . . . well, she and I . . . We saw something that was like a . . . visual phenomenon that might have been . . ." She bit her lower lip for a moment. "Mom's convinced it's a ghost, and she'd like me to dig up an explanation."

That was much funnier than electrocuting a papaya, and a chuckle sputtered out of my mouth.

Her eyes suddenly seemed to darken in shade like a creature in a sci-fi movie about to disembowel its prey. "You, of all people. I've been aching to tell you since last night, thinking I could trust you not to laugh."

"I wasn't laughing." But I said it with a barely restrained smirk.

"Whatever it was, it's synonymous to laughing."

"Only because I thought—" Christ. I was acting the same way Sienna had when I thought I'd gotten a phone call from the dead. I wiped the smile completely off of my face. "Wait. You . . . really saw a ghost?"

"I was distracted and applied the wrong software at the wrong time to the wrong plant. I mean—*Carica Papaya, Ficus Carica*. It's an understandable mix-up. Anyway—" She huffed out a breath. "To make a long story short, I think I might have triggered the visual phenomenon."

I nodded, trying to grasp what had happened. "You keep calling it a 'visual phenomenon.' What exactly was it?"

"It was this human-like figure. Floating. We have no images or recordings. But our equipment is calibrated for plant life, detecting the minutest shifts in electromagnetic and chemical signals, the subtlest of movements, and ultradian events. We found unexplained fluctuations recorded by the EM meter, radiation monitor, and infrared sensor indicating there was something tangible enough for our instruments to have detected movement. It's something that I don't want to call a ghost, even though it looked every bit like one."

"What do you think it really was?"

"I have no idea. That's why I want to study it."

"Provided nobody laughs?"

She flashed a flicker of a frown. "Provided nobody *whom I respect* laughs."

I swallowed, wishing I could rewind the last couple of minutes and start over.

The waitperson arrived and set down our orders. We both went silent.

"Enjoy your meal, sir. Madam." As soon as the waitperson left, her silence lifted.

"I don't know what to do, Bram. I'd hate to let go of this once-in-a-lifetime chance . . . but pursuing it means risking my entire career over something many clearly find preposterous."

You can just leave it all and come with me. I took a sip of wine. It was the only way I could plug up my mouth about Pangaea, having lost the opening to bring it up.

That crinkle remained on her forehead, making the wine lose its bouquet and finish.

My comfort zone was when I was solving problems. Figuring out puzzles. Calculating equations. But I didn't have a clue what to do about this. "There's over a dozen explanations out there for what people mistake for ghosts. I'm sure one of them—"

"You think I haven't checked all those out already? I have. Both Starr and I have, and there's still no explaining it."

"Speaking of Starr . . ." Surely, two biologists' heads were clearer than one. ". . . what does she think about all this?"

"She's a widow, so she's drawn to this on a very personal level. And I'm surprised you're not. I mean, what if . . ." She paused.

"What if what?"

She brushed the hair off her brow. "Aren't you even considering that it might be your friend?"

"Franco?" The memory of Sienna and her tears of glee flooded my mind with embarrassment all over again. "Only if he were still alive and playing a joke on me."

Torula lowered her gaze and picked at her food.

Sienna's response, tactless as it had been, was a much-deserved reminder of how foolish it was to believe in an afterlife. I'd had my heart and spirit broken by that delusion long ago, and it wouldn't do Torula any good to go there too.

"Look," I said. "I know you're curious, but it's not worth it. Like you said, it's putting your reputation on the line." Something no scientist—or anyone, for that matter—could afford to lose.

"But if it leads to something useful, it's a chance to make a difference in the world. You know, a chance for . . . greatness." She shrugged. "How often does an introverted botanist get that?"

She made it sound like an ambition, but I saw nothing lofty about it. "Exactly how does studying ghosts benefit the botanical community?"

"It doesn't. So it could mean a new branch of science."

I almost choked on my tenderloin. "Occult science? That's quite an oxymoron there." I eased dinner down with more wine.

She narrowed her eyes. "Okay, let me speak in a language you'd understand."

"What language is that?"

"Robots."

"What's that got to do with—"

"If you ever came across a dead Optimus Crime, wouldn't you want to know what happened to his data after he ran out of batteries?"

As extensive as Torula's vocabulary was compared to mine, robot-speak was still my territory. "Autobots don't run on batteries, Spore. They have the AllSpark. And his name's Optimus *Prime*, not Crime." I shook my head. "Obviously, you think what you're considering is bordering on criminal."

"Isn't it more of a crime to walk away when given a chance to learn something valuable?"

"Valuable . . . how exactly?"

She leaned forward in her seat, unknowingly offering me a better view of her cleavage, and I averted my gaze. "People everywhere are trying to communicate with ghosts because they want to talk with their dearly departed or simply because they want a good scare. But what if ghosts are a sign that we don't just switch off and disappear after death? And that there is no paradise waiting, and we need to fend for ourselves right here?"

I flicked some sugar crystals from a saucer to distract myself and said nothing.

"You're trying not to laugh again."

"No, I'm not."

"Then why can't you look me in the eye?"

"Because I'm trying not to look down your blouse!" I said, looking right where I said I was trying not to.

"Great." She huffed in irritation and gruffly picked up her knife. "I tell you my plans, and the first thing you do is tell me to forget them."

My insides twisted into a knot, and I kicked myself in the arse for doing to Torula what she'd never done to me. But she was in the same place I'd been just a few days ago, thinking the supernatural possible only because she hadn't found the likelier explanation . . . yet.

We both silently went to work on our food, and as I went through the motions of enjoying dinner, I pondered what I could possibly say to undo the ill effects of a chuckle.

The waitperson came by and asked, "Would you like some *carpe diem*, bro?"

I gawked at him. "What did you say?" I could have sworn I'd turned deathly white.

"None for me, thank you," Torula said. "But I'm sure he'd love some."

"Some what?" I asked, still gawking.

"Coffee, sir," the waitperson said.

"That's . . ." I looked at Torula. ". . . what he really said?"

She nodded and tilted her head, looking puzzled.

Was my subconscious trying to tell me what to do next that I was starting to hear voices?

I glanced around, looking for someone with vivid green hair but found no sign of Sienna. With a slow, suspicious nod, I said, "Yeah, sure. But . . ." I squinted at the waitperson. "I'm going to be really pissed if you come back with a half-empty mug."

The man nodded and trembled up a smile as he walked away.

Torula wiped her lips, almost done with her dinner, and here I was, still reluctant to broach the very things I'd come to talk about —as though they were cards I was holding close to my chest and couldn't lay down on the table.

Dr. Grant's piercing gaze loomed inside my head. *Is it because you refuse to take no for an answer? Or because you're used to getting what you want?*

I took a deep breath and leaned forward in my seat. "I'm at a crossroads."

She didn't even glance up from her plate. "About what?"

"I'd like to get your opinion on . . . my 'place of residence,' so to speak."

She froze, holding up a piece of prawn skewered on her fork. "You've accepted the offer, haven't you?"

"I'm not leaving NASA."

She put her fork down and frowned. "So they're posting you abroad? I didn't know NASA did that."

"It's not that simple."

"Is it Asia? Europe? The Middle East? Far is far. What difference does it make?"

"Believe me; you have no idea how 'far' far can get."

Her shoulders tensed up.

"You're upset," I said.

"Why shouldn't I be? Sixteen years, you never even came for a visit. And the minute you do, it's to say goodbye. Again."

My mouth hung open. If I said come with me, she'd ask where. If I said outer space, she'd ask how far. If I told the truth, she'd . . .

"All right, never mind." She crossed her arms. "If you're leaving, I don't want to hear about it. We can just end the night."

"What? Wait. It's just that—" *I can't risk you saying no.* "Can we just spend some time together first? Get close again?"

"Get close. Before you move even farther away?"

Shite. I knew it was too soon to lay those cards down. "Look, I'm asking you to just *be* with me for a while."

"Just *be* with you?"

"Yeah," I said, and having to ask her that suddenly lifted blinders from my eyes, making me see how foolish I'd been all these years—for not finding more time to be with her.

I glanced to my side as the waitperson laid my steaming cup of coffee next to me. It was filled to the brim.

JUST BE WITH ME

(TORULA)

I EMERGED BREATHLESS FROM SLEEP, BRAM'S COMFORTING PRESENCE ON top of me. He seemed so light, like a soothing blanket. Protective and warm. Through barely opened eyelids, I caught a blurry glimpse of his naked shoulder and his long, wavy hair.

My breath caught. Bram didn't have long hair!

Suddenly, my mind was wide awake. Bram and I had parted ways at the restaurant. I tried to move but couldn't. I struggled to speak, but my voice stayed locked inside my throat, my jaws clamped tight.

The sensation of a stranger's warmth on top of me grew stronger. I was alert yet trapped inside a dream. I strained to see from the corner of my eyes, but all I could catch was his dark hair, his face burrowed next to my shoulder.

"Just *be* with me," he whispered, sounding so much like Bram.

With all the strength I could muster, I shoved the figure off of me. He became as light as mist, and for a flicker of a moment, I saw his arm swing away as he lifted his embrace. And then he was gone.

Finally, I was able to move, but for a long while, I sat absolutely still as an overpowering sense of security and warmth wrapped itself around me. Vivid images flashed through my mind. A spray of bright blue forget-me-nots. Eyes that gleamed in fiery gold. Bronze hands slithering across my skin with a frozen touch that burned. A moan. A sigh. A whisper.

With a steady hand, I turned on my bedside lamp and noted the time. Barely three in the morning.

I left the comfort of my bed, the cloud of calm drifting away as I walked to the bathroom. Though I splashed cold water on my face, I couldn't let go of how real the apparition had been. As I looked at my image in the mirror, I asked myself why I wasn't afraid.

And that was when fear gripped me.

I hurried back into my room and turned on a few more reassuring lights. I tossed a change of clothes into a duffel bag and headed for the door. Someone had to explain to me what was happening to my mind.

10

NOTHING TO WORRY ABOUT

(TORULA)

I HAD EXPECTED A SHOCKED REACTION TO MY STORY OF A PARANORMAL paramour, but instead, all I got were a few calm nods of comprehension and a cup of hot chocolate in my hands.

"Classic case of sleep paralysis," Mom declared. "Nothing to worry about."

She'd sat me at her breakfast nook looking out at her herb and flower garden softly lit by lantern lights. Though I'd shown up at her door with barely a warning, she conducted my pre-dawn consultation dressed in a long-and-loose, pale paisley dress, her auburn hair in a braided half ponytail, and eyes alight with analytic interest.

"You make it sound like it's perfectly normal," I said, not quite believing it.

"It's common enough for people to have at least one episode in their lives, and it's not unusual for it to come with surreal hallucinations."

I shook my head. "But it wasn't surreal. It was the opposite. It felt real, and so much like Bram, I was so convinced . . ."

"That it was your dream come true?" She arched a brow. "It seems your spectral suitor was smart enough to fulfill your

Freudian wish to be with Bram. Lucky you." She tapped my mug with her teaspoon, creating a cheery ding.

I slid my mug backwards. "Mom, please take this seriously."

"I am. It's a globally-acknowledged form of parasomnia. It used to be called 'ghost oppression' in China, the 'Old Hag' syndrome in Newfoundland, and in Mexico, it's referred to as 'a dead body climbed on top of me' phenomenon. The exact cause may be difficult to pinpoint. But in your case . . ." She poised her teaspoon to tap my mug into another teasing chime.

I used my hand to shield my cup and pulled it closer towards me. "Why wasn't I scared then? Consider those labels other people have given it. Wasn't my reaction clearly aberrant?"

She pursed her lips. "You're right. Yours sounds closer to a nocturnal emission."

I gawked at her. "A wet dream? Mom, stop toying with me."

She gave a tongue-in-cheek laugh. "Oh, if anyone's toying with you, it's obviously the ghost in your bedroom. Rather than give you a sense of foreboding or a spooky feeling like you're being watched, this one simply charmed your pants off." She stirred her drink, looking as casual as someone talking about a first date.

I grimaced at her nonchalance. Did non-psychiatrist mothers also have this habit? That of trivializing matters which made their children anxious to make them believe that everything was fine. Frankly, it only made me more anxious. "Why do you think I'm not responding the way most people would? Can you at least answer me that?"

Mom laid down her teaspoon and fixed her eyes on me. "You're embarrassed more than you're afraid because you found yourself in bed with someone whom everyone would have expected you to shun."

Oh, please. I snapped two fingers to take her out of her own disorientation. "We're not talking about a person, Dr. Triana."

"Aren't we? Supposing ghosts truly are the residual consciousness of people who've passed away, then they'd probably be like disoriented humans. Feeling lost and helpless and reaching out to anyone who could see or hear them." She paused and let her gaze wander out the window towards the early morning magic of her garden, the sky warming up with a glow of the palest peach. "I imagine that's what I would have done had my near-death experience lasted longer than it did. That would have been dreadful, wouldn't it? If my sisters screamed each time I tried to communicate. Or worse, if they didn't even sense a thing no matter what I tried to do." She brought her attention back to me. "Admittedly, instinct always cautions us against the unknown. But then again, what hazardous things are ghosts known to do?"

"In a nutshell?" I clutched my hot mug of chocolate, Mom's standard balm for my childhood fear of the dark. "They scare you to death."

She waved a hand flippantly. "Most people are simply ghostist, primed and conditioned by everything from the internet to Hollywood to Stephen King. You felt no reason to be afraid because your ghost, obviously, is much, much friendlier than Casper." Mom quirked her brow.

Her arguments could have made sense, but only if one anthropomorphized these "things." And given that I'd mistaken that thing in my bed for Bram, it could've passed the Duck Test. *If it sounds like a duck, looks like a duck . . .*

Mom's gaze shifted to my hands clasping the mug close to my chest. "You're clinging to that cup as if you're about to fall off a cliff. You're teetering on the edge of believing."

I put the hot chocolate on the table and crossed my arms. "For all you know, it's genetic. Both Truth and I see something." I tilted my head. "Have you ever experienced hallucinations you haven't told me about?"

"I've never hallucinated a thing in my life," she declared with a raise of her chin. "Nor have I ever seen anything remotely like a ghost. Though one thing's for sure, I came very close to becoming one."

I groaned. "Can't you just say it's some form of psychosis? Or anything else that makes more sense."

If there was a regal way to roll one's eyes, Mom had perfected it. "Why come asking for my opinion, then reject everything I say?"

"Because none of your answers are scientific!"

"Of course, they are," she said. "Though spelled a bit differently."

"What?"

"P-S-I. Psientific."

I winced. "Great. So what we've been discussing here was purely psi-ence fiction. I think I'll just spend the rest of my morning reading Isaac Asimov. I'm bound to learn something more useful there." I picked up my mug and headed for a comfortable couch. "It's just impossible, Mom. I can't imagine how someone dead and buried could leave behind a living mind."

"Funny," she said, following me to the living room. "That's what Creationists say about Darwin's theory. They can't imagine how some lifeless clump of atoms eventually became a human called Adam."

I chuckled as I plopped down on the couch. "Who knows? Maybe one of these days, S-C-I science will learn how to explain it better."

"Well, you're in a very rare position to find the real and better explanation for ghosts. So drink up and get to work. Stop delaying the advancement of science—*and* psience—by hanging around here." She strode off and left me with my thoughts and my beverage.

I gazed out through sliding glass doors at her patio garden, dewdrops now glistening in the early morning light, and pondered the possibility—or rather, impossibility—of conscious, incorporeal life. Should Starr and I continue with our attempts to explain what it was we saw? I imagined presenting our findings to a roomful of peers who would collectively get up and exit, leaving behind a peanut gallery of hecklers shouting, "Didn't anyone tell you? Botanists don't dig six feet under!"

What the foxtrot. I can't do this. It would only take me from being the peculiar nerd who talked to plants to being the peculiar scientist who wanted to talk to ghosts. There was just no making sense of it. *Life simply can't be experienced by the dead.*

My iHub rang, and at the sight of Bram's name, the unsettling sensations from last night's dream swept through me again.

"Hello?" I said tentatively.

"I'm sorry about last night."

"Last night?" *You weren't really in my bed, were you?*

"I laughed at your story. About the ghost. I didn't mean to."

"Oh, that. Forget about it."

"I can't. That's why I called." He paused for a second. "I want to help you figure it out."

"What?"

"I want to help with your 'occult science.' It would give us a chance to—"

The deafening whirr of a vintage vacuum cleaner sucked away the rest of his sentence.

"Hang on a minute," I said, almost shouting. I scooted towards the door to get to the patio and tripped on a cord.

"Sorry." I paused to plug the vacuum cleaner back in. "In case you haven't heard, Mom, the rest of the world has gone cordless."

"You mean the rest of the still-dusty world? There's never enough power from things that run on batteries."

I stepped out onto the patio and slid the glass door shut. "Sorry about that," I said into my iHub. "Mom's still attached to her old-reliable vacuum cleaner."

"Yes, I heard. She ought to meet an Autobot. The AllSpark is far more powerful than those batteries she hates."

I peered through the sliding door as Mom restarted her loud household chore. My gaze fell on the electrical cord snaking from the appliance, and I traced its path as it curled and coiled back to the outlet on the wall.

"Anyway," Bram said. "I've got two months free. What do you think?"

Autobots don't run on batteries. I blinked in reflex to an idea that poked me between the eyes. "Wait. What did you just say?"

"Two months. I could help—"

"No, about the AllSpark."

"What?"

"Why is it better than batteries?"

"Because!" He laughed. "It's the spark of life of every Transformer that ever lived."

"Right. Exactly." I needed to end the call and chase the thought before it frittered away. "Bram, I think it's a bad idea for you to get involved in this. Besides, I'm not really in any position to grant you access to the program. It's not even my nursery. It's Starr's." I pushed the door open and let the din of Mom's duties drown out the rest of my words. "I'm sorry, but I can't talk right now." I barely heard him say goodbye as I marched into the living room and pointed at the noisy apparatus.

"Mom."

"What?" She turned the appliance off. "Are you about to scold me for keeping my house clean?"

"What's the difference between a live vacuum cleaner and a dead one?"

"The first one's much better at cleaning."

"The live vacuum cleaner has electricity coursing through it; the other doesn't. What's the difference between someone alive and a dead body?"

She scrunched up her brow. "Did I give you a hot toddy instead of hot chocolate just now?"

I strode to the outlet on the wall. "One still has life coursing through him, the other doesn't." I pulled out the plug and held it up. "Electricity doesn't cease to exist after we unplug the vacuum cleaner. We just stop seeing the effects of electricity on a machine."

Mom tilted her head. "Keep talking. I think you're on the verge of making sense."

"Our bodies are like machines. Once infused with the spark of life, we are what we call 'a-live.' And when that spark leaves us, where does it go?" I let the electrical cord drop to the floor. "Life could be everywhere, Mom. Like electromagnetism and gravity. Life doesn't cease to exist after the body goes dead—it just stops coursing through us!"

Mom stood silent and still for a while, perhaps deciding if she should indeed declare me psychotic. "Your father." She paused and took a breath. "He believed in a vital force that permeates the entire universe. He called it *Ki*. A healing life energy. But he never spoke of it this way—not as the force that animates matter."

My father. My breath caught, as though a potent dose of this "Ki" suddenly shot through me. Mom close-to-never talked to me and my brothers about our fathers. For her to have mentioned this, right now, told me how important she thought it was. "If this is true, that the energy that brings life is something merely harnessed and manifested by metabolic matter and therefore can exist outside of it, then maybe the biological process doesn't truly end where we think it does. Maybe that's how some form of 'consciousness' can persist beyond death. What if all that happens to consciousness after death is a metamorphosis? A form of life in suspension or dormancy we don't yet understand."

Mom beamed at me. "If there's any chance you can prove this theory of yours, then take it. Do something with it. Oh, sweetheart." She let go of the vacuum cleaner and walked over to embrace me. I returned the hug tentatively, unused to this effusive display of motherly warmth. "Can you believe this? My daughter could very well establish the science that picks up where medical science leaves off. You can save those who've defied saving."

I flashed an uneasy smile. Greatness, it seemed, might not be so bad, except in this case, it was bound to find me out of a job. Or out of my mind.

11

WELCOME TO GREENHOUSE 3C

TORULA HAD ACCEPTED MY APOLOGY BUT DODGED THE PEACE offering. Good thing there was some other way to bring it to her doorstep.

"It's great to see you, Bram!" Starr greeted me with her charming hint of an Irish accent. Standing at the greenhouse entrance, she gave me the kind of unbridled hug aunties give their favorite nephews. Her perfume, pleasant and fruity, wrapped me in its own overwhelming embrace.

"Thanks for allowing me to come," I said. Though all we'd ever shared were shallow chitchats inserted over video calls with Torula, Starr seemed every bit like an old friend.

"Us, meeting face to face, is long overdue." She stepped back and stood with hands on hips, giving a better view of a dress of blinding blue and garish green beneath her lab coat. "And it had to take a ghost to get you here."

"Yeah, well . . ." I grinned, grateful to have found a new excuse to spend more time with Torula. "Good thing management didn't mind an outsider coming to take a look."

"As far as management knows, Tor and I have been studying the night-blooming cereus." Her glossy lips curled into a smile, and from the pocket of her coat, she pulled out a cell phone covered in gemstones and made a call. "He's here. Like it or not, I'm bringing him in."

Like it or not? I cocked my head. I guess Torula had told her about that chuckle.

Starr put the phone back into her pocket, pressed a manicured finger on a scanner, and got an error notice.

"Oh, not again." She crinkled her nose. "This thing has been acting up lately." She dug into her pocket and pulled out a bit of paper towel.

I stopped her before she could wipe the scanner with it. "Here, let me. Paper could damage it." I took out my handkerchief and gave the surface a quick rub. "Use some window cleaner when you can. There. Try again."

She did and got a green light. "You're quite handy to have around, aren't you?" She stared at my hand as I shoved my hanky back into my pocket. "You know, that's not hygienic."

"No worries. I've got a bot butler programmed to enjoy doing laundry. Every handkerchief, for him, is another reason to go on living."

She gave a wink like a *Good Housekeeping* stamp of approval. "Welcome to Greenhouse 3C, honey." She pushed the door open and led the way in.

Tall shrubs grew in organized plant beds with cables, wires, and a mess of bric-a-brac strewn and strung amongst the branches. This had to be the botanical equivalent of an animal testing facility or something like a plant asylum where each specimen was a nervous wreck. The place was quiet, but something like the suspenseful note in movie soundtracks hung in the air—except nothing was audible. The place didn't even need a ghost to make my hair stand on end.

Starr guided me across stone paths in high heels, and she handled it better than an acrobat on stilts on a tightrope because she didn't even wobble. On top of that, she managed a conversation by tossing words over her shoulder at me.

"After you called, I thought of the perfect reason to get you clearance to be allowed in here. I told them this was the only way I could get Torula to date anyone, and they gave me the thumbs up!" She let out a laugh as pleasant as a fairy tale with a happy ending.

Effervescent. That was the word Torula had used to describe her. I guessed that meant Torula and I had one more thing in common: We had both gravitated to the happiest persons where we worked. Suddenly, the memory of a laughing Franco flashed in my mind, stirring a faint sense of sadness.

We came to an elevated workstation at the center of the nursery where Torula sat working at the console table.

"Hey, Spore," I said as I climbed the wooden stairs, snagging my shoe on a narrow step and nearly stumbling.

"You've always been horrible with stairs," Torula said without bothering to turn and look my way, acting about as friendly as someone who'd been blindsided into a blind date. "There was a reason I didn't want you coming here."

"Mind your manners, Tor," Starr said. "He's here to help."

"And I don't think he realizes what's at stake." Torula stood up and faced me. "Can you imagine what NASA would say if they found out what you came here for?"

"What's wrong with paying some friends a visit?" I asked.

Torula folded her arms. "When I told you I wanted to study this anomaly, you laughed and tried to stop me because it could damage my reputation."

"That's because . . . I . . . hadn't thought about it enough yet."

"And have you thought about what your colleagues would say if they find out you went ghost-hunting?"

I didn't have to. Sienna's delightedly tearful reaction to my phone call from The Great Beyond was forever stored in my head. "Look," I said, "there's nothing wrong with helping you find answers. I know how curiosity can grip you and not let go. I was also a victim of a hoax, and—"

"Victim?" Torula asked.

"A hoax?" Starr asked.

I swallowed. Jesus. Did I just stomp mud all over Starr's welcome mat?

"You're here to prove us wrong . . . is that what you're saying?" Torula asked.

"No," I lied. "Of course not."

"Then why are you risking your reputation by coming here?"

"Like he said, honey," Starr said, "he's here just visiting old friends. So why not act like a gracious host and make our guest feel more comfortable?" She reached for a knob on the table. "Here, let me darken the Transhade a bit for you."

I glanced around as the invisible walls of the platform area and the glass sheet suspended directly overhead slowly increased in tint on the side facing west, shielding us better from the late afternoon sunlight.

"Well, since you're 'just visiting,'" Torula said. "I'm sure you're not at all interested in seeing the data we've gathered, right?"

"Actually," I flashed what I hoped was a charming smile, "if it's not too much trouble, I was hoping you could show me the Verdabulary in action. I've never been in a talking garden before."

"That's next door," Torula said matter-of-factly. "We're in Starr's nursery, remember? She's the *only* one who agreed to let you come."

"Oh, don't be such a cold fish," Starr said. "We're in a greenhouse, not a seafood market. Come on." She sashayed to the console table and pulled a chair out for Torula. "Just access your recordings from here." She thumped the back rest in invitation.

Torula let out a hot breath, cast me a disapproving glance, then made her way to the seat. She clicked a few times on the screen, and then a deep, spine-chilling voice sliced through the air. "Your stress is affecting me."

"Whoa. What was that?" I asked.

"I call him Lurch," Torula said, finally with a tinge of a smile. "He's an *Amorphophallus titanium*."

"English, Spore."

"Literally, it translates to a badly-shaped penis. But its common names are Titan Arum or the Corpse Plant."

"You chose the perfect voice," I said. "That definitely sounded like a dead guy upset about the shape of his dick."

A chuckle escaped Torula, and Starr arched a brow. "Well now, that's a rare sound."

"The Titan's voice?" Torula asked.

"No, honey. You, laughing." Starr gave me an encouraging wink.

I glanced at Torula, who quickly turned away.

"Ooh, do Lord Ruthven," Starr said. "The one that sounds like a blood-sucking leech."

A raspy, ghoulish voice issued over the speakers. "Mmm-yum-yum-yum. Yess, yess. You are so sumptuousss, my sweetnessss."

"That was a mistletoe," Torula said.

"No way," I said. "That's what those plants are thinking when people kiss under them at Christmas?"

Starr let loose her sparkling laugh. "Of course not. That's them sucking the lifeblood out of the host trees they live on."

"Mistletoes are parasites that take nutrients and water from the plants they grow on," Torula said. "If left unmanaged, they can kill the host tree."

"Mistletoe?" I asked. "Can kill?"

"Once attached to a tree, they stay there until it's dead. Not to kill it but to subsist on its water and minerals. But when it grows unchecked, yes, it can kill."

"No."

I glanced at the two women, unsure which of them had said that. "No what?"

"That was Charlotte," Torula said, "my spider plant, talking."

"No," the plant said again. "No, no, no, no—"

Torula clicked *Mute*, silencing Charlotte. "She hasn't been watered in days, and she's been saying no . . . to something. I'm trying to build her vocabulary for when her situation gets desperate."

"It's so sad," Starr said. "Torula has to listen to her die."

"What for?"

"From what I learn here," Torula said, "I can create recordings that will allow plants to cry for help and give instructions to inexperienced gardeners on what to do to save them."

"Incredible." I swept my gaze around the nursery, captivated by its wonder—but also seeing how the "special effects" could lead one to imagine a ghost. "How does it work?"

"I explained it all to you at the restaurant, but I suppose you were distracted by your steak." She smiled. I gave a one-sided shrug. It was hardly my food that had kept stealing my attention that night.

"The main thing for us to understand is what they're feeling and why," Torula said. "We take physiological and biochemical readings of each plant in response to certain stimuli like temperature, humidity, light, and sounds. Substances in the soil and air. Even a gardener's mood or stress levels."

"Really?" I asked. "Plants can sense that?"

"There's this old superstition," Torula said, "that menstruating women shouldn't sow seeds or touch any plants because it could badly affect the plant's growth. We have results indicating it may have something to do with hormone levels of the gardener, not menstruation per se. Which, by the way, is why I'm considering that our synchronized ovulation might have had something to do with the apparition."

I understood the words . . . but wasn't sure I did. "Say again?"

"Quite likely, Starr and I were both ovulating at the time of the anomaly. Women who spend a lot of time together generally end up with synchronized monthly cycles. What regulates it is postulated to be something that can be found in our perspiration. And since Starr and I are around each other a lot, we end up smelling each other's sweat. Which is why we suspect our combined elevated hormone levels might be a factor that triggered the hyperwill to appear."

"The what?" I asked.

"Oh, *hyperwill* is a term I made up," Torula said, "to refer to the anomaly, rather than ghost."

"What does it mean?"

She glanced at Starr, who pursed her lips, then turned away.

"I'll go stand over where I was when it happened," Starr said, then made her way down the stairs. "Next to the papayas."

Torula swiveled back to face her monitor. "I'll explain the term some other time." She swept her hair to one side of her neck, her sweet, heady scent drifting towards me, easily eliminating any need for an explanation.

"I like your perfume," I said.

"Really? It's Lavender Lace."

"Lavender." I leaned closer and took a more intimate whiff of her neck. "It's good on you."

"Thank you." She laid two fingers against my jaw and turned my face towards the section beyond the workstation. "The hyperwill appeared over there. So if we can get back to the kiss you—I mean issue at hand, please?"

My mouth curled up into a self-assured grin as I blindly stared ahead. There was something I really liked about these slips of the tongue.

She pointed at an icon on the monitor, her voice all business. "See this? That's the VeggieVolt—Starr's defective program that was running in the background when I did this." She clicked on the Verdabulary icon, then opened a page containing a dizzying list of botanical names. "I selected the wrong specimen name, and when I looked over there . . ." She pointed in Starr's direction then slowly rose to her feet. I followed her gaze and saw—

Holy mother.

I froze and gaped at a floating, shapeless glow the size of a full-grown man that looked very much like a . . . a . . . prank. A system malfunction. A strange hallucination.

"Florence . . ." it seemed to whisper like a faint breeze.

It was an illusion. There should've been nothing to fear, but my heart thumped wildly.

"Who are you?" Torula asked.

A muffled moan filled the nursery, and the hair on my arms bristled. Slowly, the image grew clearer. It had clothing that belonged in another century. Lace collar. Shiny, blue silken shirt. It could have been a costume. Its lower extremities were in a haze, but the facial features slowly grew distinct enough for me to note a crooked or broken nose between striking amber eyes. Then it raised its arm and held out what looked like a cluster of blue flowers.

Torula stood motionless. Starr made the sign of the cross. Neither seemed in danger, but I braced for what might happen next. I wanted to keep my eye on the image but couldn't help glancing around to find some means for it to be projected.

The vision slowly dissipated, and before I could make sense of anything, it was gone.

Starr scampered up the steps towards us. "Oh, heaven help the poor soul. I know you're a nonbeliever but, please, spend a moment in silence with me as I pray for his quiet repose." She reached out and took our hands in hers, closed her eyes, and bowed her head. Torula gave me an awkward smile with a raise of her brows as if to say 'Why not?' then closed her eyes too.

Starr's cold fingers clutched mine as I let my gaze wander down and fixate on the floorboards, scanning them for anything suspicious. *How could anyone fake such a thing?*

The deafening clang of a metal plate falling to the stone ground blasted through the air.

Starr recoiled with a squeal and retreated towards the steps.

"Aphids dark nitrogen." A man's senseless words spilled out of the Verdabulary.

A bluish cloud, about the size of Starr, coalesced a few feet from where she had stood and moved towards Torula. I stepped forward to block it, but the smoky specter went right through me sending an icy chill slicing its way up my spine to my scalp. *Jesus Bloody H. Christ.* I huffed out a tense breath and reached an arm out—into and through the eerie figure—but there was nothing to grasp.

The glowing, roiling cloud of misty blue glided closer towards her, and she stepped backwards. I walked around the hazy figure, reassuring myself it was harmless despite my heart's pounding. As I came to stand next to Torula, the apparition faded away.

I stared at the now empty spot as my mind fumbled for an explanation. There was computer equipment on the platform and a mix of all kinds of gear scattered in the plant beds all around. I squinted up at one of the beams supporting the Transhade overhead and spotted a small, black object. "What's that?"

"A security camera," Torula said. "But we don't think it works."

"Are you sure it's a camera?"

Starr was suddenly tugging at Torula. "Let's get out of here."

Torula moved towards the console. "We need to check the data."

"Just do that from your nursery. Come on!" Starr said.

"I'll follow," I said, determined to find a logical explanation.

"We'll be in my greenhouse," Torula said, allowing herself to get dragged off by Starr. "Just one scream away."

12

USING COMPANY PROPERTY

I FOLLOWED THE TWO BOTANISTS NEXT DOOR AND WAS RELIEVED TO
find that Torula's greenhouse had a far more pleasant feel
compared to the one we'd just left. Her plants were arranged in
neat rows around her elevated work area, each one on a pedestal
and covered by a bell-shaped glass enclosure—like the enchanted
rose in *Beauty and the Beast*, except Torula's plants could "talk"
even though they weren't under any spell. But the place did look
touched by magic, with the glow of the greenhouse lights shimmering off the glass domes.

Both women were at the central platform, seated at the console
table. Starr fingered the tiny crucifix that dangled just beneath her
throat as her other hand scrolled and clicked through charts and
tables. Torula sat gnawing on her lower lip, brow scrunched,
seeming far more frustrated than frightened as she scanned
the data.

"It *is* a camera," I said, declaring my worthless discovery, "but
there's no indicator light to tell if it's working or not."

"Because they're not." Starr gestured at another black gadget
high on a beam. "Everyone thinks they're just there for show, to
keep us from lazing on the job. I mean, the only thing of value here

is the software and data, and the system itself is designed to guard all that."

"Why not ask Security if they recorded anything anyway?" I asked.

"Honey, we're chasing ghosts using company property. If they haven't found out yet, I'd rather not call their attention to it."

"But you'd at least get your hands on something to help you figure it out." I glanced at her bejeweled cell phone on the table.

Starr pursed her lips. "I've got a feeling if they did see what had happened, they'd have called me already."

I glanced around, hoping to find some idea for another avenue to take. "What about your research cameras?"

"None were on when it happened," Torula said, her eyes still scanning the data. "Did you hear it call out a name?"

"Yes," I said.

"Florence?"

I nodded. I assumed it was another one of her plants' names.

Starr looked at us, doubt in her eyes. "You heard a name? All I heard was a scary moan after you asked who he was."

"No," Torula said, finally taking her eyes off her monitor. "He said Florence before I asked for his name."

"I didn't hear it at all," Starr said.

I surveyed their equipment. Extensive but not exactly state-of-the-art. Whatever the source of these shenanigans, could it be fooling with their system? "Tell me again how the Verdabulary works. How do you get a plant to 'talk?'"

Starr gestured towards the computer monitor displaying tabulated data. "The plants' responses to different situations and stimuli are gathered and interpreted, then Torula gives them verbal translations, which are recorded by voice talents."

"And they adapt different characterizations to match the personalities I assign each plant," Torula said. "When the Verdabulary recognizes a plant's response to given stimuli, it broadcasts the corresponding spiel. But we're still at the early stages of development. All we have for now is a very limited set of recordings."

"It's possible someone could have hacked your system and is messing with those recordings," I said.

"But not all of us heard it, and the equipment didn't record it." Torula dug her fingers into her hair. "Something else is going on."

I nodded, relieved neither of them pounced on me again for implying they were being tricked.

"What about the temperature?" Starr asked. "Did you feel it suddenly get cold in there?"

"Yes, of course," I said.

"Oh, thank goodness." Starr rubbed her hands brusquely up and down her arms. "I thought it was all in my head. It's just weird, though, that the readings don't show a temperature drop."

"What? That's impossible." I went over to Starr's monitor to have a look.

"I didn't feel it get cold," Torula said with a puzzled frown. "But even isolated cold spots should have been detected by the equipment."

Starr leaned away as she allowed me to take charge of her keyboard. "That's so strange. It's like each of us experienced it differently."

I checked the data showing temperature readings that had remained constant throughout the greenhouse. "I don't understand. These should show a dip in the temperature somehow. I was convinced there was an endothermic reaction going on. Something like what happens in instant cold packs. That's why I stayed behind. To find out how it could have been rigged, but I didn't find anything."

Starr squinted at me. "Why would anyone bother to rig it?"

"Why bother with crop circles, monster footprints, and UFO videos? It's a different brand of fun for some people."

"It needn't have been rigged," Torula said. "This could have been biochemical in nature."

"Biochemical?" Was she saying it was a *natural* thing? Surely, she could tell it was a projected image of some kind.

"You're in botanists' territory, Bram." Torula looked at me, her eyes sparkling. "Around here, photosynthesis rules, and that's endothermic. Heat is absorbed instead of released." She spread both her arms out as she walked backwards, meaning to show off her greenhouse, but my eyes were drawn only to her. "That's why gardens are the coolest place to be."

"Gardens are the coolest place to be?" I curled my mouth into a one-sided grin. "I bet you saw that on a T-shirt."

"If I had a flower for every time you made me smile . . . I'd have a garden." She bit her lip coyly and made my world spin. "*That's* what I saw on a T-shirt."

Starr gaped at us, eyes agog. "I can't believe you're flirting at a time like this! And comparing this manifestation to instant cold packs and photosynthesis? Aren't you even the least bit scared of it?"

Even though it was Starr who had welcomed me here, I suddenly wished she were nowhere near us.

"Why should we be scared of it?" Torula asked. "It's something that's gotten me perplexed, actually. Why people have a knee-jerk reaction to fearing it when not a single reputable news agency has ever reported 'Death by Ghost.' And yet many people find them even more frightening than sharks, scorpions, and snakes. Mom says the world is just being downright ghostist."

Starr recoiled at the accusation. "The last thing I am is . . ." She froze, blinked a few times, then sank into a chair. "Well, it's not every day a man suddenly materializes in front of you. I mean, even Louie never did."

"Louie?" I asked.

"My husband."

Torula took a tentative step towards her. "Starr, did you ever . . . feel anything that you thought . . . could be Louie?"

Starr took a breath, closed her eyes, and nodded, reaching for the tiny crucifix around her neck.

Torula took the seat next to her friend. "What was it?"

"I've never told anyone." Starr opened her eyes and glanced at both of us. "The first time was a few weeks after he'd gone. The kids and I had come home from church where I'd ended up crying. When we entered the apartment, the TV was on, but I'm sure it was off when we left. And it was tuned to his sports channel. Something the kids and I never, ever watch." She trembled as she took another deep breath. "And there were many other incidents. Things would disappear and reappear in the most mysterious ways. And once, I even got a text from an unknown number that said 'I'm here.' I tried calling it but never got past an automated message saying it can't be reached."

I cupped a fist over my lips to keep from suggesting it could have just been a wrong send from a burner phone.

A flush rose up Starr's cheeks. "At first, all of this gave me comfort. Until I realized he was sticking around just because of me. Trying to fix a problem only I could fix."

"What problem was that?" Torula asked.

"The emptiness I refused to fill." Tears fell from her eyes. "That's when I decided to set aside the black and show him I was moving on. So *he* could move on."

I let out a heavy breath. Somehow, I'd always had a suspicion that Starr's colorful exterior was a carefully maintained mask to hide her grief. But I never would have guessed it was for the benefit of her dead husband.

I squirmed inwardly, on the verge of breaking a widow's heart all over again. But I had to dissociate her feelings for Louie from this Verdabulary bug we had yet to figure out. "Hey, now, this is obviously not anyone . . . from your past. I mean, it's not even remotely realis—"

Starr blinked through her tears as she looked at me. "Are you still saying it's a hoax?"

"Or a glitch. How do you know it wasn't just the Verdabulary?"

"The name 'Florence' isn't in my library," Torula said. "And I've been trying to find something in the data that could explain what we heard, but there's nothing." She glanced at me, then at Starr, then back at me. "You do realize what that means."

"The sound must've come from somewhere else," I said.

"No. It means *he* made the sound," Torula said. "*He* has his own lexicon."

Starr clasped her hands over her heart. "Ghosts are sentient, aren't they?"

I held up both my hands. "Whoa, hold it right there. It could've been just some noise that, by coincidence, sounded like a word. So don't call it a *he*."

"What else do you think it could be but somebody's soul?" Starr asked.

I winced. "Now let's not call it a soul either. It could just be somebody's bad joke." Then a disturbing thought suddenly struck me. *Franco's VN couldn't possibly be behind this, too, can it?* Could all this have been staged by an app? Or did Franco subscribe to some posthumous service more elaborate than a fake arrest or kidnapping? It was too ridiculous to consider but maybe worth checking at the VN site, just to be sure.

"And what if it's not a hoax?" Starr asked, brows raised. "Look at the data, Bram! The Verdabulary detected movement. It probably pushed that metal plate. And be honest about what you saw. What else could it possibly be?"

My gaze darted over all the tabulations on their computer screens convinced there was an explanation in there somewhere. "I could go through these charts all day and not know what to make of them. We need to show these figures to someone who knows what to look for."

"Like who?" Torula asked. "Trust me, there aren't any mainstream scientists out there willing to be involved in stuff like this."

"She's right, honey. You'll need to go off-road to get any 'expert' opinions."

I was willing to drive as far off road as I needed to get some logical answers. "Would it be okay if I copied the data—"

"Oh, I'm afraid not," Starr said. "We're already doing these experiments on the sly, and releasing data to an outsider would only . . ." She averted her gaze with a sudden, worried frown.

"I understand."

"My goodness." Starr glanced at a beam overhead. "What if those cameras do work and Security called Management instead? Would they consider this . . . illegal?"

"Maybe we can go back and check the sound system," Torula said, as though she hadn't even heard her friend's concern. "Find out how it managed to say 'Florence' in your voice."

"*My* voice?" I asked. "That thing sounded nothing like me."

Torula looked at me wide-eyed, as though surprised by my surprise. "I . . . I don't know." Her gaze wavered. "It could just be some subconscious glitch. My mind seems to be confusing the hyper Thomas for Bram."

"Who and Bram?" Starr asked.

"What?" Torula asked.

"Who's Thomas?" Starr clarified. "You said hyper Thomas."

"I didn't say Thomas."

"Yes, you did," I said. *Another slip of the tongue?*

"Oh, my goodness," Starr said. "Whether it's a Florence or a Thomas, it's giving us names. It's obvious we're dealing with a person here." She clutched her necklace. "Oh mercy, we're experimenting with somebody's soul."

Jesus. Starr's widowhood was obviously blinding her to all of her science. Or was I just being a "widowist?"

"We have to go back there," Torula said and moved towards the steps.

"No!" Starr said. "We have to think about this."

"About what? Torula asked.

"I don't know. It's just that . . . we're toying with somebody's life after death. And we're using company equipment to do it. This could ruin us. I'm not sure we should be doing this."

"We can't stop now," Torula said. "We may have just proven that it's repeatable."

"Well, it's my nursery," Starr said. "And my decision is that it's closed for the night."

13

HIS PURPOSE IN LIFE

I SAT AT MY WORKTABLE IN THE SPARSELY FURNISHED UNIT I'D LEASED for my stay in California. Walls and floor, off-white. Furniture, black. Windows, huge, uninterrupted glass covered with gray blinds. Simple. No nonsense. Clutter-free.

Yet I still couldn't focus.

My laptop sat in front of me, and beside it, a refillable sketchpad lay open. It was where I preferred to do my equations. Nothing compared to the raw sensation of numbers being scratched out on paper to get my mind whirring. But my work on Project Husserl had ground to a halt.

A ghost was standing in the way.

Though both Torula and Starr could have sworn I'd walked right through something otherworldly, all I could think about now was how to prove that I hadn't. Bugger. They were right to call it a hyperwill because we had no damn idea what the bloody hell it was.

It had to have been a transmission. I still saw the translucent image in my mind. Its artificially gold eyes. The period costume any theatrical actor could have worn. It must have been a 3D broadcast of some kind.

The chirpy notes of my robot, whistling as he approached, cut into my thoughts. "Here's your coffee, mate."

"Thanks, Diddit." I took the mug from the table-like surface of his cube-like body.

Then the central section lifted, exposing the smaller cube that was his head. The LED color bars that formed his mouth were curved into a smile. "Would you like some music?"

"No thanks, mate. I need to think."

"No worries." He swiveled around and resumed his happy whistling. I stared at him as he glided off, fulfilling the essence of his programming. His purpose in life, which only I knew.

Life. It struck me then how loosely that term could be used, and it was downright disturbing when biologists slapped it on too eagerly to something they still didn't understand.

I let out a gruff breath and stared at my sketchpad, ordering myself to tune out the stray thoughts and tackle the problem of Project Husserl instead. Looking through my notations, I forced my brain to cooperate. *Okay, okay. Focus.* I rubbed my hands together. Cracked my knuckles. Cracked my neck.

"With automation down," I said out loud, in hopes that talking to myself would help. "How the hell can injured astronauts call robot paramedics without having to move a limb or make a sound?" By blinking? Rhythmic breathing? Eye movement?

For a few minutes, it seemed like I could get some work done, but my busy butler whistled by again, causing a vague thought to fritter away.

"Diddit, I need you to be quiet."

"All right," the little guy answered in a sad and sinking tone, "if you say so." He hung his cubed head and slowly moved away.

I stared at the sulking robot. Although I had programmed that response, it still hit me with a guilt trip. Diddit, day or night, stayed faithful to what he was meant to do. "No, wait. Come over here."

My aluminum-and-plastic best friend perked up and returned.

I sighed at his silly, happy face and gave the command. "Open the gate. Username: Iambram333. Password: Remembrance."

A small section at the bottom of Diddit's body slid out, and I took out the small black box it held. It was light, yet it had seemed so heavy when I'd put it there—the day I finished building Diddit way back in university. I'd done it years after both my parents died in a plane crash, yet the private ritual had still hit me hard.

I opened the box and went through the collection of odds and ends. A storage disc of photos and videos I'd never revisited, along with other irreplaceable mementoes. A toy NASA super-rocket. Mom's favorite locket. Cuff links with Dad's initials.

I clutched the tiny spaceship and squeezed my eyes shut, fighting back the sorrow I had managed to keep bottled up all these years.

Night after night, I'd waited. For months after they had died. For a whisper. Or the smell of Mom's perfume. Or a soft knock on the door that always came just before one of them peered in to check if everything was all right.

But no matter how much I'd cried and begged them to come back—just to say one last goodnight—I never felt them again. Not a touch. Not a word. Not a scent.

They were gone.

As hard as I tried to fight it, tears broke through my armor.

I wallowed in the quiet emptiness for a while, then solemnly returned the trinkets into the box and gave Diddit back his heart— priceless memories kept safe but out of sight in the custody of a constant companion. It made it seem as though my parents were still around, even though I knew for certain they were not.

Diddit teetered his head left and right, pulsated the bars of light that made up his mouth, and bobbed his body up and down, doing his best to stir up some joy despite the command to stay silent. It was the essence of his programming. The reason for his being: To keep me from feeling alone.

"Go ahead," I said, swabbing my eyes dry. "Make some noise. It's too bloody quiet in here."

Diddit heartily whistled a merry tune and spun in robotic joy. As I watched him glide away, my thoughts went back to that blurry, distorted, staticky image in Starr's greenhouse. Something deceptively supernatural that, the more I thought about it, had looked much like a bad transmission.

Damn it. I hated problems I couldn't solve. *I need someone who understands radio broadcasting.* Someone to give two biologists an explanation as to how a hyperwill could have looked so lifelike—yet be devoid of life.

I checked the time. It seemed all right to give Sienna, in Langley, a call.

She answered after just a couple of rings. "Hey, Bram, what's up?"

"Hi. Uhm . . . I know this is coming out of nowhere, but . . . I'm, uh . . ." I cleared my throat.

"Finally curious about what else Franco had to say?"

Not really, but now that you mention it. "Yes, actually. Yeah." Damn. I forgot to check the VN website for any clues if this "ghost projection" could be something they could be involved in.

"He said that that childhood friend of yours sounds like a great girl."

His message was about Torula? "Well . . ." I laughed softly. "I wish he'd gotten to meet her."

"Wow. That's exactly what he said. He also told me to tell you to 'make your move'—if you haven't yet."

"Don't tell me. He ended with *carpe diem*?"

She gave no answer. After all, I did just say, "Don't tell me." I raked a hand across my scalp and let out an anxious breath. Was Franco's message as innocent as it sounded, or did it hint at an elaborate prank he'd planned—involving me and Torula? "Did he say anything else?"

"That's all he shared with me. Log into his VN, Bram. There could be stuff there that's only meant for you. Listen, I gotta go—"

"Right, wait. Hang on. Uhm, speaking of . . . the afterlife. Remember how I used to help friends design video games?" That was way back at university, but it helped me spin together a more or less credible web of reasons for my request. "Got any leads on someone I can consult on how to fake a ghost?"

———

Sienna asked someone who asked someone else and so on until I got directions to the house of an electrical engineer a few cities away—a retired lecturer from a top university who was said to be unorthodox enough for what I had in mind. Perhaps old age made a person more curious about the other side.

I pulled up in front of the Mediterranean-inspired home of a retired engineer whom they said knew a lot about séances. As instructed, I headed straight to the garage door with its pedestrian access left ajar, half expecting a room full of incense, old books, and pentagrams.

One step in, and the sweet-smelling night air was replaced by the pungent odor of motor oil. A throwback R&B song was playing when I rapped against the open door. "Good evening. I'm looking for Roy?"

"Roy Radio. That's me." From behind the raised hood of a car peered a well-toned black guy—late forties, early fifties—much younger than what I'd expected. "Come on in." Roy wiped his hands on a towel, tapped his iHub, and the music went silent.

"Hi, I'm Bram. Sorry for the late hour."

"Welcome to my office." He reached for my outstretched hand, then noticed the still-heavy oil stains on his, and curled it for a fist bump instead. "Late's okay. The place is messier and a helluva lot noisier in the daytime."

Roy stood just a few inches shorter than me and wore a cut-off shirt smeared with grease over pants no less greasy. With his tattooed arms and shaved head, he looked like a man one wouldn't want to mess with, but his cool and calm aura made him immediately come off as more than amicable.

Why would a guy like this be interested in spirits of the dead?

The spacious garage housed an impressive collection of vintage cars, among them a Benz, a Corvette, and a Datsun. Along the work tables and shelves lay a jumbled array of tools, auto parts, and electrical paraphernalia. I let out a low whistle. "Looks like you're getting these guys back on the road again. You're turning them all electric?"

"Sure am. Makes no sense parkin' 'em in the past when we've figured out how to drive 'em into the future." He gave one handsome Mustang a thump on the hood. "Even gave this the audio option to start with a good old-fashioned roar like it was still guzzlin' gas. Wanna hear it?"

"Absolutely." It was late, but I'd just been given a free pass into a toy store for the big boys, so I splurged as much time as Roy was willing to spend.

The automotive nostalgia trip came to an end with one deep, solid metallic thud as he shut an Oldsmobile door. "Easy to see why I quit my day job, huh?" Roy flashed a perfect set of pearly whites like a superhero proud to be unmasked. "So you wanna talk about ghosts for a game?"

"Huh?" It took a moment for me to recall the excuse I'd made up to get here, so I cleared my throat. "Yeah."

"Is it, like, motion-sensitive or usin' touchglobes?"

"Uhm . . ." Project Husserl's problem was the only answer that came to mind. "Voice control."

"Whatdafu? You're gonna have a bunch o' guys screamin' at each other?"

I should've thought this out better. "Uhm . . . I mean, thought control," I blurted out.

"For-fuckin-midable."

I sucked my breath in through my teeth and nodded, realizing that wasn't such a bad idea—not just for a video game, but even for Project Husserl. A vision of astronauts wearing sensors on their scalps began to float around in my head.

"But that's all a bunch o' crap, isn't it?" Roy was sneering at me. "You're not really designin' a game."

"Huh?"

"There, see? You keep sayin' 'Huh' and 'Uhm.' Sure sign of someone tryin' to shit his way through a story."

I blinked away my mental fog and owned up to the smokescreen. "Sorry about that. I didn't know how else to ask and be taken seriously."

"About what?"

"How to make a ghost."

Roy looked at me through narrowed eyes.

Okay, now he's about to throw me out.

"Well, the fact you're too embarrassed to admit it tells me you still got your screws bolted tight. You religious?"

"No."

"But you believe in heaven."

"No, I don't."

"No creed? No need for the Dalai Lama, yoga, or nothin'?"

I shrugged.

"What's helpin' you deal with life then? A shrink?"

"Ever hear of Deltoton?"

Roy raised his brow. "That high-pissin' dot org religious shingamading?"

I flinched inwardly, though it was just one of many misinterpretations I'd heard. "It's not a religion. It's a . . . paradigm. An ideology on how to deal with life like you said."

"What does that title mean, anyway? Deltoton."

"It's the Roman name for Triangulum. A constellation in the spiral galaxy Messier 33."

Roy made a face as he walked over to a table. "Thought you were a bunch o' geeks. But you named your faith after some astrology hooey?"

"It's not astrology. It's astronomy." *And it's not a faith.*

Roy clucked his tongue. "Well, I guess if it revs your motor, you gotta take it for a ride." He hefted a barstool over for me. "Ah, don't mind me. Just wanted to see where you were comin' from—

askin' about the afterlife and shit. You don't look the type to take it seriously."

Neither do you. "Do you believe in it?" I asked.

"Beer?"

"No, I'm good. Thanks, mate."

"Yeah, I guess I believe in it." Roy dug into a cooler and popped open a Bud. "It sure beats the alternative, and it's not my job to think of other options." He sat back in his chair and crossed his feet up on his worktable. "All right then. Ask away."

"Great. First question." I settled down on the stool. "Is there any existing 3D hologram technology, with no need for eyewear, that's fully-animated, life-size, and life-like, capable of interacting with you in real time, projected onto thin air?"

"Whoa, hey. One at a time there." Roy glanced up and to the side, as though reading an invisible book. "Life-size, easy. Interactive and animated in real time, sure. Life-like? No problem. But projected on thin air? 3D with no eyewear?" He crossed his arms, beer in hand. "Put 'em all together, and you got yourself the badass holodeck Holy Grail. Hell no, that technology doesn't exist. Yet."

"All right. But can you think of anything that obeys the laws of physics that could account for ghost-like apparitions?"

Roy furrowed his brow. "You got duped in a séance or somethin'?"

"I'm just looking for some answers."

"Maybe if there were sound waves . . ." Roy looked to one side and consulted the unseen book again. "Somethin' below what humans can pick up. Come 'ere." He got up and strode towards what looked like a portable soundproof booth. "This is somethin' I made myself for some classroom exercises. You're not claustrophobic, are you?"

"No, not at all." I wouldn't dream of getting into a spacecraft if I was.

"Good. Just hang in there for a few."

I stepped into the small chamber, and he shut the door. Within seconds, I got an overwhelming demonstration of what "deafening silence" meant. I shoved a finger into one ear and shook it.

Roy opened the door. "Well, did ya hear it?"

"Hear what?"

"The ringin' in your ears. That's the frequency o' the nerves in your hearin' pathway. That's its signature. For the moment, at least. Unless you got a broken hair cell in there, then that's somethin' else."

"Okay. So what's the lesson?"

"It's about low frequency signals around you. If they vibrate at the same frequency as you or a part o' you, like your eyeball—it can smear your vision and make you see things. So even a thin strand o' hair at the corner o' your eye can turn into some dark shadow sittin' next to you."

"Sounds likely, I suppose." But what we saw was no strand of hair. "So does that also mean certain frequencies can influence a person's perception of things?"

"Got a wife?"

"No."

"Well, if you ever get one whinin' in your ears, that there's a perfect example o' one certain frequency disruptin' yours." Roy walked off to fetch his beer.

"Seriously."

"Man, you don't know what serious is until you get a wife." He gulped down some beer.

I wondered if I'd have been better off with a senile retiree. "Anything less subjective?"

"A tiger's roar. It packs a punch that makes use of infrasound. It's a growl so deep, humans can't hear it. But it causes momentary paralysis. Even in people who've been trainin' tigers for years."

"No way."

"Yes fuckin' way. But it's a tricky mix. Infrasound can pass through walls and cut through mountains, but even though you can't hear the tiger's roar, you gotta be within earshot for paralysis to happen."

That didn't make sense. "I have to be within earshot of something I *can't* hear?"

"'Cause the tiger mixes the low-frequency growl with the roar we *can* hear. It's the combination that packs the paralyzin' kick. All I'm sayin' is, the influence o' one wave over another superimposes and creates altogether new interactions that's hard to predict. It's, like, not knowin' what side effects you'll get mixin' one drug with another."

I nodded but remained at a loss. "Are you saying that what we think are 'ghosts' could just be some . . . imperceptible mix of signals we don't understand?"

"Damn straight. And somethin' boosts that signal into the range someone *can* detect."

That was probably what the Verdabulary was doing. But what was it boosting?

Roy took another quick gulp of his beer. "So can you tell me why someone from NASA's askin' about the physics behind a ghost?"

Because I walked right through one. "I'm just helping out a couple of scientists who may have stumbled on a . . . well . . ."

Roy sat up like a wolf smelling prey. "Ghost? Some scientists got one? Like a real one? Are you shittin' me?"

I raised a hand to temper his reaction. "No, they don't have any idea how they generate the thing."

"They generate it? So, you mean, it's not real."

"They turn on a computer program, and sometimes it appears. They don't know how it works."

"Shit. It's a no-brainer, man. Here." Roy picked up a keychain and blew soundlessly into a dog whistle dangling from it. A few seconds later, a yellow Labrador Retriever came trotting through a doggie door.

"This is Boner, my bestest buddy in the world. He's been with me twelve long years. Bad awful eyesight, but he's still goin' strong."

I smirked. "Interesting name."

"Yeah, well, Boner was one hard-headed prick of a puppy." Roy gave his pet a playful back rub; the dog collapsed on its side, its legs turning to Jell-O. "It's all about tuning in to the right frequency. You know about the teen buzz?"

"No, I don't." This man seemed nothing like a textbook professor, but he sure talked like an encyclopedia of oddities.

"It's a high-frequency, 17 kilohertz tone only those below twenty-somethin' can hear." Roy continued to rub Boner's side. "It's an ultrasonic signal originally designed as a security device to drive away teenagers from places they aren't supposed to be hangin' out."

"What about it?"

"The ability to hear it. I think the same thing goes for people who can talk with the dead."

I had to put the brakes on the discussion and backed up to verify. "You mean those who *believe* they can talk with the dead."

"No, I'm sayin' that some people really have some special abilities that let 'em see or hear, smell, or feel those from the other side."

I shifted back into gear, easing forward cautiously. "Are you serious?"

"The dead, once they realize they're dead, come to accept the fact that they're invisible. And inaudible. And more o' less beyond our reach. But once in a while, they come across someone who suddenly reacts to their presence. Y'know, like they've been shoutin' into everyone's ears and nobody flinches. Then one day—Holy Dog Shit! Somebody suddenly turns 'is head when they walk by or gasps when they touch 'im. And once they know that about a person, hell, I suppose word gets around and more and more spirits go to that person to try and send their messages across. Maybe that software you got makes it happen. It either got your friends to hear the dog whistle or told some ghost that there's an app that can see 'em. You get what I'm sayin'?"

"Not . . . really." I glanced around, wondering if Sienna was watching through a webcam —snickering—with our entire department at Langley.

"It means your software is either actin' like a dog whistle, callin' in the ghosts, or it's helpin' those scientists see supernatural things usually beyond the range o' their normal senses."

Boner loped over to my side as if to reassure me of Roy's good sense.

"Just let 'im sniff around so he gets to know you. He mostly sees his way around by listenin' and smellin' now."

I stroked the friendly fellow. "So where'd you get all these ideas about ghosts?"

Roy gave a flippant wave of his hand. "I've never seen one myself. But I was married to someone who could, and that didn't do anythin' good for us."

"I see." So that's why I was told to come here.

"I mean, I didn't doubt she really saw some things sometimes —it's not like she has it 24/7. Her abilities come and go, and there's no predictin' when. But because people know she has the gift, they ask her what she's seein' anytime—and she obliges, even when I know she can see absolutely nothin'. I didn't like 'er dupin' people like that. Makin' 'em cry and givin' 'em hope in things she was just makin' up."

Okay, so he knows she faked it but . . . "How can you be so sure there were times she wasn't faking it?"

"'Cause the dogs see the same things she does. She'd whisper to me there's a ghost standin' somewhere, and the next thing you know, our dogs would be growlin' at nothin' at the same spot. Creeps me out even more when the dogs see 'em when she's not around."

I considered possible explanations but concluded nothing. "What do you suppose they're seeing? I mean, rationally speaking."

"Real information. Data that keeps replayin' like some poor old transmission."

I perked up at the sound of the magic word. "A transmission . . . from where?" *Gawd, I hope he doesn't say Purgatory.*

Roy tapped his hands against both sides of his head. "From here. A lifetime's memory bank exported on Wi-Fi. Brain data that somehow spilled outta bounds, burned on waves of energy that all livin' things are capable o' makin'. Hell, practically any form of energy can turn into a data storage device."

It made some sense, but at the same time, didn't. "For what purpose?"

"Shit, I dunno. What purpose do leftovers have? Ghosts are like guests who stay on long after the party's over. They got nothin' else to do, nowhere else to go. And for some reason, some people —and some dogs—have some way o' seein' stuff that we can't." Roy leaned forward in his seat. "Say . . . these scientist friends o' yours with the ghost. You think they'll lemme have a peek at it?"

"Nobody knows what it is, and it's not really 'there.' My friend just triggered it by accident, so she doesn't know how it—"

"She!" Roy's eyes popped wide open. "Well, that says a lot about why you're pourin' time into this shit."

I gave a fidget of a smile.

"Maybe I can help you get 'er some answers."

"By calling in your ex wife? I don't think so."

"Hell no! I'm tired o' takin' 'er word for it that these creatures are hangin' around everywhere. It's about time I saw one for myself. So why don't I go eyeball the ghost while you keep your eye on somethin' way prettier. You know what I'm sayin'?"

I pictured Roy dealing with this "hyperwill" puzzle while I concentrated on wowing Torula with the wonders of outer space. Not a bad idea. "I suppose I can ask—"

"O' course you gotta ask, and she'll say yes! Scientists gotta test their theories, and they need engineers to make 'em work."

14

A GHOST ENGINEER

TORULA HAD SAID YES TO LETTING ANOTHER PAIR OF EYES LOOK AT HER data so fast, the next question I should have asked was if she'd be willing to fly off to some distant star with me. Instead, all I said was "When?" And she answered, "Tonight."

Which was how I ended up at the Green Manor's basement parking lot, waiting. She came walking towards the car under the warm glow of lights, and I stepped out with a smile that held all my desires and hopes and crazy dreams to take her far, far away.

"Hey, Spore."

"Hi." She tiptoed and surprised me with a kiss on the cheek, bringing with it the sweet scent of *Lavender Lace*. It seemed I underestimated the brownie points I'd earned for having found her a ghost engineer.

From the passenger side of the car emerged exactly that: Roy— looking far more like the former engineering professor that he was, wearing a crisp executive shirt neatly tucked into dark slacks over leather shoes, smelling of soap and cologne and not a whiff of motor oil on him.

"Dr. Torula Jackson," I said. "This is Roy Radio."

"Torula. Is that Asian or somethin'?"

"No," Torula said. "It's yeast."

"East?"

"Yeast. My father's a microbiologist. So, in his honor, my mother named me after a fungal spore."

"No kiddin'."

"What about you?" Torula asked. "Were you a DJ, and Radio was your handle or something?"

"Heck no. I was baptized with it. My granddad got real famous with 'is neighbors for pickin' up an AM station with his tooth fillin' at a particular spot at the 7-Eleven store. Instead o' havin' the loose fillin' fixed, he got a name change. To celebrate 'is celebrity, you know what I'm sayin'?"

She nodded and smiled, but its sparkle quickly faded; she seemed tense, or maybe excited. "I'm afraid we'll have to hurry. I told Security you're only here to pick me up for dinner." She spun around and led us at a brisk pace to Greenhouse 3C.

Vintage lanterns hung from tree branches, casting a golden glow across the stone paths. The cool night smelled like all the colors of springtime, and in the distance, gazebos sparkled with garlands of pin lights.

"I gotta tell you," Roy said, "the last thing this place looks like is haunted."

Soon after we stepped into Starr's electrified nursery, Roy changed his tone. "Damn. This place reeks o' all the stuff you need for the heebie-jeebies."

Torula led us straight to the workstation and opened charts and tables so Roy could have a look. "We're calling the subject a 'hyperwill,' and data indicates that it might be crepuscular in nature. Or, to be precise, vespertine."

Roy sucked in his breath through his teeth. "Vespertine." He echoed the word with cinematic drama. "What a great name for a vampire villain with god-awesome fangs."

I chuckled.

Torula frowned. "What I'm saying is, it seems to be behaving like a living creature that comes out only at dusk for survival reasons."

"Say what? You're thinkin' sunlight will turn it to ashes? Phew! Never expected that from a scientist."

Irritation flashed in Torula's eyes. "I'm thinking science. You're the one obsessed with vampires." She might have kicked aside the nursery's welcome mat right then if she could. "There are two hypotheses on the table. One: It comes out at dusk because its energy source is more abundant at sunset or in the dark. Or two: Without a protective protein coating, the living data is better preserved under cooler temperatures—thus hyperwills avoid the punishing heat of the sun."

Living data. What the devil was that? I held my tongue and kept my objections at bay.

Roy scanned the charts and tabulated data. "You say you've only got two hauntings?"

"Incidents," Torula said. "Let's refrain from using such folkloric terms."

"Yeah, sure. Whatever spins your cobweb. How come you got three clusters o' data here if you only had two sightings?"

Torula shot him an acid look before answering. "The second time, it appeared twice. First as a man dressed in blue holding *Myosotis sylvatica*, then as a blurry, blue blob."

Roy's face scrunched up. "Holdin' what?"

"Forget-me-nots."

"Which are what?"

"Blue flowers."

"Why didn't you just say so?" Roy swiveled his seat and went back to surveying the charts.

Bugger. These two were off to a bumpy start, and the plus points I'd earned for bringing Roy over had probably dwindled away—possibly pushing me into the negative. I swabbed a hand over my mouth.

"Looks to me like you got a spike in electromagnetic activity each time," Roy said, "but you can't overlay the spectra generated and say they're identical. You got some visible light 'ere, none over there. More gamma over 'ere, IR over there. The only thing consistent I see is time o' day."

"Precisely," she said. "And since hyperwill incidents are commonly witnessed from sunset onwards, I'd like to test if it points to a survival pattern."

There she goes again—relating this to survival. But I didn't want this to become me and Roy against her thesis. So I folded my arms and continued to bite my tongue, though it was starting to grow numb.

Roy shook his head. "Not all ghosts are night creatures, Jackson. Lotsa people see 'em even in the middle o' the day."

"I realize that. But it could be similar to how certain bats are occasionally observed flying in the daytime. They need to make up for energy deficits—in case they weren't able to forage enough at twilight or in the night. Even though they're spotted during the day, it's still considered unusual behavior linked to survival."

I straightened up, and my objections burst out of me. "The pipes in my ceiling tend to creak at night. That doesn't make them living creatures trying to survive."

"Sarcasm," she said. "That's your rebuttal?"

"It's just data, Spore."

"Isn't DNA also just data?" she asked.

I winced inwardly, sensing that answer was about to yank the conversation into a direction I didn't want to go.

"Every known living cell contains DNA. *Needs* DNA," she said. "It replicates to preserve its own existence, and yet, based on biology's list of criteria, it's not alive. But what if it's . . ." She flicked the hair off her brow. ". . . like the AllSpark?"

"Say what?" Roy asked.

I squinted at her. "Are you trying to speak to me in robot language again?"

"No," she said. "It's a metaphor for a bringer of life-giving energy that's not from a battery or a socket in the wall."

I glanced at Roy to see if he could guess what the bloody hell she meant.

He shrugged. "It's either Red Bull or Viagra."

"It's DNA." She took a long, deep breath, like an ocean pulling away from the shore just before launching a tsunami. "After a cell membrane breaks down, some extracellular DNA can survive the hostile environment they find themselves in. That means it is naked data that holds itself intact even after cell death. Then it gets harnessed for biofilm formation, horizontal gene transfer, and several other things. I'm sure you grasp its importance."

"Not really," I said.

"It means this 'leftover' DNA actually manages to find a new purpose in life."

"I think you mean a new purpose in death."

"But hey!" Roy snapped his fingers and pointed his fingers like guns aimed at Torula. "It's still a purpose for leftovers."

I couldn't tell if Roy was mocking or supporting her, but she went on with her argument.

"If nature can grab hold of something so elemental and have it adapt, isn't it more likely with a complex and possibly conscious hyperwill? What if this incorporeal data doesn't need to be 'plugged into carbon' to survive? What if life just . . . happens to flow through it?" For a second, she seemed like a female Dr. Frankenstein with blue-violet voltage sparking from her eyes.

"That's why you're sayin' it's like the AllSpark?" Roy scratched his stubbled head. "Hell, I dunno. The only transformers we talked about in engineerin' classes were lifeless things that increased or decreased electrical voltage."

"I'm proposing that the energy that sparks biological life is *life* itself, and it could come in a variety of expressions. Like kinetic or static or potential. What if every piece of matter has the potential for vivacity, ebullience, or brio?"

"Brio? Hell, I dunno where you dig up your words, Jackson, or why you even go there, 'cause it sure as hell doesn't help you communicate."

Torula looked away, gnawing her lip, quite likely mulling a counterargument. This battle of opinions wasn't bound to go—

She gasped all of a sudden, her eyes locked onto something at the table. I turned, expecting to see some apparition sitting on the console but saw nothing.

"You have to go," Torula said urgently.

Something sparkled at the far end of the table. It was Starr's gem-encrusted cell phone.

"Whatduh? You kickin' us out just 'cause we don't believe you?"

Starr's voice cut in like a thunderclap sent by God. "No, she's kicking you out because you're not authorized to be here."

Torula looked at her, wide-eyed. "Starr, I thought you were . . ."

"I had a feeling this would happen." Starr's face was set as she climbed up the platform steps, dressed in citrusy colors of lemon and lime. "I was wondering how long you could resist . . . I just never thought it would be less than an hour." Her heels clicked sharply across the wooden floor. "I came back for this." She picked up her phone. "Perhaps God has a reason for making me forget it."

"Obviously, it's so the two of us could meet." Roy strode towards her, and Starr seemed too stunned to object when he took her hand and kissed it. "Roy Radio. Immensely pleased to meetcha."

Starr pulled her hand away and trained her eyes on Torula. "Do you realize what you've done?"

"Nothing yet," Torula said.

"You've deepened the case against us. You've let an absolute stranger in."

"Well, if you give me your name, we won't be strangers anymore, missy," Roy said.

Starr turned to him with green eyes that threatened like Kryptonite. "Do I look like I'm interested in making friends right now?"

None of this made sense. Starr was pissed. Torula looked guilty.

And Roy acted as if he were on a blind date. "Can someone tell me what's going on?"

Starr thrust both fists into her hips and trained death-ray eyes on Torula, who conceded, "Starr had asked me earlier to—"

"I didn't ask, honey. I demanded it."

Torula sighed through gritted teeth. "She *demanded* that we stop all studies on the hyperwill."

I gaped at Starr. "Stop the study? Just the other day you held our hands in prayer wanting to save what you believed was a lost soul." And I'd brought Roy over hoping to prove it wasn't.

"Well . . ." Starr softened her tone, though she still had the trace of a frown. "I admit, I was initially drawn into this for personal reasons, but since then I've found guidance in the Bible, and I've decided to let the dead bury the dead."

"I don't even know what that's supposed to mean." *Couldn't she just have found guidance in a research paper?*

"It means she'd rather pay attention to things that matter to the living," Torula said. "Specifically, the future of her children. Starr's afraid of the consequences if management finds out."

"You've done nothing wrong." I cocked my head, suddenly unsure. "Have you?"

"Of course, we have," Starr said, throwing her hands up. "We've turned millions of dollars' worth of lab facilities into a Ouija board. And if word gets out, we could ruin the Manor's reputation by implying it's interested in pseudoscience. We could become the cause for it to lose its credibility."

Torula shook her head. "You're blowing things out of pro—"

"Think about this, Tor! It's our careers at stake," Starr said. "What sort of great discovery could possibly result from this peek into the afterworld?" She raised a red-polished forefinger. "Name me one scientific breakthrough that ever came out of the pursuit of the supernatural."

"EEG," Torula said, her conviction so undaunted I had to fold my arms to keep from cheering her on.

"What?" Starr asked, her frown deepening.

"The electroencephalograph. Hans Berger was intrigued by mental telepathy. As a psychiatrist, he wanted to find something in the natural sciences that would explain how someone's emotional distress could be transmitted miles away. Asking that question led him to the discovery of the electrical nature of the brain and his invention that eventually changed the world of neuroscience."

Starr pursed her lips. "Aren't you the no-nonsense nerd who always wants to be taken seriously? Do you really think you can share findings about the afterlife and not have the entire scientific world in stitches?"

Torula gave a one-sided shrug. "I've thought about that, and I've done some reading."

"And?" Starr asked.

"Only the famous get more famous for debunking the mystical, not for proving it."

Starr blinked as though a haze was clouding her vision. "What's that supposed to mean?"

"Unknown scientists—like us—who investigate the paranormal don't get any recognition at all, no matter how legitimate their findings. Only renowned scientists who take that dubious detour end up with infamy."

"So, Berger fell into infamy." Starr nodded, seemingly with satisfaction. "Did he at least come anywhere near proving the existence of ESP?"

Torula gave no answer. Not even a shake of her head.

Starr sighed. "I'm sorry, Tor, but it's for the best that we stop this. I've been praying for a sign that says it's all right for us to go on, but so far, all I've felt is anxiety—that we're doing the wrong thing. And that means you're all leaving *my* nursery. Now."

"Wait," Torula said. "Just let Roy finish studying the—"

"Dr. Jackson?"

With one synchronized jerk of our heads, we turned towards the unidentified speaker. A manor guard stood there with no trace of cordiality on his face. "Your guests don't have clearance to be in here. I'll need to escort them out."

Torula put on an innocent smile and gestured towards me. "Oh, but he's the same guy you let Starr bring in a few days ago."

"That was a few days ago. Before the unauthorized use of this nursery was reported."

"Reported?" Starr clutched her necklace. "By whom?"

15

WHAT WOULD ISEA THINK?

LESS THAN TWENTY-FOUR HOURS LATER, ROY AND I STOOD FACE TO face in his garage, with me leaning against a grand old muscle car and him against a souped-up pickup. This was something I could have asked through a phone call. But Roy, though no longer a stranger, was still caught in that gray category between acquaintance and friend. There was a favor I needed to ask, and I needed to look him in the eye to make it harder for him to say no. *Would he be willing to go back to the Green Manor to meet Torula's and Starr's boss?*

"I know this is highly irregular," I said.

"No kiddin'? They're askin' outsiders into a disciplinary meetin' for their employees. That's just not done."

"It is, when the outsiders are part of the reason they're being disciplined, I suppose."

Roy's dog, Boner, loped over until he bumped against Roy's leg, then sat down on the ground next to him. Roy hadn't been exaggerating when he said the old guy could hardly see anymore.

Roy cocked his head at me. "Aren't you worried NASA will find out you were checkin' out a ghost?"

I snorted, even though it was the second time I'd heard the warning. "My friends will have a good laugh, and that'll be that."

"I'm not thinkin' about your friends. I'm thinkin' about the higher-ups who'll be evaluatin' you for your next promotion. Yo, it's one thing to say you believe in ghosts and another to say you're datin' a girl who wants to have one for a pet. Believe me, I know."

"It's not the same thing going on here, all right?" I tried to shake off Roy's point, but it stuck to me like bubble gum under my shoe. Still, I trudged ahead. "Look, it's this simple. We're being 'requested' to join the meeting tonight. I'm going, and I hope you will too. Torula herself wouldn't have asked, but she's really upset about having caused this trouble for her best friend. Starr's a widow with three kids to support. And us showing up is an act of goodwill that could help them. So what do you say?"

Roy clucked his tongue. "Why the hell did you have to put it that way? Now I can't say no to a damsel in distress."

We agreed to meet at the Green Manor in a few hours, and as I made my way back to my car, that small warning Roy had given me now felt like a deadly threat that could blow up all my plans. Torula's background—not just mine—had to remain impeccable if she was to be considered for Pangaea.

I buckled myself in and cracked my knuckles, unable to press the ignition.

What would ISEA think if this came out in her personnel records?

Dr. Grant had mentioned something about the heads of Pangaea being members of Deltoton. Their opinion wasn't exactly ISEA's, but it was a start.

I flipped my iHub open and tapped on the Deltoton icon—a Brunnian Link of three intertwined triangles that glinted like silver. An animated banner greeted me.

E=mc^2
What does this equation hint at
that people could mistake for God—
and why?

A new mystery in an old equation?

Intriguing. But I brushed it aside and went for the search bar. I typed in *ghost hunting*, and the results came back nil.

Deltoton didn't even think it was worth anyone's time. *But what would ISEA think of a candidate who lost her job for doing exactly that?*

16

TIME FOR SERIOUS BUSINESS

Schwarzwald, the Green Manor's administrative building, looked like something straight out of a children's illustrated storybook. Stone-clad. Climbing vines. Pin lights glowing in flower boxes at each window. Ironic that what had been happening around this fairy-tale place was turning all my plans into a horror story.

All I wanted to do was ask a woman out. To space. For life. *How hard can that be?* I'd started out thinking sixty days was an extravagance. Now, this ghost of a problem had turned me into a beggar for her time.

Torula met us at the lobby dressed in a corporate black-and-gray outfit, her hair in a neat braid. Roy and I, both wearing dark blazers, complemented her time-for-serious-business dress code. *If I could just pull her aside and tell her about Pangaea.* Surely, she'd see that her ambition to study the afterworld was nothing compared to my hopes to take her *out* of this world. Were we bound to arm wrestle over whose dream was more worthy?

She led us into a conference room that continued the old-fashioned feel. Wooden floor. Wooden table. Flowery prints on the wall.

Starr was waiting inside dressed in a dull shade of purple, clutching her necklace, standing still while looking out an arched window where moonlight streamed through.

We all turned towards the doorway as a deathly pale gentleman walked in, every strand of his blond hair slicked into place. He wore a well-tailored, double-breasted suit with high lapels and a slim necktie.

"The chairman will be here soon. My name is Eldritch Brighton." He cast a piercing look at Roy and me. "I know who both of you are." With his British accent and rich, deep monotone, he could easily have passed for an agent on Her Majesty's Secret Service who'd been raised from the dead.

The door swung open again, and in walked a silver-haired man with mellow brown eyes and thin, upturned lips that made it seem like he was always on the verge of smiling. His pale blue suit gave off the slightest sheen as he moved across the room and surveyed all of us gathered there with an expression of saintly kindness.

"Mr. Dumas," Eldritch said. "These are the people involved in the late-night activities in Greenhouse 3C."

Starr earnestly shook the chairman's hand. "Good evening, Mr. D. I mean, sir. Please call me Starr."

"A pleasure," he said.

"How do you do, Mr. Dumas," Torula said as she held out her hand, her gaze steady. "Please call me Torula."

"And you may call me Alexi. Or Mr. D. Whichever you're comfortable with, ja?" He spoke with a peculiar accent that sounded like a mottled mix of Indian and German, which in a way, went with his complexion, which was not quite brown and not quite light.

Eldritch introduced Roy and me to the chairman, and I felt no sense of added privilege even after shaking the hand of one of the richest men in the world.

"Some unusual things have been happening at the Green Manor, ja?" Mr. D gestured for us to take our seats as he settled down at the head of the table. "Could any of you explain what we're looking at here?" He nodded towards the only modern thing inside the cozy cottage-like conference room: The monitor hanging on the wall.

A video played—of me in Starr's workstation, walking into the path of a blurry hyperwill gliding towards Torula just before it disappeared.

I sat frozen, gaping.

"Holy shammalamadingdong!" Roy cried, shooting out of his seat. "You weren't shittin' me when you said a ghost walked right through you. Dawg, that's murder!"

"Oh mercy," Starr said, eyes wide. "We never thought . . ."

"It's the reason you've been staying late, am I correct?" Eldritch asked like an investigator out to extract a confession. He then played a video of Starr screaming, horrified over her fruitless papayas, without the vaguest hint of what she was looking at that had scared her. And then came footage of the three of us standing stupefied, staring at some shrubs—and no hyperwill either.

I wanted to get up, grab the remote, and examine the footage, but I was in no position to make any demands.

"I don't understand." Torula scanned the screen, searching for an image that wasn't there. "Why did the cameras only capture it on the third incident?"

"Maybe a disruption in the environment caused some electrons to get excited or somethin'," Roy said. "I hear ghosts can be recorded with infrared cameras. Is that the equipment you got?"

"Standard surveillance equipment." Eldritch narrowed his eyes at Roy. "You," he said, making that single word seem like the strike of a clock at midnight. "You're convinced that ghosts are real."

"Yeah." Roy said, raising his brow. "Anythin' wrong with that?"

Eldritch cocked his head by a fraction. "I'm interested to hear why it is you are so convinced."

I leaned towards Roy like a defense lawyer giving last minute advice before my client took the stand. "Nothing about the ex, all right?"

"No sweat." Roy straightened up in his seat. "I got only one reason: Lightnin'." He gave a confident nod. "Because when Benjamin Franklin went out fishin' for lightnin' in the rain, nobody called 'im an idiot. 'Cause everyone could see what he was tryin' to catch."

"I assume you're attempting to make a point?" Eldritch said.

"What if nobody could see or hear lightnin', except for the thousand or so people who get struck by it every year? These people are left knackered by the trauma. But what if no one believes 'em? They can spend the rest o' their lives just tryin' to produce proof. But the only answer they get is: Make it appear on demand, then we'll believe you. I know—'cause I married a woman who had to go through that."

Oh crap. I moved my leg discreetly and stepped on Roy's foot.

"Hell, that pretty much is the picture when it comes to people with ESP." Roy moved his foot away. "They wanna prove they really got it. That's why you got all these posers out there goin'. . ." Roy shifted his voice to falsetto, "I see dead people." He waved a dismissive hand. "Phew! They keep sayin' they're seein' things even when they don't. 'Cause their gift is sorta like lightnin'. Finicky as hell. Everybody thinks lightnin' strikes when there's dark clouds, or it's rainin'. But it can also happen on a sunny day and outta the blue. It can strike the tallest thing, but it can skip that and hit somethin' closer to the ground. A lotta times, it's deafenin'. Other times, it doesn't make a sound and just lights up the sky like faulty fluorescent lights. Now, how do you expect some poor fella figurin' all that biznitch about a ghost when no one besides him can see the damn thing?"

In the few seconds of silence that followed, I imagined a pin being pulled and a grenade of disgrace about to explode. "That sounds like a good point, don't you think?" I heard myself say.

"A good point indeed," Mr. D said. "And have you figured out how to make a ghost appear, Mr. Morrison?"

"Excuse me?"

"You presented a NASA ID, ja? So you have access to the latest technology and experimental—"

"Wait a minute," I said. "You think *I'm* the prankster?"

Eldritch turned to Roy. "Or perhaps it was you? An electrical engineer."

"Whatduh?" Roy's eyes popped wide open. "Are you some paranormal skep-dick? A detective out to prove that everyone's fakin' it?"

"Please don't blame anyone else in this room," Torula said, sounding out of breath. "It appeared when *I* clicked on the Verd-abulary."

"We're not here to cast any blame." Mr. D flashed Torula a benevolent smile. "You caught my interest with your theory."

"What theory?" she asked.

"That ghosts could be incorporeal data preserved after death—like extracellular DNA that survives lysis, ja?"

Surprise flared in her eyes. "You know about that?"

"I think it's brilliant."

The glow of a smile almost spread across Torula's face, but then her eyes suddenly hardened. "How did you find out about it?"

"The Green Manor has the authority to install audio-video surveillance in all its research areas," Eldritch said flatly. "The day you were hired, you signed a waiver. And so did you." He turned towards Roy and me. "It's in the fine print each time you log in to enter the premises. Which is how we know that, with your illicit use—and abuse—of the manor's facilities, you might very well produce an explanation for the occurrences."

"We're not dealing with a hoax," Torula said, her hands clasping the edge of the table. "My hypothesis is that it's a natural phenomenon that can be replicated. And that's what we've been trying to do."

"Can you?" Mr. D asked.

"Replicate it?" She shook her head. "We still have no idea what causes it."

Eldritch leaned forward in his seat. "Yes, but with the help of these two engineers, do you think you can figure it out?"

Bloody hell. My breath caught, and I gaped at the two high officials of the corporation. Were they no different from everyone else in this room? Simply curious about a ghost? "Are you saying you *want* us to study it?"

The two men exchanged glances before Mr. D got up and walked towards the arched window. "I'm afraid the Green Manor cannot risk exposure pursuing this line of study. Would you be willing to sign a contract of non-disclosure?"

Starr quickly dabbed a finger at the corner of one eye, as though she only meant to swipe aside a stray strand of hair. Torula leaned back and frowned.

The chairman turned towards us, now backlit by moonlight that glinted off his silver-blue suit. His gaze flitted across our faces until it settled on mine. "It will do more than just grant the two doctors the liberty to pursue this line of research in continued secrecy. It also frees them of all liabilities from past actions related to this matter."

I narrowed my eyes. So if Torula and Starr didn't sign, they could lose their jobs *and* be sued for damages?

There was the slightest shudder that shook Torula's body, so subtle all the others may not have noticed. "What exactly do you want us to do?" she asked.

"Find the explanation," Mr. D said.

What the devil. Did they want to rid the place of this disturbance? Clear up the Manor's name? Whatever their reasons, it was something I wanted too. "Okay," I said. "I'm in."

All heads turned to look at me. Frankly, even I would've gawked at myself if I could.

"Hell, if there's proof out there of anythin', I wanna find it. Give it 'ere." Roy gestured a "come on over" with two hands.

Eldritch rose and exited the conference room.

Torula leaned close, her voice an urgent whisper. "What are you doing?"

"Helping you get answers."

Torula shook her head. "Even if NASA never shifts the height limit, you still have a job that others would die for. Why risk your good standing on something like this?"

Because I can't step away and let them ruin yours.

"These documents should ease your fears," Eldritch said, back in mere seconds. "The confidentiality works both ways." He handed non-disclosure agreements to each of us, making me close to certain he was Mr. D's lawyer.

"Rest assured," the chairman said, "the Green Manor will make it worth your while. You and Roy will be paid for whatever time you spend here."

"No shit? Heck, I was willin' to pay just to see the damn thing." Roy scanned through the NDA and signed.

Starr sat with pen poised over paper, her brow crinkled. "I would like to make it clear that I only wish to pursue this study for purely scientific reasons."

I glanced at her in bafflement. "As opposed to what?"

"The Lord Jesus implicitly confirmed the existence of ghosts in Luke 24:39. I don't need proof they exist. All I wish to discover—or understand—is the natural mechanism in place that enables them . . . to be. And if, or how, they can still interact with our world. What I don't want is for us to conjure up the dead and consult them about the future and other things we're not meant to know."

"Duly noted," Eldritch said with a solemn nod.

Starr took a deep breath, closed her eyes briefly, and then signed.

I gritted my teeth and reached for the pen—which Torula grabbed from me.

"Bram, you don't have to," she said. "We can handle it." She signed the paper and handed it to Eldritch. "Here. You've got your research team. Two biologists and an engineer."

Damn. Why won't she let me help? "Spore, I don't need you protecting me."

"And I don't need you protecting me," she said.

"We understand," Eldritch said, his tone stern and louder by a notch. "Neither of you needs each other, but what we need is for Mr. Morrison to join the team."

"Why?" Torula frowned. "He's a robotics engineer. Why would you need him on a ghost hunt?"

The corner of his mouth twitched just short of a smile. "His presence calls upon the dead."

I froze, too stunned to say a thing. Everyone else seemed equally thunderstruck.

Mr. D glanced around at his newly recruited team of ghostbusters. "I'm appointing Eldritch to serve as the project director. He's a consultant in another facility of mine in London, so he'll be flying back and forth as necessary."

I glanced at the peculiar Englishman. *This odd bloke is a scientist?*

"I see," Torula said, pushing aside a lock of hair on her forehead. "May I know your field of specialization?"

The man raised his chin. "I am a medium and a longstanding member of the Society for Psychical Research in London."

A puff of disbelief escaped me.

"Wait. Right. Let me understand." Torula put one hand on the table as though to steady herself. "You're a . . . psychic?"

Mr. D strode back towards his seat of authority at the head of the conference table. "Eldritch is a director at my institute of research into the paranormal. He is a leader in the Spiritualist Church of England and arguably the most respected medium I know."

Respected medium? *Now that's an oxymoron for you.*

"So . . . so you . . ." Starr laid a hand over her chest as if to push the statement up and out of her throat. "You represent exactly what I said I don't want to be involved in."

"Yo, it's not like talkin' with ghosts is evil, missy."

"But it is," Starr said. "The Bible repeatedly warns us against mediums and necro—"

"Necromancers, I know," Eldritch said. He paused and took a

deep breath, his eyes losing their steely edge. "Which is why I, like you, am here for scientific reasons."

I squinted at the self-proclaimed psychic. "Scientific . . . like, how?"

"I'm hoping the facts will come to prove that our abilities are a gift from nature and not from demons. And that not all psychics are charlatans out to make a living from the dead."

"But aren't you?" I asked and motioned at his sleek Savile Row garb. "Making a killing from the dead, I mean."

The glint in his gaze returned. "This is my vocation, Mr. Morrison. It's not part of my portfolio."

Torula slumped back into her seat. "I can't comprehend this. You had us sign NDAs when in fact you openly study these things?"

Mr. D raised a cautionary finger. "Not the Green Manor, no. Its reputation of being a legitimate botanical research facility is iron-clad." He held out his hands, straightening his fingers as he scrutinized them. "These get pricked every so often for blood sugar analysis. Nearly all my life, I've been dependent on insulin shots. And the Green Manor continues to make invaluable contributions to the pharmaceutical industry towards the treatment of diabetes and other diseases that plague us. But despite all the wonders of medicine, death remains incurable. So can you blame me for wanting to know what awaits?"

"Dr. Benedict," Eldritch said, looking intently at Starr. "I assure you, I am here only to discover how nature enables our consciousness to live on after death. I'm hoping, once we understand how it works, we can then communicate with our lost loved ones so we can help them move on."

"So you're saying you're doing this purely for their benefit?" Starr asked.

He looked intently at her and nodded. "My only purpose is to help ensure that the dearly departed rest in peace in paradise."

She clasped her hands together like a young Mowgli dazzled by a serpent's speech and answered Eldritch with a subtle smile.

"In that case, if our goals are aligned, then . . . I believe it's time we explored the science behind hyperwills."

Eldritch frowned. "Why do you use that word?"

"You mean hyperwill?" Starr glanced at Torula. "Dr. Jackson proposes that we not use labels with so much folkloric baggage. So 'hyperwill' is a term derived from someone's will to survive gone on hyperdrive."

"Or like a hyperactive will to survive," Torula said, glancing my way but stopping short of looking me in the eye.

So that's why she couldn't tell me what it meant. The very root of the word was grounded on the premise that the visual phenomenon was "alive."

"Hyperwill." Eldritch grimaced like a connoisseur who'd just been offered cheap wine. "I find the term rather crass. And it already taints the subject with your own, personal lore."

"I think it's good enough to keep outsiders from knowing what we're dealing with, ja? We'll be calling this Project Hyperwill." Mr. D looked at me and nodded towards my unsigned NDA. "And with you on the team, we will have a balanced and diverse range of perspectives, ja? Torula is committed to objectively study the hyperwill. Eldritch and Roy believe in it. Starr has a stake in it. While you, Bram, are here simply because we need you. Not your credentials. Only your vibration."

All right. That does it. I'm outta here. I rose from my seat. "Listen, I don't understand why you think my coming here triggered the events—"

"It all started after your arrival, honey," Starr said with a raise of her brow.

I frowned at the absurd suggestion. "That's just a coincidence."

But then, Torula gave me a barely there grimace.

"You can't be serious." *Who the devil could convince even* her *of that?* "You're making me the cause of all this?"

"I think it's awesome, man," Roy said. "It's like you got a super power. You can frickin' summon the dead!"

"Bloody hell." I looked at Torula. "Spore, you can't go along with this. Not with a medium at the helm."

"Hey, man," Roy said, suddenly sober. "I know a lot o' psychics can be tricksters, but not all of 'em are. So whaddaya say we keep an open mind, huh?"

"With all due respect," I said, looking at the chairman, "if you're aiming to establish credibility for the project, we should be working in a more controlled environment supervised by senior scientists."

"Greenhouse 3C's setup has proven conducive to the apparition," Mr. D said. "Would you transfer a creature from the wild into a controlled environment to observe its natural behavior? And as far as leadership is concerned, no one else in this room has dealt with the afterlife as much as Eldritch, ja?"

"I don't mean to be rude," I said, though it was too late for that, "but someone in the scientific community would be—"

"More qualified to head something he knows nothing about?" Eldritch asked. "That's like saying only an atheist is qualified to prove the existence of God."

"That wasn't my point," I said.

"We understand your point," Mr. D said. "You want someone objective and neutral. Someone who has no stake in it or faith in it. Isn't that what we already have in you?"

I swallowed and glanced at Torula.

"It's a Catch 22, Bram." She shrugged. "A well-regarded scientist could give the study validity. But as soon as he accepts our project's credibility—he loses his."

"And what happens to ours?" I asked.

"I think you mean 'ours.'" Torula gestured towards Roy and Starr. "Like I said, we can handle this." She smiled reassuringly, which left me even more uneasy.

My gaze stumbled its way back towards the flimsy paper in front of me. If I left now, it would tell Torula only one thing: That strangers believed in her idea more than I did.

"No," I said and took a deep breath. "I meant *ours*." I grabbed a pen and signed the bloody paper. Now, all I had to do was figure out how to get this over with in a day or two, tops.

"Cool! Now we're in business." Roy gave a loud clap and rubbed his hands together. Starr gave a little laugh, her bubbliness inching its way back in, while Torula still had that frown marring her brow—which was puzzling. If she was concerned about NASA disapproving, the NDA should have eased her mind about that.

A knock came on the door. "Mr. D." An office person peered in. "I'm sorry, sir. We need to get going."

The chairman nodded and stood up. "If you'll excuse me, I need to leave it up to Eldritch to take things forward from here." He strode towards the door. "The manor has nearly every variation of botanists and microbiologists there are. And Eldritch has tapped some of them, so he can share scientific evidence with you that complements Dr. Jackson's theory."

As Mr. D exited, the purported medium walked towards one corner of the conference room. He stopped next to a trolley holding a wire box the size of a small microwave oven made of copper screens.

"I would like to begin by clearly stating that I do not expect you to delve into the *super*natural. In fact, I want you to stay grounded in what is nothing but natural. Just as in the example that I have with me now." With a shift in his gaze, Eldritch indicated the copper-screened box.

"It's a Faraday cage," Roy said blandly. "A radio frequency suppressor."

"Our facility in London has managed to replicate an experiment first conducted in 1995 by a microbiologist named Matsuhashi and his team. This is its reproduction. Inside are two Petri dishes that prove bacteria can communicate remotely despite airtight containers separated by a two-millimeter iron sheet."

Roy walked over and peered inside it.

"I know of that experiment," Starr said.

"So do I," said Torula. "The conclusion was that, although the bacteria were incapable of sending chemical messages, they were able to communicate by using sound waves."

"Yo, y'all back up there a bit," Roy said, pointing at the metallic box. "How the hell can you tell that bacteria are 'talkin'?'"

"Simple," Torula said. "Bacteria exposed to nonpermissive stress conditions were observed to promote colony formation and—"

Starr cleared her throat. "Allow me to explain, honey," she said, smiling at our multi-syllabic friend. "Picture this: There are two groups of prisoners sealed in airtight glass cages separated by an iron wall. Group One gets exposed to highly stressful, deadly conditions. Everyone in Group One dies. But in Group Two, a few prisoners 'acquire' the ability to survive when exposed to the same harmful conditions later on."

"The horror that happens to one group does something beneficial to the other," Eldritch said. "Survival is zero if there is no first population that bequeaths their tales of suffering. It is clear proof of a primordial form of ESP."

Now I'd heard everything. It was remarkable how Torula still kept a straight face. A comic strip popped inside my head of bacteria reading my future as they crawled across my palm.

"Heck, it's prob'ly just infrasonic communication," Roy said. "Like Morse Code that only bacteria can hear."

"One important point," Eldritch added. "We gave our Petri dishes a unique coating. They block out sound waves."

"No frickin' way."

The bacteria in my mental cartoon strip began doing semaphore. Shapeshifting to do sign language. Wearing headsets and listening to Morse Code—

Holy shite. I nearly jerked at my own thought and suddenly knew what I needed to do. *It's time to put an end to all of this afterlife bullshit.* "Can you lend us that Petri dish setup?"

"Why?" Eldritch asked.

"First thing tomorrow, Roy and I can get to work and show you what's really going on. It's right up his alley."

Roy scrunched up his face. "It is?"

"I'm afraid I have previous commitments," Eldritch said. "I can't join you, but . . ." He gestured towards the Faraday cage. "I welcome you to discover the origins of the mechanism by which a soul leaves the body and gets to speak with the living after death."

17

MY MOTHER'S HOUSE

(TORULA)

I HAD ONE CLEAR DESTINATION IN MIND AFTER WE ALL LEFT THE conference room: My mother's house. Bram may have belittled what he was risking by investigating a so-called haunting, but what I had at stake was something I couldn't brush aside.

Mom led me into the floral-scented comfort of my childhood home. Daytime had come to an end, and yet she looked as fresh as early morning in her peaches-and-cream lounge dress.

"They've legitimized the research, Mom. That means we'll keep trying to repeat the event."

"Good," was all she said, then turned towards the patio.

"That doesn't bother you?" I addressed her auburn hair as I trailed her in bafflement. "If there's any correlation between what we're doing at the lab and what Truth is seeing, then he could be exposed to it more often too."

She didn't even glance backwards when she answered. "He sees it anyway, whether or not you conduct any experiments."

He what? "How could you treat this so blithely? If it weren't for Starr's financial predicament, I would've been happy if it got cancelled entirely."

"Doctors always need to weigh the side effects of a treatment versus the progression of a disease. Not that I'm calling the apparition a disease, but you know what I mean."

"Not exactly."

Wind chimes tinkled their greeting underneath her rose pergola. Lit by warm lamplight, a porcelain tea set waited on the table, printed with dainty pink and white flowers that almost perfectly matched the ones that clambered around and above us.

Mom leveled her gaze at me, and I willed myself not to blink or look away. "Ghosts are clues. Like smoke or a scream or the smell of gunpowder, they're evidence you can't hold in your hand. They're fleeting, close to intangible and witnessed by only a few— yet they hint at something mysterious that could happen to any human being. That's why you need to investigate."

"What if it does Truth more harm than good?"

She poured us both some tea. "I'll be keeping a close watch on him. He'll be all right." She gave me a reassuring smile.

I lifted my teacup and blew on the steaming hot brew, its aroma of jasmine competing with the fragrance of roses around us.

"It's good you were able to convince Bram to help you," Mom said, pouring milk into her cup.

"I didn't. In fact, I wanted him to leave. He's up against the impossible with NASA already, with his ambition to become an astronaut. The last thing he needs is something to discredit him." I took a sip of tea in hopes it would make me as tranquil as my mother was.

"Sweetheart, you need Bram for these experiments to go on. Your feelings for him are obviously what's fueling the paranormal. His presence is affecting your psychic energy by way of your libido."

I sputtered on my tea and spilled some on myself.

"You've been thrown off balance, Tor." Mom calmly handed me a table napkin. "Something changed when Bram arrived. The eustress—the positive tension over seeing him again—has amped up your hormones. Haven't you considered that possibility?"

"Hormones, as a possible factor, is something we've considered, yes. But in the end, we saw no connection."

She gave a subtle, one-sided shrug. "Then look again. Many so-called psychic episodes are clearly associated with hormonal fluctuations. Poltergeists are most commonly linked to the presence of an adolescent. And it's prevalent among people experiencing severe emotional stress. Even pregnancy or a new baby appears to trigger paranormal activity. Find some way to test it."

"Test what?" I tossed aside the dampened tissue. "That's all just anecdotal evidence, Mom."

"Hormone treatments have been shown to increase the transmembrane protonic electrochemical potential difference by several millivolts. Bram's presence could very well be having the same effect on you."

I shook my head in disbelief. "You're equating Bram to a hormone treatment?"

"Weren't biologists the ones who introduced the word 'pheromones' to the world?" She flourished a hand down my torso. "The mere presence of a man can affect your body's chemical makeup."

"Mom, if sexual attraction were enough to conjure up ghosts, then everyone over the age of twelve should've seen one by now." I got up, abandoning my calming tea, and made my way into the house.

"Where are you going?"

"To have a talk with Truth. I'll probably have a more sensible discussion with a three-year-old."

Mom followed me as I climbed the stairs and walked down an old, familiar hallway where lavish Kashmir carpets muffled our footsteps.

"What are you going to ask him?" she asked.

"I need to find out if it scares him. I don't want to go through with this if it scares him."

The sound of a child giggling cut into our conversation. "You're funny." Truth's voice drifted towards us through his open bedroom door.

Goose bumps crawled up my arm. "Who's with him?"

Mom rushed towards my baby brother's bedroom with me right behind her. We paused at the doorway at the sight of Truth lying in bed, smiling with his bright blue eyes fixed on nothing visible at the foot of his bed.

I held my breath and waited for a man in blue to slowly appear.

Truth waved his tiny hand at the empty space. "Bye," he said, then yawned and rolled to his side.

A cold gust of nothingness moved through me as a featherlight touch stroked me beneath my chin, tracing my jawline. The hair on my scalp prickled, and I leaned away.

"Truth, darling?" Mom sat on the edge of his bed and felt his forehead. "Who were you talking to?"

He pointed at me. "Her friend."

I shuddered and took a cautious step into the room. "What does he look like?"

"Stars!" Truth wiggled his fingers in front of his face. "Many stars and gold eyes. He's nice."

I know. Despite my sentiments, I kept my face expressionless.

"Do you know his name, sweetheart?" Mom asked.

Truth shook his head and snuggled into his pillow.

"What do you talk about?" I asked.

"Stuff." Truth yawned again. "I'm tired."

Mom brushed his blond hair with her fingers, lulling him to sleep. "He doesn't have a fever," she said in a low voice, "but he's been on bed rest for days and keeps getting weaker."

"What does the doctor say?"

"Blood tests show increased blood urate levels and oxidative stress, but he can't give a decent diagnosis." Mom rose from the bed and headed out. "I'm calling your brother, Trom. Maybe an endocrinologist can figure this out better than an assembly-line pediatrician could."

I glanced around the room, not really knowing what I was looking for. "Truth, can you tell me more about your visitor?"

The soft snoring of a little boy was my only answer. I stared at the empty space at the foot of his bed—anticipating something both real and surreal to make its presence felt.

Mom was right. The incidents here kept happening whether or not we were conducting experiments, and maybe, what we planned to study could explain—and help treat—what was ailing Truth.

On my way out, I paused at the doorway and looked around Truth's room again. "Leave my brother alone," I whispered to the unknown.

Right after I'd said it, I realized it was a foolish and useless thing to do. *Stay rational, Torula.* It was easy—so easy to slip into how others handled the bizarre. I had to find a better way to deal with this than just "urging" it away.

18

A PSYCHIC'S APPRENTICE

If I had a flower for every time you made me smile, I'd have a garden. My breathing had nearly stopped when Torula said that to me and smiled. Then she had that slip of the tongue about kissing me, and she seemed to resent the possibility that NASA was sending me somewhere out of reach. All the signs told me I was on more solid ground now, making me confident to tell her about Pangaea. And yet, when I had asked her out to dinner last night, I was turned down in favor of yet another talk she needed to have with her mother.

Part of me wondered if it was her mother's ploy to block my attempts to get closer to Torula. I'd always feared Triana wanted her only daughter to follow in her footsteps to veer as far away as possible from a wedding march.

A wedding. Wow. I heaved a breath, surprised by my own thought—then surprised myself yet again when I broke into a smile.

Dr. Grant's face suddenly loomed inside my head. *Baby steps, young man. Baby steps.* I wiped the grin off my face and warned myself not to scare Torula away.

Today could be my lucky day. Despite Torula's objections, I'd shown up at the Green Manor for the start of my forty-five-day stint as a "psychic's apprentice." But she didn't know I was aiming to make it my last day too. The plan was to prove that talking bacteria had nothing to do with talking to the dead.

I'd spent much of the morning combing through all the garden plots inside Greenhouse 3C, checking for dubious devices or cables or anything that could lead to an explanation for a hyperwill. Whether pointing to a hoax or an accidental trigger, I found nothing suspicious and headed back to the central platform.

The sun shone hot, high, and bright, and all the plants seemed greener than green, spreading their leafy arms out, enjoying the morning and its humidity. Satisfying for the plants, stifling for the humans. I couldn't wait to get to the central platform with its cooling fans and darkened Transhade.

Starr and Torula stood leaning against the console table, listening to Roy's excited chatter. As I climbed the wooden stairs, Roy froze midway through a sentence. "Yo, listen. Can you hear that?"

I nearly stumbled on a step and paused in the silence.

"Hear what?" Starr asked.

Roy broke into a wide grin. "The bacteria're talkin'." Starr let loose her brilliant laugh as Roy swooped to his chair to call something up on his monitor. "Take a look at this, Morrison. The proof we wanted. We got us electromagnetic waves in the 1-kilo-hertz frequency from inside the RF shielding." He jabbed both pointer fingers towards the Faraday cage with its Petri dish setup.

"And we verified it, too, with one of the manor's microbiologists," Starr said. "She confirmed that bacteria can do radio waves."

"I suspected as much," I said, feeling smug like a detective who'd exposed a crime millennia after it had been committed. "Though I can't imagine how bacteria can do radio."

"Apparently," Torula said, "the DNA of highly developed bacteria forms in loops unlike our double helix. When free electrons traveling through those loops go through differing energy levels, they produce photons."

"Great. So our job here's done." I felt like dusting off my hands even though I never had to lift a finger. I smiled at Torula. *Maybe tonight, we can have that dinner date.*

"Yeah, we got to prove what Brighton said." Roy gestured at the Faraday cage. "We've discovered some 'primordial form o' ESP.' It's also what that shrink, Berger, was lookin' for, right?"

"No," I said, frowning at Roy. "That wasn't the point."

"They're not using ESP." Torula picked up her glass for a drink only to find it empty. "It's EEC." She put the glass back down. "Endogenous Electromagnetic Communication."

Roy cocked a brow at her. "You just made that up, right?"

"No, I didn't." Torula gathered up her thick mass of hair and clamped it up against the heat. "It's long been postulated that endogenous electromagnetic fields of organisms may act as both sender and receiver of electromagnetic bioinformation. In short, we may have merely identified—not discovered—what Hans Berger was looking for."

Roy nodded. "Yeah, and that's what Brighton thinks. That's how the dead can talk with us."

"No," I said, shaking my head. "This isn't supposed to go there."

"I agree," Torula said. "I don't think that's what Eldritch intended either."

"Great." I sighed with relief.

Torula walked to the Faraday cage. "He said this setup was to show us the mechanism 'by which a soul leaves the body.' So I think he wanted us to recognize that bacteria can indeed transmit bioinformation out of their bodies as they die. He sees it as the precursor of something more complex. That's why Mr. D said this setup supports my theory." She beamed and looked at me. "Thanks, Bram."

I gaped at her. "For what?"

"For borrowing the Petri dish setup. You showed us the means by which a person's neural data can be transmitted—out of a dying human body—and stay intact even after death."

I tried to sift through the jumble of words inside my head, none of which formed, *"You're welcome."*

"Hold on a minute, honey." Starr pursed her glossy red lips. "Jumping from bacterial transmission to soul migration is quite a fantastic leap. The material we're talking about here are very short fragments."

I nodded. *My thoughts—more or less, and sort of—exactly.*

"That's only because we're looking at transformation events in bacteria," Torula said. "Imagine how millions of years of complex evolution could have built on that process."

"Spore," I rubbed a hand uneasily over my chin. "All we have here are dying germs, not stand-ins for human consciousness."

She turned to me with eyes that wouldn't take no for an answer. "Are you saying it's impossible because it's minuscule compared to the magnitude of the eventual outcome? That's like saying discovering the existence of rhodopsin in no way helps explain the evolution of the human eye."

I dug my fingers into my scalp as I struggled to piece together what she was talking about. "Look, if what you're saying is that radio waves can make hyperwills 'happen'—then all it explains is why they appear most at twilight. It has nothing to do with—"

"Twilight?" Starr asked, her thickly mascaraed eyes widening. "You mean, you've made sense of the time factor?"

"I think so. It boils down to ideal broadcast conditions."

"How do you mean?" Starr asked, moving closer.

I glanced up, past the Transhade overhead, at the intense sunshine penetrating the greenhouse roof. "Low frequency transmissions travel better at dusk or dawn. It gives a window of a few minutes."

Torula squinted at me, and I could almost see the steam rising off the top of her head.

Roy's mouth fell open. "Holy shit. I get where you're takin' this."

"It's about time, mate." I wiped a bead of sweat off my forehead, then grabbed a stool and sat down.

"Why?" Starr asked. "What makes twilight special?"

"It's kinda complicated," Roy said. "You want the long version or the short version?"

"We don't need a doctorate on it, honey," Starr said, taking a seat too. "Just the basics."

"But not too basic either," Torula said, settling down next to her in front of Roy.

"Jee-zus. You're like a pair o' Goldilocks. Not too hard. Not too easy. Okay, here's the fairy tale version. Once upon a time, a lotta people listened to AM radio stations which, by day, relied mainly on transmitter power and antennas on the ground. But every night, magical changes happen in the atmosphere, allowing signals to travel farther."

"What changes?" Starr asked.

"In the light o' day, the ionosphere's D layer absorbs radio waves about 10 megahertz and below. But after sunset—it disappears! With nothin' to absorb those signals at night, everythin' in the lower frequencies gets to bounce back and travel farther distances across the Earth. And if the whole path were in darkness, then that radio signal can go even farther. Is that clear enough for you, Goldie? What about you, Snow White?"

"Clear as daylight, Brother Grim." Torula glanced up through the transparent roof at the blazing sky. "So broadcasting conditions improve all night? But," she looked at me, "you said it's a window of only a few minutes."

"You get peaks associated with the sunrise-sunset terminators. It's those peaks that last ten minutes at best."

Starr got up and gazed out towards the cluster of papayas where the hyperwill had appeared twice at dusk. "I don't understand," she said. "How does this explain three a.m.?"

"What's with three a.m.?" I asked.

Her eyes grew wide, and she turned towards Torula. "Honey, you haven't told them?"

"Told us what?" I asked.

Torula swallowed and flicked the hair off her brow. "This isn't right. We shouldn't be considering anecdotal—"

"Told us what?" This time, I addressed Starr.

Torula swiveled her seat and turned away, like someone avoiding having to look at her own bandage getting torn off.

"There were two incidents at her apartment," Starr said, "both at around three a.m. The first was when her brother saw it watching her sleep before it walked into the wall, and the second was when she woke up with it sleeping with her in bed, naked. Then it disappeared."

What the bloody hell? I glared at Torula. "When will you trust me again not to laugh—"

"It's not about trust." She got up and paced, gesturing with her hands. "*That* happened there; *this* happened here. Notice the difference?"

"Don't mean to scare you but . . ." Roy said. ". . . it could be an incubus."

"A what?" I asked.

"A male demon that has sex with women in their sleep and drains the life out of 'em."

Starr snorted. "You can't be serious, Roy Radio."

He raised a brow. "What if I was?"

Torula shook her head. "The incubus is nothing but a convenient excuse concocted by women in Medieval times to conceal their extra-marital affairs. Just like the succubus—a female demon that purportedly had sex with innocent men in their sleep and gave them diseases."

"Succubussss," Roy said. "Doesn't that word just capture what it does? You can almost hear it slurpin' the life outta you. And listen to the plural! Succubi. Sounds like two bisexual ghosts that come suck you in your sleep."

Starr and I laughed while Torula inhaled deeply like a fire-breathing dragon about to incinerate an unwanted guest.

Roy cocked his head at her. "Tell me somethin', Jackson. You ashamed to be studyin' this?"

Torula scowled at him. "What are you talking about?"

"There've been two other manifestations—both with you there —that you didn't bother to report. You shouldn't be holdin' out stuff like that. It could be important."

"Well," Torula said, "what's important to me could still be easily dismissed as male bovine excrement."

"Say what?"

"She means bullshit," I said.

Roy clucked his tongue. "My ex and her Pekingese used to wake up at three a.m. and make a frickin' racket about things only the two of 'em could see. The vet told me that dogs really can see, smell, and hear things people can't. Matter o' fact, he said a good guard dog doesn't just protect you from human trespassers but from invisible ones too." He shook his head. "He's a damn good vet but god-frickin' strange."

"So what's with three a.m.?" Starr prodded.

"That's the witchin' hour. My ex said it's the opposite o' Christ's hour o' death. Or that it's the devil's way o' showin' irreverence to the Holy Trinity."

"Oh my." Starr fingered the crucifix on her neck. "I say one thing's for sure. This hyper 'Thomas' is sticking to some kind of schedule we still don't understand."

"Right," Torula said. "Which means your radio waves at dusk or dawn won't explain those incidents that happened to me and my brother at three a.m."

I scratched my forehead and frowned at Torula. "What happened to that being *there* and this being *here*?"

The bold overture of the *Star Base* theme played on my iHub. I glanced at the caller ID, and my lungs deflated at the sight of it. "Bugger. It's my boss."

Torula's eyes instantly reflected my anxiety.

I spoke into my wristband and put on my most casual tone as I walked down the platform away from everyone's earshot. "Hi, Dave! What's up?"

"What are you wasting your time on over there?" came the harsh question.

"I'm . . . making progress."

"You damn well better be."

To my relief, there was no mention or question about ghost videos or psychics or anything in the *Twilight Zone*. It was a simple demand that I send in my design proposal for Project Husserl tomorrow.

It was a problem much easier to solve, but a problem none-theless; I'd hardly started. I tried to haggle for an extension, but it was nonnegotiable. I was left with no choice but to give in to the deadline.

I turned around and jumped at the sight of Torula standing right behind me. "Jesus."

"Did he ask why you're here?"

"No." I sighed. "False alarm. It's about work and this new deadline I got."

"But you're staying on and risking everything until it's more than a false alarm?"

"Of course. I mean, no. Nothing's at risk. Like I said, we're all done here."

"Bram . . ." She rolled her eyes, seemingly about to argue with me—but . . . I was wrong. Her head tilted backwards, and she swayed.

I lunged forward and steadied her. "Are you all right?"

She turned towards the cluster of papayas as I held her. I looked too, but there was nothing to see but a plot full of shrubs standing in bright sunlight.

Then I heard Franco's voice from right behind me. "Did you get my message?"

I jerked around, but of course, there was nobody there. It was all in my head.

"What message?" Torula asked, her eyes closed as she leaned against me.

Bloody hell. It's not *all in my head.*

"What . . . did you hear?" I asked.

"I can't tell you if you don't say what message you're talking about." She planted a hand flat on her forehead and opened her eyes. "I must be dehydrated from the heat."

"Let's get you back under the Transhade."

I ushered her towards the workstation as my mind scrambled to explain that voice. Radio waves? Why? And more importantly—what the hell were we hearing?

19

A VOICE IN YOUR HEAD

ALARMED BY TORULA'S DIZZY SPELL, THE TEAM AGREED TO HEAD OUT
to some place much cooler than the cafeteria for lunch. I sat, arms
folded, behind the wheel of my partially autonomous rental as it
headed down the winding tree-lined road that was the Green
Manor's endless driveway. Torula, in the seat next to me, spouted
a sentence with too many three- and four-syllable words in them,
aimed at Starr and Roy. I was too immersed in my own thoughts to
join in their discussion.

What could possibly explain that disembodied voice Torula
and I had heard? *Should I bring it up?* She still didn't know it
wasn't me, and that to my ears, it had sounded exactly like
Franco.

The Verdabulary could probably pick up stray radio waves
anytime, but Starr and Torula didn't see it as a possible explanation because of those incidents that happened outside of the
manor. And Roy might just do a dance of joy over my "super-
power" of calling upon the dead. *I think it's best they didn't know
for now.*

"I completely disagree," Torula said.

"Why?" I asked.

"Because many of the abilities we possess now have their origins in single-celled organisms."

Bugger. I'd only been talking to myself, and I had no idea what they'd been debating.

"What are you talking about?" I asked.

"Oh, don't pretend you've never experienced it," Starr said. "People say it all the time like there's a voice in their head that tells them something or other. I sometimes end up doing things I can't explain, and I just tell myself an angel whispered it to me."

Well, I'll be stuffed. They were talking exactly about the puzzle in my head.

"So it's viable, isn't it?" Torula asked. "That extrasensory perception could simply be through a biological mechanism for detecting radio waves?"

I looked into the rearview mirror at Roy, eager to hear his opinion.

"Heck, maybe bacteria sorta invented it, yeah," Roy said. "But evolution must've figured it wasn't a good gamble, so it put its chips on vocal cords and ears and all that shit, and thank God for that, 'cause now we got rock n' roll!"

"Hallelujah," Starr said with a laugh and slapped a high five with him in the back seat.

Torula remained stoic. "But it also means a biological radio can still exist, doesn't it? Maybe somewhere in our brains?"

"Not if nature was bankin' on gettin' the fittest to survive. Sound waves are the way to go. I mean, didn't the earliest life forms evolve in the oceans?"

"Yes, they did," Starr said. "Why?"

"Well, even underwater, both light and sound do a lot better 'n radio at travelin'. And as hot as you babes are, an object at your body temperature won't be emittin' much o' radio. It'd be too weak to be worth anythin'. Even the infrared you give off easily outshouts it."

"But what you're saying is—" Torula pursed her lips. "It's not impossible."

"What isn't, honey?"

Torula twisted in her seat to address them at the back. "For evolution to have fumbled with a receptor for radio signals, and then . . . set it aside. The most physicists can say is that it's impractical—but not impossible, and therefore, vestiges could still be there."

"Yeah," I piped in. "Which probably explains why we sometimes see or hear things that we think have no possible source." *Like a voice in your head that sounds like a dead friend.* It was my turn to thank Torula. "Great explanation, Spore."

She looked at me, brows raised. "You agree with me?"

"That we could have some old, abandoned radio sensor inside us? Yeah, I think it's possible."

"So you agree that there's sentience involved? That hyperwills can communicate in real time because—"

"Whoa, hey now." I nearly stepped on the brakes. "Where the devil did that come from?"

"That's where this whole discussion started, honey," Starr said. "That something triggers Thomas to appear beyond just the ionosphere disappearing."

Obviously, I hadn't been paying attention to their discussion longer than I thought. "It gets triggered, that's the point. It starts a transmission, not a conversation." The road curved and the manor gates came into view. "If you accidentally pick up an *I Love Lucy* rerun on your TV, you don't ask a question and expect Lucy to answer back."

"The hyperwill is trying to communicate but failing," Torula said. "It has a mind crippled by circumstances—"

"A mind?" I gestured at the open sky through the windshield. "There are formulas out there that exist with no intelligence at work. There are equations like . . . $E=mc^2$. The cosmos blindly obeys that formula even without any sentience to decipher it. You don't need a brain to store information or a mind to do calculations."

"Oh, my goodness," Starr exclaimed. "You're more compatible

than I thought. Tor believes we don't need bodies to be alive. And you believe we don't need brains to figure things out."

The car slowed down as we approached the manor's entrance-way, concealed sensors automatically opening the gates. As we went past the archway, I had a sudden compulsion to adjust the rearview mirror so I could watch the gates as they swung closed. Then, as the ornate panels clicked shut, an idea jolted its way through my body, and I yanked the wheel towards the shoulder and hit the brakes.

Starr and Torula gasped as they were thrust forward and jerked back by their seatbelts.

"Sweet bejeezus!" Roy cried. "What the hell happened?"

"Sorry about that. But I just had a . . . sentient moment." I made a U-turn and headed back to the Green Manor archway, not at all sure I could find the words to explain what all these back-and-forth arguments had helped click into place.

"Are you seeing what I'm seeing?" I asked as the gates swung open, hoping Roy could help me out.

Roy leaned forward and stared at the road leading back into the manor. "I just see my lunch break slippin' away."

I pulled over, and everyone got out of the car, our sunglasses on against the noontime sun. I pointed at the gates. "Think of how the data from the car sticker gets to the scanner."

Roy shrugged. "Passive RFID."

"Data transmission, involving radio waves, that doesn't need physical contact or even line of sight." I pulled down my sunglasses and peered at Roy. "It's how to trigger a hyperwill with no sentience involved." I took in all their befuddled faces and waited for at least one of them to register comprehension before slipping my shades back on.

"Holy hell and shit fire. It's just gettin' the right vibe!"

"What do you mean?" Starr asked. "In Goldilocks terms."

The faint rustle of leaves prompted me to usher everyone— particularly a possibly dehydrated Torula—underneath a nearby tree. With everyone in the cooler shade, Roy proceeded to explain.

He pointed at my windshield. "That Green Manor sticker holds data on a circuit, just sittin' there doin' nothin', until—" he arced his hand towards the reader by the gates, "a scanner hits it. Now, hyperwills are like the data in those stickers. And you . . ." he pointed at Torula, ". . . are like a scanner, emittin' EM signals that keep shiftin' in frequency dependin' on a lotta things. Your health, your hormonal makeup, your horoscope—"

Torula tilted her head.

"Just checkin' if you're payin' attention. Anyways, once in a rare while, your frequency hits the sweet spot." He thrust his fist into his palm. "The electromagnetic frequency that jives with a hyperwill. When that happens, you 'connect' and it uplinks data to you by modulatin' your signal right back atcha. And under the best broadcast conditions— like sunset—you get to read the data it's sendin' loud and clear."

"So, in a nutshell . . ." I looked at Torula and scoured my vocabulary for terms I hoped she'd find more credible. "What we call a hyperwill is data in an electromagnetic signaling system that leverages modulated backscatter in the far field when triggered by specific frequencies from a complex vibration."

She grimaced. "What?"

Oh-kay. So that didn't work. "It's just recorded info that automatically gets transmitted when hit by the right carrier wave frequency."

"You mean my signal, right?" Torula asked.

"Yeah."

"The big diff, o' course," Roy said, "is that the hyperwill isn't stuck on somebody's windshield. It's prob'ly hangin' around on some waveform, and Jackson's signal can't ever be as steady as an electronic scanner. So I guess that explains why a ghost can't linger for more'n a few seconds."

Starr adjusted the designer sunglasses on her nose. "So you're saying that's how a person could end up 'psychic' once a while?"

I nodded, conceding that was probably what had happened

when I picked up some random voice in the airwaves that my brain associated with Franco. "And when it comes to the Verdabulary, it probably detected some stray signal and converted it into a coherent radio transmission that we managed to make sense of. In other words, it turned into a transducer."

"And that isn't short for 'trance inducer,' all right?" Roy said with a snicker. "I guess you can say the Verdabulary's like some cool digital psychic."

I smirked. "With no sentience or consciousness or life involved."

"Why not?" Torula asked, crossing her arms. "Do you have solid grounds for excluding them?"

I rubbed the stubble on my chin and pondered: How to beam up someone's consciousness. Was that ever explained in *Star Trek*? "We could gather some data," I said with a sly glance at Roy. "We can build a man-sized Faraday cage and toss Eldritch into it. Let's see what conscious transmissions we can detect out of that."

It was meant to be funny, but nobody laughed. Only then did I notice that everyone's arms were tightly folded.

I unfolded mine. "Look, okay, *maybe* a hyperwill could be someone's neural data accidentally 'recorded' on an EM wave. But I wouldn't call it a soul."

Starr stared at the manor gates and shook her head. "But I agree with Tor. Thomas has to be more than . . . stuff in a sticker."

Roy scrunched up his face. "So now we're givin' the hyperdude a name?"

"I think we should. To remind us of what we're dealing with." Starr turned towards me. "With what you're saying—it's reducing someone's consciousness to nothing but data streaming across the air like Wi-Fi."

"Listen." I grimaced, hating having to say this to Starr. "I was like you once. Desperate to believe in an afterlife." I took a deep breath. "Death hurts, I know. But forcing meanings onto signs that aren't there doesn't change the fact that—"

"Yo, man," Roy said. "What's the harm in a widow believin'

her husband's still watchin' over her? Nobody knows for a fact he isn't."

I gritted my teeth. That was like asking when it was time to tell a kid that Santa wasn't real. I glanced at Starr, dressed in the brightest colors under the sun with her heart still shrouded in black. I lowered my gaze. *It was worth giving a widow all the Christmases she can get.*

"So here's what I think." Roy thrust a thumb towards the gates. "If you're right, then it means 'Thomas' could be lyin' dormant in a standin' wave somewhere with a message for some woman named Florence—just waitin' for Jackson's frequency so it gets triggered to life."

I groaned in reflex at the sound of that last word.

"In a manner o' speakin', that is," said Roy. "It's not exactly . . . 'life.'"

Torula peered over her aviators at Roy.

"Or, well, yeah, maybe it is," Roy said, correcting himself yet again. "You know, like he's hibernatin' and we wake 'im up."

"This doesn't disqualify life," Torula said, gesturing towards the gate. "It sounds a lot like basic signal transduction—a simple biochemical process."

Biochemical? Again? *My apologies to Santa.* "Look, I know you're a biologist, but this fixation on life is getting too far. Even if it were neural information from someone who was once alive, right now, it's just inanimate data, Spore. It. Is. Not. Alive."

Torula moved towards me. "I've seen him, Bram. I've felt him. He's been in my room. He's been in my bed! I can tell that he's not . . . a program." She drew closer, and even though I couldn't see her eyes through her sunglasses, I felt the intensity of her gaze. "I understand your explanation. But can you at least try to see things from my perspective? That a person's consciousness could persist and reach out to the living, devoid of a coat of flesh, the same way memory can exist outside of a brain?"

"Jesus, Spore. If anyone could talk to us after death, then even they would have done it."

"They?" Torula asked.

I held my breath as my mind constricted at the unbidden thought.

Torula stepped back, then planted a hand on her brow. "Oh gosh, I'm so sorry. I should've realized sooner. And to think I've been comparing them to fruit bats."

"What's goin' on? Who's they? Who's them?"

"His parents," Torula said.

Everyone fell silent for a moment.

Starr leaned towards Roy. "He lost them in a plane crash, honey."

"Oh man."

I let my breath out slowly and turned to look towards the distance, only now getting in touch with what I'd been feeling without knowing. "I wasn't just thinking about them. I was thinking of . . . everybody. Everyone who's passed away and all of us who will pass away. I'd like to respect their memories as that of *people*. Not zombies or ghosts or any other creature that crawls about in the dark to survive." My mind played back visions of my parents—laughing, waving, cheering, talking. Memories of my childhood that were dear to me. "I've accepted that they're gone, and I'd like to remember them as real, accomplished, wonderful people—who made me appreciate happiness, ambition, and love that can last a lifetime. Why turn them into suffering, decomposing creatures that can still think and feel? I don't see how believing in an existence like that could make death less painful to accept."

"Which is why . . ." Torula lifted her sunglasses. ". . . I would like to make sure there really is nothing for us to worry about—either because death truly is permanent, and hyperwills are nothing more than electromagnetic illusions. Or because whatever it is that lives on truly is doing well and is happy—not at all struggling to survive in the dark. Because what if it isn't so? What if, in essence, they still are conscious but helpless people? People who might be in need of our help?"

I stared at her, in no mood to argue over the definition of the word *people* found in every dictionary out there.

"Why don't we test it?" Torula asked.

"What?"

"Your hypothesis," she said. "That the hyperwill's perceptibility is triggered by a specific carrier wave frequency, because it's an electromagnetic signaling system that automatically responds to a complex vibration which I generate. Correct?"

My mouth fell open.

"How do we test that?" Starr asked.

"Obviously, we get a really big Faraday cage and toss a medium into it," Torula said with a smart-aleck smirk.

I winced, hating that I knew the fellow who'd given her that stupid idea.

"You're going to ask Eldritch to get tested?" Starr asked.

"Not him. Me," Torula said.

"Hey, now we're talkin'!"

"Wait, what?" I asked, stunned. "Now you think you're a bloody psychic?"

"To go by this RFID analogy, you need to stabilize *my* signal, right? So we can have a reliable transmitter that can communicate with Thomas?"

"Say nothin' more." Roy lit up like a furnace suddenly on fire. "It's not a Faraday shield we need. It's a frequency and resonance reader." He snapped his fingers and aimed both pointers at me. "You remember that soundproof booth I got? I'm gonna modify it to sample Jackson's signature that triggers Thomas. Let's go get it."

"I'm sorry." I tapped on my iHub, my perfect calendar now in a mess. "I was planning to leave after lunch. My boss gave me a new deadline."

"Of course, it's a *dead*line," Torula said. "If it were alive, you wouldn't be bothered."

I raised my hands in a suspended shrug, aching to say that I had to do this if I wanted to keep my good name at my job. A job that helped me qualify for a slot on a starship. Possibly two slots if she would consider leaving Earth so we could be together. For the rest of our lives. In the magnificence of outer space.

But all that came out was a grunt.

"You just go and do what you gotta do, Morrison," Roy said.

"Sorry I can't be here to help set up," I said.

"No problemo," he said. "I can have m'boys at the garage bring it over. By the time you get back tomorrow, I'll have a dog whistle you can blow so hyperwills will come rushin' to our door."

20

AT A PERFECT SPOT

I RETURNED TO THE GREEN MANOR LATE THE NEXT DAY, HOPING THAT by the end of it, I'd finally get to ask Torula what I had come to ask. The sun had cooled itself down to a comfortable companion as I ambled down the stone pathways towards Greenhouse 3C. I took in the vast, refreshing scenery Torula enjoyed every day, and I was about to ask her to trade it all in for the cramped interior of a space craft. *Did I have any chance in the world to convince her?*

This was just one swatch of the Earth that she loved. A land-scape that shimmered with dew in the morning, sparkled with pin lights at night, and now, in the late afternoon, it—

I blinked in surprise at a gazebo. Was that Torula and Starr over there? I detoured quickly to get a closer look. Yes, it was. They were both seated on a bench, their backs turned to me.

My pace quickened at the chance to speak with Torula at a perfect spot, away from all the surveillance. As I drew close enough to hear them, but before either of them caught sight of me, Starr said, "Did you ever tell Bram?"

"No," Torula said.

Tell me what? How she felt about me? What she thought about us?

I ducked behind a cluster of shrubs and strained my ears.

"I can't believe you never opened up to me about this," Starr said. "Best friends don't keep secrets from each other."

"I don't know." Torula sighed. "I guess I didn't want to reveal any kind of . . . weakness."

"Weakness? Honey, this isn't something you can help."

"I suppose. So . . . what should I do now?"

"We have to tell you-know-who," Starr said.

I puffed my chest up like a gorilla out to show who was alpha and took a step out from behind the bush. Then Torula said, "Tell Roy? It's embarrassing."

Roy? I stepped back under cover. Why the bloody hell were they going to tell Roy?

"Honey, he needs to know every possible variable that could affect your frequency. Including that other important thing."

"What other thing?"

"The significance of Bram's presence. I mean, everyone—from your mother to our own chairman—could put their finger on when all this began. Except for Bram himself."

I craned my neck to get a glimpse of Torula's face, but all I could see was hair.

She let out a long, very audible sigh. "You know I just want him to leave."

"Yes, you've made that clear enough. But I don't think you're being honest about why."

Her mother, I'll bet. I curled my hands into fists.

"Come on, honey. You have to open up to me. It's like I'm trying to diagnose a disease with the patient holding back the most crucial information."

"All right. You want a diagnosis? Okay." Torula gathered her hair up and backwards, allowing me to see her face. "I think Bram's like a brain tumor."

Bloody what? Did she know I was listening? I leaned forward to get a better look and nearly scraped my eye on a twig.

"On holocalls, he'd been benign and dormant. In person, he

turns into something malignant that infests my mind. I swear, he casts a smell over me each time he's near."

"I think you mean spell, honey."

"That's what I said."

Starr gasped. "Oh, my golly gee, that must be it! The smell of him."

"What?"

"Molecules of Bram's essence travel up your nasal passages, jolt your nerve endings, and change the way you oscillate. It's so basic, how one's scent can affect another person's biochemical makeup. You gave the example yourself. Women smell each other's sweat and regulate each other's menses."

I crooked a finger to gingerly move aside a mottled curtain of leaves.

"Bram wasn't here the first time, remember?" Torula said.

Starr thrust a fist into her hip. "But his jacket was. I threw it in your face."

Torula looked at her awry. "I think that's stretching it."

"It's primal attraction at work." Starr fished her sparkling cell phone out of her pocket.

"What are you doing?"

"Telling Bram about it."

I clutched my iHub in a desperate attempt to muffle it. Torula snatched Starr's phone away in time. "You most certainly are not."

Whew.

"It's nothing to be ashamed about, honey. It's long been established that natural body odor is more important to sexual attraction than physical appearance."

Torula groaned. "Oh, I can't believe I'm so . . . so—"

"In love?" Starr tried to grab her phone.

"Primitive." Torula clutched the phone tightly.

"The nose knows, honey. You'll have to get a good whiff of him, one way or another, before—"

"I'm not about to go sniffing around him like some mongrel in heat."

Starr tiptoed, twisted, and snatched her mobile back. "We'll need to analyze how his masculine scent affects your hormonal—"

"Analyze?" Torula exclaimed. "What do you think I am? A test orgasm?"

"Organism, dear. Calling him." Starr warbled the last two words like a singing nun.

Damn!

"No!" Torula cried, lunging but missing the phone.

I stared wide-eyed at my iHub and fumbled for the mute button. *Shite. Where the hell is it?*

"Hello, ladies!" I called out, just before the *Star Base* theme played in the air.

Torula swung around and looked more petrified now than when she'd seen the hyperwill.

Starr dropped the call and slid her phone back into her pocket while I strolled over with a leisurely wave and a strained grin on my face.

"Well, speak of the devil," Starr said.

I cocked my head. "Why is it that people never speak of an angel?"

"How . . . how long have you been there?" Torula asked.

"Uhm . . . I was just walking by when I saw you guys," I said casually, my heart thudding.

"Right on time," Starr said. "Sunset's just around the corner."

Torula tucked her hair behind one ear. "I thought you had a deadline."

"And I beat it hours earlier." I gave Starr a polite, apologetic smile. "Mind if I talk with Torula for a while? In private."

Starr gave the subtlest shake of her head, almost like a shiver. "By any chance, is your topic going to be . . . more meaningful than the weather?"

"Excuse me?"

Starr clasped her hands together as though begging for forgiveness. "It's less than an hour till sunset, so you shouldn't be talking about anything life-changing. This is the worst time to be disrupting her frequency."

"I'm sorry, but this is none of your concern," I said.

"I'm afraid it is, honey. Our task is to hail a hyperwill. The sun is setting. The time is now. And your big news could just change her vibe for good." Starr gestured in the general direction of the gates. "I'm just going by your RFID analogy. Right now, she's dancing around the same frequency she's been on since your arrival. Your next actions or words could change all that. We could lose our chances of hailing Thomas forever."

Torula gnawed her lip and paced for a few seconds. I could almost hear her agreeing.

"Listen . . ." Torula faced me and flicked her bangs aside. "I know you came here to tell me something, and it's been hanging over us, suspended, all this time. For just a little longer, it can stay there, can't it?"

"How much longer?" I asked through gritted teeth.

"Until after we successfully get the hyperwill to appear at our call. And that could very well be in just over an hour."

I took a deep breath but said nothing.

"You go on ahead, Starr." Torula's eyes never left mine. "We'll be right behind you."

Starr slowly backed away and left us alone.

I shoved my hands into my pockets. "So what do we talk about now? The weather?"

"Thank you. For agreeing to wait."

I tried to smile, but the most I could do was sigh again. The sun hung low in the sky, and a shaft of sunlight pierced its way through a tangle of vines. Just looking into her eyes, sparkling like blue-violet gems in that shaft of light, took my breath away.

"We have to go," she said softly.

I nodded. Barely.

"Before we do, there's something I'd like you to know." She walked towards me, stood on tiptoe, and whispered in my ear. "I love how you smell."

She pulled away, just as I tried to bring her closer, and rushed out of the gazebo—leaving me wishing the next hour would pass by in a minute.

21

ROY'S SOUNDPROOF BOOTH

I TRAILED TORULA AS WE ENTERED STARR'S GREENHOUSE. *JUST ONE more hour.* That was all the wait I had left in me.

We walked between plots of shrubs hooked up to one version of an experiment or another until we emerged near the base of the elevated workstation. Roy's soundproof booth, previously stored in his garage, now stood at one end of the platform like some recommissioned phone booth with wall-to-wall upholstery. But what was more interesting was the sight on the other end: Roy and Starr standing close to each other, face to face.

Torula halted at the bottom of the steps and cleared her throat. Roy glanced at her, a nervous look in his eyes. "Y'all gotta excuse me. My Boner's burnin' up."

Torula sucked in her breath. "What the Shih Tzu are you talking about?"

"He's a yellow Lab, not a frickin' Shih't."

"Boner's his dog's name," Starr said. "He's Roy's best friend, and he's really sick."

Roy gestured towards the booth. "At least that's all set and ready." He tossed us a two-fingered salute. "Gotta go. *Hasta mañana,* peeps."

"Wait, you can't go." I moved to where I could block him. "We have to do this now."

"And why the hell is that?"

"Because we're chasing sunset, that's why." I pointed up through the glass roof where a faint pastel palette was beginning to show.

"If I remember right, there's another one happenin'. . . lemme think. Tomorrow!"

"Please, Roy," Torula said in a gentler tone far more likely to convince him. "I'd really appreciate it if you could delay just a bit longer. If we let this by, it's another twenty-four hours, and sunset's just minutes away."

"What do you say, honey?" Starr asked Roy with a smile that took the place of "please." "It won't take that long."

"Long is relative," he said.

"Then it means we have to hustle." Starr lurched forward and dragged Torula towards the modified echo-free chamber. "Let's get you inside this frequency capturing thing."

"It's called the FR3," Roy said, his tone bitter.

"What does that stand for again?" Starr asked chirpily, her back to him. Torula stood tentatively at the door of the FR3.

"Frequency and Resonance Reader and Recorder." Roy collapsed onto a chair. "It's an anechoic chamber with a dedicated looped antenna in the ELF band."

"Is this going to hurt?" Torula asked as she disappeared into the cramped, padded cell for one.

"You think Roy Radio would do anythin' to hurt ya?"

Torula stepped out again, and Starr staggered backwards; the two just stood there facing each other, like partners in a dance routine who'd forgotten the next step.

Roy's brow knotted. "Yo, it's cool. The FR3's gonna do all the hard work."

Torula glanced back into the booth. "Why does it have to be so cloistered?"

"We need some kinda sensory deprivation goin' so nothin'

distracts you in there," Roy said. "That whole rig's meant to gather data from you the same way the Verdabulary does with your plants. I souped it up with a couple o' spectroscopic techniques. Also got some gold electrodes to enhance the slower EEG frequencies. All you gotta do is sit in there with dark goggles on and chill."

Starr stood at the doorway clutching small discs of gold connected to wires that snaked down and out the booth. "You ready to do this, honey?"

Torula stepped back inside, and Starr stooped down to attach the discs one by one to our "test organism."

Roy swiveled his seat towards the console, and I thumped him gratefully on the shoulder. "I really appreciate this, man. It should take just, maybe, fifteen minutes, tops."

"Yeah, well," Roy said in a low tone. "If you don't hurry up and ask Jackson what you'd come 'ere to ask, this whole show could be done before you get to pop the question."

"What question?" I asked. A bit nervously, maybe.

Roy rolled his eyes so exaggeratedly they could've popped out of their sockets.

I pulled a chair over for a huddle. "What does Torula think I came to say?"

Roy turned a couple of knobs on the equipment. "That you're goin' someplace outta reach, so you're here to say goodbye. But Benedict thinks you're here to ask 'er to come along."

I looked over at Starr still busy attaching electrodes.

"Are you?" Roy asked.

I kneaded my brow with one hand. "Been trying to."

"Shit. Isn't it gonna be isolation hell out there? No signs o' life outside o' the few humans. No civilization. Nothin' but cold, empty space?"

I froze and stared at him. *How does he know about Pangaea?* "What exactly did she tell you?"

"That they're shippin' you overseas. So it's gotta be that godforsaken place in the coldest part o' Svalbard."

"Svalbard?" My voice cracked in disbelief.

"Ny-Ålesund, to be exact. That how you pronounce it? They say the hottest days there are way below freezin'."

"Are you bollixed?"

"Man, I get it. It's top secret. But it's elementary, my dear Morrison. You're too tall to be an astronaut, so obviously you're not talkin' about outer space. And there's not many places where NASA's got research stations outta reach. So I told Benedict to JFGI, and that place came out the winner."

"JFGI?"

"Just Fuckin' Google It."

"Jesus."

"Okay, we're done," Starr called out, closing the booth's door, and Roy flicked a series of switches on. She hustled to her seat and made the sign of the cross.

"Chillax," Roy said. "Jackson won't feel a thing except boredom."

Starr fiddled with her necklace with a worried frown. "It's just that she's . . . not comfortable in there."

"Pshh! It's not like she's gonna suffocate or get electrocuted. Trust me. She'll be fine."

"Let me out!" Torula's voice blared through the speaker, jolting us.

"Whatdafuh?" Roy hurriedly turned the switches off.

Starr bolted back towards the chamber just as Torula staggered out, retching and tearing her goggles off.

I shot out of my seat but stayed rooted to my spot.

"I don't get it," Roy said scanning his monitors. "Everythin' looks fine."

Torula looked like she'd just run a race, doubled over, panting, hands on her knees. My body waited for instructions, but my mind could find no clue on what needed to be done.

"What happened?" I asked.

"She's claustrophobic," Starr said, putting a comforting arm around her friend.

That's impossible. I wanted to shake my head, but not a part of me could move.

"Jeez," Roy said. "Well, I guess it's a wrap then."

"No," Torula said, her eyes still pinched. "I can do this. Just give me a minute."

Roy glanced up at the sky through the glass roof. "That's about all the time you got."

My next breath came with some effort. Of all the unpredictable things that had happened to me since I'd set foot in the Green Manor, this, by far, had blindsided me the most. *I can't believe I never knew this.*

My sole purpose for coming here had lost all meaning. If she was claustrophobic, there was no way she could survive in a cramped spacecraft. The FR3 was roomy compared to what astronauts had to live and work in out there. There was no way I could . . .

I cast my eyes down, the very air around me having grown heavy. If Torula truly struggled with this kind of fear, then I had to consider that maybe . . . my only reason for being here now was to say goodbye.

I shook myself out of my paralyzing trance and walked towards Torula. "Are you all right? Is there anything I can do?"

She shook her head. "I just need to . . . take control again. Concentrate."

"You don't have to do this, Spore."

"Yes, I do. Waiting any longer isn't something either of us wants, is it?"

I swallowed, not knowing what to answer. "Why didn't you tell me about this?"

"What's there to tell? It's nothing."

"Believe me. It doesn't look like 'nothing.'"

"It's *nothing* I can't handle." She pushed her hair back, smoothing the mass away from her face. "All it did was keep me from playing hide-and-seek as a child." She glanced at the FR3. "And I've never had practice sitting in a soundproof sepulcher."

"Excuse me, honey." Starr clutched a few electrodes that had come off. "I'll need to reattach these."

I stumbled backwards and gave way.

"I'm sorry, Roy," Torula called out to him as Starr proceeded with her task. "I should've told you I had this . . . weakness."

"No weakness at all, sweetcakes." He tossed her a wink. "I'll just grab all the readings I can and see what that'll get us." His voice took on a deeper tone. "For vibes that lure the soul, tune in to T-O-R-U from the city of L.A."

Torula managed a smile. "I always knew you were a DJ."

"We're all set, honey," Starr said, poised to shut the door.

Torula nodded, casting one last look at me. I wanted to say something that would help calm her, but I was too bewildered to come up with anything, so instead I walked towards her, squeezed past Starr and through the booth's doorway, and embraced her— not that tight but just enough to "cast a smell" on her.

"I'll be fine," she said.

Feeling only slightly foolish for believing that a hug might somehow help the experiment, I stepped away, and Starr closed the door. Seated at the console, Roy put the FR3 back into action; I settled down next to him.

Starr took the seat next to me. "I'm sorry I had to stop you from speaking with her at the gazebo, honey. I sort of have a suspicion what you're going to ask."

My shoulders sagged. "It's just as well." I glanced around the lush nursery that was part of Torula's paradise. "Roy's right. It's isolation hell out there. She'll only be happy where life thrives in every possible corner."

"Hey, yo, now. I wasn't throwin' a wet blanket on your bonfire. I'm all for body heat, man. Just go right ahead and ask 'er. Worst thing that'll happen is that she and her girlfriend over 'ere will tackle you and kick you over the goal posts to Whatthefuckistan with a kiss o' good riddance."

"Roy Radio?" Starr protested with a raise of her brows. "Why do you think we'd do that?"

"'Cause you'll say he's bein' a chauvinist dickhead—to think Jackson'll give up all she's got 'ere to live in Svalbard."

Starr gave a charming chuckle. "Men, women, and all other colors of the rainbow can choose to give up their careers now in favor of their partners' jobs. Besides, I think Norway itself is a great place to live. So don't let it bother you, Bram. I guarantee, no botanists will be tackling you in a dogpile of rejection."

I gave a wan smile. Unfortunately, all this encouragement was worth nothing now. Space was the opposite of what a spacecraft had.

"Okay, that's it," came Torula's urgent cry through the speakers.

Starr and I rushed to the chamber door as Torula staggered out. She didn't seem as distressed as she'd been the first time, but she still looked shaken.

"Did you get anything?" she called out to Roy, her eyes begging him to say yes.

Starr clasped her hands together. "Oh, Lord, please let there be something."

Roy surveyed the data. "It looks like somethin' worth your bejangled nerves happened in that booth." He grinned and tapped on a monitor. "We got a spike in your PSD!"

He pulled a chair close to him for Torula. "See that?" We all clustered around Roy to have a look at the chart. "That's the Power Spectral Density. It tells us the power o' the EM wave you were emittin' at a certain frequency. How many watts per hertz was generated." He scratched his stubbled head. "And holybejoinkers, it's a Schumann resonance."

"What does that mean?" Starr asked.

"Holybejoinkers?"

"Schumann resonance!" Starr slapped Roy on the arm.

"It's a spectrum peak o' electromagnetic waves in the space between the Earth and the ionosphere, actin' like a waveguide."

"So, I hit a specific frequency in that space?" Torula asked.

"Seven point eighty-three," Roy said. "That's the frequency you were on when the PSD spiked. And the fundamental Schumann resonance—its lowest-frequency and highest-intensity mode—is at approximately seven point eighty-three hertz."

"In plain speak?" Torula asked.

"When you oscillated at the same frequency as the Earth's surface, your mind must've tuned in to everythin' on that frequency."

I stared blindly at nothing, coming to one hazy conclusion: If all the time I'd spent here was just worth this damned thing, then we might as well— "Go for it."

"Say what?" Roy asked.

"Let's broadcast Torula's signature and see if the hyperwill responds," I said.

"You mean we can hail Thomas now?" Starr asked, excitement in her eyes.

"Hail 'im?" Roy winced. "Who do you think he is, the Virgin Mary?"

"And we beseech thee hear us, honey. Let's test the signal now, please?"

"But I gotta get Boner to the vet!"

"Come on, mate. Just isolate *that*." I jabbed a finger at the PSD monitor. "Don't you want to walk out of here knowing if we already got a breakthrough of a bugger? Torula deserves to know after what she went through to get it."

Roy jiggled one leg, revved up and ready to leave but, hopefully, itching with enough curiosity to wait. "You're pressin' your karma with me, man." He scrunched up his face, then grabbed the keyboard. "All right. Gimme a sec."

My fingers tapped impatiently on the table as Roy accessed the Verdabulary.

"There," Roy said. "Got it."

"Sweet. Now, broadcast," I said.

"Doin' it." Roy looked over at the papayas. I turned in the same direction but saw nothing.

"Fuckadoodledickdog." Roy got down on his knees and crawled under the console table. "Shit. It's the amps."

Torula rose from her chair as she curled her fingers around my arm and tapped Starr on the shoulder, then she bobbed her head towards a pathway behind the platform. Even before I looked, her actions already told me: *We have the signal.*

My blood rushed at the sight of the hyperwill, and though I wanted to kick Roy out from under the table, I didn't dare move. Torula's grip on my arm tightened as the image hovered and, without moving its legs, turned in her direction, looking as solid as flesh and blood. If I didn't know any better, I would have thought there was a real person standing there.

The hyperwill held out both arms, palms facing upwards, and a smoky stream began to flow over its arms, as though it were holding up a slithering body of mist. The image moved its lips— but I heard nothing. Then blood oozed out of a wound on its nose.

At the sight of stark red, my mind shot out warnings of danger; I had to convince my own brain it wasn't real.

"Holy jumpin' jack," Roy cussed from underneath the console. "Damn connections were loose." He slid out from under the table and looked towards where we were staring.

"What's goin' on?"

Starr shushed him. "He's trying to tell us something."

"Who is?"

Torula drew in a sudden breath. "Turn it off."

"What?" Starr asked. "Why?"

"Turn it off!" Urgency flared in Torula's eyes.

I reached for the controls and quit the Verdabulary. In the space of a heartbeat, the image faded away.

Torula sank back into her chair as though being on her feet had sapped her strength. "Did you see him?"

"Of course, we did," Starr said.

"See who?" Roy asked.

"Did you see who was in his arms?" Torula laid a hand across her forehead, her eyes pinched.

"No one," I said. "It was all a haze."

"Thomas was crisp and clear," Starr said, "but whatever he was holding was just . . . fuzzy. Are you okay, honey?"

Torula's iHub rang. She gasped upon seeing the ID, got up, and moved away as she answered the call. "Hello, Mom?"

"What the hell did y'all see?" Roy asked.

Starr frowned at him. "What do you mean what did we see?"

"Are you messing with us?" I asked.

Roy snickered at the accusation. "Yo, that's a good one. *I'm* the one messin' with *you* guys. Really funny, Morrison." He slid his fingertips across his neck, beheading the discussion. "OK, cut the crap. I ain't buyin' it. So I'm makin' like a banana and splittin.'"

Torula returned, still speaking into her iHub. "I'll meet you at the hospital as soon as I can." She looked at me, her eyes full of dread. "Mom just found Truth unconscious. I'm meeting her at the hospital."

"Jesus." I grabbed my stuff. "I'm going with you."

"No," she said. "It might make things worse."

The three of us looked at her. "What will make what worse?" I asked, frowning.

She averted her gaze and shoved the hair off her brow. "Truth's been getting progressively weaker, ever since . . . recently."

I narrowed my eyes. "Your mother's blaming this on my being here, isn't she?"

"She's not 'blaming,' just . . ." She shook her head. ". . . correlating. What she's really blaming is the hyperwill, which just happened to start appearing when you arrived."

"What the hell? Why can't she just blame the usual stuff? Like germs or allergies."

"Truth's been talking to something only he can see in his room," she said.

"Doesn't every kid? I used to talk to Buzz Lightyear and Mike Wazowski all the time." I glanced at Roy and Starr hoping to find some allies, but they were both gawking at Torula.

"Honey, are you thinking Thomas might be behaving like a

parasite?" Starr asked. "Attaching to a living being and taking up nutrients?"

"That's impossible," I said.

"That's because you're convinced he's a dead signal," Torula said. "But don't electromagnetic waves have a malignant side to them too? They're blamed for everything from birth defects to cancer."

"Yo, now don't go jumpin' to that scary shit right away, ayt?" Roy said. "We still don't know the dynamics between ELF waves and hyperwills."

"And I don't want to find out at the expense of my brother." Torula closed her eyes and shuddered. "I saw Truth in Thomas's arms."

"What?"

"Hell no."

"Oh, mercy!"

"The haze flowing over his arms," Torula said. "It dissipated. I saw Truth's face. I'm sure of it. His nose was bleeding."

"My goodness." Starr gave Torula a comforting hug. "I'm sure it's just an illusion brought on by your trauma in the FR3 because I didn't see that."

"No one else saw that," I said.

"But just in case," Starr said, "I promise to keep the Verdabulary off until we get some answers from the doctors. And please, honey, have Bram go with you."

"Yeah. Just like you said, Jackson. There's no tellin' what effects these hyperwills have on people. So best to have a chaperone in case Thomas tries somethin' else on you on the road."

22

MEETING HER FAMILY AGAIN

TORULA TOLD THE CAR TO TAKE US TO KINGSTON MEDICAL CITY—THE hospital where her eldest brother worked as an attending physician. Only then did it dawn on me I was headed for something I hadn't braced for: Meeting her family again after sixteen years.

Torula and I hardly spoke during the entire ride, spending most of the time looking out opposite windows at passing cars, buildings, and most anything with lights in the nighttime cityscape. I might as well have been staring at total darkness with my mind a complete blank on my reason for being here. *What if they ask what I'm doing back in town?* I could say I was on vacation, even though the only places I'd been to were the Green Manor and Roy's garage. Would they even care? Maybe Torula had already told them I was visiting before leaving for a job overseas.

I let out a sigh, my mind in strange territory having lost my compass on the right way to go. I'd pictured every possible scenario of how her mother and brothers would have reacted to me asking Torula to leave Earth for good. Jesus. I might have just avoided a fist fight or two. But then again . . .

I cracked my knuckles. It would be worth all the fist fights in the world to have Torula come with me.

We arrived at the hospital, and as she and I walked down the corridors, passing nurses and doctors and patients in wheelchairs, it became obvious this was the best place to be for immediate medical attention after a brawl.

What if she could overcome her claustrophobia? I knew of astronauts with a great fear of heights who'd managed to space-walk. Heck, what could be more frighteningly high than that? I couldn't back down on a dream, right? Though this was my dream, not hers. Except . . . it wouldn't be complete without her.

I snapped out of my crazy reverie when we entered Truth's hospital room with its sky-blue walls decorated with murals of trees and flowers. Though the room was a comfortable size, it felt smaller in the presence of three Dr. Jacksons.

The full brunt of how unlike a biological family the Jacksons were suddenly hit me, with the fair and red-haired Triana, the tall and dusky Tromino, the Asian-esque Torula, and the blond and blue-eyed boy in his bed. The only one missing was Treble, studying overseas.

It was a relief to see Truth awake and sitting up in bed.

"After all these years, it's remarkable to see you again," Triana said in that mellow voice I hadn't forgotten. She sat by the bed, with a light silken shawl draped over her shoulders. Her face, her physique, her bearing made it seem as though time had stood still for her, and perhaps had even gone a bit backwards. "Trom, you remember this young man, of course?"

Tromino, though in his doctor's coat, had the unwelcoming aura of a bodyguard as he stood at the foot of his brother's bed. He stared at me for a few seconds, then spoke in an imposing bari-tone. "Bram? Is that you?" He broke into a smile, which loosened up the armor. "My, you've grown."

"Great to see you again, Trom." I found it unusual to stand taller than Torula's eldest brother. As a kid, I'd been intimidated by this guy who had taken upon himself the role of father to his siblings. It didn't help that one of my first memories of him was of one Halloween, when he'd dressed as a Klingon warrior. I'd imagined him sworn to protect his only sister from inferior humans—which obviously included me. Torula, however, convinced me that Tromino's father was most likely of Southeast Asian lineage—definitely of Earthly origin—which didn't change a thing about how I thought he might have regarded me.

"Truth," Torula said, "this is my friend, Bram."

"Hello, mate." I tossed the boy a small salute.

"I flied a kite! In my room!" Truth raised the arm not attached to an IV to demonstrate, his Rs and Ls sounding more like Ws.

"Really?" Torula looked questioningly at her mother.

"Flew a kite, sweetheart." Triana smiled. "He says that's why he fell off his bed."

"Thomas did it," Truth said. "He teached me to fly the kite."

"Who's Thomas?" Tromino asked.

"Tor's friend," Truth said. "He's dead."

Triana gripped her shawl tighter. Torula flicked the hair off her brow. Tromino eyed both of them.

"How do you know his name?" I asked.

"Mom said."

A trio of grownups stared with disbelief at the most senior one in the room.

Triana rose from her seat. "I simply told him to ask his invisible guest if his name was Thomas the next time he came to visit."

"Why on earth would you do that?" Torula asked, which was a question I'd asked about almost everything Triana did.

"Nothing to worry about," Tromino said, giving his sister a reassuring wink. "Research shows preschoolers who have imaginary friends grow up to be more creative and well-adjusted."

"But this friend isn't imaginary," Triana said. "Is he, Tor?"

"Mom . . ." Torula shook her head.

Tromino's gaze darted from mother to sister to me. "What's going on here? Do you have an explanation for the hallucinations?"

Torula clasped her hands and raised her shoulders, as though she were a child about to confess to some misdeed to her father.

"It's probably got something to do with tests I've been conducting at the Manor."

"What kind of tests?" Tromino asked. "Involving pathogens? His attending should know about—"

"No, it doesn't. I mean, yes." Torula wrung her hands as she spoke. "But they were in sealed Petri dishes. The point is—I saw . . . I mean, *we* saw . . . something. Bram and I, together, right?" She tossed me a look imploring me to continue the explanation.

I gripped Truth's bed rail, certain I was moments from ruining Tromino's opinion of me for life. "There's been a . . . visual phenomenon."

"A what?" He grimaced.

"Oh, for heaven's sake, just say it." Triana tossed one end of her shawl across her neck. "Truth's being haunted by a ghost. Somehow, the equipment Tor's been using at work has also been triggering the apparition. And now, I suspect, it's causing this lingering ailment."

Tromino stood unmoving with a deadpan expression as he stared at Triana, then, with a sigh, turned to his little brother. "Truth, you do know we have a strange mother, don't you?"

"Yup!"

"Good. Keep that in mind, and you'll end up just fine."

Triana folded her arms, torturing her delicate shawl. "His weakness could be a telepathic energy drain—the brain being the ravenous organ that it is."

Tromino grunted. "When grownups talk about ghosts in front of a child, there's no telling where his little mind could take it. You could've ended up prompting his weakness by suggesting it."

"Oh, that's baseless."

"Right," Torula said. "The same way suggesting the name Thomas couldn't possibly have influenced him either."

"It's exasperating talking with people who don't see the human brain the way I do." Triana closed her eyes and shook her head slightly like a frustrated queen who failed to understand why the peasants couldn't eat cake. "It consumes a fifth of the body's total energy at ten times the rate, half of that energy consumption going to maintaining ionic gradients." She looked at the two other doctors with her in the room. "Your brother's illness may be because of some form of energy transfer through electrochemical gradients in the brain."

Tromino grunted. "You do realize you've just compared his brain to a fuel cell."

"Which is probably what it is to the ghost," Triana said. "Truth first saw the apparition in Tor's bedroom when we slept over before my annual checkup. All this started the same night she met up with Bram. And Truth's been growing weaker ever since."

I looked at Triana through narrowed eyes. *Did she just take a potshot at me?*

Tromino scowled at his mother. "Why didn't you tell me all this before?"

"Would you have believed me then?" Triana asked.

"I don't believe it now. All I know is Truth may have been exposed to a pathogen or toxin at Tor's place. Or from you when you came back from your doctor that day. Maybe even Bram brought it over from another state entirely, triggering these hallucinations."

"I've never been to her apartment," I said.

"But you could still have triggered all of this in the first place," Triana said.

"Now wait a minute." I raised a halting hand. "You're not pinning this on me."

"Well, it's undeniable, isn't it?" Triana asked. "My daughter gets one whiff of your testosterone and poof! The ghost appears."

"Mom!" Torula exclaimed, leaving Truth's side and moving towards Triana. Tromino eased himself in and took her place beside their little brother.

My hands tightened around the bed rail. "For years, I've been away from your daughter, and the minute I'm back, you slap a ghost on my back? Is that how determined you are to get rid of me?"

Triana raised a brow. "You sound as if you think I've been standing between you and Tor."

I let out a snort of a laugh. "Well, now, isn't *that* undeniable? One whiff of your point of view, and poof! She's out of my grasp."

"What?" Torula asked. "That's your opinion of my spine?"

Triana smiled. "If you sense my daughter distancing herself from you, it's none of my doing."

"You once told her you think monogamy is for penguins. You don't think I know that?"

The eccentric matriarch leaned in closer towards me. "You may find this impossible to believe, Bram, but I've always thought that one of my daughter's grandest stupidities is not bagging you for herself the day she became capable of having children."

"Oh, shut the front door," Torula cried, then clamped a hand over her own mouth and muffled, what was most likely, a flagrant curse.

As though a cloud of puzzlement had suddenly lifted, Triana's eyes widened. "Oh, my word. Did you come back in town to ask for Torula's hand in marriage?"

"What? No."

"No?" Torula asked.

"I mean . . . not exactly. But something like it, I think."

"I see," Torula said. "Like what?"

"What?" I gulped. *Jesus. This isn't how it's supposed to go.*

"Well now, this is interesting." Tromino leaned in closer to Truth.

I refocused and centered my sights on Triana. "Don't force this discussion now just so you can be around to influence her."

"Influence her about what?" asked Triana.

"Yes, about what?" Tromino asked.

I clamped my jaw and averted my eyes from Torula's searing scrutiny. Bollocks. This was the worst possible way to go about this, but—*Here goes*. I sighed and faced Torula. "I came to tell you that I was asked to . . . go away . . . somewhere."

"Suh . . . suv . . . Svalbard?" Torula asked.

"Svalbard?" Triana exclaimed. "Where on devil's earth is that?"

I thrust an accusing finger at her. "That's what I'm talking about. I knew you'd try and stop me before I could get to my point."

"Stop you? I was just going to haggle for Venice or Prague. Whoever elopes to a place called Svalbard?"

Tromino shot out of his post next to Truth. "All right, that's about as far as I can let this go." He went to his mother's side and tucked her arm into the crook of his. "I'm taking you out of this room before you chop off my sister's hand and toss it to someone in marriage."

"I was merely expressing a personal opinion." Triana allowed herself to be led away by Tromino.

After the door shut behind them, Torula took a deep breath and shuddered. I wanted to swallow but feared the sound would reverberate around the room.

I kept my gaze on her, but she avoided eye contact, tucking her hair behind one ear. I cleared my throat. "I know it's not the ideal time or place, but could I talk to you about—"

The door swung open, and Tromino peered in with a scowl. "Torula, I need you to tell the attending about those pathogens in your experiments."

"Right. Of course." She glanced back at me, her gaze faltering, and thrust a thumb towards the doorway.

"No worries." I nodded and smiled as she made her exit, though my mind was in a gnarl of knots. I'd lost all clarity about the right thing to do. It was probably unreasonable to ask Torula to join me on Pangaea, and yet it was still beyond me to say goodbye. I'd take this question mark with me to the grave if I never asked.

I shoved my hands into my pockets and shook my head. Truth just sat there, watching me.

"Mom's strange, huh?"

I managed a chuckle. "You can say that again."

"So, I'm strange too?"

"No, of course not. You're awesome."

"I'm scared."

"Of what? All this talk about ghosts? Phew!" I waved a dismissive hand and moved to the boy's side. "It's just a bunch of talk."

Truth looked at me with big trusting eyes. "He wants me to go with him."

"Who?"

"The ghost. To make Tor happy."

Jesus. What other delusions had Triana fed him? "Hey, there's no way your sister would be happy about you going away with anybody."

"But she's coming too. He wants me to go so Tor will wanna go." Truth trembled. "She's gonna lose her blood."

"What do you mean?"

"Tor's gonna die."

I nearly jerked as a cold wave wrapped around my head and crept down my shoulders. Something about those words coming from a child made them frightening.

Tears fell from his eyes. "Can you stop it? I'm scared!"

"Hey, hey." I reached into my pocket for a handkerchief. "It's okay. It's just a dream." I probably said it to reassure myself as much as the boy.

Just as I held my handkerchief up to Truth's face, his nose began to bleed. "Oh, Christ." I dabbed nervously at the bright red trickle, staining the white linen.

"It's like that." Truth pushed my hand away to look at the handkerchief at arm's length. "I seed her blood wiped like that. Then she died!"

"You mean, you saw . . ." I cleared my throat uneasily and shoved the handkerchief into my pocket, away from his view.

"Don't tell anyone. Promise?" Truth wiped his tears on the back of one hand. "I don't wanna be strange."

23

NOSEBLEEDS

I LEANED CLOSE, FOREARMS PERCHED OVER TRUTH'S BED RAIL, AND DID my best to take the little boy's mind away from blood and ghosts and sickness. "Do you want to be an astronaut someday?"

"Uh-huh." Truth snuggled into his hospital pillow.

"Me too. As far back as I can remember, I always thought, between Earth and outer space—being out there was the more wonderful place to be. But you know what I think now?"

He nodded. "You can bring Tor with you so she won't die."

I stiffened. "Okay, mate. Time to sleep." I needed more practice making up bedtime stories.

The door swung open, and Torula strode in, looking as healthy and fearless as she always did.

"Have you been suffering nosebleeds lately?" I asked.

She flashed a flicker of a frown. "What?"

"Truth's nose just bled. And he says the same thing's happened to you."

A smile curled her lips. "He also said my friend, Thomas, was teaching him how to fly a kite."

I narrowed my eyes. "What else have you been hiding?"

"What do you mean, 'What else?'"

"You never told me you were claustrophobic."

"Oh, that." She shrugged away my concern. "It's no big deal. Mom insists it's treatable. I just never bothered."

"I should've guessed." My mind sifted through all the years we'd known each other. "That's why you hate elevators."

She chuckled. "Which is also why I know how clumsy you are at taking the stairs."

How could she think this was funny? "You haven't answered if you've had a nosebleed."

She shook her head. "When it comes to hyperwill visions, things can get misleading. At the greenhouse earlier. When I saw Thomas holding Truth in his arms? I heard a voice in my head asking if I'd be happier if Truth came with me."

"What? That's exactly what—" I glanced at the little boy, though he looked fast asleep, there was still a chance he might be taking this all in.

The door opened, and Triana glided in, flinging her shawl over her shoulder.

"Let's take this outside," I said. As Torula and I walked out, a syrupy smile spread across Triana's face.

Gleaming white walls stretched on either side of the door, a thick rail of polished wood serving as a decorative wall guard. Torula leaned against the rail, crossed her arms, and averted her gaze, as though there were things written in her eyes that she didn't want me to see.

"There's more, isn't there?" I said, leaning again the opposite wall, mimicking her stance.

She bit her lower lip before answering. "While I was in the FR3 . . . I saw myself get shot in the face."

I lurched away from the wall before I got a hold of myself. *Okay, get a grip. Stop reacting to these hyperwill transmissions as if they were real.*

"Thomas was showing me how he died, and I saw blood gushing from a wound between my eyes. I had to consciously tell myself it wasn't really me. It's possible he showed Truth the same thing, and now he's confusing Thomas with me the same way I confused you with him."

I cracked my neck and forced myself to find a logical frame of mind. "Two people, misinterpreting a similar vision. I guess that's possib—"

"Misinterpreting a vision." Torula shoved herself away from the wall. "You're so obstinate. Why can't it be an honest-to-goodness message meant for me? Thomas is trying to tell me something. What if he's asking for help? He could be dying."

"Whoa. I've heard of the living dead. But never the dying dead."

"Thomas is alive. Why can't you see it?" She gestured towards Truth's door. "The hyperwill's survival is still dependent on metabolism. Thomas is obviously feeding off Truth's energy."

"*Obviously* feeding? Shouldn't you put that up for peer review or something?"

"Think mistletoe, Bram. Like a plant living off a host, making it weak."

"Can you please stop thinking of streaming data as a living thing?" I glanced towards the nurses' station down the hall, fearing my voice might have carried that far. I lowered my tone. "There's no chance of it being alive, Spore."

"Truth has conversations with it. And it's not like how the average child plays and talks to a toy or imaginary friend. Every visit leaves him exhausted. And over time, it's made his platelet counts drop." Her eyes glinted at me. "Roy told me the communication link probably gets all its power from the transmitter. Like passive RFID. What if with each apparition—each time the hyperwill connects with Truth—it makes Thomas stronger and Truth weaker?"

"Hey, that won't happen. It can't happen."

"It's already happening."

I shook my head to reassure her, even though her argument caused enough of a dent to trigger doubt. After all, she was using my own theory against me.

She marched over and planted herself in front of me. "You heard what Tromino said in there. Mom made the brain's energy transfer sound like a fuel cell. And it's true. Even in plant life, the electrical gradient provides important motive forces in cellular activity. It works similarly in the human brain by pumping ions into or out of a cell generating ion gradients across the membrane to establish an electrochemical differential."

I gave a slow, deliberate nod, then laid a hand on her shoulder, gently pushing her—and her argument—back across the corridor and against the opposite wall. "And maybe Truth's weakness is because of some pathological reason that just hasn't been determined yet. It doesn't have to be a parasitic ghost."

She broke free and strode towards the door. "I need to talk to Mom. I have an idea."

"I don't think I want to know."

"I want Tromino to examine Truth's brain activity. And the only chance of him doing that is if Mom forces him to do it."

24

OF GODS AND GHOSTS

"So has the deed been done? Has the question been popped?" Triana flung out the questions as soon as Torula swung Truth's hospital door open.

"Mom . . ." Torula shook her head.

"Bram?" Triana looked at me, brows raised and furrowed.

"Torula just wants to ask you something."

"Yes, yes! My goodness, yes." Triana hugged her daughter. "You have my whole-hearted, unabashed blessing. I'd gladly go look for the hospital chaplain right now."

Truth giggled and clapped his tiny hands.

"Mom," Torula said, easing out of the embrace. "I just want you to ask Tromino to monitor Truth's brain waves while he's sleeping."

"What?" The bubble of bliss around her mother collapsed. "Is that all the two of you talked about?"

Torula sighed. "You made a good point about the brain acting like a power source, and I'd like Tromino to see that." She gestured towards me. "And Bram."

"Bram?" Triana eyed me and took a step closer. "Are you

telling me, despite all that's happened, you're still having difficulty accepting the reality of ghosts?"

I shrugged.

"I'm not surprised," she said. "You have the same problem about God."

I glanced at the suggestible toddler in his bed who tilted his head, as though waiting for my answer. "I . . . don't see the connection. Millions of people who believe in god don't believe in ghosts. And vice versa."

"But for someone who thrives in mathematics, proving a soul has left a dead body should be simple. You just need to compute for the energy corresponding to information that made up its consciousness from $E=mc^2$ after it leaves."

"Whatever gave you that idea?"

"A physicist. Tromino's father. And as for God, I would have thought you'd leave the door ajar for that one."

The puzzle I'd glanced at so briefly on the Deltoton website suddenly came into focus. *What was masquerading as God in Einstein's equation?* I shoved the reminder aside and shook my head at Triana. "Are you saying you believe in God?"

"Given that we can neither prove nor disprove its existence beyond question, wouldn't you say it has a fifty-fifty chance? So why slam the door in God's face?"

This time I glanced at Torula, hoping she'd butt in. But she just tilted her head too and waited for my answer. "Well," I rubbed the stubble on my chin, "there's a lot of evidence that he isn't standing there at all. And if he was, he should be able to walk right through it, or make it disappear altogether."

Triana narrowed her eyes, turned, and paced away. "Obviously, you're burdened with preconceived notions about how a god ought to be. Someone who answers prayers. Designs creatures intelligently. Omnipotent. Omniscient."

I pursed my lips, recalling why, as a kid, I'd always avoided talking with Triana. "Why call anything less than that a 'god?'"

Triana drew her shawl over her shoulders and faced me again.

"Maybe you need to relax your filters. What if God didn't make the world but simply made it work the way it does and is more of a tinkerer than a designer. An organizer rather than the ruler of chaos. A cold mathematician instead of a benevolent creator."

"Mom, could you stop picking on Bram and focus on Truth?"

"I *am* focused on your brother." Triana mussed up the little boy's hair. "Why do you think I'm pushing you and Bram to find out exactly what it is we're dealing with? Even if I'm convinced it's a ghost, I don't know what a ghost is. Nobody does. Millions of people have seen one, experienced it, and described it. But all the definitions are guesses. Just like all god-believers are guessing what a god must be like. Both gods and ghosts might be lonely, not immortal, and aching to communicate with us. Or they could be beyond the control of space and time, can read our minds, and once in a while, help us with our problems. Nobody knows for a fact. Because faith in legends does not equal fact. So stop dillydallying and go study it."

"I'm completely on your side, Mom," Torula said. "Which is why I need you to ask Trom to study Truth's brain wave activity."

Triana placed slender fingers against her temple and shook her head. "The closing aria has begun, and you're still hoping to buy tickets. I wanted to rule out sleeping disorders early on, so I've already run the test, and there's nothing abnormal in his PSG results."

"PSG or PSD?" I asked.

"PSG. Polysomnogram. It's multi-parametric, covering EEG, EMG, EOG, ECG, EIT among others."

"That's a lot of Es," I said. "I guess that means you've covered *everything*?"

"The problem doesn't happen while he's sleeping. It's when he's idle but awake," Triana said. "When he's asleep, his brainwaves go all the way down to delta. That keeps him safe."

The door opened, and Tromino strode into the room, making me lose my train of thought.

"I'm sorry," I said. "What keeps him safe?"

"Below one, going up to about four hertz," Triana said. "Those are delta waves. That's a safe region for Truth. Beta waves, at 13 hertz and above—like when Truth's solving a puzzle—that's also beyond Thomas' territory."

Tromino cleared his throat. "Correct me if I'm wrong, but are you discussing the G-H-O-S-T?"

"Ghost!" Truth cried. "That spells ghost."

"Very good, darling," Triana said.

Tromino glowered at us. "Am I the only responsible adult in this room?"

"Right," Torula said. "Let's go outside."

Mother and daughter walked out with me to stand in a huddle in the all-white corridor. As soon as the door closed behind us, I asked, "Why do you consider those frequencies 'safe?'"

"Thomas's visits most likely happen when Truth's brainwave patterns include a combination of theta and alpha waves," Triana said. "That puts his brainwaves at four to seven hertz pushing into alpha, which is eight to twelve hertz. Theta is like deep meditation, or the moment just before we fall asleep. Alpha is a relaxed state like when you unplug yourself from the world for a while. Slow your breathing, or close your eyes and relax. That's alpha. Adults go through these same wave patterns during the hypnopompic and hypnogogic states."

"When we're waking up or falling asleep," Torula translated for me.

"But for kids as young as Truth," Triana said, "they can just shift between theta and alpha all day long. Like in a persistent daydream state."

"That sounds like what it was for me in the FR3," Torula said. "The booth where they captured my signal. I was awake, but it's like I'd detached from the real world somehow."

"You were at what's called the alpha-theta border." Triana declared it without a hint of doubt. "I'm convinced that's where Walt Disney was when he thought of Mickey Mouse. And where

J.K. Rowling was when she thought of Harry Potter. You know they were both sitting in trains, daydreaming? Train rides can do that. And bus and car rides too. You get lulled into a half-in half-out state of consciousness at the alpha-theta border. It's where intuition and creativity lie."

"That would be somewhere between . . . seven and eight hertz?" I asked.

Triana nodded.

A tingling sensation rose up the back of my neck. *Hitting 7.83, maybe?*

Torula gasped and clasped my arm. "The Schumann resonance."

I gazed at her and let a smile tug at one corner of my mouth. "I swear you can read my mind."

She flashed me back a coy smile.

Triana eyed us both and folded her arms. "It upsets me to see this."

"To see what?" I asked.

"You two are such emotional clods—so immersed in science, you dodge everything that can't be predicted. Come with me." Triana marched off down the hall. Torula and I exchanged puzzled looks before following suit, jogging briefly to catch up with her.

"Do you know what the thalamus is, Bram?" Triana tossed the question over her shoulder as we paraded down the bright white corridor.

"A part of the brain?"

"It's the part that translates information for the cerebral cortex to read. It also regulates the sleep states. While it shifts between stages, it disengages." Triana took a turn around the nurses' station. "In grownups, it lasts a few seconds. Something like . . . being in between gears. It takes it a while to shift."

Triana led us into the stairwell. "It just idles for about five to twenty-five seconds on silent phase. When the thalamus is disengaged like that, that's when the adult brain is most vulnerable and open to electromagnetic influences from the outside. That happens each time it shifts through the five stages of sleep."

"And it's different for Truth?" I asked, measuring my steps as we hustled down the stairs.

"Kids his age can hover all day between alpha and theta waves, making him vulnerable even when he's wide awake."

"Where are we going?" Torula asked after we'd gone down two flights.

"A quiet place filled with concentrated emotions."

Jesus. Is she taking us to the morgue? I glanced around for a Fire Exit—and realized we were in it.

Triana exited the stairwell, walked down a hallway, and stopped at the arched doors of the hospital chapel.

Torula balked. "Mom, this isn't funny anymore."

"Really? I think watching the two of you is so laughable, it's irritating. A couple of highly intelligent individuals who can't hear anything beyond what they're thinking." Triana pushed open one of the chapel doors. "Perhaps in here, you'll finally listen to what you're feeling." She backed away and commanded her daughter— with a tilt of her head and a flick of her eyes—to walk through the doors. Torula complied, albeit slowly.

I hung back, not wanting Triana to be misled about my next move. "There's a chance I would be asking her to come away with me. If she agrees—"

Triana raised a hand, stopping my explanation. "From what I know of life so far, I'm forced to accept one conclusion. At some point in time, I won't be around anymore to take care of my baby girl." She paused and closed her eyes as she curled a hand and laid it against her solar plexus. She took a deep breath, her brows pinched, and when she opened her eyes again, they'd gone misty. "I need to find someone who could take over for me—even though she's absolutely certain she doesn't need anyone looking after her."

I couldn't believe I'd gotten it all wrong. "I must apologize. All these years, I thought you were the reason she kept pulling away."

Triana smiled warmly. "Love can't die just because someone gave an order. Nothing ever dies that way. Death is a decision, Bram. Love, like life, can only end after you decide it's over."

25

IN THE CHAPEL

A KNOT FORMED IN MY STOMACH AS I APPROACHED TORULA SEATED on one of the pews halfway down the aisle of the chapel. A candle by the altar cast a soft, flickering glow while stained glass saints looked down at us, as though eager to hear the conversation.

Torula's eyes were fixed on the altar. "Mom thinks hospital chapels are among the most emotionally charged places around." Her voice echoed in the empty place. "Because many people come here in times of despair, she thinks the prayers here are the most potent."

"Triana? Believes in prayers?" I took a seat next to her.

"She says it's a matter of affirming your belief in the possibility. You don't need to believe in God to get a spontaneous remission or placebo effect."

"She has a point." My gaze fell on the lone candle that flickered in the distance. I took a deep breath and sent out a wish . . . or was it a prayer . . . that Torula and I would make the right decisions.

"I've been meaning to ask you something. Obviously." I curled my hands into fists so tight, my knuckles cracked. "What I have to say is something only you and I can know about. I have clearance to divulge only so much information, and only to you. I'm even supposed to have you sign a confidentiality agreement—" I let out a nervous chuckle.

Her brow knotted slightly. "I understand."

I stared into her eyes. "I've been offered a mission. But there's one thing still clouding my mind about accepting it. And that's . . . what you have to say about it." My lungs constricted, making it hard to breathe, even harder to think.

Torula sat motionless, looking at me, waiting.

"It's not a short-term mission. And accepting it means saying goodbye to the life I've always known."

"What kind of mission is it?"

I rubbed my hands over my thighs. "NASA found me a way around the height limit. I got in."

She gasped. "You're going to Mars? Bram, that's—" Her eyes lit up as beautifully as the Northern Lights, and she hugged me. "I'm so happy for you!"

"No, I . . ." I shook my head and gently pushed her away. "It's not to Mars. And I can't imagine going without you."

"What?" It was almost a whisper.

I licked my lips, but it seemed my entire mouth had gone dry. "You can't imagine how difficult this is for me to ask. But if you say yes, I'm sure everything will work out."

She tilted her head. "Say yes to what?"

"First, you have to understand, I never knew about your claustrophobia. And even though they're called *space*-ships, they don't give much of it at all. *Star Trek, Star Wars* and *Star Base*. They're all far too optimistic about the size of—"

"Will you just get to the point? You never will if you keep driving in a roundabout."

"Would you consider coming with me?"

Silence followed, with both of us just staring at the other. Only the flicker of candlelight told me the world itself hadn't frozen over with my question.

The Eagle has landed. Mission accomplished. Package delivered. I let out a heavy sigh.

At last, she blinked. "You've never really said . . . where to."

"Somewhere in the constellation Ophiuchus."

Her breathing became ragged. "A constellation . . . so obscure and unremarkable, I've never even heard of it?"

I nodded. "Unremarkable to most people, I suppose. But space exploration, it's the most remarkable thing one can ever do. Carl Sagan wrote beautifully about it. Stephen Hawking always spoke of its importance. And Elon Musk keeps spreading his vision of preserving and extending the light of consciousness to other planets. We. You and I. We could be bringers of that light."

As poetic as I tried to make it sound, she seemed on the brink of cringing in horror. "What happens if I say no?"

A brick wall crashed down in front of me without making a sound. "I don't know." I swallowed, bewildered, as the dust and debris floated invisibly around me. "I probably will still go . . . or decide to stay. I don't know. I could choose to go but could still be weeded out in the end."

She looked at me . . . no, gawked at me, as though my face had become indescribably shocking.

I swallowed back the acrid taste of dread inside my mouth. "I'll understand if you say it's not possible. Your claustrophobia—"

"Is treatable, like I said. What happens if I say yes?"

A smile crept its way across my face as a flock of white doves fluttered up from somewhere deep inside me. "Then I'll submit an application to the screening committee to consider you as my partner. And only then, if you qualify, will we know for sure that you really can be among the candidates. But even after that, we'll need to go through training and screening. There's no guarantee we'll end up in the final selection."

"Really? With such a preposterous invitation, they're going to be picky about who accepts?"

"At least I know we'll be sharing a new world with good company." I flashed a confident grin, even as I squirmed uneasily inside.

Her gaze drifted towards the altar. I watched her for several seconds, trying to guess what she was thinking, then turned towards the altar too and waited in silence. My heart was pumping as though I'd just run a mile.

"How many friends or family are you allowed to ask along?"

"Just one, as far as I know. Why?" She wasn't going to ask me to take her mother along, was she? My hand tightened around hers.

"How many others have you asked before me?"

A thousand questions to ask about the mission—and this was what she wanted to know? "No one. Just you."

A pleasing tilt appeared at the corner of her mouth. "Eight and a half billion people, and you chose me."

"You had to ask?" I looked into her eyes that seemed a deeper shade than usual. "Of course, there's only you."

Her gaze slid down to my lips, and with a subtle, teasing lift of one shoulder, she leaned forward and moved closer. I held my breath, hoping that what was bound to happen next would really happen next. She laid her fingers on my cheek and planted a light kiss on my mouth. She trembled as she rested her forehead against mine, and I let the exquisite moment linger. I slid my hand up to trace the curve of her neck and buried my fingers in her hair. I pulled her closer, and she parted her lips to meet mine, this time with no restraint.

Before the intoxication could overpower me, she pulled away and whispered, "I don't think this is the right place to be doing this."

"I'm an atheist, so it shouldn't matter." I kissed her again. I wouldn't have cared if the Pope himself were standing right in front of us.

She pushed away gently. "I'm zetetic, so it partly matters."

I let her go and took a very, very deep breath, then waited for my pulse to settle down before I spoke. "I don't know what that means."

"Zetetic? It means I'm still questioning—"

"No, I meant . . ." I touched my fingers to my lips. "Was that a yes?"

"Oh . . . no."

"No?" The brick wall crashed down again—right on top of me.

"I mean, it didn't mean anything."

"Ouch." I thumped a fist over my heart, stabbing myself with an invisible knife.

"No, that's not what I meant either." She gave me a playful shove. "It's neither a yes nor a no. I need time to pull my thoughts together. It's all so . . . staggering."

"Of course." *She's giving it a chance.* "We've still got over a month before we need to give an answer."

A curious expression flitted across her face. "We," she said, as though it were a concept she'd never encountered before, then flashed a wistful smile.

26

E EQUALS MC SQUARED

T<small>ORULA, IN HER KNEE-LENGTH LAB COAT,</small> STOOD WITH HER BACK TO me. All I could do was watch as she reached down to trace the seam of her black stockings leading slowly upwards from the back of her stilettos. Just as things got interesting, Starr, wearing the same white coat, sashayed by in her red stilettos. Both of them turned to face me, revealing what they had on underneath: Nothing but slinky lingerie.

"I need some time and space," Torula said, her voice reverberating.

More women walked into the scene—each one a Torula- and Starr-clone. Every Torula in black lace, each Starr in vivid red beneath their white coats. I glided backwards for a distance, and a goal post and green turf came into focus. We were in a football field, and I heard Roy shouting, "E equals MC squared! E equals MC squared!" He was in a straightjacket, bouncing and catapulting wildly about the field, like a pinball on a pogo stick. The high-heeled clones multiplied in number, trying to block the path of the raving mad Roy.

The women pounced on top of him, but he continued to resist like a frenzied lunatic. The mass of bodies pulsated as he struggled, but I could still hear him yelling his mantra of Einstein's equation. As if to shut him up, more botanists in white coats and lingerie fell from the sky with one solid—

THUD.

I jolted awake and felt the crick in my neck as I heaved my torso off the desk in my flat. I'd fallen asleep trying to plug up the holes in my Husserl proposal—the best distraction I could find while I waited for Torula's answer.

It was a quarter past three in the morning. The witching hour. I shook my head and snorted. "Bugger." Working with Roy was driving me nuts.

"Care for some coffee, mate?" Diddit asked.

"Thanks, but I'll go make it myself." I needed to get my circulation going again. "Could you turn the TV on, mate? To a football game, but keep the audio down. Way down."

I trudged towards the kitchen for a fresh pot of coffee, images from my dream still dawdling in my head.

It's that blasted Deltoton puzzle. Asking what was masquerading as God in E=mc^2. That world-famous equation—though sometimes labeled incomplete and even controversial—was still, in Einstein's context, true. I'd only glanced at it briefly, but it seemed to have infected my mind. And Torula and Starr in a dogpile? I chuckled. My brain was defragging random thoughts from the past few days.

The brewer's quiet hiss served as the soundtrack of my dream fizzling away, and my gaze drifted lazily towards my laptop. The monitor cast a dim glow across the room as it displayed my wallpaper: A spectacular image of galaxy Messier 33 in the constellation Triangulum, a pinwheel of shimmering suns three million light years away.

A collection of Deltoton threes.

The trickle of freshly brewed coffee tapered off and dripped to a stop. I poured some out and stared at the black hole that was the coffee in my mug. I reached for the powdered creamer and let a dollop swirl into the center of the dark liquid. The creamy blotch stayed in place, its outward crawl barely perceptible.

I scooped some sugar and drizzled it around the spot of cream and watched as the crystals sank quickly to the bottom. I turned back towards the spiral galaxy on my wallpaper and was struck by its similarity to the splotch of creamer in my mug.

Cosmic Latte. What astronomers called the color of the universe.

I looked back down at my coffee and tilted my head to observe the creamer, still making its languid way through the black liquid.

Sluggish creamer. Hasty sugar. The coffee was in control.

A barely audible "Hut hut hut" managed to break through my reverie, and I looked at the television.

Saints versus Colts. Gold vs. Blue.

An image from my dream flashed into focus. Torula in black, Starr in red.

I looked down at the coffee, then back at the TV, then again at my laptop that displayed a galaxy of stars. An odd sensation bubbled up from deep inside me and quickly built up steam.

I bolted to my desk and rummaged for a pen and paper. Grabbed my sketchpad and bit the cover off my pen.

"You forgot your coffee," Diddit said.

Still on my feet, I scrawled out my jumbled thoughts.

COFFEE / SLOW CREAM / FAST SUGAR

The coffee is in control.

I crossed it out and wrote a different combination.

COFFEE / SLOW X / FAST Y

Diddit glided over and placed my mug on the table. The creamer had given up its mission to spread. The coffee was in control.

What the hell is the coffee?

Energy?

MATTER VS. ENERGY

The vision of botanists in red and black lingerie falling on a wild Roy Radio played back in my mind.

I shook my head, crossed the words out, and changed them to—

INFORMATION VS. NOISE

The girls are in control. I paused at the thought and stared at my sketchpad, blinked a few times, and wrote down, tentatively—

REDS VS. BLACKS

Whatever that meant.

I stood there with pen poised to write down my next guess. Spanning from the top of the page to the bottom, I drew one huge question mark. I chucked the pen and stared at my sketchpad.

"What the hell is this?"

"New Orleans Saints versus Indianapolis Colts," Diddit said, rolling past the television.

I glanced at the screen just in time to catch a player doing a victory dance on the turf. The huddle of huge digits printed on the players' shirts jumped out at me.

As I stared at the sea of jerseys, the cogs inside my head whirred into motion and clicked an idea into place. Focusing my eyes back on my sketchpad, I picked up my pen and added one last pairing at the bottom of the page.

ONES VS. ZEROS

Data.

Each bit was either yes or no, on or off, zero or one. Flipping from one to the other.

Why?

I laughed at my own question. I never used to think this way. Never asked why the universe had constants, why equations had givens, or how the universal laws made things more or less predictable.

But after everything that had happened, I found myself staring at a giant question mark.

How did each bit know if it was meant to be a one or a zero? Electron or proton? Living or dead?

"Hut, hut, hut!"

The quarterback's audible barely made its way to me from the television set. Who's telling both the reds *and* the blacks how to play the game?

I smiled, knowing what Torula would guess my answer to be. My god: Mathematics. My blackboard in the sky.

Everything computes. Whatever the universe did could be translated into equations. Or was it the universe that recognized equations as commands? Just like . . .

$E=mc^2$

So what did this equation hint at that people could mistake for god, and why?

I sank into my chair.

Energy and Matter controlled by . . .

A third element?

I sat up. It sounded like the perfect answer to a Deltoton riddle.

$E=mc^2$ relied on strict rules. Something told light to stick to its speed limit and made sure energy and mass regulated themselves by its square.

The equation worked because the cosmos always cooperated.

So what was the universe's unnamed capacity to record, recognize, and repeat what worked? What allowed it to remember without a brain—and how did it resist anything and everything that went against its laws?

I needed someone to bounce ideas around with. What better person to ask than the lunatic in my dream hollering Einstein's equation at the top of his lungs?

Despite the hour, I dialed Roy's number, and the guy picked up even before the first ring ended.

"Huh? Whuh—? Who? What?" Roy sounded exactly like a guilty man who'd fallen asleep on the job.

"Sorry for waking you, mate. I thought you were still working at the Manor."

"I was. I am! What the hell? You checkin' if we'll make it by tomorrow? If I said we would, then we will."

"Actually, no. I was calling about something else. It's about . . ." Bugger. *I'm not going to make any sense.* ". . . electrical resistance."

"In my setup?"

"No, in general. It's quantified in ohms, right?"

"Yeah. So?" Roy asked.

"What's it quantifying?"

"Resistance. And impedance."

"Yeah, but what's it made of?"

"Hell, I dunno. But if we can get this comm system with the afterlife to work, you can ask the ghost o' Georg Ohm himself. He's the one who thought o' measuring it so he could make sense o' his equations."

"So . . . what was he trying to measure?" *Anything resembling some scientists in lingerie?*

"Say what?"

I got up and paced. "What did Georg Ohm see in his equations that he needed to create a measurement for? I need the name of a force. An element. A principle or property that—"

"Phew! It's just like friction, man. It's the force that resists motion. What're you gonna ask me now? What's friction made of?"

"I'm tempted to."

"Shit. You know what, if this is for that deadline o' yours for NASA, it's not part o' what I'm bein' paid for. So what's this all about?"

I brushed a hand through my disheveled head. "It's really nothing, mate. Either I've had too much coffee, or I need more of it. Sorry for bugging you."

Roy groaned and ended the call.

I let out a puff of a laugh and stared at my coffee.

Is this what people could mistake for god? An omnipresent third element? Present in everything and yet was one of those factors we still couldn't see?

Omniscient because it knew all the successful patterns the world must constantly repeat—allowing water to boil only at a specific temperature, constraining radioactive material to decay at a certain rate, and a chicken egg to predictably respond to a cook's mental calculation of "heat times minutes" equals a raw, soft, or hard-cooked egg.

From my memory bank, I culled evidence that that "something" did exist. It came in different forms and was observed in different sciences. But it had no common name.

In physics, it was the potential barrier. In nuclear physics, the Gamow barrier. Chemistry called it activation energy. Quantum mechanics talked of a potential hill. In atomic fission, it was that point of criticality. In nuclear fusion, the Coulomb barrier. Then there was the Schottky barrier in electrical conduction and many other energy barriers. It was a wall everybody was climbing over, a given that no one even saw.

It was an omnipotent entity that set limits, put up blockades, and determined when conditions had been met for a bit to flip from one to zero. To accomplish this, it had to have control over every particle and wave.

Omnipresent. Omniscient. Omnipotent.

And because science had never given this element a proper name, it became known as God.

A cool sensation spread from my head to my shoulders, as though pent up steam had suddenly been released. I smiled, pleased at myself, then took a sip of coffee. It reminded me of the unassuming apple that had fallen from a tree to hint at gravity—Newton's immense concept that was just as pervasive yet elusive.

The irony made me chuckle: How it had slipped my mind to ask how the universe managed to remember.

With a curt nod, I decided it was worth the time to send out that email. Glancing at my inbox, I spotted an old message from Virtual Nexus which I'd left unopened all this time. It was probably the link to that voice recording Franco had made.

I skipped it and quickly composed my answer to the riddle.

To Deltoton:

$E=mc^2$ says that energy and matter are one and the same. But that c in the equation—the speed of light—hints at a third element in our universe. Because the faster an object moves, it appears as though part of its energy transforms into mass. Why? I propose it's because something yet undetected envelopes it. Pervades it. And stops it from going any faster than it should. It's an unidentified force that imposes not only the speed limit of light but all fundamental physical constants so that nothing decays, attracts, reacts, behaves outside of the law.

It, whatever "it" is, is a building block that is all-pervading, all-knowing, almighty, and is beyond the influence of time. It is what enables the universe to have order, predictability, and symmetry. It is what upholds the true commandments that the universe must obey for it to exist as we know it.

I clicked *Send*, leaned back, and let out a sigh of satisfaction. If this "third element" had always been in control of the rules obeyed by the inanimate—long before the inception of life—then, most likely, it was also in control of data left behind when life came to an end.

I cracked my knuckles, rubbed my hands together, and smiled. Finally, my mind was clear enough to get back to work on Husserl.

27

WAITING FOR HER ANSWER

LAVENDER.

I found a small vase of it sitting on my desk when I got to Schwarzwald the next morning. It was a quaint office custom of the Green Manor's, but these particular flowers only reminded me of someone I'd been trying not to think about.

It was the toughest challenge in the world, waiting for her answer. *How long could a guy hold his breath?*

I put the vase on an adjacent table, then leaned back into my chair and rubbed the space between my eyes, hoping to quiet my mind.

"Hey! Just the man I was lookin' for."

So much for getting some peace and quiet. "Morning, mate."

"Tell me somethin'. How do you suppose we can feed a ghost?" Roy loped over as casually as if he had just asked me what I'd had for breakfast.

"Why would we even have to?"

"Best be ready for it. Jackson thinks it's alive. Benedict wants to look for 'er husband. And I'm sure Brighton wants to have tea with a bunch of 'em. The least we could do is give 'em somethin' to eat."

I gave a sleepy grin. Maybe it was good that Roy was giving me something else to think about. "I heard some doctors arguing about it."

Roy raised his brow. "Doctors? Were talkin' about what ghosts eat?"

"Long story. But their discussion got me thinking how radiation—with sufficient energy—can produce an ion pair which can interact with surrounding matter. The reactions can be highly endothermic." I shrugged. *Don't ask me why the equipment didn't catch the temperature change.*

Roy cocked his head as he studied schematics only he could see in his head and, surprisingly, didn't chuck it in the bin. "I think Jackson can muster enough energy for that. I mean, a dog can generate an electric field of 45,000 millivolts per meter—give or take."

My mouth fell open. "Who the hell walks around knowing the millivolts of a dog?"

"My vet told me."

"And why would you talk about . . ." This guy sure had one strange vet. "Never mind. How's your dog, by the way?"

Roy's smile faded away, as though the sun had suddenly set around him. "Man, he isn't doin' so good. His age isn't helpin' in any way."

"I'm sorry to hear that." I swallowed, relating in some emotional tangent. My best friend was a robot, and just the thought of losing Diddit was something I couldn't imagine.

"Quince, my vet, says I ought to be happy that I'm the only guy who could say I've had a Boner for twelve years. He's a fool to think that's long enough."

It was funny and sad at the same time.

The doors of the elevator parted, and Starr breezed in with a swaying of hips and a tinkling of jewelry. "Good morning, boys. I've got bad news and bad news. Which do you want first?"

"Whatever rings your bell, sweetcakes," Roy said, flicking a tiny chime on her bracelet.

"Eldritch has seen the video of us hailing Thomas. He's flying over to join us when we try it again."

"And what's the other bad news?" I asked.

"Tor's brother isn't getting any better, so she's taking a couple of days off to stay at the hospital. Which is good because it delays any further testing for now." Starr picked up the small vase of lavenders and gave it a whiff. "She said she also needs some time away to deal with something else that's on her mind." She then laid the vase right back on my desk.

I stared at the feather-shaped leaves and spike-like flowers that teased me with their haunting scent, and I gave up on waiting. "Do you think you could ask her to pass by—just for a short while tomorrow afternoon? I'd like to . . . surprise her with something."

Starr's eyes sparkled like precious gems fit for a ring, and she flashed a glossy smile. "Consider it done," she said and sashayed away.

"Got a minute?" I asked Roy.

"Sure."

"The hyperwill. Can you figure out a way to block it?"

Roy scratched his head. "Man, you stood right in its path and it walked right through you. Hell, I wouldn't even wanna—"

"I'm talking about blocking its *effects*. It's for Torula's kid brother. She's worried it might be what's causing his illness."

"Hell, no." A worried frown took over Roy's face. "That's why those doctors were talkin' about ghosts, huh?"

"Yeah. What if she's right? That the hyperwill's energy demand is affecting her brother's neural network or electrochemical functions or something."

Roy nodded as he squinted at me. "So what do you wanna do?"

"Jam it."

Roy's gaze drifted to the side and defocused as he studied his invisible diagrams floating in thin air. "We can disrupt 'er brother's signal so Thomas can't use 'im as a transmitter." He snickered.

"Yo, it's gonna be like puttin' a dead zone in the dead zone. Let's do it."

28

THE SURPRISE

I TAPPED A HAND AGAINST MY CHEST TO CHECK ON THE SECRET TUCKED away in my pocket, right over my heart. I could only hope this gesture would demonstrate my promise to look after Torula and all that was dear to her—something I was desperate to make her see, now that she was deciding on our future together.

Thirty-nine hours. That didn't seem like such a long wait. But that was how long I'd been holding my breath—ever since our talk in the chapel.

When I glanced up, there she was, striding towards me from behind a row of tall shrubs in Starr's workstation. Wearing a tank top and lowriders, with her long black hair flowing over her shoulders, the mere sight of her gave me a fresh lungful of much-needed air.

She climbed up the wooden steps, took her aviators off, and surveyed the console table and its row of monitors. "So what's the surprise?"

I stood up, walked solemnly towards her, and dug two fingers into my shirt pocket.

"Oh, my Lordy me!" Starr cried, squeezing Roy's arm and

jiggling like a giddy adolescent. "This is what I've been waiting for!"

I plucked the small metallic object from my shirt pocket.

Starr grimaced, looking at my offering the size of a double A battery. "What's that? Lipstick?"

"It's something for Truth," I said. "We call it a hyperjammer."

"A toy?" Starr's face crumpled like a love letter gone to waste. She sank into a chair, all her sparkle gone. "I should've expected this from a geek."

Torula gingerly took the prototype from my fingers and examined it.

"It's gonna send out a low frequency signal," Roy said. "It'll mask 'im so Thomas can't find your brother and use 'im as a transmitter."

Torula gazed up at me with an expression I couldn't quite make out. She seemed either impressed or incredulous. Or maybe both. "You're saying this tiny contraption can render Truth 'invisible' to Thomas?"

"I guess you can say that, yeah. Just turn this . . ." I twisted the device at its base. A sliver of bluish light appeared and circled its girth. "When you see that light, it means it's sending out a signal that will keep Truth from triggering the hyperwill's transmission."

"Will it affect Truth?"

I shrugged. "It involves ELF waves. Possible side effects would be the same stuff they say you can get from electronic gadgets any given day."

"But can it do more harm than good?"

"I doubt it."

"Not unless it also jams 'is guardian angel," Roy said.

"What did you say?" Starr asked like a decommissioned satellite suddenly blinking back onto the grid.

"We wanna make the kid invisible just to the entities harmin' the boy, not the good ones helpin' him."

I frowned at him. "It's a signal jammer, Roy, not a digital exorcism."

"In a manner o' speakin', it actually is. And I don't wanna cut off anythin' more than it should, so just turn it on when the boy needs it."

Torula twisted it off.

Starr got up and stood fist-on-hip to address me and Roy. "Are you saying the jammer could affect other souls?"

Roy and I answered simultaneously. "No." "Yes."

"Possibly harm them?" she asked.

We answered the same time again. "No." "I dunno."

"Then we shouldn't use it," Starr said.

"What are you saying?" Torula asked, her voice suddenly harsh. "Are you favoring the conceptual rights of the dead over my brother's health?"

"We're not sure Thomas is harming anyone," Starr said. "And why is he suddenly 'dead?' Only yesterday, you were convinced Thomas was alive."

Torula tossed aside the comment with a flick of her hand. "I've reclassified him as among the indeterminates science and religion are still playing tug-of-war over."

"What indeterminates?" Starr asked.

"Embryos, stem cells, the brain dead, the undead. That gray area of a list where life is a big question mark."

I smirked. *I guess that's a step in the right direction.*

Starr opened her mouth, but Roy spoke before she could. "Yo, listen." He eased closer towards her. "It only works at a three-foot diameter around the person holdin' it. It's meant to keep Jackson's brother safe."

"But what will it do to Thomas?"

Torula sighed. "I'm sorry, Starr. I have to take this to the hospital."

"Wait." Starr reached out to stop her. "You can't just go ahead like this. It's irresponsible. Shouldn't we at least . . . consult an authority?"

"About what?" I asked.

"About violating sacred ground. You need to slow down and

consider this gadget you've made. Do you think it's moral? Or even ethical?"

I wanted to say she was overreacting, but I stopped myself. This was Starr; she was only doing what she probably felt a good soldier of God would do. I sighed. "Hyperwills are accidentally preserved data, Starr. They don't have rights or feelings."

She aimed her Kryptonite eyes at me, and my breath caught.

Jesus. Did I just say that to a widow?

"Yo, man," Roy said. "That's what they said about dogs 'til the SPCA came along. Even dogs have souls, y'know."

Torula hefted the hyperjammer towards Starr. "What do you want me to do? Throw this away? What if Thomas starts sucking the life out of your children? What would *you* do? Call a priest? Isn't that something you do only when someone's about to die?" She turned to leave but paused and looked at me, holding up the gadget. "Thank you for this."

I shrugged. "Roy helped me with it."

"Thank you too, Roy Radio."

He gave her a wink; she smiled warmly, then hurried out.

The second Torula was out of earshot, Starr stood akimbo in front of me. "Why didn't you tell me what you were up to?"

"Excuse me?"

"A surprise. That's all you said about what you had for Torula. You had me fooled."

"Starr," I said, "I know you have concerns about your husband, but—"

"This is more than just my husband. This is about protecting every lost soul out there who deserves to rest in peace, protected from human-inflicted injury." She pointed a bloodred fingertip at my jugular. "You knew I'd object, didn't you?"

"Hey, nobody's tryin' to dupe anyone around here, ayt? Morrison was just thinkin' about Jackson. That's all it is. It's all for her. So don't take it bad, missy."

"Stop calling me 'missy.' I'm a missus." She held up her left hand and brandished the golden wedding band still on it. "I may be a widow, but in my heart, I'm still very much somebody's wife, and I will do what I must to protect what is dear to me. So help me God." With one last angry glare at me, she turned and stormed out of the nursery.

29

A SURROGATE CHANNEL

I STOOD ON THE CURB NEXT TO SCHWARZWALD AND STARED DOWN THE rocky path leading to Greenhouse 3C. Torula was due back at the Green Manor today, and even if she tried to dodge the topic all day, she was bound to give clues to her thoughts about Pangaea. The morning was sunny, but it seemed cloudy. Cool and breezy, yet it felt stifling. That about summed up what lay ahead today as I hoped for the best and braced for the worst.

A car drove by, and the solitary passenger—a man wearing a black shirt with a clerical collar—looked at me with a stranger's scowl, as though he had glimpsed my soul and didn't approve. I thought of only one person who would have had such a guest.

I hurried to Starr's nursery. Nearing the workstation, I heard Starr and Torula's voices raised in a tense argument.

"What were you thinking?" Torula asked. "We signed an NDA, then you turn around and tell a bishop?"

She bloody what?

"He won't say a word," Starr said. "Trust me. He's family."

I strode around a plot of tall shrubs, and the platform came into view. "Did Eldritch authorize it?" I asked, looking straight at Starr.

She left a long, uncomfortable silence in the air before answering. "We need outside guidance. We're all too close to this to see the bigger picture."

"Bram," Torula said, the anxiety easing from her brow as I approached the platform. "Truth's doing much better. His condition has improved remarkably."

Now that was good news I wanted to hear. Unfortunately, there was no time to relish it.

"That's not reason enough for us to be reckless," Starr said. "You'd be risking two lives by agreeing to hold this test. Your brother's and Thomas's."

"Oh, please," Torula said. "It's just a signal jammer. It's a cloak, not a weapon of mass destruction."

Suddenly, I got a whack on the shoulder blade. "Yo, Morrison. You ready to rock n' roll?"

"Hang on, mate." I thrust my hand out and stopped Roy from going past me. "Can the hyperjammer stand up against the Verdabulary during this test?"

"O' course."

"You sure about that?"

Roy shrugged. "Isn't that why it's called a test? 'Cause we aren't sure about anythin' yet." He strode on by then trotted up the platform steps.

"Mornin', ladies! I'm stoked. You're hot. And this is gonna be one helluva day." He stood at the top of the steps, chest out, shoulders back, proud as a superhero, and said, "Let's show the world how to ghost-hunt in broad daylight."

I walked slowly up the stairs, my mind caught in a knot of uncertainties.

Was this bishop going to end up being more trouble than he seemed? Now that Truth was doing better, was Torula ready to talk about Pangaea, or was she going to prolong the torture?

I tripped on a step, glanced up, and looked straight into Roy's befuddled face.

"For such a bright and sunny mornin', everyone sure is glum around 'ere."

Starr and Torula turned away, unsmiling, and settled down at their stations.

I took a seat at the other end of the computer console and pretended to work. I cast a covert look at Torula, waiting for her to glance my way, but she just sat staring at her monitor.

Roy straddled the chair next to mine. "So where the hell's Brighton?"

"I'm here."

Starr let out a stifled squeal and twisted around to glower at the deathly pale Eldritch who had walked in soundlessly behind her.

The man let his gaze alight on each of us. "I am here today not as an observer but as a participant."

"What do you mean?" Torula asked as the rest of us exchanged glances.

"You have given your brother a device. A barrier depriving the spirit access to your brother's life force. His source of strength. I am here to take the boy's place—as a surrogate channel."

A few seconds of silence passed, then Roy blew out a raspberry of a laugh. "You're shittin' us, right?"

Starr frowned. "Eldritch, I don't think we should go through with this. We need to slow down and consider the consequences—"

"Consequences of what, Dr. Benedict? Of your decision to expose our studies to the Church?"

"Yo, hell, you did what?" Roy's eyes bulged out at her.

"I didn't expose anything. The bishop who was here is my uncle. I happened to mention to him that my greenhouse might be haunted."

"Happened to mention?" I asked. "Like a ghost story casually spilled out of you."

Starr lowered her gaze and brushed her hands over her skirt, as though the sleek fabric needed further smoothening. "He asked how things were at work, so I told him. Then he insisted on coming here so he could pray and bless the spot where Thomas appears."

I squinted at her. *A blessing from a bishop.* Was that the full extent of her threat? Definitely not something that could do any damage.

"He's a bishop. He coulda done a lotta damage!" Roy cried, and I gaped at him. "He might've shooed our research subject away."

"I extremely doubt that," Torula said.

"Hell, Thomas better not be gone, 'cause there's still a helluva lot I gotta learn from 'im," Roy said, brow knotted, lips pursed. He seemed to have gotten more invested in this project than I'd expected.

"Then let's not delay any longer so we can see if we still have a hyperwill project on our hands." Eldritch planted his icy gaze on Starr. "Shall we begin?"

She clutched her tiny crucifix pendant as she gazed at the cluster of papayas. "Psalm 121, verse seven. The Lord will keep you from all harm. He will watch over your life." She made the sign of the cross, and then sat down.

"I'll take that as a yes," Roy said and settled down into his post at the console. "This is Roy Radio, broadcastin' live over the Dead Zone."

I clicked on my dashboard too, activating the Verdabulary, and a hush fell over the place. We all glanced around—scouring the surroundings for any sign of an apparition like hunters waiting for a camouflaged creature to emerge from the wild. Even the plants seemed to be holding their breath in anticipation.

While the others hoped for some ghostly revelation, I was fearing the effects on Truth. What if the hyperjammer couldn't hold off the effects of EM signals boosted by our equipment?

Seconds ticked by, but nothing happened.

"You think the amps might have come loose again?" I mumbled at Roy.

"No way."

I was about to check when Eldritch spoke. "Are you familiar with biathletes, Mr. Radio?" The so-called psychic closed his eyes, inhaled deeply, and released a long-drawn-out exhale.

"Uh . . . yeah?" Roy said.

I checked the readings on the monitor.

Eldritch continued to talk in a slow, rhythmic—almost hypnotic —manner. "Those Olympic athletes thunder down a ski slope . . . hearts pounding . . . then in seconds, calm themselves to fire a rifle . . . with extreme accuracy." He paused, taking in a lungful of air, and exhaled. "Mediums do the same thing. We close our eyes . . . steady our breath . . . and bring ourselves to the alpha-theta border . . . in seconds."

I nudged a dial ever so slightly on the console, just before Eldritch opened his eyes.

Roy gulped. "Do you see anythin'?"

Eldritch looked at the foot of the stairs, shifted his gaze to the shrubs nearby, then squinted and tilted his head. "He's very dim. Like a man standing in the shadows."

"I see him," Torula whispered.

"Me too," Starr said. "He seems weak."

"Whatduh?" Roy said. "I don't see a damn thing."

I stared at the same spot, and a distorted image of the hyperwill faded into view, like a diffused reflection twisted and crammed into a warped and slender mirror. And then I felt—more than heard—a deep and palpable sigh that came without a sound. My hair bristled. Even though my mind knew this was just some old transmission, it was impossible to remain unaffected. It was the reason horror movies would never die.

The image grew in clarity, and Thomas's face became recogniz-able. A prickling sensation traveled down my spine as the image rotated, afloat, and looked at Torula with its amber eyes.

A pleasant male voice issued from the Verdabulary. "Dry not do iris cold."

"Shit," Roy said. "What's goin' on?"

"He's just standing there, looking at me." Torula took a step towards the stairs. "Are you all right?"

The apparition moved its lips, but no words came.

"Do you need help?" she asked.

It gave no response, and then Torula winced and staggered back. "I think . . . I need to sit down."

Christ. I dragged a chair over. "What's wrong?"

She laid a hand over her brow as she took a seat.

Eldritch spoke with urgency. "You must break the connection immediately. Otherwise, Thomas might attach to you."

"Nuh," Torula said. "Abbey fan winsome vilify meek arson."

"Spore?" I asked, bewildered.

"Hurry, take her outside," Eldritch said.

I expected her to resist, but she meekly put one foot in front of the other as I ushered her down. Her knee buckled, and I held her fast. Jesus. What was this experiment doing to her?

"They stink in snow and whirl," she babbled as she walked. "I'm dirigible."

I held her tighter with every labored step to get her outside. I looked back at the hyperwill just as its jaw detached, dangled, then fell to the ground.

"Turn it off, Roy," Starr cried. "Hurry!"

The figure floated towards us. "Tell her . . ." The words resonated in my head just as the image held out blue flowers. Then its arm came off, and the vision crumbled to ashes.

30

USING SYMBOLS

TORULA SAT RECOVERING ON A LOW STONE BENCH ENCIRCLING THE base of a tree, the thick canopy giving us ample shade against the sun.

"How are you feeling?" I asked.

She nodded, with head bowed, but said nothing. That didn't reassure me one bit.

I glanced at the nursery entrance about fifteen meters away. What if the Verdabulary was magnifying the effects of EM fields on her instead of Truth?

Starr hustled over and handed Torula a tumbler of water. "Say something, honey."

"I'm all right. Thank you."

"Oh, heavenly mercy." Starr clasped her hands together and heaved a sigh; it seemed her concern for her friend now outweighed all her other worries. "You sound normal again."

"What are you talking about?"

"You were speaking in tongues," Eldritch declared, as though it were an undeniable fact.

Torula gave me a questioning look as she took a sip of water.

"Your words were jumbled," I said.

"Slurred, maybe, but not jumbled. I was just asking for mefenamic acid. I thought I was going to get a full-blown headache, but it's gone now." Torula put down the tumbler. "I need to call my mom so I can—"

"Truth's all right," I said. "I've called and checked."

"Looks like our hyperjammer did its job, huh?" Roy punched me lightly on the arm.

"That doesn't make these experiments any less dangerous," Starr said. "It did this to Tor, and God only knows what it's done to poor Thomas. I saw him turn into ashes." Accompanied by a faint rustle of leaves and a strong scent of flowers, that last statement sounded eerier than it should have.

"Thomas is fine," Torula said, using one hand to tame her hair against the breeze. "What you saw was an exact replay of a vision I had in the FR3."

"Do you understand what it means?" Starr asked.

Torula shook her head.

"He's communicating by using symbols," Eldritch said, turning to look towards the nursery. "Spirits use images and memories they pick up from the medium's mind."

A bit of unverifiable trivia that gives psychics something to do. And get paid for.

"The departed have no choice but to make do with what they can connect with," Eldritch said. "That's why the meaning often becomes blurry. Sometimes, the message could get lost entirely."

"Like how?" Torula asked.

"They could use another person to represent someone you don't know. Or they could move objects around or hide them to send a message. A missing watch could be a reminder of an important appointment. Misplaced eyeglasses could mean there's something you need to see. In communicating with the departed, you must look for themes or meanings beyond your personal interpretation."

Make things up, that's what he means.

"He always tries to hand me forget-me-nots." Torula spoke

looking at the green grass at her feet, as though trying to find a translation written on the ground. "And he said, 'Tell her.' But I don't know who 'her' is or what he wants me to say."

"Florence," Starr said. "Didn't you once hear him say Florence?"

"Does it even matter anymore?" I asked. "It's like a replay of an old SOS message from a ship that's long sunken to the ocean floor."

They all looked at me like I was some party pooper who'd just crashed their Ouija get-together.

"Hey, man," Roy said. "If you got a message from outer space, would you care less if the aliens sent that message light years ago? You'd still wanna know where it came from and what they're tryin' to say."

"Yeah, because searching for life outside our planet makes sense. But picking up shreds of information on stray EM waves—it could just be something that spilled out of YouTube."

Eldritch turned his icy gaze on me. "You seem to think ghosts are petty, Mr. Morrison. No apparition has yet taught anyone how to cure a disease. Or solved a mystery science can't explain. That's why all this seems irrelevant to you."

I let out a tired sigh. "I'm glad you see my point." Though it was clear he was only beginning to make his.

"The tragedy of death leaves the departed distraught over seemingly mundane matters. About not having said goodbye to one's parents. About leaving behind children, friends, loved ones. Who will care for them, comfort them, make sure they end up fine? That's the reason they stay on. It's for the everyday things that matter most to the very few. And they can't leave until they know they've set things right."

"Set things right?" Pent up feelings surged inside me, and I clenched my fists as I struggled against a sudden seething. "My parents died when I was fourteen. They had a lifetime of things left to help set right for me—things as petty and mundane as they come . . ." I shook my head as I sifted through a turmoil of words in my head.

"Bram." Torula laid a hand on my arm. "Nothing like this ever happened to me either, but things changed. Maybe, when your parents passed away, the conditions were . . . just not right." She looked at me, her eyes seeing the pain no one else did; she was the one I had leaned on the most when I had come close to falling apart.

"Yo, man." Roy laid his hand against his chest. "It's an ability I don't have either. But just 'cause you can't hear a dog whistle doesn't mean no one's been blowin' it."

"Your friends are right, Mr. Morrison," Eldritch said. "Hyperwills commune directly with our minds. It's an ability for us to receive the messages. And if a spirit is able to move objects around, it's by tapping into the medium's latent telekinetic capabilities—even without the medium knowing."

Starr's eyes grew wide open. "You mean, my husband could have been . . . tapping me? Or my children?"

Roy scowled. "Then why do they all skip me?"

"These psychic abilities lie in our genes," Eldritch said. "*We* have the capacity, and you either don't have it or your ability is too weak."

"You're sayin' it's not in my DNA?"

Torula snorted. "There's no such thing as a 'psychic gene,' Roy."

"Paranormal abilities run in families, Dr. Jackson," Eldritch said. "You have the gift, and so does your brother. The reason we're called 'Mediums' is because we can also mediate communication for those who need their vibrations 'fine-tuned,' so to speak." He turned towards me. "In your case, Mr. Morrison, you managed to see Thomas because of Dr. Jackson. Away from her presence, you wouldn't be able to detect a hyperwill even if you walked right through one again."

"Hey! That's just like inducin' intermediate frequency translation." Roy thumped me on the chest with the back of his hand.

"Y'know, like havin' one energy wave influence the characteristics of another."

"Which is why," Eldritch continued, looking at me, "your parents may have tried to reach out, but you simply don't have the genes to perceive them on your own, and no medium was around to assist. I can help if you would be open to—"

"You caught it on video," I said, shoving the evidence between him and me. "I doubt your camera has the genes that Roy and I don't have."

"Good point," Torula said, and we all looked at Eldritch to wait for his rebuttal.

"It took me a while to figure that out," he said. "But I got a clue when Dr. Jackson referred to that bluish manifestation as a *third* incident—distinguishing it from the one we couldn't see a few seconds earlier. I believe, instinctively, you had sensed they were not the same entities."

Torula heaved a deep breath and gave a subtle nod. "It scared me. All the other incidents didn't."

"What are you sayin'? We got two hypers hauntin' us? Git outta here."

"It's the only explanation that makes sense," Eldritch said. "That second specter had appeared after you were all startled by a piece of metal falling to the ground. Unfortunately, why the metal fell is beyond the scope of the camera, so we can't tell if the spirit itself had caused the metal to fall."

"And what if it had?" Starr asked.

"It would indicate a spirit driven by mischief, something not at all a characteristic of Thomas. It would show that this one fed on fear, using it to generate enough energy to be visible to the naked eye."

"Damn. It does make sense," Roy said.

Only if you believe in the sixth kind. I glanced at Torula, thinking of grabbing her by the hand and leading her out the manor's gates. As though to escape my hidden plan, she got up and walked towards the sun-dappled path leading to the greenhouse, just to the edge where the shade given by the tree branches ended.

"Please don't go any farther, Dr. Jackson," Eldritch said, approaching her like a bodyguard advising caution. "Be afraid of spirit attachment. It's the reason why, with your brother protected, I had opened myself up, lowered my defenses to become the new channel. But it has obviously formed an attachment to you already."

"Maybe we should give 'er a hyperjammer too," Roy said.

"No." Torula abruptly turned to face us. "Thomas is weak enough as it is."

"So what're you plannin' on doin'? Offer yourself again for 'is next meal? What if we've turned it into a cy-vamp?"

"That's what I'm worried about," I said.

"What?" Torula looked at me in disbelief. "You think Thomas has become a . . . cybernetic vampire?"

"No. I'm worried the equipment might be amplifying the signal—and the side effects that go with it. That's why we shouldn't be doing any more experiments until—"

"He's draining her of hormones," Eldritch said like the self-declared authority on the undead that he was. "That's what's happening. A spirit will always sap your strength when he drinks of your life force. It's a primary source of nourishment. They're attracted to high levels of it."

"Oh my," Starr said. "Tor's mother has the same suspicions."

Torula bit her lip and cocked her head, and I had no clue what to make of that response.

"Spirits are very dependent on the emotions they stir," Eldritch said. "You can almost identify a spirit by the flavor of emotions it leaves behind with each manifestation. The frightening ones feed on fear. Lustful ones feed on passion. Happy ghosts feed on joy."

I gritted my teeth and glanced at Starr, hoping she'd heed the Bible's warning about consulting with mediums, but she looked so engrossed, Eldritch might as well have been a priest.

"Does the manor have evidence that supports this theory?" Torula asked.

"No. It's a conclusion I made on my own," Eldritch said.

"Based on what?" Torula asked.

"The witching hour."

Gawd. I rolled my eyes.

"That's three a.m.!" Starr exclaimed.

"You gotta be shittin' me."

"It's also called 'The Devil's Hour,'" Eldritch said. "When demons and ghosts are said to be at their strongest. It's when many people wake up, inexplicably, to experience the supernatural. The legend of the witching hour was born because of a shared manifestation among people of different cultures and faiths, from all parts of the world. It's Mr. D who, inadvertently, helped me figure it out."

"How?" Torula asked.

"He's diabetic. And he told me that his doctors had once advised him to set his alarm to three a.m. to check his blood glucose at that hour."

Torula nodded as if the psychic's mumbo-jumbo made perfect sense to her. "It's the dawn phenomenon."

"I don't get it," Roy said. "If you see ghosts at three a.m., you're diabetic?"

"No," Torula said. "The dawn phenomenon happens to everyone, regardless of age, gender, or geographical location. In the middle of the night, our body releases growth hormones, epinephrine, cortisol, etcetera, to help the body repair and restore itself. This can cause glucose levels to rise in diabetics, but those with no problems with insulin are unaffected by it."

"Or they wake up and see ghosts?" Roy asked.

"Or dream about them," Starr said, raising her brow at Torula.

Torula turned abruptly towards the greenhouse. "I think I know what's going on. I know what to look for." She straightened up and tugged her shirt down firmly. "I'm going back in."

"Like hell you are," I said.

"Are you insane?" Starr cried.

"If Truth was able to hold up against the parasitism for days, surely I can take it for a few more minutes."

"Jackson, it was milkin' you dry and scramblin' your brains. Even you would stop milkin' a cow if it started speakin' in tongues."

Torula darted her gaze from one stone path to the other, looking every bit like a cornered criminal about to make a run for it.

"Let's go to your nursery instead, Dr. Jackson." Eldritch held his arm out towards one path and blocking the way to another. "Perhaps the data you can access there will show us what you're looking for."

31

WE'RE NOT HARMING THOMAS

Roy and I walked behind Torula as Eldritch led her safely away from Greenhouse 3C. Torula paused along the stone path and looked behind us at Starr who hadn't budged. "Aren't you coming?"

Starr stood alone in the shade of a tree, trifling with her necklace, while the rest of us waited in the sunlight. "Part of me wants to stay away, but another part says it will be wiser if I watched over what you're doing."

I almost smiled; it was ironic that we were at odds despite feeling exactly the same way about Project Hyperwill.

"Heck, I got into this gig just 'cause I was curious," Roy said. "I still can't see the damn thing, but now I go to sleep and wake up thinkin' about it."

I rubbed the stubble on my jaw and wondered why he did.

"Come on, Starr," Torula said. "We're not harming Thomas. More than anything, I think proceeding with this study is the only way to help him."

"And other lost spirits like him," Eldritch added.

Starr looked at me, though I had nothing to say. Was she waiting for me to stop her too? Frankly, I thought it would be easier on everyone—including Starr—if they just let her walk away.

"All right," Starr said and pointed a polished finger at me as she walked towards Torula. "But no more anti-hyper gadgets."

I sighed and let everyone else lead the way to Torula's nursery. We all filed in, clueless as to what piece of information Torula was chasing now. As we walked past the neat rows of glass-enclosed plants surrounding the elevated platform, I imagined them turning their leafy heads to guess what their botanist friend was up to now.

"So whaddaya wanna see?" Roy asked as he positioned himself at the workstation.

"What the FR3 captured of my brain activity," Torula said.

As Roy opened a selection of charts and diagrams, a deep voice resonated from a hidden speaker nearby. "I'm thirsty."

Roy jumped. "Whatdafuh! You got a ghost in 'ere too?"

"Relax," Torula said, smiling, and gestured towards a specimen plant in its glass dome. "It's my Spathiphyllum. The Verdabulary will take care of giving him water." She sat down and surveyed the graphic representation of her brain waves on the monitor as the Spathiphyllum let out an appreciative sigh. "Ahhh . . ." Like a tired gentleman sinking into a warm bubble bath.

"There, see?" Torula said. She pointed at a relatively calm section of the graph, where the wave patterns were midrange in density.

"What about it?" I asked.

"That's when my PSD spiked."

"When it matched the alpha-theta border," Eldritch said.

"Right," Torula said. "Now, show me the electrochemical readings shortly after that."

Roy displayed another chart showing a corresponding spike.

"I knew it." The glow of a smile spread across Torula's face. "The transmission triggered a higher metabolic rate, induced by increased brain activity. That's the correlation between heightened hormone levels and increased paranormal observations. Do you get it?" she asked, her eyes wide and bright.

All of us gaped in confusion. Even her Verdabulary remained speechless.

"Hyperwills feed on *electricity*," she said, "not hormones. Having elevated hormone levels is what allows our brains to produce more electricity. Simply put, the more hormones produced, the more millivolts—the more power the hyperwills can use."

"How?" Starr asked.

"A single brain cell has a transmembrane potential of 70 millivolts, and hormone treatments have been shown to increase the transmembrane protonic electrochemical potential difference by several millivolts."

That sounded familiar. "Is this based on that fuel cell analogy your mother gave?" I asked.

"It's not an analogy, Bram. It literally is the production of electricity in living organisms. It's called electrogenesis." Torula swiveled her seat to face Eldritch. "My mother's a psychiatrist. She's convinced these apparitions are influenced by some sort of hormone modulation. There's about 300 millivolts of energy present around the membrane of a cell. With higher hormone levels, you can boost it."

"Are you saying a hyperwill can frighten you just to modulate your hormones?" Eldritch asked.

"In a manner of speaking," Torula said. "Like how a lab rat gets to associate pushing a certain button to get food, hyperwills might associate scaring someone with an energy surge." She cleared her throat and stood up. "And speaking of lab rats, I'd like to go to the clinic."

"What's the matter?" I asked, instantly worried. "Are you feeling something?"

"I feel perfectly fine. But I want them to get vitals and a blood sample from me. All this time, we've been examining the transmission being sent by the hyperwill. But we haven't analyzed me. The transmitter. The antenna. The transducer or whatever else it is you think I am." She tapped her chest. "We need to study what effects hyperwill-driven electrogenesis might have on my system."

Eldritch nodded. "Every medium will tell you giving a spirit access to your life force is a draining experience."

"I believe," Torula said, "that what primarily drains the medium—or transmitter—of energy is driving ion pumps to restore an electrical potential, something crucial in the process of electrogenesis that requires more ATP."

Starr frowned and shook her head. "Surely, Thomas didn't mean to cause any harm. He wouldn't have done so if he knew his life depended on keeping you well."

"I agree," Torula said. "Like mistletoe, I'm sure the hyperwills are unaware of the ill effects of their basic need to feed. In fact, they probably don't even know they're feeding."

"Jeez. It's like people have had a gut feel about it all along. Except we ended up jumpin' to weird ideas like vampires suckin' blood, succubi harvestin' sperm, and zombies eatin' human flesh. I think deep down, we sense what the hyperwills are doin'— harnessin' energy our bodies produce. But we ended up bein' too creative. We get subconscious hints and we . . ." Roy snapped his fingers. "What's that word? Extrapolize . . . extipolate?"

"Approximate? Extrapolate?" Torula asked.

"Extrapolate, that's it," Roy said.

"Oh, Christ," I said. Only after the others turned to look at me did I realize I'd actually said the words out loud—four cardinal directions of confusion, resentment, disappointment, and disbelief. "Look, the last thing I want is you to think I have no regard for the dearly departed. It's the opposite, believe me. That's why I don't understand why it gives you satisfaction to picture them like parasites sucking the life out of our bodies."

"That is not how anyone wants to picture them, Mr. Morrison," Eldritch said. "Unfortunately, most people have been poisoned by what fiction has fed their minds. That's why we need to work together to uncover the hard facts."

"The problem is, Bram . . ." Starr said. "You were never interested in the research. You didn't come here to learn or to work. You only came to woo my friend."

I opened my mouth, wanting to deny it—but couldn't.

"Yo, you can't force a guy into a game if he doesn't wanna play." Roy had spoken in my defense, but somehow the words also carried the sting of an accusation.

Torula gave me a sad smile. "I know you think this someone that we're seeing is a some-*thing*. And I understand why you can walk away from it—in fact, I've been encouraging you to. But I can't. Not until I understand why he's reaching out to me."

I found it hard to meet her gaze. "You must know, I'm doing my best to help. I *want* to believe."

"No, you don't." Torula sighed. "What you want is to help—without having to believe." She moved towards the stairs. "I'm going to the clinic."

"I'm coming with you," Starr said, and all I could do was look on sullenly as they left the platform and headed out.

I slumped onto a tall stool, guilty of having promised wholehearted support yet coming in with half a heart.

Roy clucked his tongue. "Can't figure you out, Morrison. You can see the damned thing. Shit, you even walked right through it. But you still don't think it's what it is?"

"I'm not surprised," Eldritch said. "Skeptics can ignore facts to defend their non-belief as passionately as believers cling to scriptures to defend their religion."

"Hey now," I said, straightening up. "I've been far more open-minded about this than I thought I'd ever be."

"Nah," Roy said settling down into a chair. "Your mind's just ajar—and only 'cause Jackson's foot is keepin' you from closin' it."

Eldritch gazed out at the potted plants around us, their glass domes glinting in the sun as though they were his audience instead of us. "For most people, a psychic experience comes just once in a lifetime. One incident of clairvoyance, telepathy, telekinesis, or any other supernatural occurrence. One inexplicable moment that never happens again. So people end up giving it some flimsy explanation and file it away, until it turns into nothing but a dim and curious memory. A fluke." He glanced at Roy. "Like a lightning strike that no one else heard or saw."

"Yeah," Roy said with a nod. "What was it like for you, Brighton? The first time you saw one."

Eldritch paused a long while, then exhaled audibly like a man tired of trekking down an oft-beaten path that led him nowhere. "I've lived with these visitations as far back as I can remember. But the first contact I made that others could attest to was in my mother's office. I was still very young, and my mother had asked me to wait on a couch while she finished a meeting with her clients. They talked about having problems locating their father's last will and testament, and my mother remembers that I had dozed off during all that. In the car ride home, she says I told her that I'd dreamt of their father in a wooden house, pointing at a particular drawer of a table underneath some stairs." He shook his head, as though he regretted what had happened next. "I don't know why, but my mother actually told her clients what I'd said."

"And they found it?" Roy asked.

Eldritch nodded. "It was at the bottom of a drawer—of a table I'd never seen, in a summer house I'd never been to, that belonged to people I'd never met before or since. After that, my family no longer doubted my abilities." He looked straight at me. "I admit, for a while, it was tempting. It became easy to trick people into believing. Until my father gave me a good dressing-down. He told me to respect the gift and not corrupt it with my vanity—to ensure people will not lose their respect for me." His gray eyes, usually expressionless, were now a shade of melancholy. Perhaps heeding his father's advice hadn't done much to spare him the scorn.

I considered this man who believed in things no one else could see. Accused of having conversations with hallucinations. Who formed friendships with figments of his mind. Suddenly, I understood the icy pallor around him.

"Listen," I said. "This ability of yours, it's drafted you into some . . .'cause' you didn't volunteer for. I've no doubt you see things—"

"But you still don't believe they're people," Eldritch said. "People whom we can help."

"And I've been trying to explain why. It's data. It's old data. Obsolete data. And absolutely not conscious or alive. But all my explanations seem to be falling on deaf ears."

Eldritch scrunched his brow. "Are you sure it is us who are deaf? Or is it you who refuses to see, Mr. Morrison?"

I shook my head in aggravation. *What can I do to make them all break free of this delusion?* How could I open *their* eyes so that so they could see—

Holy Christ. That's what I needed to do!

"I can make everyone see it," I told Eldritch. "Even Roy."

Roy gaped at me. "Say what?"

"If the cameras saw it once, I can make anyone see it every single time. I just need to . . ." I patted the console table like Torula had, ". . . fine-tune things a bit."

32

THE 3D CHAMBER

I STOOD AT THE TOP OF THE PLATFORM AND WATCHED ROY AS HE PUT the finishing touches on the 3D chamber. Measuring nine feet square, taking over two plots in Starr's nursery, like a giant aquarium with a translucent cylinder housing a tilted mirror at its core, it was where the hyperwill manifestation would appear when "hailed." Soon, if all went well, the dark interior would light up with the apparition and put an end to everyone's mystery. Everything about this so-called Thomas would be revealed.

"I never would've believed you knew any religious hymns if I didn't hear it myself, honey."

I looked behind me, not knowing who Starr was talking to.

"What?" Torula asked, seated next to her at the console.

"That tune you were humming. They sing it every day at the missions."

Torula shook her head, eyes still fixed on her computer. "No, that wasn't me. I don't . . . hum."

"*El Cantico del Alba*. There's no mistaking it, dear."

"Well, I've never heard of it. So don't accuse me of anything."

"It's not an accusation." Starr stood up. "Goodness, you make it sound as though knowing a church hymn was a crime." She walked past me with a roll of her eyes and headed down the plat-form, her shocking pink shoes clicking on the steps. Despite her initial reservations, Starr was back onboard—hoping to confirm that the hyperwill was still intact even though we'd seen it crumble to ashes.

I glanced at Torula, riveted to her monitor at the console table. "We're just waiting for Eldritch, right?"

"Uh-hmm," she sort of replied. A discreet movement of her hand told me she had switched the display on her monitor.

What's she up to? I walked over to my seat and feigned a yawn, my eyes straining to catch a glimpse of her computer screen, but I was too far away to read the fine print on her open tabs.

I reached for a tablet and pretended to work, ending up opening my inbox. A subject heading caught my eye: The Deltoton Riddle.

Well, what do you know. It seemed like such a long time ago when I'd answered the brainteaser about Einstein's equation, when I'd proposed that $E=mc^2$ hinted at a third element in the universe which people mistook for a god. Feeling as though I'd stumbled on an old toy I'd long forgotten, I clicked on the message.

I found your answer quite intriguing. Can you prove it?

Live by the trine,
Yonn Benerak
Co-Founder, Deltoton.org

I guessed they liked my answer. I glanced up, grinning, and was surprised to find that Torula had left her seat and gone to join Starr and Roy by the 3D chamber.

Her deserted computer monitor beckoned. I stood up and pretended to stretch a sore back then took a few casual steps and riffled through some items on the desk and dropped a pen "by accident." I picked it up and just so happened to sit on Torula's newly vacated seat. I glanced at her to see if she'd noticed. She was oblivious, engrossed in conversation.

I checked her search engine history and turned completely deaf to everything going on around me. I sat slack-jawed and stared at the recurring topic: Exobiology.

Torula had been surfing about the study of life outside the Earth.

"Wo-how!" I shot out of her seat and grabbed my coffee mug, turning around just in time to catch the trio look my way. I pointed at the empty mug in my hand. "Coffee. Hot."

I sauntered back to my seat and made one restrained fist pump, mouthing a silent "Yes!"

———

By the time Torula joined me back on the workstation, I'd concealed my silly grin behind a mask of detachment.

She looked at my bone-dry mug. "You downed that burning hot coffee really fast."

"Well, yeah, uhm . . ." I traced a zigzag across my eyes. "I'm falling asleep here."

She smiled, cupped my cheek, then leaned over to kiss me on the mouth.

That's just got to mean a yes! "Hmm . . ." I licked my lips, forcing myself to look all cool about it. "Keep that up, and I won't need another cup of coffee."

She dazzled me with her eyes. "Mom was finally able to bring Truth home yesterday."

"That's great." It was an odd segue, but it was still great news. "What's the diagnosis?"

"ITP." Torula pulled a chair over and took a seat. "An idiopathic thrombocytopenic purpura, compounded by hyperkalemia."

"English, Spore."

"A bleeding condition of unknown cause, plus an abnormally high concentration of potassium in the blood. Mom's turned the hyperjammer off and is giving Truth lots of puzzles and mental exorcisms to keep him on beta waves."

I didn't let on that I'd caught that slip of the tongue, but it told me enough of what she thought of Truth's illness.

She laid a hand on my thigh. "Thank you."

I raised my brow in a silent query.

"If you hadn't thought of that hyperjammer, I don't know what condition Truth would be in by now."

I squelched my smile, downplaying the sense of achievement that puffed up my chest. "You're welcome."

"I mean it." She squeezed my thigh. "I've been spending all my time just thinking of the best way to thank you."

In a split second, I thought of a thousand possibilities—all of them on a starship headed towards another sector of the galaxy. "I've got a few ideas."

A man's voice suddenly cut in. "Are we all set?" Eldritch asked like a sudden cold shower.

"Almost. Sorry to cut in, lovey doves." Roy bounded up the platform steps. "Come on, Jackson. You've been exiled to Schwarzwald."

"What do you mean?" Torula asked, frowning.

Roy opened his hand and dangled a necklace with a hyper-jammer for a pendant. "I'm not gonna hail any hyperwills until you and your kid brother have your jammers on. Hell, I called my ex about this 'spirit attachment' thing, and she says she's always scared of it happenin' to 'er dog 'cause they usually prey on weaker subjects—like pets or little kids."

"You called your ex?" I asked. Was Roy's enthusiasm for this project fueled by something personal?

"Don't worry. I didn't say anythin' about what we're up to here."

Torula moved her seat backwards and away from me, her eyes like daggers. "You knew about this?"

I gave a reluctant nod. In truth, it was my idea to send her to another building. But I figured she'd have an easier time accepting it if it was for the benefit of the experiment than because I was worried about her. "You won't miss a thing," I said. "You'll see everything clearly on the monitor we set up there."

"Let's go, honey." Starr waved her over from the base of the steps. "I'll keep you company."

Torula glared at her. "I thought you didn't even approve of using the hyperjammer?"

"I don't. Especially not where it can harm Thomas. But I don't want you speaking in tongues again, so come on." Starr bade Torula towards her with her brightly painted nails.

Eldritch checked his wristwatch, then tugged gruffly on the cuff of his sleeve. "Shall we get started?"

"This isn't fair," Torula said. "If it weren't for me, none of you would be seeing any of this." She snatched the hyperjammer from Roy and grumbled as she tromped away.

I stared, barely breathing, at the dark glass chamber as we waited for Torula and Starr to make their way to Schwarzwald. This was to be my parting gift for the Green Manor after a short two-month stint. Torula's closure. My final step. The completion of her spectral quest.

I rubbed a sweaty palm over my pant leg, feeling like an artist just before his first sculpture was to be unveiled.

A ghost for a work of art.

"You know what I'm thinkin'?" Roy said. "With all the stuff we've added to the system with a faulty VeggieVolt still runnin' in the background—and now it's talkin' for plants *and* ghosts—it should have a new name. Like *Verdamalgam* or somethin'."

I imagined Torula cringing and shook my head. "We're sticking to Verdabulary."

"We're all set, dearies." Starr's voice came over my headset, coming all the way from Schwarzwald's conference room.

"Okay, peeps," Roy said. "Buckle up and enjoy the ride."

With the faint hum of a machine coming to life, the tilted mirror at the core of the central cylinder began to spin. It built up speed and soon became a blurry vortex. When the mirror hit the optimum spin rate, Roy gave me a thumbs up. "You're on, Morrison."

I initiated the modified program, and several tense seconds went by with nothing but an unchanging vortex to look at. I laid my hand on the console table, mentally giving the Verdabulary the push it needed.

Come on, you can do it.

Slowly, almost imperceptibly, a breath of color spread over the hazy twister. Then a blotchy image appeared, difficult to discern. Eldritch stepped closer to the chamber, and I lay my fists on the console table, urging the system to correct itself and . . . extrapolate.

At last, in the middle of the 3D chamber stood the vivid image of Thomas.

Roy rose to his feet. "Holy Mother o' Moses."

A sense of achievement, like a warm shot of whiskey, coursed through me. The hyperwill looked exactly as I'd expected it would. Complexion: Rich and ruddy. Garments: The finest of his era. His stance: Like a nobleman captured in a period painting.

Even though I was the one who had sent Torula away, I wished she were right next to me, admiring my handiwork first-hand.

And then, Thomas spoke.

". . . (static) . . . help me . . . (static) . . . floor . . . ins . . . (static) . . . tell her . . . (static) . . . never forget."

The hair on my arm stood on end. This was no longer a borrowed voice from the Verdabulary; it was, presumably, the hyperwill's own record of what Thomas had sounded like—if that were truly its name. Though garbled and gritty, it still preserved enough of a pleasant quality.

The specter's lips made subtle movements, but never in synch with what we heard. The audio signal looped, each playback lasting for less than a minute, most of it meaningless hissing and garbage.

Starr's voice came through our headsets. "This is unbelievable."

Eldritch gazed at the apparition. "At last we have proof."

Roy and I exchanged fist bumps.

"He's so handsome," Starr said.

"O' course he is. Morrison grabbed images from Hollywood movies and made a composite. Recognize the actor? He's from that Mafia versus aliens movie."

"I just gave him longer hair," I said.

Eldritch turned towards us, his eyes boring right through me. "What did he say?"

I jabbed a thumb towards the large monitor at the base of the platform showing exactly what they were seeing in the conference room. The image of Thomas in his blue silken shirt and britches stood unmoving, staring blindly at nothing. "What we're looking at here is just Pepper's Ghost—a technique to create an optical illusion—and that's its 2D representation."

"A representation?" Eldritch asked.

I nodded. "When I recorded the stream of information of the last apparition, I ended up with mostly damaged data. So I gave the computer what it was missing. Sort of like planting a memory in there so it could extrapolate."

"Yeah, it's like how you catch a glimpse o' someone's eyes or mouth or somethin' and your brain fills in everythin' else so you recognize who it is."

"Exactly," I said, gesturing towards the console. "I gave the computer the ability to fill in the gaps based on what I remember of what I'd seen—or at least, what I think I'd seen. So now, when the hyperwill appears, even when the data's missing, damaged, or isn't in the visible spectrum, the software does a fix and translates it for us."

The hyperwill turned its head slightly to one side and hardly anything else, though it probably blinked.

"There really is an 'apparition,'" Roy said, "but it doesn't look like what we're seein'. In fact, Thomas isn't even in the chamber. It's still just a projection."

Eldritch strode towards us, hands curled into fists at his side. "Are you saying all this is a parlor trick?"

"No, it's a reconstruction." I raised a calming hand. "We really are receiving a hyperwill signal from somewhere out there. The computer harvests that data and selects just what we need to get a 2D image. Then, using a high-speed, high-brightness projector, we cast that 2D image onto the spinning mirror inside the chamber, turning the hyperwill into a virtual 3D image. So what we get is this optical illusion using reflection and light and transparent surfaces."

Thomas continued to stand motionless, like a man daydreaming while waiting for a subway train, oblivious to his surroundings. Using the computer tablet, I zoomed the camera in.

Eldritch stared at the composite. "Exactly how much of this is . . . extrapolated?"

I tapped on the tablet, and in the blink of an eye, Thomas' image blurred. All the color receded into grayscale, then the very structure of the man dissipated until its opacity faded away. All that was left was a smoky, floating film of what looked like a five-foot-tall, whitish blob with a few barely discernible highlights and shadows that might have served to define Thomas's image of himself.

"That's all there really is of him?" Starr asked through the earpiece.

"It's as good as it gets with today's radio wave videography," Roy said.

"And since we can't actually 'see' radio waves," I said, "we can only interpret the data as a black and white image."

Torula stayed silent, probably still pissed for having been exiled.

Eldritch walked closer to the chamber wall and gazed at the smoky specter. "All this equipment. All this so-called 'science.' And all you give me is a hoax?"

I'd shattered the man's hopes; I almost felt like apologizing. "I've reconstructed it as best as I could. Look, I even broke its nose."

"You did what?" Eldritch asked.

"Well, he had to, honey," Starr said. "It's the most obvious thing that ruins Thomas's face."

I brought back the full simulation and zoomed in on the facial detail as Eldritch moved closer to the huge monitor. Thomas's amber eyes nearly filled up the screen.

"That wound must be related to the circumstances of his death," our psychic "supervisor" said. "Spirits usually portray their mortal wound when they manifest. Many powerful hauntings are from those who were brutally wrenched from their lives."

"Why'd you take away the flowers?" Torula finally spoke. "He's usually holding flowers."

"Forget-me-nots, right?" I asked. "I had a hunch this guy didn't walk around with a bunch of them all the time. It just wasn't normal. But now I've got another hunch. Just listen." I raised the volume of the playback.

"... (static) ... help me ... (static) ... floor ... ins ... (static) ... tell her ... (static) ... never forget."

"Never forget," I said. "It wasn't a symbol. Your brain was extrapolating too. You heard meaningless words, and since the brain is programmed to make sense of things, your mind made an assumption and turned it into something relevant to you."

"And he never really said Florence, did he?" Torula asked. "It's just a jumble of apophenia and pareidolia. I was seeing substance in meaningless syllables."

"And is this EVP a reconstruction too?" Eldritch asked.

"EVP?" I asked.

"Electronic Voice Phenomenon. Ghost recordings," Roy

explained. "No, it's legit. The software's just digitizin' and cleanin' up the data, then boostin' it into the range we can hear."

"What about the name Thomas?" Eldritch asked. "You can't 'extrapolate' it from anything in there."

I muted the hyperwill's playback. "I have to admit, the human brain is a far more sophisticated instrument than anything we've got. So I wouldn't be surprised if there's more data in there that's decipherable to Torula but not to our equipment."

"That's because you've digitized his message," Torula said. "The body transmits data in analog. By cleaning up the data, you also took away most of it."

Roy clucked his tongue. "We did what we could, Jackson. This is the best we can get outta what's left of 'is signal. He's just dead as a dodo."

"No, he's not, Roy," Torula said. "He's just a mistletoe that's been tossed from its tree. He needs a host so he can eat."

A shuffling sound came through the speakers.

"Honey, what are you doing?" Starr sounded alarmed. "Tor, are you crazy? Bram, she took her jammer off and left!"

Damn it, Spore. I rushed out of the nursery.

As soon as I spotted Torula charging down the path, I called out to her. "You know I can't let you in here."

She didn't even slow down. "We need to talk to him."

"Jesus, you're reckless." I moved to block her advance. "Reckless and insane."

She stepped backwards, away from my grasp. "*I'm* reckless and insane? *I* am?" She glanced behind her, then lowered her voice. "Who's the one thinking of flying off to godforsaken outer space?"

"That's different."

"Of course, it is. Compared to leaving my home planet with absolutely no chance of rescue, what I'm about to do now is a walk in the park."

"But there is," I said.

"There's what?"

"A chance of rescue. There'll be three batches of three ships, to be launched every nine years."

"Oh." She seemed to relax, and I let out a breath. "So if we're battered by asteroids, we get rescued in nine years?"

"Or . . . sooner." Bollocks. "The assumption is, technology will advance so the next triads will travel faster."

She folded her arms and stared at me. "If I grow weak in there, how long do I have to wait before you pull me out?"

It was probably a rhetorical question, but I answered anyway. "Not one second."

"Thank you," she said and marched towards the nursery.

33

WHERE ARE YOU?

One step past the nursery door, and Torula's pace slowed; her breathing grew labored, her eyes pinched.

Starr came hustling in behind us. "Tor, stop being ridiculous. You can't be in here."

"Look," Torula said, showing us her arm. "It's my pilomotor reflex to Thomas's energy transmission."

Goose bumps. She thought it would be enough to distract me? "Come on. You have to get out before it gets worse."

"I just need a little time to test—"

"Thomas has sensed you," Eldritch called out from where he stood by the glass chamber. "He's moving."

Torula surged forward, and when we came in view of the hyperwill—I couldn't believe it. It bloody smiled at her. Not in any dark or sinister way. But like some wimpy kid who got noticed by the prom queen.

"Oh, mercy me," Starr whispered.

"I'll be damned," Roy said.

Torula smiled back at the image, as though she, too, were glad to see an old familiar face. "I knew he'd come. Follow a trail of ants, the flight of a bee, the growth of a plant's roots and branches. All living things go where there's food."

"So to catch a hyper, you need bait?" Roy glanced up, as though reading notes he'd scribbled on an invisible ream of papers in his head.

Torula took a step forward, but with that single move, she wobbled.

I reached out to steady her, and at the same time, the hyperwill held out its hand in her direction. Bloody hell. Was it responding to her in real time?

The pleasant, male, Verdabulary voice Thomas had chosen for itself echoed through the nursery. "Dewdrops urea thyme."

Torula grimaced and laid her fingers against her brow. "Where are you?"

The image moved its lips—but we heard nothing.

"Say it again. Where can I find you?" Torula said.

It mouthed another soundless phrase, looked to its side, then back at Torula.

Torula squinted and tilted her head. "I'm sorry. I don't understand."

"He said, 'Tell her,'" Starr whispered, then staggered back and gasped. "Do you see it?"

I glanced at the hyperwill but saw no reason for her to be alarmed.

Torula grabbed my hand. "I can't see," she said.

"I can't see what she's seeing either."

"No." Torula turned towards me, her eyes focused on nothing. "Bram, I can't see."

Jesus. What's happening?

Starr rushed forward and advised Torula to bend at the waist. "Let the blood go to your head, honey."

I clenched my fists, grasping at thin air. *Do I force her to walk out now or let her recover first?* "Roy, turn off the—"

"No," Torula said, head bowed, palms on her knees. "Just give me a minute."

I stared at the hyperwill. Though it made no sound, it seemed to be talking—engaged in conversation with whatever it was that nobody could see.

Torula straightened up, and I put my arm across her shoulders. "How do you feel?" I asked.

She retched and swayed, and the next thing I knew, she was limp in my arms.

Everything around me dimmed, and I grew deaf to what the others were saying; all I strained to hear was the sound of Torula's breathing as I lifted her into my arms. My eyes focused on the fastest way out as I rushed her away from there. Someone ran past me and opened the nursery door.

Out in the sunlight, my senses normalized, and I made my way underneath the shade of a tree a short distance from the greenhouse. I laid Torula down on the grass and cradled her head on my lap.

I stared at her chest, and only when I saw the normal up and down rhythm of her breathing did I relax my arms, but every other muscle in my body remained clenched.

Starr crouched on her shins and leaned over to slip Torula's hyperjammer back on. A cool breeze brought along the scent of fragrant bushes nearby and mixed with Starr's fruity perfume. It seemed enough to nudge Torula's eyes open.

"Tor, can you see me?" Starr asked, bowing low to peer into her friend's face.

Torula nodded. "Amply," she said, her eyes on Starr's cleavage.

"Oh, thank goodness." Starr clasped her hands together, and I managed a normal breath.

"You okay, Jackson?" Roy asked.

"I feel pins and needles up and down my arms, but other than that, I'm okay." She raised her head a bit.

"You're not okay," I said through gritted teeth. "So don't get up yet."

"Take my blood sample," Torula said, relaxing back down on my lap.

"I'll go get the kit," Roy said and jogged back to the greenhouse.

Eldritch's black wingtip shoes crushed blades of grass as he approached. "That was foolhardy of you, Dr. Jackson. I've already warned you about spirit attachment."

"What did you see, Starr?" Torula asked. "Was he trying to show me something?"

"It wasn't very clear. Just a woman's silhouette. A hazy figure in a long, flowing dress." Starr sat back on the grass, smoothening her skirt over her knees. "But what more did Thomas say to you? I didn't hear anything besides, 'Tell her.'"

"I couldn't hear a word at all," Torula said. "Your jewelry was making too much noise."

"What jewelry?" Starr brandished both her arms. She had a watch on one wrist and a chunky pink bracelet on the other. "These don't make a sound, honey."

Torula shook her head. "But I could've sworn . . ." She pushed aside a lock of hair that the wind had blown across her face.

"Perhaps it was another message," Eldritch said, his slicked-down hair impervious to the breeze. "The sounds you heard might hold a deeper meaning for the hyperwill. Remember, they speak in symbols."

"What symbol could there be in my jewelry?" Starr asked. "Could it be something Florence had worn?"

"Florence isn't real," I said. "Torula put two random syllables together in her head. That's all it is."

"What if—" Starr paused and suddenly clutched her pink bracelet. "A woman . . ." Her eyes grew wide. "Of course! Thomas wants us to find a woman named Pinkie."

"Pinkie?" I nearly choked saying it.

"I'm sure you recognize the painting Thomas looks like. The Blue Boy? And my jewelry was calling attention to itself with sounds. Maybe he's trying to tell us that he's looking for the spirit of—"

"The Pink Girl?" I asked, in disbelief. "What are you doing? Getting spiritual guidance from a bangle?"

"Let her speak, Mr. Morrison. She needs to explore all its possible meanings," Eldritch said.

"Explore? You mean guess, don't you? Make things up like it was a game?"

"Gordon Bennett! I've had enough of this." Eldritch glared at me. "Every day, you come here and watch us take wild swings, and all you do is scoff at our attempts. You're like a popcorn seller who doesn't care which team wins or loses. You're just happy to get in for free to be with Dr. Jackson."

I jabbed a finger at him. "Let me tell you who ought to be selling popcorn—"

"Oh, look!" Starr cried, louder than she needed to. "Roy's here!"

Roy ran over and handed her a small medical pouch. "Here you go."

"Thanks, honey. I used to be a candy striper. Now, I'm just a candy snacker." Starr's sparkling laugh did what it could to lighten the atmosphere.

Eldritch turned and stepped away to gaze at the greenhouse, clipping his hands behind his back—as if to say "conversation over." While Starr put a tourniquet on Torula's arm, Roy called the clinic. To distract—and calm—myself, I listened to his every word as he gave instructions for someone to come pick up the blood sample.

"All done," Starr said, tapping on the tube of freshly collected blood.

"Not bad," Torula said, flexing her arm. "I hardly felt it." She pushed herself up. "Believe it or not, I feel perfectly fine."

"Well, I don't believe it," I said.

"Okay, I concede," Torula said. "I'm probably borderline anemic, but then, I'm close to that time of the month, so maybe it's just PMS."

I frowned even as I helped her up. "Just have a seat for a while anyway. You scared the bollocks off of me." I ushered her towards a stone bench encircling the base of the tree.

"I'm sorry," she said as she sat down. "But I had to . . . test a hypothesis."

"That you're more stubborn than an ass?"

"That when presented with the nourishment he preferred, Thomas would feed. You can't deny the effect. When I came in, he energized. He responded to me."

"Spore, he looked life-like even to me. But I just put skin and clothes on a ball of smoke. It's a graphic simulation."

She tilted her head questioningly. "It got cold in there. Was that part of your simulation too?"

"It couldn't have been." Starr glanced at me. "Was it?"

"I didn't do anything," I said. "And I didn't feel anything."

"Yo, I felt it too," Roy said. "But I checked the data. There was no temperature drop. It's frickin' crazy."

Torula glanced around at all of us, her expression both teasing and tentative.

Oh no. I knew that look.

Roy squinted at her. "Y'know what's goin' on, dontcha?"

She quirked her mouth. "I looked through some of my mother's research papers on the nervous system and came up with a shaky hypothesis."

Roy plopped down beside her on the stone bench. "Shake it away, Jackson."

"Cutaneous thermosensation is mediated by unmyelinated fibers that respond to frequencies within the range of a hyperwill."

Roy snorted. "Y'know what. It's your turn to talk to me like I'm Goldilocks. With nothin' more than two syllables."

Starr laughed, and we all waited for Torula's "translation." Even Eldritch turned to face us, staying at a distance, this time clipping his hands in front of him.

Torula tempered a smile. "All right. Here goes. Most of our nerves have a white, fatty coating that helps them conduct signals faster. But . . ." She paused and looked at Roy. "I can't give you its name because I'll go beyond my limit."

"I'm givin' you a pass. Just this once."

"Myelin. And there are a bunch of nerves called C fibers which don't have this coat. And they're found in human skin."

"Go on." Roy nodded.

"C fibers respond to cold. Meaning when it gets cold, it tells the brain it's cold, so you feel it."

"So you're sayin' hyperwills are cold creatures? So our skin reacts—"

"No, they're not. You know how capsai—" She paused again, probably subtracting syllables from her thoughts. "A compound in hot peppers. Our brain tells us it's hot even though it's not."

"You mean like if I shove a thermometer into a habanero at room temperature, it'll read normal, but one bite and it burns my tongue off?"

"Right. That's because the nerve sensor for heat is the same one that picks up the signal from peppers. The brain reads both as hot even though the other is not."

"And the C fibers read for cold?" Roy asked.

"Yes, and unlike other nerve fibers that respond to hundreds or thousands of hertz, the naked C fibers respond to less than 10 hertz."

Sweet Jesus. Did she really just make sense of it?

"No shit." Roy swabbed a hand over his stubbled head. "Hyperwills resonate with those naked fibers in our skin?"

Eldritch unclipped his hands and moved a step closer.

"Precisely," Torula said. "Unmyelinated, C low-threshold mechanoreceptors are activated by a five to ten hertz stimulus. Which is why the Verdabulary didn't pick up a temperature drop. It's because the stimulus wasn't cold at all. It was an electromagnetic signal at a frequency that activated the same afferent nerve fibers that transduce, encode, and transmit information at innocuous, cold temperatures."

"Goddamn. I can't believe I understood that!" Roy cried.

"Bravo." Starr applauded with a laugh, and a bird overhead twittered.

"So," Roy said, "the cold isn't because of any endothermic reaction goin' on. No energy's gettin' generated that way?"

Torula shook her head. "Bioelectrogenesis. That's the power source, Roy. And my blood tests can give you a clue as to what the process does to my body's resources."

"Your blood tests, huh?" He looked like he was jotting it down in that notebook in his head. "Can dogs do the same bioelectroma-jingle thing?"

Torula crinkled her brow. "I . . . would assume?"

From down a stone path, a nurse came jogging towards us. "Hey there," he called out. "I'm here to collect the blood sample of Dr. Torula Jackson?"

"Here you go," Starr said. "Thanks for coming over."

"No problem," the nurse said as he took the vial from her. "Oh, and uh, you're supposed to change the frequency."

"Frequency of what, honey?"

"I dunno. The guy who called just told me to pick this up and tell you to change it."

"Yo, I'm the one who called," Roy said, raising his hand. "I didn't say anything about any frequency."

Alarms and a red flag suddenly went wild inside my head.

The nurse shrugged. "Just repeating what I was told. Gotta go."

"Wait," I said. "Can you remember the exact words of the caller?"

"Exact words?" The guy shrugged. "Uh, like . . .'We're right outside Greenhouse 3C. Could you please send someone over to pick up the blood sample of Dr. Torula Jackson.' And he said thanks."

"Right. That's what I said."

I nodded. That's exactly what I'd heard Roy say.

But the nurse continued, "Then you asked if I could—"

"Yo, that's all I said, then I hung up."

"Uh, you said thanks, and then you asked if I could hear you.

When I said yes, you said, 'Bro, you gotta tell them to adjust the frequency.' *Then* you hung up."

A cold sensation coursed through me, in one intense sweep from head to toe. *Could this—all this—still be part of one elaborate VN prank?* "Did it sound like him?" I asked, bobbing my head towards Roy. "The one who said to adjust the frequency."

The nurse shrugged again. "Why wouldn't it? It was the same call." He held up the vial of blood. "Okay if I go now?"

"Sure," Starr said. "Thanks, honey." She waited until the guy had jogged a good distance, then turned and addressed Torula and Eldritch. "Okay, can either of you explain why Thomas is impersonating Roy now?"

"Clearly," Eldritch said, "the spirit is desperate to get his message through, and he's telling us, through an engineer, what needs to be done."

"What are you sayin'? He possessed me? Possession my ass. It was obviously just a split pairs fault in the service network that caused some crosstalk. What the hell kinda ghost would use the word 'bro?'"

I swabbed my hand over my mouth. I knew exactly who would —but I needed proof before saying a thing, or else I'd be taking potshots just like they were.

Eldritch squinted at me. "You seem to have another explanation?"

"Me?" I raised my brows as innocently as I could and shook my head.

Eldritch glanced around at us. "It appears you have all forgotten that we may be dealing with two distinct spirits here. One is Thomas, and the other, the one whose manifestation was caught on video. For all you know, the Verdabulary could be opening up channels to even more."

I rubbed at an itch that I didn't have on my nose.

"We need to recalibrate." Eldritch turned towards Torula. "Meanwhile, you need to go to the cafeteria immediately. Eat to replenish your strength."

"I feel fine," Torula said.

"You mustn't allow yourself to stay weak after a psychic episode. You need to stay strong to fight it off in case it chooses to attach again. Dr. Benedict, please make sure she eats."

"I'll be more than glad to show her how it's done, honey."

Eldritch then addressed me and Roy. "I need you to figure out what this 'change in frequency' means, but more importantly, how you can ensure that communicating with hyperwills using the Verdabulary will not bring harm to humans, particularly Dr. Jackson. Let me know what you'll need."

Eldritch headed down one path as Starr tugged Torula to walk down another. Roy and I turned towards the greenhouse, but Roy stopped in his tracks, spun on his heel, and trotted after Eldritch. "Yo, wait a sec, Brighton. Gotta ask you somethin'."

That left me, alone and reluctant, heading back to deal with this creature they called Thomas—or to uncover if it was nothing but an elaborate practical joke from somebody I once knew.

34

VIRTUAL NEXUS

It did look like a grown-up version of the kid in *The Blue Boy* painting.

Standing atop the workstation of Greenhouse 3C, I stared at my 3D caricature of Thomas—the manufactured image of a memory that refused to die. I had tossed this together to prove a point.

Could Franco have orchestrated some audio version of this together? Just for kicks?

I sat down at the console and navigated to the Virtual Nexus website and searched for Franco's account. It asked for my password—which I quickly found in that unopened email I'd ignored all this time.

Franco had left me one message. The same one Sienna had told me about: Him telling me to "make my move" on that childhood friend of mine whom he thought sounded great, then ending it with, "Carpe diem, bro." But that was it.

I clicked on VN's support chat box and asked where I could find the files of phone calls. The person on the other end searched all records related to Franco's account and found nothing else addressed to me. Franco had never recorded any messages, whether audio or video. Not for me. Not for anyone.

As I slowly turned to gaze at the image in the chamber we had come to call Thomas, goose bumps made a chilling crawl from the nape of my neck. Was it . . . could it . . . It couldn't be. There was no way that hyperwill was Franco. There was nothing about it that pointed to him in any way.

I moved to the control panel and turned off all the hyperwill's computer-generated layers, leaving behind the blob of a cloud that everyone else considered alive. I walked down the platform and approached the chamber, stopping right in front of where I assumed its "face" would be.

It rose higher from where it hovered as if to look me in the eye. The mist roiled dreamily, its shapeless coils unfurling and twisting back.

"Franco," I whispered. "Is that you?" I leaned in close, my eyes scrutinizing the display for any indication of life. Any overt movement. A pattern or rhythm. Anything besides chaos.

As I watched, two smoky tendrils coiled close together, uneven whorls about to form eyes. I held my breath as they darkened— poised to coalesce. But the misty ribbons spiraled apart and disappeared into the haze.

I sighed in disappointment, ready to be convinced but finding nothing. If this wasn't a hoax, then—"What the bloody hell are you?" I took a few pondering steps backwards, then turned away and headed back to the console.

My gut told me this hyperwill wasn't the man I'd worked, laughed, and marveled about outer space with. But it also told me something else. There was some probability it was Franco's hyperwill that had made that call to me after he'd died.

Some.

I huffed out a breath, caught off guard by my own willingness to accept the unlikely. The memory of Sienna laughing her head off blinked on in my mind. But what the heck. My conclusion stood on flimsy evidence from my past few weeks here. Thin as ice, but it still gave it some ground to stand on.

Some.

I shoved away the annoying image of Sienna—and the echo of her laugh along with it—collapsed into my chair, and observed the misty cloud inside the chamber. It was a haze of meaningless data that at one time could have been a record of someone's life. No matter what these "hyperwills" were, I wasn't going to let myself fall into the same trap Torula had. I wasn't going to think of them as "people."

Neural data. That's what they were. Left intact outside a protective body after death. What in nature could possibly store that with any stability at all?

I reached over and shut down the Verdabulary. Still wrestling with my thoughts, I kept my eyes on the rotating mirror at the center of the transparent cylinder, mesmerized by the spiraling motion—slowly circling, spinning, and winding to a halt.

And then it hit me. "A vortex." The image of a whirlpool spun around in my mind, turning into a spiral galaxy, and cosmic hands closed in to encase it in a colossal Petri dish. "Yeah, that could work."

"Thanks for the vote o' confidence," came Roy's unexpected reply.

I jerked around. "My vote of confidence on what?"

Roy fidgeted, looking as guilty as a stooly who'd just blurted out the wrong thing. "Thought you heard me talkin' to Brighton."

"No, I didn't."

"So what did you say could work?" he asked.

"A vortex. What did you think I was talking about?"

Roy glanced at the darkened chamber and said nothing.

I eyed the chamber too. "I hope you're not planning anything stupid with that con artist."

"Yo, Brighton's legit, man. Don't turn him into a bad guy just 'cause he's got no control over 'is gift. He's like a faulty CB radio—where the band keeps changin' and all the citizens are dead."

I narrowed my eyes. "So you *are* planning something with him."

"No."

"Why don't I believe you?" I shook my head. "Just don't come running to me when it blows up in your face."

"That's sworn to and guaranteed," Roy said, raising his right hand as he gave his solemn oath. "Not lookin' at you for any help. At least, not until Sunday."

"What's with Sunday?"

Roy quirked a brow. "What's with a vortex?"

I almost dodged the question, but it was about time I stopped dealing them popcorn. "I think . . ." I cleared my throat. "I might have an equation that explains what happened to Thomas."

35

ORBS AREN'T MADE OF DUST

"I LOVE IT!" ROY CRIED AND GAVE A WHOOP. "THIS IS WHY THE world needs guys like us."

I winced as his voice walloped against me. My head had all the oversensitive symptoms of a hangover as I greeted the new morning with barely any sleep. "What are you talking about? I did all the work."

"Yeah, but I had to keep you awake to finish it. You think that was easy?"

I yawned and slouched in my seat, propping my legs on an adjacent chair.

"Man, I can't believe you figured this out. Sure can't wait till Sunday so you can help me figure somethin' else out."

"What's up on Sunday again?" I squinted up at him; the opaque setting of the Transhade overhead still left the workstation far too bright for me.

Roy eagerly nudged a tablet towards me. "JFGI. 'Orbs in barn' by Mac Maniac. It's a video of ghost animals."

"Orbs are nothing but the retroreflection of light off dust particles," I mumbled.

Roy planted my mug of hot coffee on the console table with a rousing thud. "Drink up n' wake up. You gotta see this. It proves that orbs aren't made o' dust."

I took a sip and settled back down in my seat.

"It's this video from someone here in California. He's got ghost animals in 'is barn. It happened where a horse gave birth. So I figure that place'd be reekin' o' hormone-propelled energy, right?"

I did my best to hold my droopy eyes open and watched the video.

"See that?" Roy pointed at the long rays of sunshine on the black and white footage of an empty barn. "The sun's low in the sky, so I guess sunrise or sunset—that makes the time just right. Then the orbs . . . there, see?" He pointed at a bright ball of light bobbing on the screen. "That one's actin' like a horse that's just stickin' its head outta its corral. Now, here, wait for it. Wait for it . . . There! I think that orb's a dog."

The movements didn't look like dirt floating in the air at all. "You're right. It's not dust."

"Bet your ass it's not."

"It's a spider. Crawling so close to the lens, it's turned into a moving dot."

"What the fuck, man! That's just one bug that crawled across the top. Glue your goddamn eyes on the bright orb floatin' all over the place. See how it's sniffin' exactly around that wet part on the ground, where the horse had the foals. Like it's tracin' the edges. That one really reminds me o' my Boner when he finds a wet spot he's interested in."

I grimaced. "Why can't you just call him your dog?"

"So whaddaya think? Worth checkin' out? Brighton says animals can definitely become hyperwills too. He said animals can have a memory o' their lives but without self-awareness. Meanin' they can appear as weird monster-like things, disembodied eyes, colored lights or orbs just like that. They remember how to behave but have no idea what they looked like."

Roy continued to watch the badly scratched video, devoid of

any sound and obviously captured in analog. "The orbs look like they got shadows, but I'm sure it's just gen loss and noise . . ."

He kept on babbling as my eyelids acquired a will of their own and refused to obey me. The last thing I remember hearing was, "C'mon. It's not that far . . ."

The next thing I knew, I woke up to the sound of Roy cussing at something. "What the hell kind o' question is that? Why else would a guy like him bother with shit like this?"

"But he doesn't believe in ghosts or souls. And nothing I say seems to change his mind."

My breath caught the second I recognized Torula's voice.

"Do I have to spell it out?" Roy said. "Y-O-U. That's why he's doin' it. And the reason you were tryin' to kick 'im out? H-I-M. You were takin' care of 'im, so he won't lose 'is job."

"That's exactly my point." She sighed. "I don't understand why he's risking it for something he doesn't believe in. And as he would say—it doesn't compute."

"Doesn't compute? Hell. He's a man. You're a woman. One plus the other equals only one thing. That's the simplest equation I know."

In the silence that followed, I forced myself not to move and kept my breathing steady. *Come on, Roy. Keep her talking.*

"Hello, there, honey bunches!" came a cheerful but oh-so-incredibly ill-timed greeting from its unmistakable source. "My, it's a gusty morning out there today."

I opened my eyes to the sight of Starr pushing stray blonde tendrils back into her bun. I glanced at Torula who had a tentative smile on her lips as she looked at me, as though she wasn't quite sure of her opinion of what she was seeing.

I smiled back awkwardly and brushed a hand through my hair for some attempt at grooming.

"Yo, Benedict! You'll never guess the surprise Morrison's got for us today."

"Ooh, I hope it's something sugar-free."

"Somethin' way sweeter. He's figured out that all hyperwills hitch a ride on sinusoidal waves at the start."

"At the start of what?" Starr asked.

"The afterlife."

"I beg your pardon?" Starr slowed down as she climbed the platform steps.

I stared at Torula as she approached and lowered herself into the seat next to mine. She was that close, but I still couldn't read what she was thinking. So much for ESP or EEC or whatever else Hans Berger might have missed. I reached for my coffee mug and took a quick sip, then grimaced at the room temperature brew.

"Have a look at this." Roy invaded the space between Torula and me and reached for the keyboard. "Morrison worked on it all night so we can show you what happens to your memories—after you die."

Starr clutched her pendant and moved closer and peered at what looked like a pillar of gray smoke on the monitor. "Isn't that the radio wave photo of the hyperwill?"

"Hell no. It's the simulation of a soul! Morrison thinks Thomas is livin' inside a soliton."

"I never said 'living,'" I said.

Both women turned to look at me; one seemed amazed, the other appalled.

"C'mon man. Show 'em. It's wicked cool."

I shook off what remained of my grogginess and took over the keyboard. "Our senses deal with data in analog, right? So I made a simulation of the body shooting out its neural information in analog." On the monitor, the cloud of gray began to undulate. "That's a simulation of how a real hyperwill probably behaves if it were visible at the point of death, with a sine wave initial condition." It was mathematically sound, and it was upsetting—what the equation said. That this could be the fate of all our stored memories after death.

The image eddied and swelled until a red-orange streak appeared, arcing through the cloud. "That reddish band demonstrates how solitons eventually come out of the single-mode initial condition. Tiny imperfections appear and grow exponentially."

At its core, feathery plumes of swirling coils appeared. "See those random shifts that decay into individual vortex rings? Those 'breakaways' are bound to increase over time. It's predicted by numerical studies of time evolution. But fluctuating temperatures can also trigger scattering."

With everyone's eyes locked on the screen, the simulation of the original wave slowly degenerated.

Roy clucked his tongue. "That's the problem with analog signalin'. With the invasion o' noise, the original wave breaks up into separate standin' waves. Eventually, the noise becomes dominant. And that leads to signal loss and distortion—makin' the original data impossible to recover."

"Impossible?" Starr asked.

"Impersonate?" Torula asked almost at the same time.

"You mean impossible, dear," Starr said.

I puzzled over the misused word. *Another slip of the tongue?* Torula kept blinking as though deep in thought, her eyes fixed on the monitor. *Was she trying to work out how this wave could be a person?*

"What does this all mean?" Starr asked.

"Simply put, it means, over time, a soul just falls apart."

Starr looked at me with troubled eyes. "It can't be . . . that simple."

I turned back to the screen and let the simulation show it. "The analog electromagnetic waves the human body generates are unstable and eventually break up into a stream of solitons— new objects that spontaneously appear in a system when conditions are right for it." I pointed at whorls in the simulation. "These smoke rings are closed loops of vortex filaments, which prove to be better, if not excellent, candidates for transmitting information. The dark cylindrical core is stationary with extraordinarily stable properties." Stable enough, I thought, to have held fragments of Franco's neural data intact long enough for us to keep receiving snippets of them after he'd gone. But *how* that transmitted data ended up in phone calls? That was just beyond me.

"That, m'dear ladies, is the physics o' the soul as calculated by m'friend, Bram Morrison." Roy slapped me on the shoulder. "It explains why ghostly apparitions, soon after a person's death, seem like they still got all their faculties together. But over time, they break up into smaller but more stable pieces. That's why all we got left o' Thomas . . ." he gestured towards the dark and gloomy chamber, ". . . is only what we got left o' Thomas."

Torula remained silent, still staring—mesmerized by the image on the monitor.

Starr fiddled with her crucifix pendant. "This also demonstrates that the soul emerges as a complete 'packet' of all our memories, right?"

"Sure does. It's just a matter o' catchin' it in time. But as far as poor ol' Thomas is concerned? Nearly everythin' that he was—if he was an artist, a playboy, a genius—that's all gone. All we got left o' him is the part that's still holdin' on to those damn blue flowers. Sure stinks like shit if that's what's gonna happen to my soul."

"Don't be silly," Starr said, frowning at the screen. "This is just the simulation of a guess."

"It's a mathematical fact." I nudged my sketchpad over. "Every radially symmetric standing wave solution is unstable if perturbations are equal to or greater than one plus four over n."

Starr let out an irate breath, refusing to even glance at my scribbled equations.

"But all hope isn't lost," I said. "If p is greater than one and less than one plus four over n, then they could remain stable. Which is probably why some hyperwill segments last longer than others."

"Which also means souls have the capacity to be virtually immortal." Roy sent Starr a reassuring wink. "Given idyllic conditions, that is, missy. I mean, missus."

"Idyllic, like paradise?" Starr asked.

Roy nodded, then glanced up at the glass roof. "Sad fact is—as long as they're lost out there, they're as mortal as the rest of us."

Torula stood up and gripped the edge of the console table as though to steady herself. "It's not impossible."

"What?" Starr asked.

"The original data. It's not gone for good, so it's not impossible to recover."

"Honey, did you just drift off and miss everything we've talked about?"

"Maybe that's how they reproduce," Torula said. "When a hyperwill breaks up into independent sections, it's like cacti. Stems with weak joints fall off and reproduce asexually."

I gaped at her, unable to believe she'd just taken my digital simulation and turned it into a sign of life.

"Hell, I don't see how this leads to producin' baby ghosts. But it does show an entity breakin' up into pieces. Pretty much everythin' that holds itself together for a long time relies on things bein' constant. And judgin' from your visions o' Thomas fallin' apart, I don't think he has that kinda stability."

"How much time do you think he has?" Torula was looking straight at me. "Regardless of whether it's alive or dead, how long can that data stay intact unprotected like that?"

"The answer could be anybody's guess," I said.

She shrugged and flashed a charming smile. "I'd like to hear yours."

It was enough to coax the answer out of me, and I tapped on the keyboard to show her. "Vortex solitons can hold tons of energy in the circular motion at the core. And under ideal conditions, that energy could last quite a long time." The display changed to footage of the planet Jupiter's turbulent surface. "The Great Red Spot. It's been raging for about 350 years."

"That's a storm," Starr said.

"That's a vortex," Roy said. "A very stable standin' wave."

"But that thing's huge, honey. Solar-system huge. And Thomas is just a tiny little smoky thing."

"We get invisible standin' waves in small recordin' booths all the time. They're the worst thing in studio acoustics. The smaller the studio, the worse it gets."

"So you think Thomas is living in a standing EM wave nearby?" Torula raised a halting hand at me before I could object. "I know. You didn't say 'living.'"

I shrugged to acknowledge the truce.

"He can't be that close," Roy said. "He used to have to wait 'til sunset to be able to broadcast this far."

"But in case you can locate its source," Starr said, "we can bring Eldritch there, right? So he can send him into the light."

"No," said Torula. "That will kill him."

"It will save him," Starr said. "Thomas needs a protected environment, and he won't have that here on Earth. That's the help he's asking for."

"And you're pinning your hopes on paradise?"

"Of course, I am." Starr's conviction shone like an angel's golden lamp for the benefit of lost souls. Torula, on the other hand, was like the PAWS police, fighting to save a stranded animal.

"My mother's been there and back. She entered that so-called light in her near-death experience. She didn't like what she saw."

"She saw hell?" Roy asked.

"She saw nothing."

Well, that makes sense. I reached for the keyboard again.

"It's what God allowed her to see," Starr said.

"It's probably what data looks like after it's been erased." I changed the computer display to a pristine white screen.

"Shit." Roy grunted. "Death by erasure. That sucks."

Torula pointed at the blank screen and looked at Starr. "Don't try to send Thomas into that light. Not until after we get some answers."

"I already have my answers. It's in the scriptures. In the church. In the hearts of everyone who believes. What about you? Where does your faith lie?" She gestured towards me. "In mathematics?"

Torula moved to block me from Starr's aim. "If you want to

attack my point of view, then address me. Don't drag someone else in just to—"

"As a matter of fact, yes." I got up and offered myself as an open target. "Life *is* a matter of calculation. Every living thing, from bacteria to terrorists, to the savior around your neck. They live or die by the same equation."

"What equation?" Starr asked.

"The one that answers which gives the greater advantage, my death or my life?"

Starr's eyes locked on me. "And where did you find this life-determining formula? In an atheist's bible?"

"Nature abounds with formulas. Equations rule the world."

"And pray tell." Starr thrust a fist into her hip. "Who do you think wrote those equations?"

"Touché," Roy said.

I wasn't about to fold on that. I huffed and lowered my gaze, feeling like a bull pawing at the ground before it charged. "It's interesting, this recurring story of a barrier to the afterlife. The pearly gates to heaven. The River Styx." I looked at Starr. "Do you know the slash we put across an equal sign to denote when values aren't equal?"

"What about it?"

"It's the symbol of a barrier. When the right factors are in place, things happen. When they're not, the barrier stays." In my mind, I held the picture of a phalanx of female football players in lingerie, and a bit of a smile escaped me as I glanced at Torula. "I think hyperwills form only when the right factors are in place. How long they last also depends on a lot of variables. But what the equation proves is . . ." I directed my gaze at Starr. "Not everyone who dies generates what you call a soul."

Something that sounded like a stifled scream escaped from Starr, and she glanced at Torula, then back at me. "The two of you are Adam and Eve all over again. Plucking forbidden fruit that will get us pushed farther out of Eden."

"What makes you think we're defying God?" Torula asked. "If

intelligent design got us this far, then that design has brought us to the threshold of finding out if hyperwills do manage to stay conscious and alive."

"If they do, then it is by God's will that they do so. It's not our business to interfere—"

"If there's a natural law we're about to break, then something's bound to block our way," I said, the image of black and red football players all crouched into defensive positions inside my head.

Starr centered her sights on me. "She never used to think like this." She jabbed a finger at me. "You've pushed her over the edge. The same way some godless lawyer pushed Darwin to question the omnipotence of God."

"Now wait a minute—"

Torula laid her hand on my arm to appease me. "Stop aiming at Bram because he's the only atheist within range. This is what *I* believe. Genesis and evolution agree on one thing: Life started out biologically immortal—and then we lost it. What if what we're going through now is God finally revealing the science on how to claim his promise of eternal life?"

Starr took a step back and, for a moment, teetered on her high heels. Then she raised her chin, her eyes glinting with resolve. "God has given us His promise of salvation, and it's in His hands how we get to earn our immortal life. I can't let you step in like this just because you think God isn't doing His job right." She turned and left in a harried gait. "I'm going to tell Eldritch to put an end to this."

"Don't do it, Starr." Torula followed her, dashing down the stairs. "You're throwing away our only chance to study this."

36

FOR HUMANKIND'S SAKE

(TORULA)

THE BLUSTER OF THE MORNING ASSAULTED ME AND STARR AS SOON AS we exited the nursery. Starr whipped around, sending her skirt in a whirl as she confronted me. "Why are you so blind to the consequences, Tor? We should be helping Thomas move on, not trap him and dissect him like some specimen to appease your curiosity."

I ignored the wind that tousled my hair. "You know this has gotten far beyond curiosity about a ghost. Or the health of my brother. Or creating computer programs to talk with the dead. It's a study for humankind's sake now. It's so people would understand death and not have to fear it anymore."

"Then leave me out of it. There's a reason people fear death. It's because it comes with judgment. Eternal life is meant to be a gift, not a science experiment." She strode away, fists clenched by her side.

"Do you really want to leave the study of the soul in the hands of agnostics and atheists?" I called out. "Didn't God give the key to genetics to an Augustinian monk? That should tell you something." *And Mendel was a botanist too, like you and me.*

Starr paused in the middle of the stone path.

"I need an ally, Starr. Bram and Roy think a hyperwill is software in need of a gadget. But you believe Thomas is alive. You believe that of every soul."

Starr turned and thrust one of those fists into her hip. "You want to know what I believe? I don't think it's logic guiding your actions anymore."

"What are you talking about?"

"Remember what Eldritch said? Happy ghosts feed on joy. Angry ghosts feed on fear. And Thomas probably feeds on . . . lust? Love?"

I scoffed at the implication, even as a knot tightened inside my chest. "So this is your new angle of attack? That Bram's feelings for me aren't real?"

"Think about it, Tor. Why did it take him so long to open up about why he came here? Or even just to tell you about Svalbard? Maybe he really just came for a visit to say goodbye but then slowly reconsidered."

I opened my mouth, but my mind ended up flashing back to all the times Bram had stuttered and stammered whenever I'd asked why he had come.

Wind chimes jangled in an angry chorus in the trees as Starr continued her cruel assessment. "I think even you've been influenced somehow. You used to talk of Bram as just a friend. The friend who never cried for you. But he's obviously more than that now, isn't he? Thomas has probably been stimulating and feeding on those strong feelings you now have for each other."

I snapped out of my defensive stupor just in time to keep Starr from having the last word. "You're accusing me of being blinded? What about you? Can't you see I'm trying to be a Good Samaritan? I think Thomas has been left for dead on the roadside, and he's asking for our help. I can't believe the first thing you want to do is send him faster to his grave."

"But he's already *in* the grave!"

"Not in his mind, he isn't. He hasn't accepted it. Take a long, hard look. Death is something even the dead would want to escape." I marched forward and past her, trying to block out her words that now spun in my head.

The wind made it hard to breathe. Hard to think. What I felt, what I knew, what I wanted. What Bram wanted. I couldn't tell what was true anymore. Things changed when this hyperwill appeared. I'd been perfectly content, and now I was considering leaving it all for someone who had once left me? Maybe it was best to bring things back the way they were and put my heart away where Bram couldn't reach it. Or hurt it.

Far is far. What difference did it make? *I have to let him go.*

37

JUST TAKING A BREAK

SOMETIME AFTER TORULA WENT CHASING AFTER STARR, ELDRITCH showed up in the greenhouse. He gave no greeting. Asked us nothing. Barely even looked our way.

Roy and I simply sat down and watched him from the central platform as he paced in front of the glass chamber, staring at our 3D composite of a ghost.

As we waited, Roy slid his chair next to mine, leaned over, and asked, "So what about Sunday? I got somethin' to show you in my garage."

I shrugged. "Yeah, sure." I could do with some beer as he showed off his souped-up creations. After all, the only thing I was waiting for was an answer from Torula—and all I had to cling to for hope was her search engine history.

Eldritch called out from beside the chamber. "You said the hyperwill transmission is still coming from somewhere out there?"

"Yup," Roy said.

"Can you pinpoint where?"

Roy scratched his shaved head. "Not exactly. But based on Morrison's simulation, he's gotta be in some secluded area. Some enclosed and empty place. Away from lotsa noise. With a cool and steady temperature."

"That message to 'adjust the frequency,'" Eldritch said. "Would making such an adjustment help us communicate better? Can it help you locate Thomas so that—"

The sound of boots angrily crunching on gravel had us turning our heads to check who'd arrived. Dressed in a black tee, camo pants, and army boots, Torula looked like someone about to start a private assault instead of a conversation. The hyperjammer dangled from her neck like a rifle bullet with a sliver of blue light near its base.

I got up and switched off the Verdabulary before it could do her any harm. She stopped about an arm's length from Eldritch and stood there, panting, with a frown on her face.

"Is everything all right?" I asked.

"Of course, everything's all right." She gripped the hyper-jammer and aimed her piercing gaze at me. "I'm wearing this thing around my neck, aren't I? My trusty defense against that mindless transmission of inanimate data that has no influence over me. Or you. So everything's perfectly all right, right?"

My head throbbed just trying to process her answer. "Uh . . . right."

"Did you manage to convince Dr. Benedict to reconsider?" Eldritch asked.

"Reconsider what?" Roy asked.

Torula shook her head. "If anything, she convinced me. I came here to ask to be excused too."

"What?" I asked. Excused from what?

"Your disagreement with your friend has upset you," Eldritch said. "I can sense the aura of gloom around you."

"What's going on, Spore?"

"It appears both she and Dr. Benedict wish to step away from the project for a while," Eldritch said.

Step away? "Do you mean . . . leave?" I stood frozen, gawking.

Roy clucked his tongue. "Yo, I know we can't keep Benedict in the party if she doesn't wanna dance anymore. But Jackson, it's *your* party."

"No. It's her nursery, Roy," Torula said.

"But it's not 'er ghost. If anyone can claim ownership, it oughta be you guys. It's only around 'cause o' both of you."

"Give this more thought, Dr. Jackson," Eldritch said. "And some time."

"I just need to process things." She glanced at the darkened glass chamber. "Away from that. Away from all this." Then she looked at me. "Away from the smell of you."

Roy leaned towards me and sniffed.

"What did Starr say to you?" I asked. "Something about me being a demon to be exorcised from your life?"

"She thinks . . . this has all gotten out of control. Like, *we're* not in control."

Eldritch stepped closer towards her. "Please tell Dr. Benedict she has my word. We will not entrap any spirits and will only work towards finding a reliable means of communication with the other side. If she agrees to stay on the project on those conditions, I hope you will too."

Without another word, Torula spun around and left as irately as she'd arrived.

"Did she just quit?" If that was the case, I was leaving too.

"She's just taking a break," Eldritch said.

"From something I got into—only because of her?"

"Like I said, she's just taking a break. She knows the importance of what we're doing, as I hope you do too, Mr. Morrison. We need to find Thomas."

I let out a weary sigh, wondering if my stay here in California had just gone from pointless to even more pointless. "Look, even if we could locate it, all we'll find is a faded tangle of broken threads." I gestured at the 3D chamber. "You asked me to play the game, and this is how I played it. I've made the most of the cards we've been dealt."

"Then obviously we're not seeing all the cards," Eldritch said.

"We only get to see what you've programmed for us to see. But what if there's more to him than—"

"Holy shit, that's it!" Roy cried, looking at me wide-eyed as he pointed at the chamber. "We aren't seein' the whole goddamned deck! Sweet bejeezus. I think I know what we gotta do!"

I wanted so badly to back away and fade into the background. Just disappear without having to say goodbye. "Listen, if Torula's going to quit—"

"She's just taking a break!" they both cried.

I swabbed a hand over my mouth, wondering if goodbye was even necessary.

Roy grew somber and approached me. "Hey, man. Don't just do this for your girl. Do this for everyone alive. You gotta see this for the big thing that it is. It's us, puttin' an end to death."

"I get it. You're trying to stop the dead from dying."

"No, man. It's us! It's us not ever losin' anyone anymore. It's bein' able to keep everyone special to us from leavin'. It's just like you said. You don't wanna think o' your parents suffferin' after death. Nobody wants to think that of anyone they lost, or anyone they're about to lose. You showed it in your simulation. There's a chance for us to save 'em."

That's what I tried to do. With remembrances kept inside a robot. "It's just storing data so you can hold on to something. It's not saving lives. It's saving memories—to be relived like old home movies. Recordings. Playbacks of the past that have no hope of a future."

"Not if they remain alive, like Jackson says. We still aren't sure they aren't."

"The living dead." I shook my head. "It just makes no sense, Roy."

"You're right, Mr. Morrison," Eldritch said, moving closer towards the platform. "Death has never made sense. Not even to the dead. They walk around confused about their own existence. They remember what they've lost, and they know they have no future here. They're living memories paralyzed in time. If you can see and hear them the way I do, you would want to help them too." Eldritch stared at me, unmoving, and I imagined him trying to use some pseudo-mind trick on me. "In your few remaining days with the Manor, will you help us? Try to come up with a way to find Thomas?"

My forehead twitched involuntarily as I considered the words of a man who had grown up believing that the only people who relied on him were dead. I glanced at Roy and saw a kid looking at me trustingly, suspended high up on the other end of a seesaw I was ready to abandon.

In my few remaining days . . . As though stung by a nasty bug of compassion, I gave a barely perceptible nod. It was enough assurance for Eldritch who broke his gaze and walked away. The mind trick had worked.

I glanced sideways at Roy. "So I'm guessing you have a plan?"

"Damn straight. First is to stop thinkin' o' Thomas as human. I mean, he's not in a body anymore. He's an electromagnetic wave— not constrained to seein' light that's visible to our eyes or hearin' only sounds human ears can pick up. He's surfin' across everythin' with no need for a medium to go anywhere." He paused. "Ehrm . . . by medium, I don't mean the deep-breathin', alpha-theta borderin' kind."

"We're on the same page on that one, mate. So what's step number two?"

"That crosstalk glitch gave me an idea. I got a feelin' Thomas has got more things to tell us if we listen every possible way. So far, we've just been listenin' to a single frequency band. So, I'm thinkin'—what if a hyperwill's part ultrasound, part infrared, part ELF, part gamma, part this n' that." He tapped on his temple. "Need some time to rummage through the engineerin' scrap yard up 'ere on how to go about it."

I blew out my cheeks, feeling incredibly tired. "Sounds like a plan."

"Yeah, well, in the meantime, I need you to do the most important thing to make all o' this worth anythin' for you."

"What's that?"

"Get your girlfriend back in the game."

38

THIS IS IT

I COULD HAVE CALLED TO ASK IF SHE WAS READY TO TALK. OR IF SHE'D like to have dinner. Instead, I'd driven to Torula's apartment on a gamble she'd be home.

Holding a finger over the doorbell, I took a deep breath, then rang it.

This is it.

I shoved my hands into my pockets and glanced down the empty corridor. With its high, arched ceiling, modern art, and contemporary lighting, the hallway should've felt hospitable, but it only grew increasingly stifling as I waited.

The door opened, and she stepped out in torn jeans and a loose sweatshirt—worn-out masculine pieces that, no matter what, always looked fresh and feminine on her. "You should've called first."

"I did. From the lobby." I grinned, trying not to look nervous. "May I come in?"

She folded her arms and looked down the same corridor that was now gloomier and stuffier than a few seconds ago. "It would probably feel this awkward all evening."

"Why?" I failed to breathe in the long pause that followed.

"When you first came back here, you said you were at a crossroads."

"Yeah."

"Did you mean, at the time, you were still deciding between staying or going? Or did you mean, you still hadn't decided if you'd ask me along or not?"

"What?"

She gazed at me with eyes that held a thousand questions. "When did you know for sure that you wanted me to come along? Before or after your exposure to the hyperwill?"

"The second I was given the offer."

"To work on the hyperwill?"

"To go on the mission! What's going on, Spore?"

"Why didn't you ask me sooner?" she asked with a frown. "Is it because you weren't sure when you first got here?"

"Of course not." I tried to sound sure of myself but couldn't stop myself from swallowing.

She stared at my Adam's apple.

Bugger. "Look, it was a huge dilemma. I don't want to leave without you, but it also means redefining your life. And then, I found out about your claustrophobia—"

"Which I said is no major concern. I can start treatment anytime if I want to." Her shoulders rose and fell as she sighed. "I need to know—Did your feelings change *after* you saw Thomas?"

"What the hell?" My mind erupted with objections charging through like an angry mob. "Is that what Starr planted in your head? That that . . .'thing' possessed me and is controlling my mind? No bloody way!"

"Eldritch said hyperwills manifest depending on what they feed on. They can feed on fear. Or joy. Or . . . feelings, like . . . what it's making us feel."

"*Making* us feel?" I cracked my neck. Cracked my knuckles. Anything to dispel the need to punch a goddamned ghost in the face. "Damn it. Whatever that psychic has to say has got nothing to do with us. I know what I've always felt. Always. And that's never changed."

"All our lives, you've stayed at a distance. Then a hyperwill comes along and suddenly you're—"

"Whoa." I raised my hands to stop her. "Did you just say I've stayed at a distance? You're the one who keeps—"

"You left."

My mind stalled at her words that were like two solid rocks lobbed at my chest. "I was. . . " Helpless. Grieving. ". . . fourteen. I had no choice." My legal guardians, who'd been good friends of my parents, had come to take me to live with them. Torula knew that.

"You didn't even cry," she said.

I squinted, disoriented. Did that comment even belong in this thread? "What?"

"When you came to say goodbye, you didn't shed a tear."

"Because I never said goodbye."

"Well, you came by to say . . . something. And you didn't even grow misty."

My mouth hung open for a while—because I had no bloody idea what the hell needed to be said. "I don't . . . understand . . . the problem."

"When your parents died, you cried a river of tears. An ocean of tears."

"They *died*. You can't possibly be comparing—"

"And what about Franco? You cried for him too. And he was just a friend, like me."

"He died too! What the—"

"*I* cried. For you! And I couldn't stop. But you just stood there. With that heartbreaking, lopsided grin of yours like . . . like . . . you didn't care."

Like I didn't care? Suddenly, it clicked into place. And I remembered her twelve-year-old version sobbing as I stood at the curb those many years ago, her mother beside her, my guardians behind me, waiting to take me to a far-off state on the east coast.

"Don't you remember?" I asked. "I was on a video call with you that very night."

Torula took a deep, shuddering breath. "It's not the same. It's never been the same."

"Yeah, it's because . . . I've been working to make things better. To make *me* better." As a kid, I'd felt both lucky and awkward talking with this smart, well-bred, and mysterious seatmate with stunning eyes. But just as things got comfortable, I became an orphan who had no choice but to get hauled off half a country away.

She flicked aside her bangs. "You could've come back when you were eighteen. Or flown over for a visit. Or you could've invited me to come visit you anytime. Why did you have to wait for . . . all of this to happen? Now I can't tell what made you ask. If it's the hyperwill, you turning thirty, or just the reluctance to live the rest of your life on a spaceship full of strangers."

"The hyperwill is nothing. And turning thirty? What?"

"What if Pangaea hadn't come along? What would've happened? Would you have left the country for another job? Left me?"

I struggled to find an explanation—or tell her about plans I'd made that involved her—but I had neither. I'd been biding time, maybe waiting for those astronaut credentials to come boost me into her league.

She held the doorknob, probably struggling for a way to let me down easy. I sucked in my breath, already feeling the sting of the rejection.

"You asked me why I didn't ask you sooner—to go where I wanted to go. But I did."

"When?" she asked.

"All these years. Since we were kids, I've been asking."

"Those weren't serious."

"Says who? Do you even remember the times I asked?"

She lifted one shoulder in a coy shrug. "Once, you said you wanted to be king of the stars."

"And I asked you to be my queen."

She smiled and lowered her gaze to the floor. "I remember."

The seconds ticked by in silence at her doorway, her hand on the knob, the door still closed. I reached out and took her hand. "All my life, I've been chasing two dreams. One involved outer space, the other involved you. For years, I thought both were out of my reach. And now, suddenly . . ."

She looked up at me, tears sparkling in her eyes. "Oh, Bram. The Earth is so magnificent. All the people, all the cultures, all its possibilities. How could you think of leaving it all behind?"

"Anyone can offer you a future among those people and places. But no one else can set sail across an ocean full of stars and give you a chance to discover life forms the rest of mankind would never see." I pulled her close. "It'll be you and me, Spore. *We*."

I smiled. She squirmed. And in that moment, I understood—she would say yes only because of me. She would never fathom the call of what was waiting out there.

If she went with half a heart and things went wrong . . . *Sweet Jesus*. I wouldn't want to look in her eyes and see sadness there. Not in outer space, with no chance of bringing her back to where her happiness lay.

But can I go without her? The thought suddenly seemed foolish.

With a deep breath, I said what I didn't realize I was more than prepared to say. "If I had to choose just one dream, it would be you."

"I . . . what?"

"If you want to stay on Earth, then this is where I belong too."

She gasped and tried to pull away. "I can't have that on my conscience."

"It shouldn't. It's my choice."

"But it's always been your dream. To be king of the stars." Her tears fell. "I can't be the one to take that away."

"I can give up the stars." I wiped her cheeks. "As long as I still have my queen."

"Gosh." She laughed softly. "You're still as cheesy as ever."

"And you're still pushing me away. But this time, I'm not going anywhere." I folded my arms and stood my ground like a man who couldn't be moved.

She bit her lower lip as I held her gaze. "You could sail an ocean of stars . . . and you chose me." She said it in such a low voice, I almost didn't catch her words. Then, she slowly turned the doorknob. "So do you want to come in?"

39

THE DELTOTON RIDDLE

TORULA SAID YES. EVEN AFTER SHE'D SAID IT THRICE, I STILL COULDN'T believe it. *She would leave Earth to be with me.* The moment almost made me believe there was a god.

It had been hours since she'd given her answer, but I still lay awake, watching her sleep. There was no way I could force my eyes to close, so I slipped my pants on and left the room. Mere acquaintances might have expected army-inspired interiors, but the cozy pastel atmosphere flecked with greenery was exactly how I had pictured her place to be.

I made some coffee, grabbed pen and paper, then settled onto a kitchen stool to do some calculations. Figuring out the details of what Roy and I were working on for Eldritch was the only thing I could think of to bring back the calm.

A floorboard creaked, and the sight of her in black panties and a white tank top obliterated all equations from my mind.

"Coffee, at two in the morning?" She slid into the stool across from me at the kitchen nook.

"Helped myself. I hope you don't mind."

She glanced at my equations. "Tell me about 'Coffee, slash. Slow cream, slash. Fast sugar.'"

That was nowhere on my piece of paper. "Where did you hear that?"

"Your sketch pad fell off the table at the workstation. It opened to that page."

"You looked at my notes?"

She arched a brow. "You looked at my search engine history."

"I . . ." My solar plexus tightened defensively. ". . . have no excuse."

She smiled and bit her lower lip. "Is it related to Project Hyperwill? Those notes."

"No. But . . . it sort of helped me figure it out."

"Really? How?"

I stiffened in my seat, convinced she'd find it petty—my exercise of solving the Deltoton riddle. "It's nothing." There was a huge chance she'd only find it ridiculous.

"No matter how ridiculous it is, I promise not to laugh."

Jesus, how does she do that? "You want to talk about that—at this hour?"

"At least I'd yawn rather than laugh." She propped her chin up on her fist.

"Good point." If we were spending the rest of our lives together, I ought to share my way of dealing with the world. "Ever hear of Deltoton?"

Her gaze flitted to the side as she pursed her lips. "Starr once told me a priest had warned their congregation against joining it. Are you part of it?"

I nodded and chuckled. "It's just a dot org with its own ideology." I poised both hands in front of me, about to steeple my fingers to form a triangle, but changed my mind and clasped my hands instead. "Its paradigm is founded on ternions."

"Sets of threes?"

"Yeah. In relation to the physical, the logical, the visceral. Body, mind, emotion. Action, vision, passion. Permutations of the same. Say, for instance . . . for anything to succeed, you need to work hard at it, think things through, and put your heart into it. Sweat, strategy, and spirit."

"Got it."

"Deltoton posed a puzzle and, I think, I gave a good answer." A twinge of embarrassment threatened to stop me from sharing anything more.

"What was the puzzle?" She seemed honestly interested.

"Something like, 'What's masquerading as God in the equation $E=mc^2$?' In other words, what's the third element that makes our world work?"

She pursed her lips. "Lithium?"

"Matter. Energy. And a third one."

"There's a third one?"

"That was the question." I scratched my temple in a moment of self-doubt. "At least, I think it was."

She laughed a soft, amiable laugh. It put me more at ease. "Anyway, one day, I watched some creamer drop into my coffee and thought, 'So that's how it works.' That's how the world keeps the laws in place."

Torula glanced at the coffee cup next to me and tilted her head. "You saw a drop of creamer in your coffee and you understood . . . God?"

"Whoa, back up a bit. I'm just saying there's stuff out there that fills in some blanks. But to find them, first we have to see the blanks."

"Blanks." She echoed the word as though it's all she could see as she stared at my coffee.

I shook the cup and the liquid inside quivered. "Everything in the world jitters and vibrates, right? From virtual particles to spinning galaxies—everything is in motion. So there must be something in the universe that creates *order*—something that keeps those vibrations coherent and maintains the harmonic waveforms."

Torula crossed her arms on the table, blocking my view of her breasts beneath her shirt. The motion helped force my thoughts to stay on track.

"Matter, energy, and the organization of living systems. Was that your answer?" she asked.

"No. I'm talking about what imposes laws—even before life makes an appearance. From the moment of the Big Bang." I pushed the cup towards her. "Imagine the creamer I put in here to be our universe. A few drops of meaningless energy that exploded into . . . something that surrounded every particle of it and told it how to spread in all directions until it's one uniform thing." I pulled the cup back towards me and pointed inside it. "The coffee in the cup. That's the 'blank.' That's the obvious thing all around us that we don't see. Do you get it?"

"I'm afraid not. I'm sorry." She straightened up and ran her fingers through her bed hair, mesmerizing me with her shapeliness and silken skin. "Maybe you could try a different analogy? Coffee doesn't work for me."

I paused and took in the moment. There she was, gorgeous at two in the morning, willing to talk about math, science, and theories, in her underwear, over a cup of hot coffee. Just some of the reasons why I couldn't imagine leaving her. I glanced at the couch a few paces away.

"Well?" she asked.

"Well, what?"

"Is there anything besides coffee on your mind?' She folded her arms again, obscuring part of the temptation.

"Ohhh, yeah." I sighed and pushed my cup aside, along with some steamier thoughts. "Picture a raving lunatic getting tackled by female football players in lingerie and high heels."

Torula raised a brow.

"It was a dream I had."

"Too much porn, I gather?"

"I think my subconscious was puzzling over the things I wasn't consciously bothering to puzzle about. And I realized . . . the raving lunatic could be the tiniest speck of matter there is."

"Quarks?" she asked. "String?"

"Whichever one, it's in constant flux. Always vibrating. The tinier the slice of matter of this universe that you observe, the wilder and more turbulent it gets. Why do you suppose that is?"

"Because the quantum world is weird?" She put on a wry face.

"Because the most fundamental quantum particle is a raving lunatic. A mad infinity of possibilities. The more you detach each morsel of matter from whatever it is that constrains it, the wilder it gets—the freer it moves. And as bodies get bigger, the more restrained—the more orderly they become."

"Isn't that because of the natural forces? Gravitation, electro-magnetism—"

"Yes, but even those fundamental forces need to be controlled with precision." I grabbed my pen and drew an equal sign, then a slash down its middle. "That's where the football players come in. They block and tackle actions that violate the laws."

She stared at the unequal sign I'd drawn. "So these football players . . . they're like walls of energy preventing reactions. Like a barrier of energy that needs to be surmounted before a chemical reaction can take place."

Anticipation bubbled inside of me. Her example would take her exactly where I wanted her to go. "What's the barrier made of?"

She shrugged, as though the answer were so obvious. "Activation energy."

"No, that's the amount of energy you need to get over the barrier. So what makes up the barrier?"

"Some other kind of energy."

"So there's no proper name for it? In your entire Torulan vocabulary?"

She paused in thought. "Look up the Arrhenius equation. That's a definition you'd understand."

I drew an equal sign and encircled it. "It's in an *equation*. Exactly." She had arrived at my intended destination. "We can't see the football players, only their effects. The equations prove they exist."

"To do what?"

"To pile up all around us. In layers of dimensions around us to impose the laws. That's why by the time you get to observe an atom, it looks like an orderly system—with electrons following strictly quantized orbits in a clouded space that's never devoid of energy."

She was quiet for a moment, then her lips pursed as her brow furrowed. "That phalanx of football players." She laid her hands flat on the table then leaned forward, her breasts calling attention to themselves. "Why are they in stilettos?"

I shrugged, my inadvertent glance at her cleavage worsening the defensiveness I felt. "It's . . . just something . . . subconscious. Nothing meaningful."

Her eyes narrowed into slits. "You think it's weak."

"What?" I tried to look surprised, and hopefully, guiltless.

"This . . . mysterious element. You think it's a very weak force, which is why you need an entire football field of *women* to constrain one tiny lunatic of a particle."

I raised my hands in mock surrender. "Hey, I also said it's the force people mistake for God. So it has almighty strength in numbers, okay?"

She nodded, but rather slowly. "And you think those football players—that element—is what?"

"Rembrance." I licked my lips like a connoisseur testing the texture of the word against his tongue.

"Rembrance? I've never heard of it before."

"That's because I made it up."

Her brows raised a tiny fraction. "What does it mean?"

"It's sort of rooted in 'remembrance,' but more of the ability to *make* something indelible. It records accidental strokes of luck that work, so successes get to repeat themselves, and it takes note of failures so it can steer away from them. By recognizing and classifying patterns, it creates harmony over the dissonance."

"I see." Her eyes sparkled as though reflecting the facets of a gem. "Remembered dissonance or resonance. I like the port-manteau."

I had no idea what that word meant, so I just let my lips curl into a smile.

"So . . . what is it, exactly?" she asked.

"A form of energy that gives the universe the capacity to create order out of chaos."

"How?"

"It recruits data and puts them in uniform."

"What?" Her lips parted with a barely there smile, but she kept her promise of not laughing.

"Data could just be running around in waves leading a mean-ingless existence—naked and raw—until it's recruited by an observer, and it puts on a football uniform, turning it either red or black. Then, it joins the game and jumps into formation and becomes 'in-formation.' Do you get it?"

Now, she laughed. "I love your mind."

Flattered and somewhat flustered, I flexed my bicep. "I was hoping you'd go for my body, but—"

She gave my arm a playful slap. "You went through all that just to make sense of hyperwills, didn't you? You had to put some mechanism in place to make it plausible for the information that makes up consciousness to hold up over time."

"Maybe. But it also shatters Starr's ideal of eternal souls. Rembrance holds the equations that determine how long it takes for something to decay, dissolve, or disintegrate in this thermody-namic world. And entropy is a value that keeps rising, making it more and more difficult for all those football players to hold up against the outcome."

Her gaze drifted off to the side. "Any chance you can make those almighty football players keep Thomas in the game a little longer?"

So we're back to talking about that again? I leaned away and sighed. "It's never going to end, is it? Your fascination for this . . . thing."

"It's a mixture of goodwill and self-interest, really. That 'thing' could be us someday."

"I doubt it. I have no desire to stick around as stale data in a standing wave." I picked up my coffee and took a sip of my own analogy before *it* grew stale.

"Maybe it's not for you, but many people would appreciate it— if death was imminent, but you could keep their consciousness alive."

"It's not alive, Spore. You can save it, like any bit of data, but it's not alive."

"So you can?" Her voice rose with excitement.

"I can what?" I froze, feeling like I'd just stepped on a Bouncing Betty.

"Save him."

I was right. My own words had detonated another bad idea. "Look, saving Thomas is like trying to salvage a video game after it's been played. It's long been 'game over' for him, and we're just grabbing the recording."

She arched a brow. "Did you hear what you just said? Video games make it so simple to press 'reload' no matter how many times you die. Who's trying to figure out how we can do that in real life?"

"Whoa." I put my cup down and raised both hands to stop her wild thought from advancing. "I thought you just wanted to study the thing. Not 'reload' it."

"If consciousness itself were immortal, maybe we can find a way to keep death from happening."

I shook my head. "Death happens when it happens. It means one crucial bit of life flipped from a one to a zero."

"If that were true, wouldn't you want to find a way to keep that bit from flipping? Given that you don't believe in a god, your stance already supports my cause."

"What cause?"

Her voice became low and breathy. "We can make our own Heaven here on Earth."

I imagined her tearing her shirt off, shoving my coffee to the floor, and lunging at me from across the table. Despite the vivid image of my own version of Heaven, I managed to stay motionless.

"Don't you see?" she asked. "We got a ghost for a clue, pointing at a stone left unturned that no one has bothered to look under. And what we've found is something we can leave behind for eight billion people and their descendants to benefit from."

Looking under rocks. I smiled to myself. Well, that was something botanists on Earth and astronauts in space did in common.

"If there was one last thing we could do here," she said. "You know, in case we leave for 'Svalbard?'" She fixed her sparkling, teasing, beguiling eyes at me. "It could mean the science of Immortology. The study of our immortal soul—or how to make it immortal, if it isn't." She reached for my hand. "You once spoke of Elon Musk's vision to preserve and extend the light of consciousness to other worlds. My vision is to preserve and extend it here—in our Afterworld. See this through with me, Bram, and this could be our legacy. For Earth. A means to study what happens to consciousness after death."

I cocked my head. "And if that science ever came into being, can you actually bring yourself to walk away from it?"

She chuckled. "If that science ever came into being, I'd rather have it do so after we've lifted off. That way, I'd be too far out in space to hear anybody laughing."

A comforting warmth traveled up from where she touched me, and I smiled. I wished I'd known the reason behind her new obsession sooner; it would have spared me a lot of distress.

A legacy for Earth. "Okay, we can give it a shot." I shrugged. "It's data. So to save it, I guess all you need is a disc. Roy and I can try to whip one up at the Manor."

She pursed her lips. "No, not at the Manor. If Starr finds out, all hell—or maybe, heaven—will break loose. And I'm sure Eldritch will side with her about the acceptable way to save a soul."

"No worries. I'm going to Roy's place this Sunday. I can tell him about it tomorrow and ask if we can work on it there."

40

THE FIRST PROTOTYPE

"HOLY HITTIN' THE NAIL ON THE HEAD WHILE SLIDIN' FOR A homerun!"

That about summed up how Roy felt about the idea of making a storage device for a hyperwill.

"How the hell do you come up with these things? Gimme that!" He snapped a photo of my sketchpad with all my notes and calculations on the feasibility of the idea, then all I had to do next was stroll through his garage door Sunday morning, all set to put together what Torula and I had agreed to call a willdisc.

The workplace was deserted, but the vintage and muscle cars continued to preen like metallic exhibitionists, and I was the admiring audience of one as I headed towards the screened-off area at the back. I wondered which of these Roy had wanted to show off. They all looked incredible.

He sat at a table, soldering, next to some equipment I'd never seen before.

"What's all this?" I asked as I examined the gear up close.

"Invented some and rented some," Roy muttered hunched over his work.

A soft whimper issued from a padded wicker basket at the

corner. I walked over and got down on my haunches. "Hey, old guy. How you doing?" I stroked the Labrador, now seemingly a different fellow from the inquisitive one I'd met a few weeks ago.

Roy took off his goggles and stared at Boner. "Got started on the willdisc the same day you told me about it. The first proto-type's almost done."

Already? "Wow. You're in more of a rush to get this over with than I am." I almost laughed until I realized the implication. "Hey, you're not planning on leaving the Manor the same time I am, are you? I was hoping you could stay and help Torula for a while." She wouldn't have to leave until after ISEA gave a green light.

"Jackson goin' with you to Svalbard?"

I clenched my jaw, hating that I had to lie to the guy. "Not right away but . . . eventually, yeah."

"Yee-hah!" Roy raised his hand and exchanged a walloping high five with me. "Good ass fudge! Yeah, sure. I'll stay on with 'er. I'm deep into this hyperwill shindig, as you can see." He gestured around at his paraphernalia.

"All this . . . is for that?" Roy's actions simply baffled me. "Why?"

"Look around you." He used his soldering gun to point at the cars in his garage. "I've devoted years to gettin' these classics back on the road. If I can feel that strongly about things made o' steel and rubber, how much more for somethin' that's flesh and blood?"

"Oh-kay." I nodded even though the pieces didn't fit. "But hyperwills don't have flesh or blood."

"What can I say? It's a labor o' love."

Love of what? The ex-wife? *Is he trying to win her back or something?*

A click and a couple of high-pitched beeps cut into my thoughts. Roy walked over to pluck a metallic component ejected from a machine.

He closed one eye as he examined it. "This is for the ionizin' mechanism in the titanium core. I gotta say, it was a clever modification you gave that solved a lotta issues." He laid it down in front of me and headed back to his worktable.

"What issues?"

He just pursed his lips, slipped his goggles on, and went back to soldering.

I picked up the circular piece of metal the size of three stacked quarters. "How'd you manage the titanium casing?"

"I just grabbed a handful, along with these, from storage." He held up something like a Petri dish rimmed by a miniature crystal hula hoop.

"You had those just lying around in storage?"

"Not mine. The Green Manor's."

My stomach lurched. "You mean you swiped them?"

"Recycled 'em. They were just gatherin' dust."

"But I told you the willdisc is none of the Manor's business. That's why we're working here!"

Roy peeled off his goggles and glared at me. "Well, you're a frickin' idiot if you think we can start from scratch and finish this all in one goddamned weekend. You're jumpin' ship, and I'm not gonna be left paddlin' around 'ere on my own. So we're gonna finish this, right here, right now." He shoved the crystal dish and titanium core at me. "Now put these together while I go finish the plasma injector."

I gaped at the items I held in my hands and had to agree. They did look far better than what we could've managed on our own.

By midday, with my back gone sore and Roy's playlist still blaring, we initiated the final step: Injecting the crystalline ring that edged the disc with an odorless, colorless, multicomponent plasma.

"And there you have it, folks," Roy said as he held up the crystal willdisc, its shiny white metallic nucleus powering the miniature vortex around it. "The world's first and only storage device for the soul. This gives the term S.O.S. a whole new meaning." Tiny, colored lightning bolts appeared wherever his fingers touched the transparent crystal. "If this thing works, we can practically FedEx a ghost."

I smirked. "So you're planning a new dotcom now?"

"What for? We can do it through Amazon." He set the disc down carefully into a thin, metallic case lined with fabric. "Okay, you all set to test it?"

I rolled a stiff shoulder. "We'll need to locate Thomas first, don't you think?"

"No, I mean test it before we find 'im."

"I thought using it on Thomas *was* the test."

"How about catchin' us somethin' at the farm?"

I cocked my head. "What farm?"

"That video o' ghost animals in a barn. The orbs I showed you. That's why I asked you to come today. I messaged the guy who put the video up, and he's—"

"Hang on a minute." I held up a halting hand. "Your plan is to ghostbust some animal orbs? Isn't that something you just do in cartoons?"

"Hell, I told you about this days ago."

I started packing up. "I'm sorry, Roy. I hardly even remember the video. Besides, I'm against animal testing."

Roy scowled at me. "You think I'm jokin'? We're on the verge of a scientific breakthrough, and you think I'm jokin'?"

I chuckled. "You do realize it's funny, right? That what you're planning to do has been done by Scooby Doo?"

"Scooby Duffus, my ass." He jerked his head towards the exit. "Just get the hell outta here. I'll go do it on my own."

41

WHAT THE HORSE DICK ARE YOU DOING?

TORULA AND I ARRIVED EARLY AT THE GREEN MANOR, THE PICTURE OF a perfect pair. With no one around, we walked hand in hand down a sun-dappled path as birds chirped their hellos. We paused for a moment and kissed. I'd never known a Monday morning as sweet as this—exactly the kind kitchy clichés were made for.

We entered Greenhouse 3C, and it was as balmy as a tropical paradise. Good, and warm, and comforta—

"Holy shiznickumitch!" Roy burst past some bushes. "What the horse dick are you doin' here so early?"

Torula and I staggered back and ended up slack-jawed over a strange sight floating in the glass chamber.

"What the hell is that?" I asked.

Thin waves of kaleidoscopic light hovered where Thomas' holographic image should have been.

"I drove to the barn and caught it. The guy who posted the video o' the orbs was only too eager to help."

"You caught . . . what exactly?" Torula asked.

"A horse's hyperwill." Roy grinned.

I gaped at the ribbon-like rays that billowed at about the height of a full-grown man. "Bullshit."

"It can't be," Torula said, advancing with me towards the glass enclosure. The chamber's central cylinder with its tilted mirror was missing; it was standing to one side of a plant bed. What now stood in its place was a slanted, transparent, makeshift screen.

Roy's overboard enthusiasm didn't just puzzle me now. It worried me. He could get Torula in trouble all over again with the Manor.

"Yo, watch how it moves. Extrapolate a bit. Can you tell it's a horse?"

Torula squinted at the undulating image and nodded. "If I mentally superimpose a galloping steed over it, yes. I suppose it can be a horse."

"Or an octopus," I said.

"Or a bioluminescent jellyfish," Torula added.

"Well, my bet's on a horse. That thing was transmittin' into the barn, but I didn't find it there. I found it at the farmhouse, in the cellar. Pretty smart for a horse to think o' goin' underground for safety."

Torula looked at Roy. "Did you say you 'caught' this image? How? With a radio wave camera?"

"No. I designed a special standin' wave detector to look for it around the farm. Then I directed it there." Roy gestured towards a device at the far end of the console table. "I call it the iCube. C'mon, I'll show ya. Just lemme shut down the display." He bounded up to the workstation, and soon the flurry of light inside the chamber faded away.

I examined the cube contraption—a smooth, white plastic box about nine inches on each side. At the front of the pristine gadget was a sticker of the white Apple logo.

Torula pointed at the sticker and smiled. "iCube. Cute."

"Nice touch, huh?" Roy said. "iCube's short for Immortality Cube."

At its top, right at the center, was a barely visible tapered point resembling the tip of a pen. "What's this for?" I asked.

"That nib's an electrode for generatin' seed electrons. It ionizes the surroundin' air creatin' plasma around it. The nib swivels, adjustin' to the geometry and gradient, makin' sure the ionized region continues to advance until a completely conductive path is formed so you got a continuous arc from the hyperwill to the positive corona."

"So . . . what does it do?" Torula asked.

"It makes the air conductive, burnin' a path through the air for the hyperwill to follow—straight through the nib and into its new home. Kinda like a tunnel o' light. You gave me the idea. Sorta."

"I did?"

"You said—to catch a hyperwill, you need bait. So that's what I got ready. A power source waitin' inside the iCube. And the ionizin' electrode's the red carpet to dinner." Roy pressed a recessed button on the side of the iCube, and the top slid backwards. There, seemingly levitating atop the interior cylinder, sat the willdisc.

The willdisc?! I stepped closer, hoping I could still obscure it from the cameras.

"That's the recording device, right?" I said, desperate for damage control.

"No, don't you recognize it? It's the—"

"Disc drive. Of course. How could I forget?" I tossed a furtive glance towards the beams overhead then glared at Roy.

Torula whispered in my ear. "Is that what I think it is?"

I nodded.

"Can I touch it?" she asked.

"Be my guest," Roy said. "Just don't drop it, or you'll lose the horse."

Torula took the willdisc between her fingers and multi-colored sparks danced across the transparent ring. Roy looked on like a proud father.

Despite the wonderment in her eyes, she delivered a bland remark. "Well . . . you certainly had me fooled. I thought it was the real thing."

"Say what?"

"Well, aren't we all busy quite early," came an unexpected greeting from behind us, and Torula sucked in her breath. Roy plucked the willdisc from Torula's fingers and placed it in the iCube. It hovered over its receptacle.

Starr came up the platform steps, ready to start her work week in an ensemble of orange and green. "I'm surprised to see everyone already hard at work." She glanced at the iCube. "And what's that new thing over there?"

"That?" Roy reached over and pressed a button on the device. "That's just somethin' I tossed together."

As the cover began to close, Starr dashed for the willdisc and snatched it up before the iCube shut.

"Holy fuck!" Roy lunged and tried to grab the willdisc from her. She twisted away, her elbow nicking Torula's arm, knocking the willdisc out of her grasp. It fell to the floor with a gut-wrenching crack.

Starr gasped.

I froze—like everyone else—and stared at the broken device. Slowly, I bent down and picked it up. No sparks came in response to my touch, and even though I wasn't entirely sure of what it had contained, I felt a subtle pang of regret over its loss. "Whatever was in here—it's gone now."

"Holy goddamnfuckery, woman! Do you know what that cost me?" Roy thrust his fists against his forehead, as though his brain were about to burst. "Goddamn motherfuckin' shit." He plopped into a chair and kicked at the one next to it, toppling it over. "Dammit!"

"I'm sorry. I'll pay for it," Starr said.

"Cost me truckloads o' luck, balls, and all-night headaches to get it. Try and pay for that."

"Why'd you even grab it, Starr?" Torula asked, her eyes full of disbelief.

"Because you were hiding it from me, so I suspect it can't be good." Starr frowned at us. "What was it?"

"A horse's soul." Roy got up and righted the chair he'd kicked by smashing it down.

"A wh . . . what?"

"A recording of a horse's soul," I said.

"No, it was the real soul of a real animal." Roy jabbed a finger towards Starr. "I figured if you're erasin' Thomas soon, I might as well get me a backup of another hyperwill to test."

Starr's gaze flickered for a moment. "You're bluffing. Horses don't have souls."

"Oh yeah? Well, I know for sure dogs have souls. It's the source o' the werewolves legend. It's dogs possessin' humans."

Torula cleared her throat. "It's called clinical lycanthropy, Roy. A psychiatric syndrome wherein—"

"And there's a passage in the Bible," Roy said.

"What passage?" Starr asked, her frown deepening with doubt.

"A legion o' demons begged Jesus not to send 'em into the deep, so they went and possessed a herd o' pigs. Doesn't that tell you—" Roy's eyes suddenly bugged out. "Pigs!" He clapped his hands and aimed two pointers at me. "Maybe we can make a willdisc from pig brain. I always see it in crime shows. They use pigs as stand-ins for human cadavers all the time. That's gonna be way better than somethin' made o' crystal."

"Oh, heaven help me. Now you're thinking of storing souls in bacon?" Starr's voice arced a pitch higher.

"It's just a joke," Torula said.

"And I can't believe you're treating this like a joke!" Starr said. "I've been ignoring this voice in my head telling me I may have been wrong—telling my uncle about these apparitions. But this . . . this . . . 'horsing around' has pushed me over the edge. That's it. I'm leaving you heathens to make a call." She groaned her disapproval as she stomped down the platform steps.

We stared after her departing figure—a rumbling cloud about to rain down fire and brimstone on all of us.

"Who's she gonna call this time? The Pope?" Roy asked, hell-bent on being turned into a pillar of salt.

"I wouldn't be surprised," Torula said. "Half her clan is in the clergy."

Despite that NDA we'd signed, this supernatural circus was getting out of hand. I raked a hand across my scalp. "Any chance they've all got a vow of silence?"

Torula's iHub rang, and Roy's eyes grew wide. "Yo, tell me that's not the Vatican."

She smirked as she picked up the call. "Hello?" She listened for a moment then glanced at Roy. "Yes, he's here." Her eyes opened wide. "Who did she say she was?" She fixed a disbelieving look at Roy. "What else did she say?"

Now what? I narrowed my eyes at Roy, wondering if he'd asked his ex-wife over for a ghost of a time.

"No, it's all right," Torula said into the receiver. "I'll let him know. Thank you."

She turned to Roy with a puzzled tilt of her head. "Someone called the office at Schwarzwald looking for you. Good thing the person who answered didn't know about you and only found out you're with me after she'd put the phone down."

"Why is that a good thing?" Roy asked.

"It was a reporter from an online magazine called *THEORY*."

"Bloody hell, Roy. A reporter?" I clamped a hand over my temples, fearing the worst already.

Roy jerked back. "Hey, I didn't say anythin' to anybody!"

"Oh really?" Torula said. "Well, she wanted to confirm if the Green Manor was into studying animal souls. Any idea who might have given them—"

"Hell, I just gave my name to the farm owner and nothin' else. I said I was an amateur inventor, caught the horse, and left. I didn't say anythin' about the Manor. I swear!"

"Do you think someone could've followed you here?" Torula asked.

"I drove to my place before I came 'ere. It was dead o' night. The streets were empty. If anyone was followin', I'm sure I woulda noticed."

"The car you used . . ." I said, thinking of one telltale marker. "Was it the one with the Green Manor sticker on the windshield?"

Roy's mouth fell open. "Jesus H. Yeah."

"Oh no." Torula glanced with dismay at the camera. "I have to tell Mr. D. and talk with the people at Schwarzwald in case that reporter calls again."

"What'll you have them say?" I asked.

She turned to leave. "I have absolutely no idea."

42

I CAN'T MAKE IT WORK

Roy and I accompanied Torula out of the nursery but parted ways with her just a short distance out, enough to get away from the microphones and cameras. I paused along a stone path, next to a tall hedge.

"What the hell's wrong with you, Roy? You know we're keeping the willdisc under wraps. Then you bring it here, and worse—you leaked it to a reporter!"

"I didn't mean to." Roy raised his shoulders in a tense shrug. "I needed to check if the willdisc works, that's all."

"Why are you so obsessed about this? Are you trying to get your ex back or something?"

"Why the fuck would I wanna do that?"

"Then give me one goddamned reason why you would—" Suddenly, the thought of another possibility jolted me. "Jesus. Don't tell me you're thinking of selling ghosts on Amazon."

"No . . . I'm not." Sober in a heartbeat, he rubbed the top of his head glumly and ambled off the path.

I paused and gave him space; this was more serious than I'd thought.

"I need to put my dog to sleep . . ." Roy winced and pinched the space between his eyes.

"Oh man."

"Boner's got some infection, and the doctor says he's too damn old. Not strong enough to fight it."

His back to me, I laid a comforting hand on his shoulder. "I'm sorry." I couldn't think of any other words to say that would make it hurt any less.

"I can't just let Boner go." He turned to face me but avoided eye contact, his arms crossed tightly as though he were cold. "So I made a modified Faraday cage big enough for 'im and put the iCube together, but it had a lotta issues until your idea of a vortex in a willdisc solved all o' that. Then I used the horse to check if it can work on animals, and now I know. It can."

"It can what?"

"Do what I need it to." He sniffed and rubbed his nose but kept his eyes averted.

A tight knot formed in my gut. "What exactly are you planning to do?"

"Kill my dog. So I can save 'im."

"Jesus Christ." The afternoon air suddenly grew cold around me. "I mean, Jesus Christ, Roy!"

"I'm out of options, man. My best friend's dyin', and I'm tryin' to save 'im. But I don't know what I'm doin' wrong. I can't make it work."

"I don't understand. Make what work?"

"I caught a horse's hyperwill, right? But I did somethin' else. I asked my vet, Quince, to put a real sick dog in the Faraday cage and let 'er die there in 'er sleep. But I didn't get any stream o' data to form anythin'."

Bloody hell. Roy was actually planning to *make* a ghost? I swabbed a hand over my mouth. "Listen, I know you want to keep him around. But it's his time, mate. It's just how life was programmed to go."

"Didn't you see all those cars in my garage? I told you there's no sense buryin' 'em in the past since we've figured out how to take 'em into the future. Well, I got a chance to do it for my closest friend. So I'm doin' it. I'm savin' his soul."

"No. You've always known my stance on this. A hyperwill isn't alive. It's a fossilized memory stream of some kind. It's a data transmission, not a soul."

Roy shook his head repeatedly, refusing to listen— to me and probably even to his own conscience telling him it was madness. "I just wanna make sure that when I put Boner down, he'll head straight into a willdisc and not go into the light. I know I said I wasn't gonna ask, but . . . will you help me?"

I could barely swallow as a lump of dread constricted my throat. "Roy, even if it works—and I doubt it will—but even if we do manage to capture any data, it won't be any different from me keeping my parents' memorabilia inside a robot or getting post-humous phone calls from VN."

"Yeah, well, I'm gonna go through with it whether you help me or not. I got no choice but to put 'im down—but I'll be damned if I just sit around and let 'im down."

43

HELPING A FRIEND

A FULL MOON HUNG LOW IN THE SKY, LIKE A BAD OMEN TELLING ME I had to stop whatever was about to happen.

Afraid of any lurking reporters, I'd peeled off the Green Manor sticker from my windshield and drove up and down Roy's street, scanning the parked cars and checking out the early evening joggers. But it was all an act of procrastination before pulling over to face my challenge of the night: To help a friend accept the death of his pet.

Silence greeted me as I walked into Roy's garage. The day had just ended, and the smell of hard work still hung in the air. A small section at one discreet corner at the far end had been cleared, and the modified Faraday cage Roy had built for Boner sat there like its centerpiece. It looked like a miniature of the 3D chamber at the Green Manor with about the same dimensions as an oversized office table. The clear glass bore a tinge of gray with metal foil taped along its seams. A small camera on a tripod stood a short distance away.

"I'm callin' it a Motown." Roy's voice cut through the silence. "'Cause it's more than just a Faraday cage now. It's gonna be the only place where a decent dawg can get some soul."

Though it sounded like a joke, I didn't laugh. There was no trace of humor on Roy's taut face.

"I got a really fine mesh in there, fully integrated into a transparent mu-metal foil, incorporated to block the entry and escape o' EM waves. So at the moment o' death, the Motown would protect Boner's soul from any electromagnetic interference and keep 'is sinusoidal signal from escapin'." Roy muttered it all like a professor rattling off a lecture he didn't have time for.

I glanced around the spacious garage. "Where's Boner?"

"Over at the vet. He's really in bad shape. Practically just forcin' him to hang on." Roy ushered me into his office: A cramped and cluttered area with just enough room for a table, a chair, one cabinet and a little bit of air. I squeezed myself in and checked out the data displayed on the computer.

"That's what we got from the poodle that died in 'er sleep in the Motown. Whaddaya think?"

I frowned at the near absence of data. "What's there to think? There's hardly any signal here to speak of."

"That's what I'm worried about. You once told Benedict that not everythin' that dies generates a soul. Boner's gotten really weak, so I need you to figure how to fix the setup."

"Well . . ." I cracked my neck as I prepared to dash a man's hopes. "I really don't see how it —"

Roy's iHub rang, and he dashed out as he answered it.

". . . could work," I finished lamely, staring at a now-empty doorway.

I slumped onto the chair's backrest, lost on what to do. Roy had already done so much, but he had kept it all secret because he knew how things usually went. *Share a crazy plan and people will try to stop you.* I knew that well enough.

But sometimes, stopping someone was the right thing to do.

Suddenly, Roy was back at the doorway, panic in his eyes.

"Boner's had a seizure. I gotta get 'im here before it's too late." He handed me a willdisc case. "I've already put one together. All it needs is the plasma injection. Can you finish it for me, man?"

I took the small case from him. "Yeah, no worries." *What am I saying?*

"I need you to promise me . . ." Roy trembled as he spoke. ". . . you'll figure this out. You're gonna make it work, right?"

"Hey, I . . ." I balked and shook my head. "That's not something I can promise."

"Dammit, man. Just think about it! It's what you do better than anybody."

"But I . . ." What else was there to do? Argue? The dog was dying. Roy was desperate. And I was . . . right there. "Okay, I'll think about it."

Running on autopilot, I dug out my sketchpad—my trusty security blanket in times of trouble. I flipped through the pages and found the equations I'd used for the simulation—this set of assumptions that had allowed me to predict how a sine wave could lead to an energy transfer at the point of death.

Roy must have adapted the calculations to the energy levels his vet had told him a dog could produce. But that sick poodle had died without producing a hyperwill—so maybe the electrical impulses were simply too weak.

How the hell do you boost neural signals in a dying dog?

I glanced at Boner's empty wicker basket. *But why even do it?* We should just let the old guy go in peace.

A sense of gloom pulsed inside me as I stood, unable to move, in Roy's deserted garage. There was no way I could give him a definitive answer on how to do it. The closest I could get would be a guess.

My iHub beeped, and I hoped it was Roy saying we were too late. But no. It was Torula.

"Eldritch just called," she said. "We have an emergency meeting tomorrow morning, and he's requiring all of us to come—including Starr."

"What's it about? The willdisc?"

"He didn't say. But the latest thing that's happened was that leak to a reporter. So please tell Roy to come. If the topic's related to him, he needs to be there."

"Sure, no worries."

"Okay, then. I'll see you—"

"Wait, hang on a bit. Could I ask you about that idea your mother had? About hormone modulation and how it affects electrogenesis. Could it help boost neural signals?"

"What's this for?"

Roy needs to kill his pet. I grimaced. "It's for the willdisc. Roy needs to . . . know." *Please don't ask why.*

"Why?"

I grimaced even more. "I think it has something to do with . . . uhm . . . this thing . . ."

"The iCube?"

"Yeah."

"What about it?"

"Er, it's got something to do with how it manages to . . . save a soul, I suppose?"

"I see. But boosting neural signals isn't something we could use when it comes to Thomas anymore. Are you asking about the medium's neural signals then?"

"No, Roy's more like . . . curious about how the hyperwill came to be. Something about what happened at the point of death, I guess?"

"Oh! It's great timing then. My moribund spider plant, Charlotte? She has tons of data to share on that."

"But that's a plant."

"Right." She sighed. "You're talking about electrogenesis in humans."

I gritted my teeth. *Mammals would be more accurate.*

"I'm afraid I can't answer that," she said. "But I'm sure Tromino can. I'll send you his number."

In mere seconds, I had her brother's number in my iHub.

Tromino. The one person in Torula's life who intimidated me. And here I was, about to consult with him on how to catch a dog's ghost. But Torula was right—an endocrinologist would give me a better chance at getting a clue.

Sketchpad in hand, I wandered over to the screened-off section in the garage where the equipment was. I sat on a stool and fiddled with my wristband as I stared at Boner's empty dog basket.

How do I ask Tromino about this? Fat chance my cover of working on a video game would help here.

I huffed out a breath, tapped on my iHub, and made the call. After a brief exchange of pleasantries, I dove in.

"I'm working on this project for NASA. It's a life support system for the Mars mission, designed to deploy automatically."

"Interesting," Tromino said.

The specs of Project Husserl rolled smoothly off of my tongue. "But if automation breaks down, we need a backup system the astronauts can trigger even when they're incapacitated. We've considered voice activation, but it's limiting. I've also sent a proposal exploring thought control."

"Even more interesting."

"But the big downside is—it would require the astronauts to constantly wear headgear to capture the impulses. Not very comfortable."

"I can imagine."

Okay. It's now or never. I clenched my fist until my knuckles cracked. "I was wondering if you could give me an insight on designing a sensor that could detect naturally-occurring signals from a distance. Like bioelectrical impulses—electromagnetic signals produced by the body which we can boost when death is inevitable." *Don't say "huh." Don't say "uhm."*

"And the experts at NASA couldn't come up with an answer?"

"Uhm . . ." Bugger. "I thought it better to ask the best endocrinologist I know."

"I'm the only endocrinologist you know."

"That's why . . . you're the best." I facepalmed and winced.

Tromino chuckled. "Well, much as I would want to be part of the glory, I don't think designing equipment for Mars is up my al—"

"Something like a sine-wave generator." I got up and paced. "Over at NASA, we have a three-phase sine-wave generator circuit. It's used in studies of the propagation of traveling waves in plasmas. I'm looking for something like it in the human body."

"A three-phase what?"

"Sine-wave generator circuit. It's used to power the plasma equipment, combined with three high-voltage transformers and three power-amplifier channels."

"Why the sets of threes?"

"It's what works."

"NASA, huh." Tromino said the acronym like it was amusing.

That was an odd response. "What about NASA?"

"I heard a lot of its top guys are with Deltoton. Have you heard of it?"

"Of course." *I hope he's for it*. "Are you a member?"

"Only recently, yes. But don't tell the wife. She thinks it's pagan."

I laughed. "I get that too, sometimes."

"Ah, a kindred soul."

With that casual revelation of common ground, conversation became easy. The talk rambled on around Deltoton and then, out of nowhere, Tromino said, "Try the HPA axis."

"Excuse me?"

"It's the closest thing I can think of—to mimic your sine wave contraption."

"What is it?" I flipped my iHub screen open and typed a quick search for the HPA axis. I landed on a chart of the human body, showing a couple of teardrop-shaped glands and a kidney highlighted in color.

"The hypothalamic-pituitary-adrenal axis," Tromino said. "It's the crucial team in the neuroendocrine system that controls the body's overall response to stress."

I pressed *Record* on my iHub. "How is it activated?"

"It's a complex cocktail and sequence of events. Though I doubt it would come into play if the astronauts are unconscious. They would have to be under duress. Glucocorticoids rise activating the hypothalamus. Then you have the corticotropin-releasing hormone triggering the pituitary to release ACTH . . ."

I let Tromino ramble on, with more than half his words unintelligible to me. All Jacksons seemed to talk the same way.

"Cortisol might have a lot to do with it too," he said. "In other words, you need the right combination of hormones in conjunction with a highly agitated human heart. One cardiomyocyte can pack a powerful electrostatic punch, enabling the heart to generate the body's most powerful, rhythmic EM field."

"That's how I get my sine wave pulse?" I asked.

"Maybe. And both NASA and Deltoton would be happy. It's a set of three."

I finished the willdisc. Just as I was storing it in its case, Roy came trudging into the garage with his dog in his arms. Boner's eyes were open by a crack, his tongue poking out of his gaping mouth with every labored breath. Roy looked like a tired and punished man with a face stripped of all memory of joy.

"You got the willdisc ready?" he asked.

"Yeah. I've . . . I've got it." I couldn't get over the transformation of both man and beast.

"He ain't gonna make it through the night."

I reached out and stroked the old Labrador. From the dim interior of the garage came the faint sound of footsteps.

"The vet's here," Roy said. "We gotta do it now."

44

WHAT TROMINO HAD TOLD ME

By the dim light of a solitary lamp at the back of Roy's garage, I did my duty of relaying what Tromino had told me. I wasn't sure what all of it meant, but it made perfect sense to the vet.

Roy listened with a blank expression, as though numb. Perhaps it was the only way he could go through with this—by not letting anything change the fact that he'd already made up his mind. "I'll go set up the iCube," he said, then left me with the vet to discuss what needed to be done.

Quince sat on the floor, across from my perch on a stool, and caressed the sleeping dog. The gaunt man, with a chin too long for his face, seemed to be in his mid-thirties, though it was a difficult guess. He looked like a Goth guru from the temple of tattoos with his eyes heavily lined in black. Skin art peeped past his sleeves on the back of his hands and crept up one side of his neck. The piercings underneath his lower lip and over one eyebrow glinted in the lamplight; one earlobe displayed a row of small silver rings, the other a black ear cuff for his iHub. Quince smelled clean, but he looked dirty.

I broke the long silence. "Mind telling me why you think it makes sense?"

"The HPA axis in aging dogs. It's like a siren song in a sad three-part harmony." Quince's eyes stayed fixed on the yellow Lab. "It exhibits progressive dysfunctioning."

His words were like half prognosis, half poetry. "I don't understand."

"In older dogs, the hormone receptors act up, especially those for cortisol, aldosterone, and ACTH—hormones often produced because of biological stress."

"So how does it make sense?"

"Older dogs get increased basal hormone levels. And there's a heightened responsiveness. It's almost like they're primed to set off the HPA axis faster. Maybe 'cause to them—death comes easy, man. Like the body's always ready for Code Blue."

He sounded like he knew his stuff, but it was difficult to trust the guy after hearing Roy's weird stories involving him. His grungy appearance didn't help in any way. "So do you know what you need to do?"

Quince started grooving to a beat only he could hear, then I realized that was his way of nodding. "Fraught with panic and pain. That would have to be this one's end."

Panic and pain? "Wait, what?"

"It's the most efficient way to activate the HPA axis. Just like a violent death, dude. It sends the body's defenses on hyperdrive."

"Hey now, wait a minute." I got on my feet as a grave unease rolled up my back. "You're going to hurt the poor fellow?"

The vet's expression remained deadpan. "Sudden cardiac arrest induced through an injection. It'll be quick. Though each second might feel like forever."

"Hell, no. There's got to be another way."

"This is the closest to humane, man—though still far from it. But that's what I need to do if we want the HPA axis playing hardball."

I glanced at the aged dog battling just to breathe. *Why punish him more?* "This is going too far."

"Think of me as your echo, man." Quince held two fingers in a peace sign and tapped it over his heart. "I'll go explain things to Double R and try to convince him to let the poor guy go. What do you say?"

I guess I'm your echo too. "I'm with you on that one, mate."

I walked over to the resting dog and got down on my haunches to caress him. Though it seemed like a callous thought, I hoped Boner would suddenly stop breathing right then—so Roy's mad plan would come to an end.

Quince came back and plopped down on the floor next to Boner. "He said okay."

"Okay what?"

"He says it's okay for me to do it."

"And you agreed?" I got up, stunned. "Why?"

"It could help other dogs someday. And the people who love them."

I shook my head. *Would anyone else really want this for their pet?* "Think about it, man. What you described—what you have to do. It's not just illegal, it's cruel. Precisely why it's illegal."

Quince shrugged. "I'm an ex vet as it is. I've stopped practicing." He placed one hand flat against his chest, all his nails painted black. "I'm a chicken heart in the company of dogs."

"What?"

"I lost my own dogs in a fire. All five of them in one freak accident. The only thing I could do to get me through it was commemorate them with tattoos. The pain of the art became part of the grieving. You wanna see?" Quince unzipped his jacket.

"No, no. It's okay."

"I opened a tattoo shop instead. Now, I can lose myself in the stories of the people who come in to get their stamp. You could say —Ink became my liquor. My business is my catharsis."

"I see." I settled back uneasily into my seat.

"Double R's ex, Karen, you know her?" Quince asked.

"Never had the pleasure."

"She comes around once in a while. Just to visit—and wow my customers with her gift. You know about it?"

I nodded.

"Karen says those who embrace their death go straight into the light. She keeps telling me my dogs are still around because they died trying to get out, fighting to survive. People always say that about those who die unprepared, and it's been acting like a jack-hammer on my mind. It's hard for me to believe they never left because I don't feel them. I can't tell if they're really there."

Quince's words struck a chord, and I lowered my gaze. I'd gotten to thinking about my parents' death again lately. Had they really been incapable of lingering in any way? Or did they try to transmit to me, but like Roy, I just didn't have the "antenna" to receive it? Did I lack a gene—a gene neither of my parents had? And unable to connect, their messages just . . . faded away? A cold wave coursed through me, and I shoved aside a sudden throb of grief.

"Boner's my last patient. I never did stop looking after him. So I think it's only right that I be the one to do this."

Roy hustled in. "Okay, I'm all set. You guys know what you gotta do?"

Quince rose to his feet, letting Roy take his place on the floor by Boner's side.

"Hey, man. I gotta make sure you understand what we have to do to get your gadget to work." Quince shoved his hands into his jacket pockets and rolled his shoulders once to loosen them. "I'll need to deliver an intracardiac injection that will induce extreme stress and, eventually, cardiac arrest. It's a far cry from peaceful, so this procedure doesn't fall under the definition of euthanasia."

Roy kept his eyes on his pet. "He really likes it when you stroke 'im on his forehead, just between 'is eyes." He scratched the dog's brow, and Boner gave one feeble thump of his tail.

"Listen, mate," I said. "You're not just asking me to play along with ideas anymore. You're asking us to help kill your dog. To experiment on—Christ." I raked a hand through my hair. "I don't even know why you're considering this. It's not just about the law. It's downright cruel."

Roy kept stroking the dog's pale coat as though trying to memorize what it felt like. "What would you have done if you had the chance to save your parents?"

"It was impossible."

"Well, what if it fuckin' wasn't? What if they were sick and old and dyin'? What if you had a willdisc and—"

"I still would've given them a bloody choice, Roy. I would've made sure they understood. Your dog isn't capable of understanding. All he'd want is for all the pain to go away."

Roy looked at me, his eyes a mixture of anger and sorrow. "Do you think doctors should stop treatin' babies 'cause they don't understand why it's gotta hurt before it gets any better? I'm tryin' to save 'is fuckin' life, man. He's a dog, and I'm 'is best friend, and I have no goddamn way o' tellin' him why. Why, why, why!"

Boner whimpered, and Roy held back a sob.

"Hey, listen, man," Quince spoke in a calming tone. "If I'd been there, I would've done anything, too, to save my dogs from the fire. But the thing is—based on stuff Karen's told me—some spirits get trapped in their moment of death. We don't know what it's going to be like for Boner."

"He won't be trapped. He's gonna remember everythin'."

"You don't know that," I said.

"Yes, I do. You proved it to me."

"Me?" I recoiled at the statement. "I never—"

"Your simulation." Roy hauled himself up off the floor. "You showed us that at the moment o' death, we could capture a complete soul. And if we keep it safe, we could keep it from breakin' up into solitons." He strode to the table, grabbed my sketchpad, and shoved it in my hands. "It's somewhere in there. Your proof that we could save my dog's life. Not 'is body. But everythin' he remembers about 'is life."

I clutched the ream of calculations—the foundation of Roy's

faith. It felt heavy in my hands. I laid it down on the table over a small pile of tools. It slid and hit the lamp, toppling it over, casting the room into deeper gloom.

"Yo, listen, I get what you're sayin'. But Boner—he's more than a friend. He's family. Maybe it's hard for you to get that." Roy trudged towards the table and righted the lamp. "If you don't wanna stay, I understand."

I kneaded my temples with my hand, overwhelmed and over-powered by the profound bond between a man and his dog. All I had was a robot—but one thing was for sure, if I got on Mission Pangaea, I'd be damned if I didn't try to bring all of Diddit's data along with me.

"All right. Fine."

"Fine?" Roy asked.

"Bloody fine. If I'm the cause of all this madness, then I ought to see it through."

45

A FRAIL OLD FRIEND

Roy bent down and kissed his pet on the ear. "You ready, boy?" His fingers clutched Boner's coat, as though trying to stop the sick, immobile dog from going anywhere.

"Listen," he said, leaning close to his best friend. "I know you're gonna get damned scared. But it's just gonna last a few seconds." He glanced at Quince. "Right, doc?"

The vet nodded in his groovy way then reached out to detach Boner's collar.

"See? And I'm gonna be right here, waitin' for you to get back." Roy hugged his dog as tightly as a man could hug a frail old friend. "I need ya, boy. A man needs 'is best buddy 'is whole life." He caressed the dog's muzzle, and Boner's tongue flicked out to give his most precious human one last lick.

Roy sniffed loudly as he got up. "Okay. Let's do it."

As Quince helped Roy lift Boner into his arms, I squeezed into the modified Faraday cage, ignoring the burning sense of wrong eating into my gut. Squatting on my heels, I deposited the willdisc into the iCube; the machine sucked it in with a swoosh, a click, and a faint, melodious hum—a sound that contrasted starkly with how everyone felt. I backed out of the cage and helped push Boner and his basket in.

Roy sat inside the chamber for a while, the quiet shaking of his shoulders telling us to leave him be.

I glanced at the vet, who seemed completely unaffected by the prospect of dealing his last patient a dreadful death. "How're you doing, mate?"

"I'm cool," Quince said with clinical indifference. "They say old dogs never die. We're just making it real."

Roy crept his way out of the chamber and wiped his face on his sleeve. With a forceful exhale and a shudder, he looked Quince in the eye. "Okay. Do what you gotta do."

Quince grabbed him by the arm. "I think there's something else you can do to help make this work."

"What?"

"You need to keep calling out to him."

My gaze darted to Quince's face. "What? You can't—"

"Okay." Roy said like a soldier grimly accepting his orders.

"Command him to stay," Quince said. "Instinct would tell him to end the agony and run to the light. You need to make sure he doesn't."

This is cruelty to both man and dog.

"For how long?" Roy asked.

"I don't know. But Karen believes that ghosts can hear us better than they can read our minds. And what I know for a fact is that hearing is the last sense to go. So for as long as the brain can accept auditory data, there's still a chance you can call him back. Keep him fighting against his own death."

Roy looked dazed.

"Be brave—for the both of you," Quince said.

I laid a hand on Roy's shoulder. "Listen, mate. I . . . I'm right here."

He thumped my hand and nodded, letting me know he understood what I'd really meant to say.

He walked to the side of the chamber and knelt down, leaning in as close as he could to his dog lying inside, and rested his hand on the glass. "Hey, Boner. I got your back."

I held the chamber door open as Quince crept in with his equipment. Roy watched, unmoving, as the ex-vet attached electrodes to monitor Boner's vital signs. When Quince held the syringe aloft, Roy spoke in a voice that quivered. "I love you, buddy."

A soulful howl emanated from the chamber, and it was as though the entire place suddenly grew icy cold.

"I'm right here, boy!" Roy cried. "I'm right here."

Monitors beeped wildly as Quince hustled out of the Faraday cage. I shut the door and worked fast to seal the gaps with mu-metal tape.

"It's okay, Boner." Roy's voice rose above the din. "Everythin's gonna be okay."

The dog's eyes shot open, in panic over a scene that unfolded in his mind. His gaze darted around, frantic. He tried to get up but couldn't. He yelped and kicked then went into a contorted convulsion.

"Jesus God!" Roy cried.

"Command him to stay," Quince called out. "Make him choose to stay."

The dog's back arched, his body gripped by the paralyzing force of a punished heart fighting to survive. His eyes widened in fear and then, with one last breath, glazed over.

The suffering was at its end, but Roy had to issue his final command.

"Stay with me, buddy! Stay, you hear? Come 'ere, boy. Come 'ere!"

The poor dog went limp and the piercing tone of a flat line cut through the air. "Oh God, no. I'm sorry! I'm sorry." Roy stared unmoving, with bloodshot eyes, his mouth agape.

"Keep talking," Quince said.

I could barely breathe. How could Roy even speak through this?

His chest heaved. "C'mon, be a good boy. Stay with me. Just stay, okay?"

The monotonous note of the EKG monitor maintained its bleak and final pronouncement.

Roy pressed both hands against the glass. "Don't you fuckin' leave me, y'hear? Come back." His voice went down to a whisper as he gazed at his pet's lifeless body—eyes still partly open, but empty. "Stay . . ."

I wiped the sweat from my upper lip and strode to the console, squinting as though walking through smoke as I forced my mind to focus on the task. Settling down into my seat, I thumped a fist against my chest to help ease the tightness inside. Quince was nowhere in sight. I surveyed the computer screen displaying the wave oscillations inside the willdisc.

The data patterns weren't shifting.

"Come on," I muttered. "You've got to bloody work."

Quince reemerged, his black eyeliner smeared, and turned off the EKG monitor. He took his jacket off and used it to clean up the black gook from around his eyes. His arms still seemed covered with sleeves because of the ornate artwork featuring the likeness of several dogs.

Roy went back to stand by the chamber, his shoulders heavy and hunched. After a long moment of silence, he strode towards the wall, turned off the overhead lights, then knelt by the chamber to peer at the iCube. "See that?"

In the darkness, a pinprick of light became discernible at the top of the cube, a luminous dot of blue-violet barely visible at the nib.

"Is that . . . it?" Quince asked.

Roy shook his head. "It's just sayin' we got an electric current goin'—ionizin' the air molecules for Boner to follow like a trail. It's like a yellow brick road to 'is new home." His gaze stayed fixed on the iCube. "The box itself should light up when it starts receivin' somethin'."

Quince took a seat next to me as Roy settled down on the floor.

The silence grew thicker by the minute. I kept my eyes on the empty status bar on the monitor and clenched my teeth.

"Do you want me to go in and . . ." Quince motioned towards the chamber, ". . . carry him out now?"

"No," Roy said. "We gotta keep it sealed until the upload's done."

Five minutes went by. Then ten—without a spark in any of the readings.

When trying to save a life, how does one decide when it's over?

Suddenly, Roy let out a piercing whistle, jolting Quince in his chair, his elbow slipping off the armrest.

"Whatcha waitin' for, boy? Get your ass in that willdisc!" He pulled out his keychain and blew a dog whistle.

Quince leaned over and whispered. "Has it been too long?"

I cocked my head tentatively, caught between an "I don't know" and a "Maybe."

"Boner's been weak a long time," Quince said, still in a low tone. "Maybe that's why it didn't work."

"We're not done waiting," I said.

Quince nodded but managed to muster only enough patience for another minute of quiet. "Dogs don't really die, you know. They just go to sleep in your heart." He picked up his jacket and put it on. "Karen says it's sudden death that drives ghosts to linger. Like, they know it's not their time, so they fight to stay. But Boner—his mind's been primed to die. He was ready for it. Just like that sick poodle was." He zipped up his jacket, the sound of the teeth closing ripping through the silence.

"Well, goddamn it. I never listened to 'er when we were married. So I'm not listenin' to 'er now."

"There's no hurry. It's only been . . ." I glanced at the monitor. "Thirteen minutes." *Christ. How much time does a "soul" take to leave?*

"I'm just saying, a dog's short life is his only fault." Quince got up and shrugged. "You're better off knowing he's resting in peace than living a life of pain."

"Pain?" Roy rose from the floor. "If you don't shut the hell up, I can show you pain."

"I'm just helping you embrace your loss."

"How would you like to embrace my fist with your face?"

Roy charged. I shot out of my seat. Quince fell backwards in his chair onto the floor.

I held my arm out to block Roy. "Come on, mate. Let it go."

Quince, still sprawled on the ground, opened his mouth again. "I think—"

"Shut up, Quince," I said.

"But—"

"I said shut up!" I barked.

For several seconds, nobody moved. Then, Quince slowly, cautiously raised a finger towards the Motown. "Look," he said.

Roy and I turned our heads and saw a faint glow emanating from the bottom of the iCube.

Roy rushed to the chamber. "Atta boy. Good dawg, Boner!"

I checked the computer readings and winced at the looped symbol for infinity: The estimated time left for the—*What do I call it?*—the "upload?"

Quince got up, righted his chair, and collapsed in a spent heap onto it.

The status bar popped to life. "Oh, Jesus," I said. "It says 1,052 days left. That's almost three years."

"You're shittin' me."

"Now it says ninety-five days." I grinned sheepishly. "Sorry, mate. Should've known better. It's going to keep moving up and down for a while."

"That's still three fuckin' months!" Roy turned to the chamber and bellowed. "C'mon, Boner. Hop to it!"

46

FULL-FLAVORED FREQUENCIES

JUST AS I WAS ENJOYING THE BEST PART OF MY DREAM WHERE I WAS commanding an intergalactic mission, Roy nudged me awake. The iCube status bar that kept track of Boner's upload was less than an inch to the top.

I squinted at Roy through my groggy state. "How're you doing?"

"Flyin' like a golf ball aimin' for a hole in one." He said it with a faint smile, his eyes brimming with hope as he stared at the iCube. It seemed impossible, but he really did look like he already felt better than I did. Quince let out a loud burp and crumpled his beer can.

Roy switched the TV from the movie he and Quince were watching to closed-circuit mode then got up and opened what I thought was some vintage refrigerator positioned next to the Motown.

"This 'ere's what I call The Cellar." The top shelf was empty, but right underneath was a black version of the iCube attached to vials and canisters set up in neat rows all the way to the bottom. "This whole setup is designed to pump energy into the iCube so it never runs out. I got me some nonlinear stuff down there servin' as frequency doublers and triplers so the food Boner gets is full-flavored when it comes to frequencies. You know what I'm sayin'?"

I nodded. "Because you don't know exactly what range he'll need, you're giving him everything."

"Damn straight. It'll be churnin' out EM waves at varying frequencies, so it resonates through the whole EM spectrum—from ELF to IR, UV, all the way up to gamma."

"Why do you call it The Cellar?" I asked.

"'Cause the temperature inside is regulated, and everythin' there's protected from harsh light and vibrations. So it's kinda like a wine cellar for the soul."

I shook my head in amazement. "I'm gobsmacked over how you figured this all out."

"You kiddin' me? I just followed the trail o' puzzle pieces you guys were tossin' behind you at the Green Manor. You just didn't have an old dog chasin' your tail to put it all together to be worth anythin'."

We stood clustered together, watching the status bar as Roy counted down after it hit the ten second mark.

"Three . . . two . . . one."

Completely lit, the iCube gave off one bright pulse which settled down to a cool and steady glow.

"Sweet hello hallelujah," I whispered. Quince bounced on the balls of his feet, while Roy beamed like a dad about to greet his new baby.

"Okay, Boner. I'm comin' in." Roy opened the chamber door, and a rank odor drifted out—the smell of fear, sickness, and death combined in an unseen fog. He took the iCube out then placed it on the top shelf of The Cellar, connected it to the black cube, then shut the cellar door.

"Let's rock n' roll!" He dashed to the console and turned a knob. Just like the Transhades at the Green Manor greenhouses, the glass at the rear of the Motown darkened. "Whatever data the system gets, it's gonna project it onto that panel. We'll see it on that monitor too." He cocked his head towards the TV. "It's not as fancy as our 3D chamber, but it'll do." He gave me two thumbs up.

With a deep breath, I activated the Verdabulary and triggered Boner's computer-assisted reincarnation. We all stared at the chamber. Seconds ticked by, but nothing happened. Even the TV screen remained blank.

"Holy fuck, man. He better be in there."

"Maybe the cables are loose," Quince suggested.

"The cables are fine," Roy said.

I cracked my knuckles, aching to fix computer codes but didn't know where to start. I tugged my chair forward and the keyboard closer, pointless motions to help the process along.

Roy banged his hand down on the table. "What the hell's takin' so long?"

Quince backed one step away from Roy.

"Okay, let's just . . . catch our breath here," I said. "It's still early in the game. Maybe the program's still—"

"Extrapolatin'? Extrapo-fuckin' my ass!" Roy punched and kicked on the door of The Cellar, cracking it open, then he charged towards the chamber and raised a fist at the glass.

"No, don't!" Quince shouted.

Roy froze and slowly lowered his hand, laying it down gently on the glass chamber. "Goddamit, Boner." He fell to his knees and talked to his best friend's body through the glass. "I know you gave it all you got. But we just never had practice. I never got to teach you what to do." His shoulders slumped, and he wept in silence.

I bowed my head and struggled for something to say. I recalled the most comforting thing people had said to me when I myself had been grieving.

If there's anything I can do . . .

I swallowed. It wasn't something I wanted to say now. Because I'd done enough.

Like a tired old man, Roy hauled himself up to his feet. "I guess it's time to lay him in his grave out back. Give 'im his peace."

I stood beside him and laid a comforting hand on his shoulder. His grief was just beginning. *The worst will be when he realizes what "permanent" really means.*

Quince and I helped bring Boner's body out of the chamber. There was hardly a sound as Roy placed him in a box and covered him with a soft flannel blanket.

He laid his hand on the sheet. "I'll see you in heaven, buddy." His faith in my equation having been shattered, he'd gone back to believing in the one thing that would make Boner's death bearable.

"Here," Quince said, handing him Boner's dog collar. "He won't need this where he's going."

I turned away from the sad reminder that keeping remembrances was the most anyone could do. Then from the corner of my eye, I caught movement in the huge TV monitor. I took a closer look and jerked back at what I was seeing—or thought I was seeing. I darted a glance at the chamber but couldn't detect anything from where I stood, so I moved closer. As I watched, breath on hold, a pinprick of light floated from the top and descended until it hovered over the floor. It slowly expanded until it looked every bit like the faintest of orbs.

"Well, I'll be stuffed," I said softly as I stared at the image.

"Whoa," Quince said, stepping closer. "Is that what I think it is?"

"What's that?" Roy asked with a frown.

The dim, translucent sphere circled where Boner's body had lain. I looked at the TV where it was far more visible—flickering between shades of yellow, blue, and gray.

"Close the door!" Quince pointed towards The Cellar. "He might escape."

"No, he's safe in the willdisc," I said. "And I think . . ." I eyed the cellar door Roy had kicked open, ". . . he needs to sense Roy to transmit."

"Hell, that can't be *all* we got o' my dog. What the hell is it?"

I went back to the console to check the readings. "All's good, as far as I can tell."

"Goddamit." Roy charged towards the chamber. "Don't fuck with me, Boner. Show me all you got." He hunkered down and inspected all the cables snaking across the floor. Then he checked all the connections in The Cellar and those leading out of it.

I squinted at the TV where the orb seemed to be moving in unison with him and remembered the time when Thomas's hyper-will had responded to Torula in real time. On a hunch, I opened a simple video editing app so I could superimpose one footage over the other. The camera Roy had set up on a tripod was aimed at the chamber. I manipulated it and set it to track Roy as he moved around, then—keying out the dark background of the floating orb—I superimposed it over Roy's image. The ball of light moved alongside him.

I grinned at the little orb that glowed like a flickering sign of hope.

"Dude, this is like . . . wow." Quince, diluted by beer, was stripped of all poetry.

Roy went down on all fours tracing the cable lines underneath the console, and onscreen, the glowing sphere hopped up and down next to him.

"Roy?" I said.

"What?" Roy answered with his nose to the ground.

"I think you'd want to see this."

Roy shot up like a meerkat craning at something in the distance.

"Walk around," I said. "It's following you."

Roy got up and strode away from the chamber and back again, then went from one corner to the next. The orb turned every which way he went.

Quince grinned wide. "This is killing me, man. It's pumped up rad."

Roy, arms akimbo, gaped at the screen. "That's it? That's my

Boner in the afterlife? A tiny pipsqueak of a wiener? You gotta be shittin' me!"

"He's a dog," Quince said. "Of course, he's small."

"And maybe . . ." I hated to admit it. "Eldritch might be right. Maybe animals don't have data on what they look like. No self-awareness."

Quince nodded to a much faster inner beat. "Yeah, makes sense. Dogs bark at themselves in the mirror. They can't tell it's them. Come to think of it . . ." He moved closer to the monitor. "The colors of the orb . . ." The ball oscillated from brown to yellow to gray to blue. "That's about the full spectrum of what a dog can see. Just yellow and blue and smudged-up shades of those."

Roy stood silent, eyes to the ground, then slowly turned to look at his dog's body beneath the flannel blanket.

"He may have no idea what he looks like," I said, "but he sure remembers you."

Quince glanced at the tattoos on his arms and gave them an inconspicuous rub.

Roy bent down and held out his hand at thin air. On the monitor, the small opalescent ball glided forward. Roy wiggled his fingers, as though rubbing the area atop Boner's head. The orb began to fluctuate side to side—seemingly wagging in pure canine bliss.

"Hey, boy. Is that really you?" Roy knelt down, and the orb bounced all over him. He looked up at me, tears in his eyes. "He's alive, man. What else can I say? He's alive."

47

THE EMERGENCY MEETING

DESPITE HAVING SPENT ALL NIGHT FIGURING OUT HOW TO RAISE A DOG from the dead, I'd managed to show up on time at Schwarzwald for Eldritch's emergency meeting. With caffeine filling in for consciousness, I slouched down in a conference room chair and yawned. I was so groggy, I felt tipsy, and the country-cottage atmosphere and garden-scented air weren't helping at all.

Torula leaned over and whispered, "Can you try a little harder to look alive?"

She had no idea what Roy and I had been through, and there was no easy way to explain it. With a grunt, I pushed myself up on the chair.

Eldritch, dressed in his dapper version of death, sat next to the rainbow-clad Starr, facing the hi-tech monitor in the old-fashioned meeting room. I apologized on Roy's behalf that he wouldn't be able to join us.

Eldritch frowned. "That's unfortunate because I wanted him to explain something." He picked up the remote control. "I saw footage of a horse's hyperwill and everyone trying to pass it off as a recording. But more notably, there's a snippet of Mr. Radio saying this."

He played an audio clip of Roy saying, "Maybe we can make a willdisc from pig brain!"

Eldritch turned his ice-cold gaze towards me. "This willdisc. Is it something you plan to use on Thomas?"

I looked back at him through woozy eyes, relieved the topic was the willdisc after all—and not a reporter spilling our secrets—and pointed at Starr. "She broke it."

She arched a brow. "And I would do so again, honey, if you attempt to use it to trap a human soul."

I pondered the possibility. "Maybe if we could get our hands on some pigs . . ."

Starr's eyes flared wide. "Can you believe this irreverence?"

Torula stared open-mouthed at me for a moment. "What he means to say is . . . it was a fragile prototype, but . . ." She cleared her throat and faced them, sounding all business-like. "It's an opportunity we should explore. Think of Thomas as a vulnerable life form. Like a hermit crab that's lost its shell. The willdisc is an electrochemical environment that could save him from—"

"Are you sure it's to save him?" Starr asked. "Or is it to dissect, preserve, and display him like a naked crab in formaldehyde? I know, more than anything, you want to study him, Tor. He's a human being, no matter what you think. So treat him like one."

I scrunched up my brow against the fluorescent lights that punished my eyes. "What about saving dogs? Cats have nine lives. Why can't we give dogs another?"

Torula nudged my coffee mug closer to me. "What he means, I think, is . . . this is like teaching an old dog new tricks. Why can't we give this new technology a chance? Challenge old assumptions and—"

"Because it's breaking the law," Starr said. "It is God's law that we join Him in paradise and not linger here. We must guide every lost soul we find into that haven. Not to yours that's made of glass."

"It's crystal, actually," I said, believing it mattered.

The door swung open and in walked the benevolent-looking

billionaire, Mr. Alexi Dumas. "It appears someone in this room has turned my hobby into a headache." He stopped directly across the table from Starr and addressed her. "You know the reason I'm here, ja?"

Starr clutched her necklace. "The T.R.O.?"

Torula looked at her friend. "What T.R.O.?"

So this is the real emergency? I straightened up in my seat.

Mr. D enunciated each word. "A Petition for Injunction with Prayer for a Temporary Restraining Order." Though his eyes showed displeasure, his amiable countenance remained. "I have been issued a document demanding that the Green Manor suspend Project Hyperwill until after a proper evaluation of its . . .'scientific, ethical, and social implications.' The plaintiff is a Bishop Isaac Benedict."

Torula drew in her breath. "Starr? You couldn't have. This was our chance to study it." She shook her head. "Our one chance."

Starr averted her gaze and said nothing.

"You broke the NDA," Eldritch said.

"I broke man's law instead of God's." Starr looked him in the eye. "You have the right to fine me and to fire me. But what you're doing is trespassing on sacred ground."

"But our aim is to *save* a soul," Mr. D said. "Surely, the church would approve of that, ja?"

"Not if you see things from his perspective." Starr turned accusing eyes towards me. "Isn't it your belief that the human soul is nothing but lifeless data?"

Only yesterday, I would have given a decisive yes, but after last night, I wasn't sure anymore. Boner's "orb" was capable of real-time interactivity—repeating actions learned while still alive. But it was information stored in a vortex sine wave, feeding off energy supplies kept in a temperature-controlled cellar. *It couldn't be called a living thing, could it?*

"Is that hesitation I detect?" Starr asked. "Have Thomas's mani-festations convinced you of his sentience?"

"Thomas?" I shook my head. "No. Not at all."

Starr rose from her seat. "Then I believe stopping things where they are is only right." She addressed Mr. D. "If I may be excused, sir. I believe you understand my sentiments. There's nothing more I can do for this project."

"By all means. You've done quite enough already." At her departure, Mr. D sat down across from her empty seat.

"So where does that leave us?" Torula asked, trying to salvage a dream.

"At a grinding halt, I'm afraid." The chairman's default expression of a smile barely showed.

"And we can't do anything?" she asked, and it tugged at an old, familiar feeling inside me—that of wanting to breathe life into what others believed to be a dead ambition. "What if we set up identical conditions at another greenhouse?"

"Project Hyperwill has been effectively manacled," Mr. D said. "The rest of the Green Manor will be in danger of suspension if we challenge—"

"Not necessarily," I said as the fog of sleeplessness lifted from my brain. "The willdisc wasn't made for the Green Manor."

"I beg your pardon?" Eldritch asked.

"The only thing we signed here was the NDA. And all it did was bind us to secrecy as we studied the apparitions here. We were never hired to invent a storage device. So technically, it's Roy's and my intellectual property."

"You have a warped definition of ownership, Bram," Mr. D said. "You used materials from the Green Manor, which makes my corporation the rightful owner."

"The parts, yes. But the technology is completely ours. If Henry Ford got parts from someone else to build a car, that someone can't claim to own the car, can he?"

Mr. D leaned forward and pointed a finger at me. "But you are under contract with me."

"Only to explain the anomaly," Torula said, the glow of comprehension spreading across her face. "I was the one who asked Bram to make the willdisc. The Green Manor had no hand in its creation. You weren't even supposed to know it exists."

Mr. D cocked his head. "I see." He glanced at me, and his smile regained its saintly glow. "Now, indeed, I see. So even though the corporation has been restrained, you as *individuals* have not."

"But what about the parts?" Eldritch asked. "How do you skirt that technicality?"

The chairman shrugged. "They were discards. Obsolete supplies. We turned those parts into garbage, making their finders their keepers, ja?"

Torula rose to her feet. "Then tomorrow, we—as individuals—can go find Thomas and save him."

"Tomorrow?" I asked. "We haven't even begun looking for it."

"That's all right," she said with a glimmer in her eye. "I think I know where he is."

"How?" I asked, baffled.

"Thomas told you, didn't he?" Eldritch asked, perking up like a man spotting a friend in a crowd. "Did he show you by using symbols?"

She nodded, almost imperceptibly. "Remember when I asked Thomas where he was, and all I could hear was Starr's jewelry? I just kept seeing her crucifix, and when I closed my eyes, I heard bells. I realized they weren't small, tinkling bells, but more like distant church bells." She gestured at Starr's vacated seat. "And she also once heard me humming a church hymn I never knew. So I think Thomas is in one of the California missions."

"Are you sure about that?" Eldritch asked.

"Strangely, yes. I am." She looked at me, her eyes brimming with such conviction that I couldn't help but nod to say I believed her.

"Then you must go there," Mr. D said, "and find him."

"To do what?" asked the psychic who couldn't foretell the obvious.

"What's there to explain, Eldritch?" asked the chairman.

"I gave Dr. Benedict my word. We are not to go entrapping souls with that device. And I agree with her."

"Then don't come with us," Torula said. "We never made that promise. Besides, as Roy once said: Thomas is not her ghost. And that if anyone can lay claim to it—"

"No one can lay claim to anyone's soul," Eldritch said. "They need to be free to settle unfinished business so they can cross over. And now you plan to put him in a cage?"

"Believe me, he won't feel caged at all," I said, picturing a bobbing canine orb. "Like Torula said, it'll be more like giving a hermit crab a brand-new shell."

"A shell that confines him," said Eldritch.

I shook my head. "Not if you know the properties of crystal."

He turned earnest eyes towards the chairman. "Alexi—"

"Eldritch," Mr. D said and paused as the icy one simmered. "You will have your chance to communicate with Thomas. But tomorrow, let's have them test *their* technology, ja? Let's learn the most that we can—before you send him where you believe you have to send him."

48

COULD IT BE CONSIDERED ALIVE?

THE SOUND OF CRICKETS GREETED US AS I USHERED TORULA DOWN Roy's driveway. She craned her neck as we walked past his front lawn, sparsely lit by moonlight.

"Lovely garden," she said, taking in a lungful of the fragrant breeze. "And he's got a *Brunfelsia Americana* in full bloom."

"I suppose *you'd* notice that, even in the dark."

Roy greeted us at his garage's pedestrian entrance and led us in, towards the back, where it seemed as lifeless as the rest of the deserted work area.

"I see you've been busy." I bobbed my head towards The Cellar that now had a see-through door.

"Yeah," Roy said. "Ditched the metal for fused silica."

"Great," I said. "Now, you've still got the inside protected while staying transparent across the whole EM spectrum."

Torula smirked. "I suppose *you'd* notice that, even in the dark."

I grinned right back at her.

The Motown had been set aside, and now at center stage was the huge TV monitor. Roy pulsed his brows teasingly at Torula. "Are you ready for this, Jackson?"

She tilted her head. "Ready for what?"

He flashed his superhero smile. "Come 'ere, buddy." He bent down and started stroking thin air. "Good boy."

Torula looked at me with a scrunched brow. I pointed at the TV. Onscreen, where the camera should have shown only three people, there appeared a ball of light hovering in front of Roy's knee.

Torula glanced from the screen to Roy and back again. "What am I seeing there?"

I swallowed, part of me still not wanting to tell her, but I had to. "Last night, we did something that I hope you'd understand. Boner's condition took a turn for the worse, and Roy had to put him down."

"Oh dear, no." She clasped Roy's arm. "I'm so sorry. Is there anything—"

"Don't worry about me." Roy flicked an uneasy gaze towards me. "Just go on and tell 'er."

I let out a nervous breath and carefully—truthfully—narrated what we had done and why Roy had chosen to do it that way. Torula gnawed on her lower lip, her brow in a knot as she listened to me admit that I'd stood by and helped Roy do it.

"That wasn't euthanasia," she said in a low tone. "I don't think there's even a word for what you did." No doubt, she had a few words in mind to describe our actions but was too kind to mention them.

"How do you feel about it?" I asked.

She was silent as she kept her eyes on the TV screen showing Roy moving around while the orb, invisible to the naked eye, continued to trail him. Finally, she shuddered and took a deep breath. "I can see how . . . not wanting to lose someone can lead you to make reckless decisions."

I realized the full meaning of her words, and I reached for her hand. "You're not upset?"

Her eyes shone like candlelight in the dead of night. "Why would I be? You did it, Bram. You actually did it. You proved that an afterlife exists."

"Hell yeah," Roy said. "It was just a matter of us findin' a way to detect it."

If there was such a thing as a stammered smile, I suppose that was what I gave them. That orb was information salvaged from a dying dog, and now Boner—his brain, body, and all—was dead and buried in Roy's backyard. The dog's hyperwill data was in a temperature-controlled storage cabinet and being translated by a computer, so how could it be considered *alive*?

"What's troubling is," Torula said, "it implies that a peaceful demise means we simply fade away. That's just so . . . so . . ." She seemed to dip deep into her well of words and came up with ". . . sad." Her downcast eyes made me want to apologize for mathematics' heartless conclusion.

"There could be another possibility, though." I cracked my knuckles, hoping to give my equations a sympathetic side. "Maybe a peaceful death is a mathematical concept that doesn't happen."

Torula and Roy looked at me with hopeful eyes.

"Death is a crisis, no matter what," I said. "Even if you overdose on sleeping pills, or if you were in a coma—your entire system is hardwired to find some way to fight it."

Torula nodded. "Even a dehydrated Spider Plant would say no to it. Repeatedly."

"There you go," I said with a grin. "An equation—where the impetus to fight death is at or near zero—just doesn't occur in real life. It's only in my sketchpad."

"But what about that poodle who died in 'er sleep?" Roy asked. "We didn't get a jot o' her soul."

I rubbed my stubbled jaw. "How long did you wait?"

He shrugged. "Long enough."

Torula squinted and tilted her head. "Maybe when the organism isn't under duress, it just takes longer."

"Shit. You mean, she coulda been tricklin' out?"

"Who's to say?" she said with a chuckle. "After all, we're using software intended for botanical life, not some . . . other kind."

Roy's brow shot up. "Ooh, almost forgot. Speakin' o' other

kinds o' life." He grabbed a sealed envelope from a table. "I went to the clinic to get some info about your electrogenesis results, and they asked me to give you this."

She scanned the note. "They want to talk to me about my blood test results."

"I knew it!" Roy gyrated, rubbing his tummy like a badly trained belly-dancer. "All those dizzy spells and the nausea? Somethin' tells me you two are gonna have some company when you head off to Svalbard."

I stopped breathing for a moment.

"Don't be ridiculous," Torula said. "It could be so many other things." She sounded glib even as she flicked the hair off her brow.

"Let me go with you." I was ready to insist if she said no.

"Right. Okay," she said after just the slightest pause. "After we catch the hyperwill."

49

A HISTORIC TOURIST ATTRACTION

IN THE DEAD OF NIGHT, TORULA, ROY, AND I STOOD GAZING AT THE California mission. Built two and a half centuries ago, the church had been rebuilt and restored to become a historic tourist attraction. But we needed it deserted for what we had in mind.

"Three a.m.," Roy griped as he pulled on a beanie. "Twenty-four hours in a day, and you had to choose three a.m."

Torula buttoned up her coat against the chill. "When aiming to catch an elusive creature in the wild, would you do it when you think it'll be sleeping?"

"That depends," Roy said. "People usually wait for Dracula to sleep before—"

"All right, listen up." My breath turned into visible puffs of warmth as I spoke. "We need to look for places that rarely get disturbed. Ideal places for standing waves. Like attics, cellars, small rectangular rooms."

"Only rectangular rooms?" Torula asked.

"Ideally, but not necessarily having parallel walls. As long as a multiple of half the wavelength of the room resonance fits between the opposite walls."

"Right. As if that actually helps me. Let's go." She led us

towards the churchyard, stepping onto a grassy area and walking close to the rough, stone wall. "I think we should look near there." Torula pointed towards the belfry.

"Why there?" Roy asked.

"That was how Thomas told me he was in a church. With the sound of bells."

"All that clangin' and bangin' isn't bound to keep a wave standin' around. I'd put my chips on the basement."

"The basement?" Torula asked. "But . . ."

"The floor plans we got say the entrance would be over there," I said, pointing in another direction.

"Right." Torula sighed and looked as though she had to pull her feet out of quicksand before she moved. We came to a hatch on the ground partly concealed by low bushes. It had no lock. As I lifted it open, the rusty hinges rasped in the quiet night. I glanced nervously at all the darkened windows around and overhead.

Turning his flashlight on, Roy descended the rickety steps then shone the beam on the stairs for Torula.

She stayed glued to where she stood.

"You claustrophoberizin'?"

I flinched inwardly. *Crap. How could I have forgotten?* I pulled out my car key and offered it to her. "You should wait in the—"

"No. I just need to . . . concentrate."

"Have you started your treatment for this?"

"It's only tough for me in dark and tight spaces," she answered with a stilted smile. "I'm sure it's roomy down there, and there's bound to be some light."

"Turn the lights on, Roy," I said and climbed down part of the way then held out my hand for her.

She leaned over and held on. Her grip was tight—too tight. I offered my other hand too, but she froze, crouching there, unable to take a step.

Roy cussed from the darkness below. "No lights down 'ere, dammit."

The dim glow of Roy's flashlight caught the terror in Torula's eyes as she made her slow and shaky way down. Her breathing grew quick and shallow.

"Are you okay?" I asked.

She retched then stumbled her way back up.

"Jesus." I bolted after her.

She tugged at her coat collar, pulling it away from her throat. A loud cough escaped her, and we glanced up towards a window in time to see a light go on. Torula grabbed my shirt and yanked me backwards into the basement hatch. We clambered down the stairs, but I missed a step and twisted in despair to help Torula keep her balance. Roy lunged forward, caught us in time, and helped break our fall.

With all three of us crumpled on the rough ground, Roy let out a crisp but quiet, "Fuck."

"You've always . . . been horrible . . . with stairs," Torula said, her eyes shut tight.

"Are you hurt?" I asked.

She shook her head but was panting—struggling to control her breathing.

"Man," Roy said, "this gig is a bad idea for someone pregnant."

I glanced up at the open hatch, expecting someone to either look down at us or lock us in. I raised myself on one elbow and leaned over her. "How are you feeling?"

She looked at me, her eyes betraying her anxiety. I laid a hand on her abdomen, aching to protect . . . whatever might be . . . as we lay there waiting for calmness to return.

Torula took a long, deep breath, shuddered, and sighed. "I think I can get up now."

"I'll take you back to the car," I said, helping her up.

"You need me here to lure Thomas. But . . ." She looked up at the hatch where some moonlight streamed through. "Maybe I can just sit here and . . . keep an eye out."

"Great idea." I handed her a flashlight and flicked another towards her pendant but was surprised not to find it there. "Where's your jammer?"

"I left it in the car."

"What the hell. Why'd you do that?"

"We're looking for Thomas, and I'm the bait. Now, will you please get on with what we came here to do?"

"Damn it, Spore. The last time you were this stubborn, you went blind." I had to grit my teeth to keep from raising my voice.

"I'll be fine." Torula strode towards a spot next to a pillar. She sat on the ground, cross-legged, and leaned against the wall. "I'll sit right here—relaxed and rested—until you get back. Now go. Find Thomas."

Roy grabbed his knapsack and pulled some antique-looking contraption out of it—like an odd assemblage of spare parts without a shell, about the size of a big man's shoe.

Torula gave it a dubious frown. "What is that relic?"

"A standin' wave detector."

"Eldritch uses EMF detectors surely far more advanced than that. And he says even those don't give him much help."

"It's 'cause they aren't *standin' wave* detectors. This one is, and it's calibrated for hyperwills." Roy disappeared into the gloom.

I contemplated manhandling Torula out of the place, but there'd be a steep price to pay if I did. "Give me a call as soon as you feel anything wrong, you understand?"

"Aye, aye, Captain Morrison, sir." She gave me a salute, and I could only crack my neck in frustration.

I turned around and promptly hit my head on a beam. "Bugger." I stooped my way in and soon caught up with Roy. The floor was uneven, and with every step, bricks wobbled or crumbled underfoot. Wooden planks stood exposed against the rough-hewn walls and the stale air smelled of forgotten time. Around a corner, the space narrowed sharply, and thick support beams grew dense. The pillars formed a broken, narrow alleyway towards a boxed-in area.

At the mouth of the cramped alcove, Roy checked his meter reading and let out a low whistle. "I think we found the sweet spot. My naked C fibers are shiverin' down 'ere."

He took out the iCube and edged towards the tight opening. Stuffing himself through the gap, he pushed the iCube in as far as he could. "Okay, it's in place." He heaved himself out and collapsed backwards on the floor. "Jesus H. This is like waitin' for a heart attack to happen."

I was afraid he was right. I imagined Torula fighting off her fears with a flashlight for a sword.

Roy reclined on the floor as though on a picnic blanket in the park. "Hey, would you have believed anyone if they told you a few weeks ago you'd be sittin' in the dark somewhere aimin' to catch a ghost?"

I shook my head. "There are a lot of things I never would've believed possible just a few weeks ago."

"Damn straight. I've changed my mind about how haunted houses are just places with strong EM fields. Or that spooky corridors just have infrasound givin' people the creeps. 'Cause I used to think, if you take away those things, then all the spooky stuff disappears, so that proves there were never any ghosts. But hell, now I see it's the wrong cause-and-effect. I mean, if you kill all the bamboo trees and then all the koalas disappear, it isn't right to say there never were any koalas."

That got a chuckle out of me. "I think you mean pandas. Koalas eat eucalyptus."

"Whatthefuckever. If a standin' wave is their habitat, and electricity's their food, what happens if you take all that away? They disappear. Except when that happens to pandas, you get dead pandas as evidence, but when that happens to ghosts, all you get are a bunch o' scared people swearin' they saw somethin' white with black circles where their eyes oughta be." Roy glanced inside the nook and jerked back. "Holy hypershit. The gauge just came on."

"Sweet."

"But we got a long wait. It took me nearly an hour to corral the horse's soul."

"We're not waiting. We'll leave it and come back tomorrow."

"You got my vote. Let's go get your girl."

We started to back up when Torula's shout echoed around us. "No, don't!"

Fear sliced through me, and I half crawled, half stumbled my way out. I was in a nightmare, not moving even though I was running as fast as I could. A beam of light swung towards me from up ahead.

"Bram?" Torula called out.

The sight of her standing safe where I'd left her released me from the bad dream. "Are you all right?"

"It's Thomas. He's taking Truth—" She swayed and staggered forward then collapsed in a heap on the ground.

"Spore!" I rushed forward and lifted her in my arms. *Goddamn it. She needs the jammer.* I clambered up the stairs and carried her out, laying her gently on the grass and resting her head on my lap. "Spore, can you hear me?"

Roy emerged from the basement, and I pulled out my car key and tossed it to him. "Her jammer's in the car."

He caught it and froze, gaping at a spot behind me. I clenched my fist, just as I heard a stranger's voice say, "What seems to be the problem here?"

I whipped around to see two police officers walking down the pathway towards us. Human cops, not robots. Good. We had a chance to reason our way out of this.

I glanced up at the small window where the light had turned on earlier—which now suddenly turned off. My hands tightened protectively around Torula as I forced my breathing to calm down.

"She fainted," I said. "We need to get her away from here."

"Were you out drinking, sir?" the policeman asked.

"Heck no," Roy said. "She might be pregnant."

"She's claustrophobic," I said. "We went into the basement, and she couldn't handle it."

"That section is off limits to the public, sir."

"Yeah, well . . ." Roy cleared his throat. "We were just huntin' for ghosts. That's not illegal, is it?"

The cops exchanged doubting glances. "Did you say ghosts, sir?"

"Technically, just one," Roy said. "One ghost."

"You grulmrulmrulmi," Torula mumbled.

"Ma'am, are you all right?" the female officer asked.

"A protocol Manhattan tavern her," Torula said, but only half her mouth moved.

I clenched my jaw and fought to keep my composure.

The officer moved closer and peered at her. "Could you raise both arms, ma'm?"

Torula raised her left arm, but the right one remained limp on her side.

"Both arms, Spore." I stared nervously at her right arm.

She just lifted her left arm higher.

"She could be having a stroke," the officer said.

My heart thudded, and a trickle of blood oozed out of Torula's nostril.

"Jesus." I reached into my pocket, and the officers reached for their weapons.

"Keep your hands where we can—"

"It's just my handkerchief," I said. Cautiously, the officers allowed me to take it out and wipe Torula's nose. The frank red stain on white linen blasted a tunnel through my mind, bringing back the memory of a frightened toddler's dream. *I seed her blood wiped like that, then she died!*

50

AT THE EMERGENCY ROOM

I LIFTED TORULA IN MY ARMS AND CHARGED LIKE AN ANGRY BULL towards the road. The officers shouted out warnings at me until they realized where I was headed. Torula regained consciousness as we neared the police car. I set her down, and the female officer helped ease her into the backseat.

Roy brandished my car key. "Listen, I gotta get somethin' really important—"

"Please, get in," the officer said.

Roy sighed, shoved the key into his pocket, and complied.

As we drove away from the overpowering effects of the hyperwill, I glanced back at the church. *She should get better now.* But instead, Torula moaned and began to shiver. I held her close.

I glanced at Roy. He shook his head. Without the hyperjammer, neither of us knew how to help her.

At the emergency room, the police kept Roy and me confined in the crowded waiting lounge. The staff whisked her away, and I clenched my fists, clinging desperately to absolutely nothing.

Why isn't she getting better?

A resident arrived and asked me a flurry of questions. I craned my neck each time the emergency room doors swung open. The young doctor's words sounded muffled, as though filtered through gauze. What had the patient been eating? Had she been drinking? Taken any drugs? Any recent injuries? Other syncopal episodes?

"Other what?" The unknown term jumped out and rose above the melee in my mind. That's when I was told: Torula had lost consciousness again.

"What's wrong with her?" I fought the urge to push aside the petite intern and charge into the emergency room. She said she would return as soon as she had answers.

I need to get the hyperjammer.

I glanced at the exit. *What if I made a run for it?* A police officer loomed into view and wiped the plan off of my mind. I glanced around, like a man who'd misplaced his purpose, and my gaze landed on Roy, who'd been watching me.

"You okay, man?" Roy asked.

"She needs the jammer."

"Been tryin' to figure out how to tell 'em that." Roy bobbed his head towards the cops. "But there's no twistin' a tale that'll make any sense."

I paced, aching to do something. Anything, besides wait. A phone call came in, and I answered my iHub only to find out it wasn't the one ringing. Eyes on my wristband, it dawned on me to call up Torula's mother to tell her where I was and why.

The officers approached and said a caretaker from the mission had confirmed the church wasn't going to press charges. We were to be let off with nothing but a reprimand—to grow up.

Roy hitched a ride with the cops back to the church to get the car, and I stationed myself by the emergency room doors. I peered through the view panels and saw too many curtains, too many people. I stepped back. The sign on the wall said "one companion for each patient." *Then why am I outside?*

A nurse bustled by, and I stopped her. "A patient, Torula Jackson. Dr. Torula Jackson. She's alone inside. I need to—"

"Sorry. We're filled beyond capacity. We need to restrict who can be allowed companions at the moment."

I took a seat, stood up and paced, sat down again, then repeated the cycle. Just when I was about to call Roy to ask what was taking so long, he came striding through the entrance.

The crowd seemed to part as Roy approached, the hyper-jammer on its chain dangling from his hand. Time slowed down as Roy lifted his hand and—

A tall blonde woman stepped into his path, and Roy shoved the jammer into his pocket.

I charged forward, but just as I neared him, Roy raised his voice. "Now what's a damned reporter from *Theory* got to do with me?"

I veered to the side and walked on down the corridor.

Damn. Getting the jammer to Torula was more important than whatever I thought NASA might think.

I turned back and locked eyes with Roy who was walking towards me, still arguing with the reporter. The chain dangled freely out of his pocket.

I strode past him, eyes forward.

"Don't believe everythin' the cops tell you. Now, go bug somebody else."

I zipped past him, and my fingers hooked around the chain, yanking the hyperjammer cleanly out of his pocket and into my hand. My purpose was restored.

I glanced back at Roy marching out of the hospital, the reporter by his side.

Clutching the hyperjammer like a talisman, I pushed the emergency room doors open. It was like diving into a turbulent sea, but I welcomed the chaos. It kept me invisible as I searched for Torula. Above the hubbub, or perhaps beneath it, I heard her moan. She lay on her side on a gurney pushed against a wall along a walkway.

"Hey," I said. Her lips were pale, but her eyes were a deep shade of anxiety. "How're you doing?"

"Caribou sleigh?" she asked.

"What?" I leaned closer.

"Can you soufflé?"

I forced out a comforting smile. "You're going to be fine." Gently, I lifted her head and slipped the chain around her neck. I twisted the jammer, checked for the ring of light that confirmed it was on, then tucked it beneath her shirt.

"There," I said, my tension easing. "You'll be all right now."

She nodded, and I sighed with relief. Then her shoulders began to shake, and her eyes rolled up into their sockets, her body wracked by a convulsion.

"She's seizing." Someone pushed me aside before I could say or do anything. A nurse ushered me outside—back to the waiting area where everyone was reduced to useless.

I stared, mouth agape, at the emergency room doors as they swung shut, as though telling me, "You should have stayed out."

My heart pounded, barely able to keep up with my thoughts that ran wild.

Did our experiments lead to this? Manipulating EM waves. Capturing her resonance. Testing her fears.

My head began to throb. I found a seat and surrendered to the wait, all the while wrestling with myself whether I should take the hyperjammer back or leave it be.

After a long while, a familiar voice cut into the gnarled thread of my thoughts.

"Bram, how is she?"

I glanced up, surprised to find Triana there. Then I remembered I had called her. As I shared the little that I knew, the intern returned, and Triana introduced herself as the patient's mother.

"Her condition has stabilized. But we found a small lump in her neck during the routine examination. Did you know about that?"

"No," Triana said. "Have you taken a biopsy?"

"Yes. We're just waiting for the results."

Triana was then subjected to the same questions I had been

asked. For the first time, I found things out about Torula's father she herself probably never knew. He was French-Japanese. A microbiologist who died in a sporting accident when Torula was five years old. As far as Triana knew, he had no family in America. They were all either in Europe or in Japan.

"I need to be with her," Triana said.

"I'm sorry," the fledgling doctor said and gave some reason we had no choice but to accept.

Triana glanced at me. "I'll be back," she said then stalked off.

I sank into my seat and did my best to ignore the caustic thought that this had all begun with my return. I tried to crack my knuckles, but I'd exhausted every pop and snap I could get out of them.

When Triana returned, her mouth was set in a grim, straight line. "Come on. We're leaving."

"Leaving?"

"We're moving her to Tromino's hospital."

51

AS THOUGH NOTHING WAS WRONG

TORULA'S HOSPITAL ROOM BORE THE SOOTHING COLORS OF AUTUMN, with drapes and furniture dipped in shades of gold and brown. A homey atmosphere, no doubt meant to be calming. Still, the ground beneath my feet trembled as I walked, and I put on a relaxed smile as though nothing was wrong.

"Nice place you got here," I said, taking a seat on the daybed, which looked much like a regular couch.

"Glad you like it," Torula said from her hospital bed, still wan but doing her best to be her usual self too. We had an unspoken agreement to treat her condition as if it weren't there. After all, we still didn't know what it was. The only thing we knew for certain was that she wasn't pregnant. It was a relief to us both, though a part of me was somewhat disappointed.

"Mustard curtains. Mayonnaise walls. Furniture the colors of coffee and burgers." I breathed deep—half-expecting the smell of a deli but inhaled citrus-scented disinfectant instead. "You'll gain weight in a place like this." Since laughter was the best medicine, I doled it out as much as I could.

She smiled, and blood slowly oozed out of her nostril.

"Jesus." I rushed to her side and handed her a tissue box from the bedside table.

She closed her eyes, tilted her head back, and stanched the trickle.

"Should I call a nurse?" I couldn't keep the act of nonchalance any longer.

"No. They're coming to get me for some tests anyway."

I slipped my hand into my pants pocket to clutch the hyperjammer. I had removed it from Torula and turned it off before the ambulance ride. Her condition had started when she wasn't wearing it and worsened when I had turned it on. It was probably doing more harm than good or, more likely, serving no purpose at all.

Torula sniffled and looked at me. "I know what you're thinking."

"I doubt it." I'd lost all comprehension of my own thoughts hours ago.

"You're worried Truth's dream might be coming true."

I smirked to hide my fears. "No, I was actually thinking . . ." I looked at the blood-stained tissue in her hands. ". . . ketchup."

She almost chuckled but winced instead and laid her fingers against her temple. "Don't . . . make me . . . laugh."

"Sorry." I didn't know what else to do.

The door swung open, and a nurse with a wheelchair walked in.

"I'll come with you," I said.

"No," Torula said. "Stay here and rest. You look—"

"Awful, I know."

She smiled, but the pinched corners of her eyes told me she was covering up her pain. "You need some sleep. Stay here and wait for Mom. She just drove Truth over to my aunt's. She'll be back soon."

The nurse wheeled her away, and in the sudden emptiness, I realized it wasn't the ground that was trembling. It was me from exhaustion. I sat back down on the daybed, closed my eyes, and let waves of slumber lap over me.

Just as the heaviness lifted off my shoulders, the swoosh of someone entering the room snapped me back to wakefulness.

Tromino, in his white doctor's coat, grunted a greeting as he snatched the cliPad from its holster. I watched in uncomfortable silence as he tapped through Torula's medical records.

He scowled. "I need you to confirm this. It says she may have had a TIA, but she never saw a doctor about it?"

"What's a TIA?" I fought to keep my eyes open as I looked up at him.

"Transient ischemic attack. A mini stroke. It says here she experienced temporary blindness, aphasia, paresthesia—"

"I . . . I don't know those terms."

"Difficulty speaking, numbing or tingling of the limbs. You were there when these happened?"

"Yes."

"And you didn't do anything?"

"She recovered."

"For God's sake, her words were slurred, and she had transient vision loss. That didn't alarm you?"

I scrambled through the cobwebs that clouded my memory, uncertain why everyone else had just let it go. "We thought it was just because . . . she was about to pass out."

"Just because?" Tromino glared at me like a flabbergasted principal about to expel the school dunce. "Why would you think it's normal for anyone to pass out? What was she doing? Sitting in a centrifuge at NASA?"

Jesus. Where was my mind?

"What was she doing?" he asked again.

"She was . . . at the greenhouse." I kneaded my forehead trying to recall when Torula had lost her vision. "It was an experiment involving EM waves and holograms."

"How many others in the staff exhibited the same symptoms?"

I swallowed. "None." I felt the dunce cap fall over my face and smother me.

The door swung open, and Triana walked in. Tromino gruffly slipped the cliPad back into its base.

She glanced at the empty bed. "Where's Tor?"

"Getting more tests," I said.

She turned towards her son. "And what do we know so far?"

He walked towards the door. "I'll call her attending and have her explain—"

"No," Triana said. "Tell me."

Tromino let out a heavy sigh. "Better have a seat then."

She sank down next to me on the couch, and Tromino took the chair beside her.

"What Torula had this morning was another TIA," he said. "Not a full-blown stroke, but it's a symptom of something else. Tor has a rare disease of the distal internal carotid arteries called Moyamoya."

The faintest frown flickered on Triana's brow.

"What does that do?" I asked. "What does it mean?"

"It's a progressive cerebrovascular disorder caused by blocked arteries at the base of the brain. The only treatment is surgery for revascularization, a bypass to improve blood flow to the brain." Tromino's face remained stolid, marking him as a veteran at separating his profession from his emotions.

"How does one get . . . Moyamoya?" I asked.

"The etiology is unknown, although there's some indication it could be hereditary."

"Not from me," Triana said, vehemently.

Tromino nodded. "It's more common in Asian populations. Particularly the Japanese. But one more problem is—her condition's concurrent with a thyroid tumor."

"Papillary carcinoma?" Triana asked.

Tromino nodded. "A common form of thyroid cancer. It should be easily treatable."

Cancer? No! A hole opened up beneath me sending me straight into hell. "What do you mean by easily treatable? It's not serious, then? She's out of the woods?"

"I think we discovered it in time, but—"

"But what?" I asked. "She's a strong girl. She can fight this."

Tromino glowered at me. "And you think I believe otherwise?"

"Because you said 'but!'" I got to my feet, the tension too much to bear.

"But?" Tromino also rose from his seat. "I say 'but' and you think I've given up on my sister? How many foolish conclusions do you come up with in a day?"

"Foolish is when a doctor gives up even before the patient does."

Tromino moved a step closer. "You've got some nerve to say that. You're the genius who completely ignored her symptoms."

"Boys!" Triana's tone was sedate but potent enough to dilute the tension in the air.

Fighting would be much easier than having to deal with how I felt, but I opted to turn away from the battle. So did he.

"What's the prognosis?" Triana asked.

Tromino stared at his mother before giving a reply, as though weighing his answer if it was something she could take. "With the hemorrhage and ischemia, she's in poor clinical condition. And there's biochemical evidence of hyperthyroidism caused by the carcinoma which could explain the rapid decline. Though we'd rather wait until her condition improves, we've scheduled surgery for Wednesday. But . . ." He glanced at me.

But? I narrowed my eyes.

"But they see only a 3 percent chance of success."

52

BASED ON STATISTICS

TORULA LAY SLEEPING IN HER HOSPITAL BED, HER TEST RESULTS READY to point at the next step to take. I tried to wrap my head around that 3 percent chance. What did it mean, really? I'd heard of people with no chances of surviving at all who still made it. Christ. There'd been patients declared dead before they got up and walked again. So 3 percent still meant she had a chance, didn't it?

I sat with arms crossed and stared at the doctor seated on the couch. The man tasked with saving Torula's life. He looked bronzed and pale at the same time—an olive-skinned man who never got any sun. Black-haired yet almost bald.

We kept our voices hushed as we talked.

"That's it?" I asked. "That's how doctors calculate the chances of a patient surviving a treatment? Based on statistics?"

He nodded, his eyes sparkling with intelligence from beneath thick brows.

"You must have some elementary particle of life in your equations," I said. "Something like photons, electrons, gravitons?"

"You're asking if life has a counterpart to those?" His eyes narrowed as he pursed his lips.

I cracked my knuckles in the silence that followed.

"No, I don't believe it does. But then, I'm not the doctor of biology in the room. She is." He glanced at Torula and was about to say something more when the door swung open, and Triana entered the room.

"Oh, thank you so much for waiting, Germs." She touched her cheek against his then walked over to Torula and gently roused her. "Sweetheart? The neurosurgeon's here to explain the procedure. Are you up for it?"

Torula opened her eyes by a slit. I came to stand at the foot of her bed and smiled to reassure her. Encourage her. I don't know, maybe to let her know I was worried like hell but knew everything would be all right.

"Tor," Triana said, "this is Dr. Najafi. He's the best man alive to perform this operation."

Torula slowly turned her head to meet her designated savior.

"Hello, Torula," Najafi said.

"Did my mom just call you Germs?"

"Yes, unfortunately, she did." He chuckled. "My real name's Jeremiah."

"I've called him Germs since pre-med," Triana said. "He was so afraid the nickname would stick, he'd never get any patients."

Torula sighed as though she were bored. "Will I end up a vegetable? Scale of one to ten. Ten meaning I'm a turnip."

Najafi was silent for a moment. "There have been very few case reports of papillary carcinoma of the thyroid associated with Moyamoya making this difficult to predict."

"Try."

He smiled, his bedside manner unwavering in the face of a patient angry at her disease. "The overall prognosis depends on how rapidly vascular blockage occurs, and in this case, it's happening too fast. Revascularization is most successful when performed under non-emergent conditions." He paused. "Ideally, we should wait, but a seizure or a major stroke could put you in a coma at any time."

"So you're saying—there's no time to waste, but we should wait?" she asked.

Seconds ticked by with no one speaking, as though this was the wait we all needed.

"So why can't we?" I finally asked. "She was fine just yesterday. She can fight this. Move the surgery to when she's stronger."

"There are no known drugs that can reverse the blockage fast enough," Najafi said. "Even now, we risk potentially irreversible neurologic deficits."

"Or worse, right?" Torula said. "So if I don't die waiting, I could die from surgery done too soon."

"Don't say that," I said.

Triana shook her head. "Don't even think that, dear."

"Seems I've got nothing to lose. Except . . . everything." Her eyes seemed to go blank.

"No." It sounded more like a snarl than a word when it came out of my mouth as the hospital walls closed in around us. "You're stronger than the doctors think, Spore. I know you."

Torula shut her eyes tight and shook her head.

Her mother stroked her hair.

"Army igloos stink," Torula said. "We Donatello Picachu on trial." She opened her eyes and looked at Najafi.

He grabbed his penlight and shone it in her eyes.

"What did she say?" Triana asked.

I wished I could move closer. "This has happened before. A couple of times. No one could understand her."

Torula kept blinking as she stared at Najafi's face, gesturing with a hand and smacking her lips.

"Can you hear me, Torula?" Najafi asked.

"New shoulder bee sting solstice around a eunuch."

Triana glanced worriedly at Najafi. "It's Wernicke's aphasia, isn't it?"

"While having an atypical absence seizure," he said.

"What's going on?" I asked.

"Why? What happened?" Torula looked at me, as though *she* were concerned for *me*.

"Say something again, dear," Triana said.

"About what?"

"Can you hear me now?" Najafi asked.

"Of course."

Najafi checked her pupils again. "It seems you've just had an absence seizure."

"Don't be ridiculous. I was just . . . talking to you." She glanced at me as though waiting for confirmation of a reality she could no longer grasp.

I swallowed and struggled to hide my nervousness. "You were talking, but we couldn't understand you, Spore."

"Petit mal seizures can last for mere seconds," Najafi said. "Those having them may not even be aware they're occurring and recover quickly as though nothing had happened."

"You mean it could've happened before, and I didn't even notice?" My mind flashed back the past several weeks and found many occasions to blame myself for not having paid better attention. What an idiot I was!

"Oh darling." Triana clasped her daughter's hand. "There's no delaying the surgery. Bram's right, you know. You're strong enough to fight this."

I nodded my encouragement.

Torula looked at Najafi as though waiting for him to cast his vote about her chances.

"I promise to do everything humanly possible to make sure it's a successful procedure," he said.

Torula scrunched her brow and froze, her eyes suddenly fixed, seemingly blinded. "Something's happening," she said.

"What are you feeling?" Najafi asked.

"I see . . . sparkles. A sphere. A glowing sphere."

"Like an orb?" I asked.

Triana moved closer. "Is it Thomas?"

I reached into my pocket. "I'll turn the jammer on."

"No," Torula said. "It's . . . not out there."

"It sounds like a migraine aura." Najafi reclined her bed. "The byproduct of a famished brain. Don't worry, I'll give you something for the pain." He tapped his wristband and dictated his orders.

Torula gripped her mother's hand. "Mom, help me."

"I promise." Triana clasped her hand over Torula's. "I'll use medicine, blackmail, sorcery, and prayer to make you strong again."

I eased closer. "You'll be all right. You're going to win this."

My comforting words seemed to give the opposite effect. Torula gripped her bed rail as though on a raft about to go over a waterfall, her feet scraping the sheets as she tried to edge away from her fate. Her eyes were fixed on some haze inside her mind. She was staring at her symptoms, drifting swiftly down a turbulent river, increasing in speed, and no one could do a thing to stop them. She turned to me, her hands sliding on the rails. "Bram, save me."

Her plea was like a blast of icy wind that engulfed me.

She turned to Najafi. "Find another way. Delay the surgery."

The doctor shook his head. "We can't. The immunologic stimulation of the thyroid—"

"I want another way!"

Triana leaned closer. "Darling, surgery right now is the best option we have."

No. I clenched my fists as Torula grimaced in pain. *Not with a 3 percent chance.*

Torula threw up. A nurse charged into the room and headed straight for her IV. Through narrowed eyes, Torula looked at me and clasped her bed rail in despair. "Make sure . . ." she panted as she spoke, ". . . they find another way."

"I will." I gripped her hand over the rail and held tight until her sedative took hold. "I promise."

53

THE FAILED TALISMAN

I STOOD IN THE MOONLIGHT STREAMING IN THROUGH TORULA'S hospital window. She'd been asleep for several hours now, and I kept the lights dim as I stared outside without really seeing anything. The hyperjammer felt cold between my fingers like the failed talisman that it was.

The memory of her grasping at her bed rails, asking her mother for help, calling out to me to save her—I wanted to crush the jammer in my hands the way her words had crushed me. All our lives, she'd been the one saving me. Now, it was time I paid her back.

She cleared her throat, and I was by her side in a heartbeat.

"How're you feeling?" I asked.

"Much better. The hyperjammer must be working."

"This piece of crap?" I shoved the device into my pocket. "I've a mind to throw it out the window. Turn it on or off, it doesn't do a thing."

"It's keeping Truth safe. Is that where Mom is—with Truth?"

"Yeah. She'll be back soon."

"Has she talked to Najafi about delaying the surgery?"

"I'm afraid *she* needs to be convinced first." I swallowed knowing it was the crucial first step that lay ahead for me.

"Then get to work on your sketchpad. I'm looking for a solution to my problem, and I need you to show her."

"My sketchpad?" That made no sense.

She pulled herself up but hardly budged. "Bram, you've figured it out. How life gets decided on. You know there's something that makes it all work."

"What do you mean?"

"I heard you talking to Najafi. I've had this notion that, like electricity and gravity, life is everywhere. But you think it has its own quantum, and I think you're right. Life should be measurable in a quantized form, and when the right quantity satisfies the equation, then energy or matter comes alive—or stays alive. Rembrance holds the formula that determines when someone lives or dies."

I jerked back at the sound of the word. "Listen. Rembrance. It's something I made up. Don't turn it into a fact."

"It's your mathematical theory that needs real-life proof. And you can prove it—through me." She breathed deeper with excitement. "There's an equation that doctors need to know about. Which shows life can be measured—not in years, but in quanta. And there's an equation for someone to find. I'm hoping you can find it through me."

"No, Spore." I couldn't let her grasp at mere straws. "That's not the answer you—"

"Like you said, equations rule the world. Maybe you can find out what my real chances are. Go beyond the doctors' data and experience and statistical analysis. Prove that 3 percent isn't all I have. Maybe then they'll agree to wait."

"Wait for what?"

"For my chances to get better. What if they can address the carcinoma first, then let me regain my strength. What if there are drugs out there still under trial? What if I fight as hard as I can—"

"Spore." I shook my head. "Even if an equation proves that

you're overflowing with life—which you are—the fact remains that you're at risk of a stroke at any time. They need to operate right away."

"Then they'll kill me doing it."

My face contorted in anguish beyond my control. "No. You're going to make it."

"I know." She smiled. "I know all my memories will." A tear fell from her eye. "But not my body."

I grasped her hand. "I promised you . . ." I took a ragged breath and willed myself to say what I wasn't sure I should be saying. "I promised I'll make sure the doctors find another way to save you. I think I have."

She gazed at me unblinking, the glow of expectation in her eyes.

"Do you trust me?" I asked.

"With my life," she whispered.

My heart pounded. "Only if you will let me . . ." I gripped her hand in both of mine. "I can make you a willdisc—and *save* you."

54

PAST THE SIXTY DAYS

I SAT ON THE STEPS LEADING UP TO ROY'S PORCH AND STARED UP AT A sky ablaze with starlight. I breathed in deep, wishing I could smell the scent of stardust as I stared. And stared. And stared. Up at the cloudless night.

Man, it's beautiful. The unchartered ocean Torula and I could have sailed across.

I clutched my iHub, unable to bring myself to press the dial pad. I needed more time to sit. And stare . . . and stare. At the stars. The planets. The galaxies. And all that space! *There's just so much of it.*

But what I needed was more time. To be with her. To give her strength. And try to save her soul.

The door behind me swung open, letting out a shaft of light from Roy's foyer.

"Hey, bud. You okay out 'ere?"

"Yeah. Please tell Triana I'll be in in a minute. I just have to make a call."

"Sure, no prob."

Somehow, I managed to dial my boss's number to ask for more

time past the sixty days I'd been given. To see someone through to the end. And help with things . . . after.

Sympathy came through from the other side of the line, and Dave graciously agreed to let me extend my leave.

After I ended the call, I looked back up at the sky's open invitation still blinking far above. Later tonight, I would have to send an email to Dr. Grant canceling my second appointment. I bowed my head and accepted the truth. Whatever Torula and I had decided, it was out of our hands now.

I bundled up all thoughts of regret and sorrow over lost time and broken dreams, locked them inside a steel case somewhere inside me, and walked into Roy's home. I mustered a polite smile and a curt nod at Triana. "Sorry to keep you waiting." I'd brought her here to show her that there was another path her daughter was daring enough to take, and Torula was hoping I could convince her mother to let her take it.

Triana looked calm and comfortable, even as she sat with back straight and ankles clipped, next to Roy on the couch. Positioned across from her was a huge CCTV monitor showing her loosening the silken scarf around her neck.

Roy's living room, with its wooden beams, stucco walls, and arched doorways, struggled to keep its relaxing, inviting atmosphere after being invaded by an assortment of TV screens oddly scattered around the place.

With one click on a remote control, Roy produced an orb on the monitor facing Triana. It glowed next to his feet onscreen, even though nothing was visible to the naked eye. "That's m'dog, Boner. Now, I can't do Morrison's kind o' 3D magic, so I just grabbed whatever footage I could get and slapped 'em on." He clicked again, and the video image of a young yellow Labrador Retriever pasted itself over the orb.

Triana blinked in mild surprise. I leaned against an archway and crossed my arms, intrigued, though a bit anxious over what I was seeing.

"With this system, I can walk with 'im around the house, see?" Roy moved across the room, and the footage changed to a big and hefty Lab trotting next to him. As he left the range of one camera and entered another, the onscreen view automatically switched to that of the next camera. "He needs to sense me, though. If he doesn't, he sorta . . . snoozes, you know what I'm sayin'? So I threw together a signal booster, and for as long as I'm within 50 meters o' the iCube, he's good."

Roy walked back to us and plopped down into an armchair. "Sit," he said, and the dog abruptly changed to a much smaller Lab with a lighter coat sitting down. "I just started buildin' the library, so it's kinda hoppin' around a hodge-podge o' yellow Labs of all ages for now. But dependin' on how the Verdabulary interprets Boner's actions, the program grabs hold o' the right image to act as a coat over 'is orb."

Triana displayed a smile that stopped just short of her eyes. "I have to say, what you've achieved here is remarkable as it is. But . . ." She clutched the scarf around her neck. ". . . are you saying this is also what's in store for my daughter? A stream of home videos with bad editing?"

I looked intently at Roy, hoping for some reassurance myself.

"No, o' course not. Boner doesn't really have a good idea o' what he looks like or looked like. That's why I gotta help 'im along. But your daughter? She's one o' the architects who built this bridge to the other side. So she's gonna rock."

Triana clasped her hands on her lap as she swept her gaze around the network of television screens that were visible even up to the second-floor hallway. "Will we still be able to consider her . . . alive?"

"My dog's alive," Roy said with an emphatic nod. "I don't know how to explain it. I can't touch 'im, hear 'im, or see 'im like I used to. But it's like my best friend never left. He's right there." He gestured at the empty space at his feet. "I'm still figurin' out how to get audio and all that. But, I know—this is just the beginnin'."

A spasm seemed to course through Triana, and she clutched a hand over her chest. "Oh, I can't believe I'm considering killing my own daughter."

She'd finally said out loud the horrible reality I'd been denying. I clenched my gut and gritted my teeth so hard, every part of me hurt.

"Yo, now, you shouldn't be thinkin' of it as 'killin'." Roy moved towards her and cupped a hand on her shoulder. "It's more like helpin' someone 'transition.' You take someone from bein' a mortal to bein' an electromagnetic entity in a disc. That makes 'em *eMortal*." He grinned. "See what I did there?"

Triana closed her eyes, laid her hands over her solar plexus, and took several deep breaths. When she opened her eyes again, she nodded and smiled at Roy. "Well, I've no doubt your best friend is happy and content, even now."

"Damn straight." Roy held two thumbs up. "Death sucks, but we can lick it."

I sank onto the couch with a sigh—and it came out louder than I'd expected. I glanced at Triana and found her eyeing me. Probably gauging my ability to do what needed to be done—or my resolve to go ahead with it.

She leaned closer and tapped me on the knee. "Do you know why I wholeheartedly believe every person has a soul?"

I nodded. "Because of your near-death experience."

"Because I'm one of a set of triplets." She opened her purse and took out her cell phone and began scrolling through its files. "My sisters—Ana and Diana—and I were split from the same egg. But I'm different from them. My mother said my sisters were born laughing. I was born thinking." She handed me the phone showing a photograph of three baby girls, two of them smiling, the third one staring at the camera with brooding eyes. "As I grew up, I realized it's because I was born with memories and fears that neither of them had."

"Whaddaya mean 'memories?'" Roy squeezed himself onto the couch to have a look at the photo.

"I grew up with an irrational fear of getting beaten up—but only by my father. In fact, everyone thought it's why, as a toddler, I wanted to be called Triana Malarney. They assumed it was a name I made up to dissociate myself from my phobia." She dug for something else inside her bag. "I was a teenager when I died and saw my body from above. I heard and saw things going on around me even after my heart had stopped beating. Then it's as though an unseen force sucked me up through the ceiling and into a peaceful darkness, heading towards an unearthly light." She pulled out a letter envelope from her bag and held it with both hands on her lap. "Then I found myself in a sunny, beautiful place full of flowers and trees. And I could hear people and glimpse them in the woods all around me, waiting for me with such over-whelming love and joy, I felt it even from a distance."

She paused and shuddered as she sighed, as though still savoring those feelings. "Years later, in medical school, I figured out all those sensations had come from my brain, making sure that I relaxed and didn't get in the way of my body's efforts to save itself. It was a natural high to sedate me. That is, until I came to a brook. A barrier I had to cross, like a deadend." She looked Roy and me in the eyes. "I think this was when my 'hyper will to survive' came into play. I believe, at that point, my brain had shut down."

Roy inched forward in his seat, while I stayed frozen waiting for the rest of her story.

"Someone appeared beside me. At first, I thought it was my mom, then I realized it was a younger version of my grandma who'd passed away years ago. She told me to go back and be the good mother I was meant to be. But I didn't want to. Not because of what she'd said but because of something I felt. Something right there, in the woods, and I had to keep going to find out what it was."

The envelope in her hand teased at my curiosity.

"Everything was brighter on the other side of the brook, and I couldn't see beyond the glare. I put one foot in to test the water, and things started to feel awry. It seemed like my other foot got rooted to the ground, and I couldn't tug it free. And then I had this . . . suctioning sensation. As though the water in the brook was flowing stronger and its gurgling grew louder until it was all I could hear. I strained to see something beyond the light. Or hear something beyond the rush of the stream. But there was nothing."

She closed her eyes for a moment as if to relive her own death. "I pulled my foot out of the water, and things grew calm again, and I found myself suddenly gifted with hyperthymesia. Quite the opposite of amnesia, because suddenly, I remembered everything. Knowledge. Skills. Things I'd long forgotten—and other things I thought I never knew. It was a panoramic view of all my memories —both conscious and subconscious. As though my brain had lifted all its checkpoints, detours, and road blocks so I could have access to every conceivable reason I had to live. In a singular moment, every teardrop. Every smile. Every love was put within my grasp. To jolt my will into fighting for a reason to stay." She paused and breathed deeply. "It was a lifetime in a glance. In fact, it was more than one lifetime because that's when I chanced upon Stuart."

"Who the heck's Stuart?" Roy asked.

"Apparently, he was my son—from a previous life."

"No shit."

I glanced at the envelope again, even more intrigued.

"Of course, I had no idea who he was right away. Because suddenly he was just there. I was walking down a path, then I turned around and saw this little boy running towards me being chased by a man whom I knew was my father. But not my *real* father. It was some other man I'd never seen before, and I saw him hold up a stick about to hit that boy.

"I screamed and called out his name then ran back to save him. Then I realized, at that instant, that boy was my son, and I couldn't leave him with that man. The next thing I knew, I was being sucked back through a sea of white light, until I could hear the doctors and nurses again. And I begged them, in my mind, not to let me die so I could find a way to help Stuart."

She handed me the envelope, and what it held was a yellowed reproduction of a newspaper clipping from the early 1930s. The article spoke of a preacher man who had beaten his stepdaughter to death. The woman was survived by her "bastard son"—a boy named Stuart Malarney.

The story could have just been something she'd heard as a child, which had stayed hidden in her subconscious until it resurfaced when she'd "died," and yet it had wielded power over her life's choices ever since. "Is this why you never married? To protect your children from their fathers?"

"Four different men. Four different reasons, Bram," she said curtly.

Roy tugged the paper for a better view of it, and the image of the Labrador on the TV monitor ambled over as if to have a look too.

"The good news is, I never felt any fear towards my real father again. Eventually, I traced their death certificates and learned that the boy, Stuart, had died from pneumonia the same year his mother did. The preacher man died years later in prison."

She took the clipping from Roy, folded it, and slipped it back into the envelope. Boner settled down and scratched at fleas that didn't exist.

"I'm not alone, Bram. Many others can find evidence that their past-life memories can be traced to someone real. Do you realize what all this means?"

"That our memories don't die with us?"

"And that they seek to live again!" She said it as though she'd just made the discovery. "Past-life memories manage to reintroduce themselves into living, breathing human beings. As phobias. As recurring dreams. As unexplained memories or even skills from a previous life. How else do you think instinct was born?"

"Say again?"

"Not everything you know was taught by an elder. Millions of creatures are born and left to fend for themselves without a single lesson on how to survive. They're born with the knowledge to avoid the terror of a fall, the scent of a predator, the taste of poison —valuable information one normally acquires at the brink of death. Past-life memories are tiny morsels of ingredients stuffed into the recipe that makes up who we are. Sometimes those morsels enrich the broth, but others—like phobias—simply spoil it."

"You're shittin' me. You're sayin' there's parts o' hyperwills inside all of us?"

"They fight to stay alive. That horse's soul you found in the barn. Thomas in the church basement. Stuart's mother in my memories. And, I believe, my daughter's unfounded fear of dark and tight spaces. These are all fragments of souls that sought refuge in different places, by different means, some way, somehow —because they never crossed the barrier." Triana looked at me with eyes that were like a balm to my spirit. "This willdisc can be a repository for Torula's soul. It can buy time for medical science to repair her body—until she can move back in." She held the envelope up towards me. "To find the strength to escape death, all my daughter needs is someone like this."

I cocked my head, quizzically.

She tapped the envelope against my chest. "You're her Stuart Malarney. You're her reason to fight to stay alive."

Her words seemed to suck the air from out of me; I could barely breathe.

"The Japanese have a word for it," she said. "*Ikigai*. Torula's father had taught it to me. It means 'that which makes life worth living.' And I realized its power—while I was dead—and it became clear to me. All that life needs to do is to find the reason and the will to say 'no' in order to go on living." Triana gazed at me with wisdom that sparkled from inside. "That's all it is, really. Life is the ability of any bit of matter—or energy—to say no to the god of physics when it gives the command to decline into disorder. Life, simply put, is the ability to disobey. We prevail. We adapt. We heal. We fight to maintain our present existence. Even bacteria use that ability. Even viruses do. And I bet—so does a hyperwill."

And so will Torula. That's what Triana's eyes seemed to say. If only I could completely believe it, because all I saw ahead of me was dark, unknown territory, and I was too scared to take another step.

"I need to bring her back," I said. "Back into her body after she heals. I still don't know how to do that, or if it can even be done."

Triana grew silent and stared at the Labrador on the screen. Boner's image glanced at her, as though sensing her apprehension. "You said it took several hours to upload the dog's hyperwill into the willdisc?"

"Yeah," Roy said.

"Well, if you can find a way to work around that problem, the rest of it should be easy."

Did she just say "problem?" Acid bubbled in my gut. "What . . . problem?"

"Like you said, we need to put Torula's mind back into her body. It's not something you had to consider for Roy's dog. But with Torula, we'll need to bring circulation back within four minutes, or else her brain will start to die."

She might as well have loaded a gun, cocked it, and aimed it right between my eyes. I desperately riffled through the formulas in my head, but all were tied to the factor of time. The conclusion was resounding: A peaceful death for Torula would be out of the equation.

"HolyshitOMGfuck." Roy had said all there was to say.

Triana took a deep and calming breath. "For her to come out without any neurological dysfunction, whoever performs this procedure will need to lower her body temperature to 18 degrees to buy you time."

"How much time?" I mentally recalculated with the factor of temperature in mind.

"As far as I know, about half an hour. But someone must have figured out a way around that limit by now."

"Someone?" I stood up and paced as if walking would help me get past a deadend. "No number of experts can come up with an answer that doesn't exist."

"I'm not saying no one has the answer. I just don't know of anyone who does." Triana shrugged. "But I'm sure the two of you can figure it out."

"Hell, I don't have a frickin' clue either."

"I wasn't talking about you. I was talking about Bram and my daughter. He'll work on this side, she from 'the other side.'"

"Oh, sweet Jesus." Pain gnawed at the wall of my stomach, and I rubbed over where I felt the acid eating its way through. "I've been reading about other options out there for extending life beyond death. There's whole brain emulation. Computer-Brain Singularity. 4D Brain Engin—"

"Hell no," Roy said. "Think o' the soul, man. Think o' the soul! Listen to all the stuff you just said. They're all just focused on the brain. Nothin' but the brain. But your nerves extend to the ends o' your fingers and the tips o' your toes. And we got an EM field extendin' way beyond what our body hair can reach. It's a mistake to think the human mind is stuck inside the skull."

"I agree," Triana said. "What lies in the homo sapiens sapiens' head is a most elegant and logical processor—but it doesn't do the data gathering. It just sits there in the dark, waiting, untouched by light, and yet it lets you see. No pain receptors, and yet it makes you feel. We can observe the brain giving the orders, but it listens to an army of mindless advisors that have never ever been inside a skull." She glanced at the image of Boner on the TV screen, scratching his imaginary fleas. "Just look at him. Full of memories of the life he left behind with no brain getting in the way."

"What's that supposed to mean?" I asked.

"That three-pound gray and white organ in your head comes loaded with features the soul absolutely doesn't need. It has mufflers and blinders to ensure you don't get distracted from what matters most for survival. Accidental savants, people who suddenly become prodigies or speak in a foreign language after a head trauma? I'm convinced these are people who suddenly have a damper or two unlocked—sometimes temporarily, others permanently. As for the rest of us with blinders intact, our past-life talents and abilities are held at bay by our brain because we don't need all that irrelevant information to survive. It's the same reason we're all blind to the existence of ghosts."

Roy glanced at the invisible orb at his feet and petted it. "Heck, I'm not anymore."

Triana smiled and looked up the video of a dog that plopped down on its back for a belly rub. "The soul has a mind of its own, Bram. All your decisions are greatly influenced by a foolish proverbial heart, a mysterious gut feel, and a tingling in your loins. When you save a soul, you preserve even those things the brain doesn't consider part of its job of keeping you alive."

I sank back onto the couch, afraid to embrace her assumptions —as comforting as they were—knowing it was a logical mind that Torula needed from me in order to survive.

"Yo, why don't we get Thomas to help?" Roy said.

"Don't be funny, Roy," I said.

"No, I'm serious. There'll be all of us bashin' our heads together over here, why don't we give Jackson a brainstorm of 'er own on the other side?" He turned towards Triana. "Like I was tellin' you earlier, I went back to that California mission, and the people there were kind enough to let me retrieve our 'ghost bustin' equipment' from their basement. I bet Brighton can sneak you into the greenhouse so you can have a look at what we got in the willdisc."

"That would be grand," Triana said. "It would ease my mind tremendously if I could see a human hyperwill thriving inside a willdisc."

"Hell, yeah. And if you get to speak with Thomas, you can offer 'im the job."

I gaped at them as my mind danced around the bizarre idea of recruiting an old friend of mine instead. Someone better qualified. Someone I had no bloody idea how to find on "the other side."

Triana raised a brow. "I must say, that's not a bad suggestion. What have we got to lose?"

"Not our minds, that's for sure." I raked a hand over my scalp. "Because we've all bloody lost ours already."

Roy edged closer. "Just one thing. You know that Brighton wants to talk to the hyperdude to set 'im free, right? So you just gotta make sure he doesn't."

"*I* have to make sure? Don't you mean *we*?" I said, waggling a finger between him and me.

Roy then jabbed his own finger around at us to emphasize his pronouns. "*We* don't have a reporter on our tail. It's just *me*. So that leaves *you*. But I'm thinkin' you'll need Jackson." He glanced at Triana. "I mean, your daughter Jackson. Thomas responds only when she's around."

"That's out of the question," I said.

"Then maybe you can bring 'er baby brother instead 'cause Thomas likes 'im too, right?"

Triana tightened the scarf around her neck. "If you need a Jackson, then you'll get one."

"No way," I said. "You can't expose Truth to—"

"I'm the Jackson you need. My genes are the common denominator between your two mediums."

I balked at the suggestion. "Triana, you know how this thing debilitates its hosts."

"I need answers, Bram. All the answers I can get so I can convince Tromino to help us. You need him—and all his connections—to do what you need to do."

55

THE PSYCHIC AND THE PSYCHIATRIST

WE KEPT THE NURSERY IN DARKNESS. EVEN THOUGH ELDRITCH trusted the guards who had let us in in the middle of the night despite the TRO, there was no telling who would tell. Training the tiny flashlight of her mobile phone on the stony path, Triana followed me through the maze of electrified shrubbery, and there, by the 3D glass chamber in Greenhouse 3C, the psychic and the psychiatrist met for the first time.

"How do you do," Triana said as they shook hands. "I'm so pleased to meet a counterpart of mine for the undead."

I thought she was being sarcastic, but I should've known she was being sincere.

"Many people struggle to find happiness while they're alive," she said. "And if they end up still stuck here on Earth in the after-life, I don't see why things should be any different."

"I appreciate your point of view." There was a sudden hint of warmth in Eldritch's icy gray eyes, as though engaged in friendly banter at a cocktail party. She and Eldritch did seem dressed for it, compared to me, in my gray pullover and faded jeans, with a satchel holding the iCube slung over my shoulder.

"Mr. Radio had advised me that you've volunteered to come and take your daughter's place as a conduit to Thomas."

"Yes, and I'd like to thank you for agreeing to help us," Triana said.

He took a deep breath. "I do so with great reluctance. These experiments have taken a toll on your children's health. Why risk your own?"

"If this is the only chance for my daughter's research to reach any fruition—for her to find the answers she's seeking—then I'd like to ensure it has its best chances."

Had they been holding champagne glasses, they might have shared a toast.

Eldritch cocked his head. "I must emphasize, though. I only agreed to risk the TRO for the chance to set Thomas free and guide him to the other side." He bowed slightly at Triana. "But as agreed, I'll wait until after you've asked him what you need to."

Triana nodded, smiled, then averted her gaze, turning towards the empty glass chamber. Eldritch hadn't been told about Torula's real condition and why Triana was willing to face any consequences in order to see Thomas. All he knew was that Torula had fainted during our "ghost hunt" and that she was still too weak to come view the hyperwill today. "I'm ready," Triana said. "How do we begin?"

I walked up Starr's workstation platform, set up the iCube, and activated the Verdabulary—but this time, I disabled all computer-assisted "extrapolation." The hyperwill we'd captured in the church basement would make an appearance inside the pitch-black glass chamber in whatever time-ravaged state it was in by now. I'd expected to feel more enthusiastic about seeing it, but maybe because I'd reconstructed it from head to foot, the mystique had all but faded.

A glowing vortex descended like a lazily spiraling mist, turning into a shapeless swirl that slowly coalesced. "Okay, brace yourselves," I said. "If the information has deteriorated beyond what the Verdabulary can read, I don't know how ugly the sight's going to be."

I waited for the tattered remnants of a turn-of-the-century man in blue to fade in, but then . . . What the devil? I gaped at the image that appeared. *Who the hell is that?*

I faltered towards the stairs. Mouth open. Mind frozen. I miscalculated the first step and half-tumbled down. Limping my way towards the chamber, I stopped once I came within the glow of the unfamiliar apparition. It stood nearly motionless and unresponsive, just like Thomas's hyperwill had done, but all the similarity ended there.

This manifestation looked like a twenty-something-year-old man from the early 1900s, attempting to look well-dressed minus the means to do so. He wore a rumpled brown suit with a wide necktie, trousers a tad too big, and a cloth hat that belonged on Sherlock Holmes's head. No blue flowers. No bright blue clothes. Everything was as drab as the Great Depression, but the image, down to the details, was intact.

"Well, that's good," Triana said, staring at me. "You look like you've just seen a ghost."

"I have. I am. That's . . . that's . . ." I pointed at it. ". . . the wrong ghost."

"No," Eldritch said. "I can sense this is him. This *is* Thomas."

"What are you talking about? This bloke's from the wrong century altogether!"

"Don't be distracted by how he looks to us now, Mr. Morrison. What we were seeing before was how he had chosen to communicate with Dr. Jackson. He was sending her a message. Remember, they speak—"

"In symbols. Yeah, yeah." It was a great excuse for not understanding what the hell was going on. I shook my head as I stared at the apparition of a man who seemed lost in thought on the wrong side of the road, waiting for the stoplight to change so he could cross over. *I wonder how long that stoplight's been stuck on red.*

The hyperwill blinked and seemed to sigh.

"It's disorienting, where he is," Triana said, observing the motionless apparition. "Perspectives get distorted. Focusing is a challenge. And communicating to the living? I had no clue how to do that."

Eldritch raised his brow. "You had an NDE?"

She nodded. "Traveled all the way to the barrier. And I was convinced that if I'd gone through that barrier, there was no turning back. My life would've come to an end." She raised her chin. "An end, Eldritch. That's why ghosts make sense to me. They're not interested in crossing over, because it means this life—this precious one they're desperately holding on to—would come to an end."

He sighed. "It is, indeed, a point of no return, but it's not the end. It's the entranceway to our next existence."

"But what if I don't want the next one? I want this one. I *love* this one. This is where I've built my home in every deeply mean-ingful sense of it. And then there's all the knowledge I've gained. All the experiences and relationships I never want to forget." She turned towards the hyperwill inside the chamber. "Which is why I would want to have a talk with Thomas. I want to find out how he feels about that barrier, and if he'd be interested in . . . an option."

"What kind of option?" Eldritch asked.

"To stay on in the willdisc."

His face hardened. "To keep him trapped in your crystal cage?"

"It's not a cage," I said. *It's not something I'd consider for Torula, if it were.* "Do you think your skull is like a prison for your brain? It's protection. That's all it is."

"Poor man," Triana said, waving a hand in front of the hyper-will's eyes and getting no response. "He's down to the barest minimum of what he needs to stay alive."

Eldritch peered at Thomas' expressionless face. "Do you really think he is? Truly alive?"

"He could be, but barely. Like someone in a hypoglycemic coma. The body shuts down in response to a severe shortage in fuel for metabolism."

Triana studied the image closer like an art aficionado absorbing details of a masterpiece. "See those little ticks and movements he still has? It's similar to what a person in a coma would exhibit. They could just be autonomous reactions programmed into memory. It doesn't mean the patient is awake. But it also tells you the patient isn't dead. He's just waiting—for his strength to return."

I swabbed my hands down my face, torn between optimism and confusion. "Look, I'm telling you, this isn't the hyperwill Torula was studying. I can show you the composite I made of it."

"Please do," Triana said.

I hurried to the workstation and, on the TV monitor, played back footage of the likeness of Thomas I'd digitally put together. "I made it as close as I could to what we saw."

"That looks like *The Blue Boy*," Triana declared the moment she laid eyes on it. "By Thomas Gainsborough. Except you have a man, not a boy."

A prickling sensation traveled up my spine. "What did you say?"

"The painting was of a boy not a—"

"No. The artist's name," I said.

Triana's eyes widened. "Oh, my word."

"I understand it now," Eldritch said, his voice registering some life. "He wasn't showing us what he looked like. He was giving us his name."

With the look of a man enlightened, Eldritch strode towards Triana. "Perhaps all we need is a little bit of 'fine-tuning' to get more answers from him. Would you mind?" He held out a hand towards her. She stared at his open palm for a moment then reached out and clasped it.

"Breathe with me," Eldritch said and began to inhale and exhale in a slow, relaxing rhythm.

Triana closed her eyes and followed his lead.

I cracked my knuckles, not quite used to the complete absence of objections in my mind. There was no voice declaring this a waste of time. No pressing desire to distance myself from the absurdity. I got up and watched them and let the ritual take its course.

Then, the hyperwill turned towards Triana, and in a voice I now recognized as Thomas's, the image spoke without moving its lips.

"Please help . . . tell her . . ."

Triana gasped and opened her eyes.

"It's using the Verdabulary," I said walking down the steps towards them. "It's a playback of something we recorded before when we first hailed it."

The image flickered and twisted like a transmission losing its connection.

"Stay calm," Eldritch said. "Stay with me."

Triana clasped a hand over her solar plexus and took a deep breath.

". . . (static) . . . help me . . . (static) tell her . . . my promise . . ."

"Oh, dear me," Triana said. "Are these his dying thoughts?"

It was saying things we hadn't deciphered from the recording we had. The hair on my arms rose as I listened to every word.

". . . I'm bleeding . . . (static) inside the church . . . (static)." The image glided towards Triana. "Tell her . . ."

"What's her name?" Triana asked. "Give me her name."

We waited, but no answer came.

Eldritch closed his eyes and clasped Triana's hand in both of his, drawing her closer. The hyperwill's lips moved, voiceless, and yet I heard his words . . .

I narrowed my eyes at Eldritch who was now speaking in a different, younger-sounding voice, devoid of his British accent. "Help me. I'm bleeding to death. On the floor, inside the church."

I shook my head. *He could just be making this all up.* Just like Roy's ex-wife used to do.

"What's her name?" Triana asked.

Eldritch gave no answer.

"Give me a name. Yours or hers."

"I need to tell her," Eldritch continued in his borrowed tone. "I'll never forget my promise . . ."

"Is your name Gainsborough?" Triana asked, feeding it an answer like she'd provided her toddler son the name Thomas. I curled my hands into fists. *This isn't right.*

Eldritch, eyes closed, tilted his head, scrunched his brow, tilted his head even more—but said nothing. It was obvious he'd run out of symbols to stab in the dark.

"Okay," I said, "let's not force things if there's really nothing there."

Eldritch slit his eyes open and glowered at me. "The spirits can sense distrust. It sends a message to them that they're not welcome."

"Oh, I doubt the spirits even care," Triana said. "It's not unheard of for nonbelievers to suddenly see a ghost despite their skepticism." She sighed and patted Eldritch reassuringly on the arm. "Come on, this is probably just stage fright. Concentrate and bring Thomas back."

"Dr. Jackson, it's not that simple."

"I'm not saying it is. But my daughter needs answers to convince others that this is real. And I think you can get them from that ghost." She looked earnestly into his eyes. "I believe you can. I know you can."

Eldritch took a deep breath and nodded then turned and stepped closer towards the glass, holding out his arms as though they were divining rods. Triana looked on patiently as he inhaled and exhaled towards the alpha-theta border, while I struggled against a nagging feeling that we should just pack up and leave.

Fix the frequency. It was like the thought hadn't even come from me. I glanced over my shoulder, imagining the suggestion had come from . . . maybe . . . Franco? Then suddenly, the words made perfect sense. Both Triana and Eldritch were new to this equation; we weren't on Torula's frequency anymore.

"I have an idea," I said bounding towards the platform. "But you need to come up here. Both of you."

I scrambled around the workstation looking for the gold electrodes Starr had used on Torula. I found them stuffed inside a box under the table. As Triana and Eldritch approached me at the console, I dragged two chairs and positioned them right next to the iCube. "Sit down."

Fumbling with the electrodes, I stuck some on their temples and scalp to course their brain signals into the Verdabulary. I double-checked the jacks and cables, tightened connections, and gave the setup one quick scan to make sure the settings were right, and then I realized the adrenaline—and skepticism—coursing through me weren't part of the cocktail this experiment needed. So I slowly backed away towards the stairs.

Eldritch eyed me with blatant distrust.

"Just give it another go," I said as I continued my quiet, backward exit from the platform. "And I suggest you put your hands on top of the iCube."

Triana surveyed all the cables and wires attached to her and asked, "Are you sure that's a wise thing to do?"

I stopped and reconsidered my retreat and marched back to stand between them. "Here," I said, putting my hand on top of the cube. "Put your hand over mine, and once you're more comfortable, I'll back away."

After another moment's thought, Triana complied, and Eldritch laid his hand on top of hers.

"Now what do we do?" she asked.

"Release your mind," Eldritch said. "Don't think. Don't listen. Just breathe."

I paused and took a breath, preparing to step away, and when I glanced up, Franco was standing right there.

I blinked—quite a few times—expecting him to be a figment of my mind. But he stayed right there like flesh and blood. Olive-skinned with thick black eyebrows, looking back at me, rubbing his close-cropped beard and dressed in something smart yet casual that he'd have worn to work.

He looked better than I remembered. Neater. Younger. And . . . alive.

My mouth hung open, frozen like the rest of me.

"Where are you?" my mind managed to ask. Was he floating around the ionosphere? In somebody's basement? In some kind of "Heaven?"

"Bro, there's no telling space or time here." His lips didn't move, and yet I heard him loud and clear.

"I can hear him," Triana said.

The moment she spoke, Franco's image dimmed and quivered.

"Hang in there, mate." I kept my eyes on him, afraid he'd disappear.

"He's repeating everything he said earlier," she said. "But now I understand every word. He's saying . . ."

Eldritch joined in, and they spoke the next words in unison. ". . . tell her to look under the floor. Inside our room. The money is for her and our son."

They were still communicating with Thomas? My heart thudded a strong, confused, excited rhythm. *Why can't they see you?*

Franco shook his head, pointed a finger upwards, and twirled a circle in the air.

"What does that mean?" I asked out loud, without meaning to.

"It means he's unaware of the passage of time," Eldritch said. "He doesn't know it's been decades since his death."

"No." "No!" "Niet." "Non." "No!" The speakers echoed denial in a dozen different Verdabulary voices.

"Oh, this is too much to bear," Triana said and pulled her hand off the iCube.

Like a bubble that burst, Franco disappeared.

"What are you doing?" I cried. "He's not finished."

"I'm afraid he is," Triana said. "I felt his pain. His fear of leaving behind the people he loves. It's too cruel to keep having him relive it."

"But you didn't see . . . everything." I tapped on the iCube. "We need to reconnect."

"I saw enough. Thomas is too far gone, Bram. That fragment is all that's left of him. He's no longer equipped to care for anything else."

"Then we must set this part of him free," Eldritch said, "so that he may be whole again."

"No, wait," I said, my breathing gone frantic. "You need to keep him talking. I need to think."

"Think of what?" Triana asked.

A circle in the air. What did Franco mean? I raised my own finger and twirled it around as I tried to decipher it.

"You want us to go around?" she asked.

I glanced at her, thought about it, then shook my head.

"Try again?" she asked. "You want us to try again?"

That made some sense. "I suppose? No matter what, we need more answers." I placed my hand back on the iCube. "For Torula."

Triana sighed and nodded then laid her hand on mine.

I glanced back to where Franco had appeared just a while ago, but there was no sign of him. Then I heard a child's giggle, and Triana sucked in her breath.

Inside the chamber, the hyperwill image had changed to that of a little boy flying a kite—a boy with dark hair who strongly resembled Truth.

Eldritch spoke in a cold, imposing voice. His real voice. "The boy is this woman's child. Leave him alone. Your actions are hurting people."

The hyperwill answered through the Verdabulary. "Please help. Tell her. Both of them." Then a blurry image of a woman in a long flowing dress appeared next to the boy. She looked towards us, and a cold jolt ran through me at the sight of her blue-violet eyes.

Holy Mother of Jesus.

I rushed down the steps and towards the chamber, as though all that was dear to me had been threatened, before it registered in my confounded mind these were nothing but muddled memories. Corrupted data—damaged and desperately repaired. I slowed down, realizing there was no way of—or point in—grabbing both the child and woman out of there.

Coming to a stop by the chamber, I looked back, and my heart sank. My impulsive dash had cost me my connection to Franco.

Eldritch addressed himself to the chamber. "I have some sad news to share, Thomas. Your wife and son, they're both gone now. They've both passed away."

The images of the woman and child disappeared, leaving behind the hyperwill in the ill-fitting suit, frowning. "No." His lips continued to move, but no sound came.

"He's insisting that he sees them living amongst us," Eldritch said.

"You're mistaken," Triana said, looking at the chamber. "Those are my children whom you see."

The image grimaced as though in pain.

Suddenly, I sensed a presence behind me, and then a familiar, overwhelming fragrance that could only be . . .

I turned and was stunned to find Starr standing there, tears glimmering in her eyes.

"It's time for you to go into the light," Starr cried towards the glass chamber. "It's time for you to join your Maker."

The Verdabulary issued a pleasant greeting. "Good evening. Where is Torula?"

"Leave Torula alone," Eldritch said sternly. "You're hurting her."

The hyperwill let out an agonizing moan, followed by the deep voice of the Corpse Plant. "Your stress is affecting me."

The image in the chamber crumpled and distorted, transforming into a fourteen-year-old version of me, smiling. I stepped back and gaped at the sight of myself through Triana's eyes from those many years ago—that last day, when I had to leave after my parents' death. "See you around, Spore." Then a wound opened up between his eyes—my eyes—and blood slowly oozed down.

"He's saying goodbye," Triana said urgently.

"No!" I said. "We have to stop him." He could be a bridge to

Franco. What if this was our only means to reach him? What if . . . What if . . . "We still don't have our answers." I looked desperately at Triana. "We need to show something to Tromino."

"Please, Eldritch," Starr said, her hands clasped. "Guide him into the light. It's the right thing to do."

"No, Bram's right," Triana said, rising from her seat. "He's proof the world needs—that the afterlife is real."

"You're breaching a holy boundary," Starr cried. "All of you. This isn't part of God's design."

The psychic frowned, one hand on the iCube, the other gripping the chair's armrest, as he glanced from Triana to Starr to the image in the chamber.

"Set him free," Starr called out.

"No, we need him." Triana reached out and touched Eldritch's hand. "Please . . ." she said looking intently into his eyes.

The hyperwill's image exploded into a thousand shards of meaningless data. "I'm thirsty," groaned the Verdabulary. Where the young man had been standing, the likeness of Truth appeared, blood dripping from his nose. Then it twisted and morphed into Torula, pale and weak, with blood oozing out of her nose too.

The next instant, a blinding white light burst inside the chamber. I shielded my eyes and turned away, but the light remained; it shone inside my mind. Then just as quickly, it imploded into darkness.

From out of the sudden, somber gloom, a familiar voice spoke crisp and clear. "Now, it's my turn."

Starr glanced our way. "Who said that?"

"You've been ignoring me," said a vivid image of Franco that suddenly appeared right next to Starr, looking at her. "I told you it's the wrong bishop."

She shrieked and staggered away. The next instant, he was gone.

56

OUR OWN VERSION OF SALVATION

GET THE DATA AND RUN.

Those words flared in my mind as soon as I noticed the Green Manor's security guards in their black and dark green uniforms. They were standing in the shadows some distance behind Starr.

What did Franco mean by "It's the wrong bishop?" Was it him who gave Starr the idea to tell her uncle? Would she tell us now if I asked?

"You're in contempt of court," Starr said, still breathing heavily from the shock of Thomas dissipating and Franco appearing and disappearing.

I heard Triana's voice from behind me along the stone path. "A Petition for Injunction with Prayer for a Temporary Restraining Order. Who else but you would come swooping down to grant the church's prayer?"

I mustered my most unruffled grin as I struggled to find some way of getting my hands on the Verdabulary information.

Eldritch took a slow pace descending the platform, his eyes to the ground, brow furrowed.

Damn. I wished he'd stayed up there. I needed his high-level security codes to be able to copy any data.

Starr lowered her arms to her sides, as though bracing for a showdown. "I believe in the Lord's promise of eternal life. That's why I'm here to make sure that every soul remains free to receive it."

"Do you mean that?" Triana asked. "Every soul?"

Starr's meticulously shaped brows crinkled. "What are you implying?"

"Cite me one passage from the Bible that says even a nonbeliever can have an immortal soul," Triana said.

"A nonbeliever?" Starr blinked several times. "Well, I certainly don't have every word of the Bible memorized."

"Really?" I asked, honestly surprised. "Nothing off the top of your head?"

"Well, there is a passage from John. That whoever does the will of God lives forever."

"And God's will is for us to believe, isn't it?" Triana glanced at me. "So what about us? Shouldn't we start looking for our own version of salvation? If we're not meant to go down this path, God can just step right in and stop us."

Starr gestured at herself and the manor guards behind her. "Well, this is God, stepping in."

"Why?" Triana asked.

Starr looked up at the starry sky through the glass ceiling, as though listening for whispered guidance from the divine. "And as it is appointed unto men once to die, but after this the judgment." She focused on Triana. "For the wages of sin is death, yet salvation in Christ gives us eternal life." She laid both hands on her chest. "I believe that, in my heart of hearts. What you're trying to do is only for God to give."

I scratched my jaw, like I was getting a rash from all the scripture flying around like pollen. "Could you quote us something written within this millennium, not two thousand years before my grandparents were born?"

Starr charged towards me, a crimson fingertip pointed at my chest. "*Every* culture has a complex belief in the afterlife. *Every* religion, a version of an eternal spirit. Belief in the hereafter is part of being human. It's burned into our DNA as a species. Atheists are the aberration."

"Does that mean we're the next step in our evolution?" I considered it a compliment. "You're calling me a mutant."

"I'm calling the police," Starr said. "You've violated the restraining order."

"Let them go," Eldritch said.

"Them? You're among the guilty."

"Dr. Benedict," Eldritch said, "what has just happened has made it clear that the Verdabulary is attracting other souls who wish to communicate. And this last spirit's message to you was to stop ignoring them. Don't take away this new link between our world and theirs."

"*Were* you ignoring him?" I asked. "Has this last hyperwill shown itself to you before?"

Starr raised a brow. "Why are you so curious? So you could capture this new spirit to take the place of the one who's crossed over?"

I swallowed. If I confessed that I knew the "new spirit," it would be the same as saying yes.

"I urge you to reconsider from the perspective of science," Eldritch said. "All these years, I've been guiding spirits into the light. Whether they were believers or nonbelievers, I never asked. Because *I* believed there was something waiting beyond the barrier. But I never really had a basis for that belief. Especially now that you've reminded me that that gift isn't meant for everyone. At least, according to the Bible."

Starr nodded. "It's also in the Book of John. 'Whoever does not believe stands condemned already.'"

Eldritch lowered his gaze. "I never knew where I'd been sending them, but it seems to be a place many souls choose to avoid."

"You've been doing the right thing, Eldritch." Starr's eyes softened. "Don't misunderstand what's going on. Christ wasn't avoiding reuniting with His Father when He stayed on to finish His business with His disciples. He remained on Earth, but after forty days, He ascended."

"But the Bible is for believers," I said. "Science isn't bound to accept the idea that there are souls lingering out there dealing with unfinished business. Give us the data that's been gathered tonight so we can uncover the facts."

"And you think science will pay any attention to you?" Starr crossed her arms. "None of you have the credentials to make this study any more credible than it's ever been." She flicked her gaze around the three of us, from Triana to Eldritch to me. "She deals with crazy people, he talks with the dead, and you're a wannabe-astronaut who wants to talk to aliens."

Triana huffed in frustration. "I can't believe my daughter considers you her best friend. You have nothing in common."

Starr's eyes narrowed to slits. "Be grateful that something good came out of this evening. The hyperwill we called Thomas has been set free. Because of that—and because *I am* Torula's best friend—I'm allowing you to leave. But have no doubt, all the data gathered during tonight's illegal activity will be deleted."

57

HE WAS MY FRIEND

Eldritch, Triana, and I were escorted by manor guards to our cars, and from there to the gates. Triana and I remained silent until we were out on the road; that's when I said, "At least, we still have a chance," at the exact same moment that Triana declared, "Well, that was a complete disaster."

"What did you say?" we both asked each other.

I smiled. "You first."

She looked at me, brows raised. "We've lost Thomas and will probably never get access to the Verdabulary again, and you're still hopeful?"

"I know the guy who appeared afterwards. I mean, I knew him. Know him. He was my friend. Or . . . is." I scratched my head.

"How do you know him? Or did."

"He was a colleague at Langley and a good friend. He died in a car crash just a few days before I came here. And I think it's a good thing that Thomas opted to . . . do what he did because I think that's what allowed my friend to get through. He was waiting for his turn." I twirled my finger in the air. "And he's the better ghost to brainstorm with Torula on the other side."

Jesus. *I can't believe that last sentence really came out of my mouth.*

Triana closed her eyes and inhaled deeply as if to savor the aroma of what I'd just said. With eyes still shut, she asked, "Please tell me you know how we can find him again."

I couldn't. So all I managed to do was swallow.

She must have heard me gulp because she asked, "At least, tell me you have a plan."

I didn't. So all I managed to say was, "I'll work on it."

———

Just as we arrived at the hospital, Triana received a call telling us to head straight for the ICU. But rather than take us to Torula's unit, an intern led us to a small meeting room next to the ICU section.

It had a table just right for six and a monitor on the wall. No windows and no attempt at décor of any kind. Even the plastic-and-metal chairs weren't all that comfortable because, I guessed, no one was expected to sit here for very long. This was probably where doctors met with family members to give them heart-wrenching news. Or where they were left alone to discuss if it was time to pull the plug.

I felt nauseous as I sat down to wait next to Triana.

Tromino walked in with an invisible dark cloud that defied the stark bright light of the room.

"How is she?" Triana asked.

"She's been moved to ICU. What else could that tell you?" Though his mother had asked the question, Tromino's eyes—brimming with hostility—were trained on me. "You. Are poison. You've pinned my sister's hopes on a lie."

"Stand down, Tromino Jackson," Triana said. "Is she conscious? What happened?"

He huffed a hot breath and took a seat at the end of the table, next to his mother, away from me. "Her latest MRA showed a sudden progression of another steno-occlusive lesion. Her risk of fatal stroke has gone up tenfold. That surgery is her only chance, and yet she's canceled it—because you gave her faith . . . in a hard drive?" He looked at me as though he couldn't believe I had any semblance of a brain.

"It's real, Trom," Triana said. "The willdisc is real. I've seen what it can do."

"Oh, yes, absolutely," he said with a sneer. "She's told me all about what it can do, and that Bram had to kill a dog to prove it." He spoke through gritted teeth. "This is barbaric."

"It's all part of medicine. Part of the oath to defy death," Triana said. "We saw off limbs, drill through skulls, and cut babies out of their mothers to save lives."

"Your solution isn't medicine. It's murder."

"No," I said, shaking my head. "It isn't murder when a doctor stops a patient's heart and cuts it out so he can replace it. We need to do this so we can save her."

"How? By pressing Ctrl+S?" Tromino glowered at me. "Torula's made of a genetic code, not a binary one."

"Hyperwills are alive," I said and sensed a heavy load suddenly lifting just by saying the words. "The hyperwill we saw, it—*he* had emotions. Sentience. He had a vision of a future and chose to give it up when denied what he wanted most. He may have been just a fragment of a lifetime, but whatever he was made of? It was enough to make him feel."

"I think, therefore I am," Triana said then laid a hand over her heart. "I feel, therefore I live."

Tromino got up and paced then faced us again with eyes filled with sorrow. "What kind of future will my sister live stuck inside a disc?"

"I can bring her back." My heart thudded with dread over my own claim. "Not as a disc full of data, but as the living, breathing woman we all know." Triana's gaze bore through the side of my skull as she watched me conjure up an empty promise—a promise Torula blindly believed I could fulfill.

"How can you be so sure when no one's ever done it before?" Tromino asked.

"Do you think it bothered Neil Armstrong when he was told to take a walk on the moon?" It was a left-field rebuttal, but it made sense to me. Torula was, in a way, going to take a giant leap for mankind.

Tromino gaped at me. "You think you can bluff your way through this?"

"Oh, give him a break, Trom." Triana waved a dismissive hand. "We all know it's never been done before. Every breakthrough medical procedure had, at the outset, never been done before. So stop being a bully and let Bram resurrect her."

"Resuscitate her," I corrected, and rose to my feet. "After she transitions her data into the willdisc, we buy Dr. Najafi the time to do what needs to be done surgically. Then, we allow her body to heal before she transitions back and we revive her—making it all part of a life-saving medical procedure."

"Of course." Tromino looked at me with a withering frown. "The surgeon couldn't possibly kill her because you've already done the job."

I heaved a breath and forced myself to calm down. "I have a design—a robot called Petey. A physical therapist for astronauts in suspended animation. It's even caught the attention of Dr. Rubin Grant of the Johnson Space Center."

"And how does that help us?"

"Petey could help Torula recuperate from post-mortem surgery."

"Post-mortem sur—" Tromino's face contorted. "You mean 'autopsy,' you idiot. And your influence has caused my sister to lose her mind."

"She's not losing her mind . . . she's losing her life, and she's doing all she can to fight it."

"Tromino," Triana said in calming tone. "Your sister is willing to risk her body so we can save her soul. That way, even if the operation doesn't succeed, we wouldn't lose her. We'll have time to find another way to make it work."

"That's the whole idea," I said. "To buy time to figure it all out.

Damn it, Tromino, don't cut her open just so she could die fighting."

"So why don't you just let her do that?" Tromino asked. "Let the operation proceed. And if there's a problem, you can step in."

"But you told me yourself," I said. "A peaceful death is out of the question."

"I told you?" Tromino scowled. "What kind of twisted—"

"The HPA axis. You said it needs to be under duress to trigger a strong enough sine wave pulse. A set of three, remember?"

Tromino's expression shifted from disbelief to sheer hatred. "You manipulative son of a—" He lunged. I stood my ground, but Triana rose and shoved her hand against her son's chest.

"Stop blaming Bram for all that's happening. It's not his fault your sister got into this. It's mine. I pushed her into it."

"What are you talking about?" Tromino asked, glaring at his mother.

"*I'm* the one who wanted her to study death. *I'm* the one who told her to go and chase the ghost. How could I have known that the price for understanding death might be her own?"

He shook his head weakly and moved away. "We're doctors, Mom. Our job is to fight for life, not study what comes after it."

"Look!" Triana thrust out her hands as though staring at putrid boils and lesions. But besides age spots and varicose veins, all I saw were fair and slender hands. "Past the peak of our reproductive years, our body believes its job is done and stops bothering with nonessentials. It begins to build up aches and pains, dulling our senses, making life progressively miserable. We age until each birthday just becomes another tick of the bomb. And our brain—including society's collective mind—helps keep us sane by convincing us there's a Great Beyond where Heaven waits just beyond the barrier. But I know it isn't there."

"Then put your faith in science," Tromino said. "Tell her to have the surgery. Don't pin her hopes on this foolish wizardry."

Triana grabbed her purse and started digging through it. *Is she bringing up Stuart Malarney again?* I rubbed my jaw uneasily.

She laid out bottles of pills, lotion, and sunscreen on the table. "This. This and this. *These* are what I call wizardry. Mesmerizing all of us into believing that delaying the inevitable is the best we can do. But now, with the willdisc, we have another choice. At the point of death, we can capture the powerful electromagnetic pulse our body uses as its data recorder. And just like that—we are saved."

"My God." Tromino's eyes locked on me like heat-seeking missiles that just wouldn't quit. "You've got even my mother wrapped around your finger."

"It's technology, Trom," I said. "The human body's like a machine. To fix it, you sometimes have to take it apart. The willdisc simply allows us to back up all her data in an external drive, but it's still conventional medicine that will have to step in to fix the hardware." I swallowed, having no choice but to admit the truth. "I can't do this . . . without your help."

"Good. That's why you're not getting it. Torula will not be turned into software. She's flesh and blood. *My* flesh and blood. And I'd like to keep things that way. So no matter your good intentions, I want you out of what's left of my sister's life."

I held his angry gaze. "You can't make me leave."

"Tromino," Triana said. "This is the worst step you can take."

He laid his fists on the table and leaned towards me, his next words like a knife carving a thin line across my neck. "If you don't leave, the illustrious Dr. Rubin Grant will get a message from me. Telling him about your state of mind, your recklessness, your pseudoscience in pursuit of the occult. Let me see you salvage your career—and your future in NASA—after that."

Triana touched her son on his arm. "Your sister needs Bram to go on. Without him, she could die of a broken heart."

"Open your eyes, Mom. It's the love of her life who's stepped up to the plate to kill her." A vein on Tromino's brow bulged as he thrust a threatening finger at me. "Make sure you get Torula to drop this delusion and accept the best that medical science can give her. If not, I will personally get in touch with Dr. Grant and have you fired on grounds of insanity." He snarled and strode out the door.

I collapsed into my seat and dragged both hands through my hair as I scrambled for some next course of action. Without Tromino's help, there was no moving forward on this.

"You can't leave," Triana said. "If you do, she would have no choice but to settle for surgery."

"Is that so bad, really? At this point, a 3 percent chance is far better than . . . than the zero options we've got. We have no medical team. No equipment. No plan."

"I thought you were working on it?"

"What?"

"The plan." She raised a finger and drew a circle in the air. "To find your friend on the other side."

I squinted as I stared blindly at nothing, finding no reason to look for Franco if we didn't even have a medical team that would take the first step with us. Even if we had a ghost, we didn't have a chance.

Triana sighed. "Could you at least stay until all this is over?" She picked up her purse. "Your presence may somehow boost that 3 percent to a much higher number." She then collected the bottles on the table—the potions and pills that were her secrets to slowing down time—calling my attention to her aging hands as she tossed them back into her bag. Then a faint tremble of a thought nudged my gaze up to the tiny wrinkles on her face and the flecks of grey her hair dye had missed.

A jolt ran up my spine. "I need to go to NASA." I blurted it out even before the thought had completely congealed. "I think . . . maybe . . . I can still chase an appointment there."

Triana looked at me with sad bewilderment in her eyes. "You can't do this. You can't put your career ahead of her life. I'll talk with Tromino—"

"Believe me, this has nothing to do with Tromino, and everything to do with her life."

58

A SUDDEN CHANGE OF PLANS

DEATH OR NASA. THOSE WERE MY ONLY WAYS TO ESCAPE LIFE ON Earth. The second had always seemed the better option because I'd assumed it always meant I'd be able to come back.

But now, I was going to try to turn things the other way around so that—even with death—coming back becomes an option.

Amidst the cutting-edge technology and the future-here-today ambience of the Johnson Space Center, Dr. Rubin Grant's office—with its antique displays and Persian rug—stood out like the anachronism that it was. Free of his knee pain and his cane, the man had his aura of strength and dominance restored as he strode from behind the massive wooden desk.

"Your original appointment was scheduled a week ago, am I correct?" Grant asked.

I stood by the door, laptop bag in hand, desperate on the inside, calm on the outside. "I apologize, sir. And I'm grateful you were able to squeeze me in with such short notice."

"What's this about? A sudden change of heart?" Grant took a seat on a tufted leather armchair and gestured at the matching sofa next to it.

"No, sir. There was just . . . a sudden change of plans." I cleared my throat as I took a seat, clutching the strap of my laptop bag as if it were a lifeline. I let go of it and went into freefall. "If you don't mind my asking, sir—of those you've invited to join Pangaea, how many have accepted?"

"Are you here to tell me I can count you in?"

I smiled and shook my head. "I'm guessing you're dodging the answer because it's not a number worth boasting about. Am I right, sir?"

Grant raised his brow. "Are you showering me with 'sirs' to keep from offending me? Just get to the point . . . *sir*."

I nodded, swallowed, and plunged right in. "You've been trying to recruit men and women in their prime, asking them . . . us, to leave Earth for good. I can't imagine the tough sell that is. You're aiming for a crew with excellent physique, who're emotionally stable, highly educated, responsible, ambitious. People at the peak of health with the brightest futures. Exactly like who *you* used to be . . . several decades ago."

Grant twitched in his seat. "I take it back. You don't give a damn about offending me."

I held up a hand in apology. "I didn't mean that as an insult. It was the deepest compliment."

"Enlighten me. I don't see how calling me a 'has-been' translates to flattery."

I reached for my laptop, hoping the facts would set things straight. "May I?"

Grant nodded and, for the next half hour, listened intently as I took him through my experiences of the past two months. He learned about everything Tromino had threatened to expose to ruin me. From my witnessing the apparition in a greenhouse to the software I had modified to decode it. I had managed, with Eldritch's help, to acquire videos of the apparition captured by the manor's cameras, including that of me walking right through a specter. Grant watched playbacks of the hologram I'd manufactured, footage of Boner when he transitioned, and how he "lived on" in a willdisc in Roy's garage.

Grant interrupted me frequently, asked questions, clarified details, double-checked the facts. I felt heartened by his enthusiasm. The director may have seemed like a man who relished the past, but deep inside, he was a child enthralled by every new thing that gave him a glimpse of the future. No wonder he had dedicated his life to pursuing the untried.

Unfortunately, the most compelling evidence I could have had —the consecutive apparitions of Thomas and Franco, a man whom Grant could have traced back to NASA—no longer existed. I didn't even bother to mention them because they would have sounded no different from a psychic's sideshow. So instead, I pulled out a willdisc and held it up for Grant to see. Light glinted off its titanium core and limned its curved edge. Tiny, vein-like sparks forked within the plasma wherever I touched it. "This is a willdisc. A storage device for a soul."

Grant gazed at the device and shifted in his seat. "You've given me a dramatic . . . or perhaps I should say disturbing, presentation. And it bothers me that this sales pitch started with you calling me old." He gestured at the disc. "I hope you're not suggesting I bury myself in that thing when my time comes."

My mouth twitched, unsure of how to respond. "Someone dear to me has fallen gravely ill, and her chances of surviving an operation are grim, to say the least."

Grant nodded, sympathetically. "Yes, I understand it was the reason you'd canceled your appointment. How is she doing?"

"Dr. Torula Jackson was scheduled to have surgery, but she's asked that it be postponed—until after we've moved her neural data into this." I laid the willdisc down on the table directly in front of him. "We're about to embark on a procedure that's never been done before. And if we succeed, it can change the entire future of space travel."

He jerked in surprise. "I'm afraid I don't follow."

I leaned forward. "Dr. Grant, I'm offering you a new breed of astronauts for Pangaea."

"I beg your pardon?"

"Dr. Jackson is prepared to make a test flight. Her body has grown frail, but her spirit remains strong. She can make the trip."

His brow quivered in seeming confusion. "Have you gone mad, Mr. Morrison?"

"Yes," I said, with a roguish smile. "As mad as all of you were when you thought of asking me to leave everything I have on Earth for a wild adventure to some pinprick in the sky. What's crazier? Sending ninety-nine astronauts to some hazy constellation? Or guiding one determined spirit into a remarkable new future, right here?"

Grant stared at me, dead silent.

I kept talking, just hoping the man didn't already consider me a lunatic by now. "Even the tiniest bacteria can prove that data from a dying organism can be transmitted on electromagnetic waves from one soundproof, airtight Petri dish into another. And today, technology all around us constantly harnesses radio waves to carry information, practically error-free, from sender to receiver and back again. The data in our minds behave similarly, and we've proven that it can be captured and stored."

Grant eased forward in his seat and touched the edge of the willdisc. "That's quartz crystal, am I right?"

I cocked my head, surprised he knew. "Yes, it is."

"We've had similar experiments involving living cells, proving they code their messages on EM waves. Quartz possesses the UV and IR transparency needed to transmit data from one sealed Petri dish into another. Glass, on the other hand, blocks them."

I had to make sure I got that right. "NASA has conducted studies on this?"

"Yes, but no credit due here. We merely reproduced findings the Russians had back in the '70s in Novosibirsk."

It was unbelievable. "What . . . what were the studies about?"

"I don't know why the Russians did it. We, on the other hand, were probing the possibilities of thought control." Grant leaned back and pursed his lips as he pondered.

He believes it. He believes memories can be captured on a wave. I reined in my excitement.

"Correct me if I'm wrong," Grant said, "but what you did to that poor Labrador. That is what your friend wants for herself?"

"As step one, yes. Then, we heal her body. At step three, we bring her back to life."

Grant paused then shot out of his seat with more agility than expected. For a moment, I feared he was about to call security. The doctor paced, his brow knotted, then he called someone up on his iHub. "Yes, one quick question," he said. "That project Sioux and Fein were transferred to, what's it called again?" Grant put on reading glasses and jotted something down. "Yes, of course. How could I forget? Might as well throw away those memory pills."

I stood and waited for Grant to settle back into the armchair before taking my own seat again. It was good to have been on my feet for a while. Though my heart was pounding, it felt like I'd lost all circulation in my limbs. My fingertips were ice cold.

"Level with me," Grant said. "Do you know what you're doing?"

My gut tightened. "Yes, I can definitely say—"

"Please don't oversell yourself. I need you to be forthright with me. Do you know how to bring her back?"

I swallowed and bobbled my head.

"I take that to mean you have no damn idea?"

I bobbled my head the same indeterminate way.

Grant clucked his tongue and leaned back in his seat, rubbing one knee with his hand.

"If . . ." I gritted my teeth. "*When* we succeed, it could be the breakthrough Pangaea needs to get its crew. After Torula transitions, she'll prove that, given a stable environment, consciousness can stay alive indefinitely. It will be one small step that's another giant leap for all mankind."

Grant winced. "Ach! You've just made Neil Armstrong turn in his grave."

"If he'd had a willdisc, he could be joining Pangaea." I buffed the promise I was holding until it gleamed. "Why cast a wide net when you can just reach out and pluck the low-hanging fruit around you? The smartest and brightest achievers who are far more than ripe for the picking."

"About to rot in our graves, you mean?" Grant's response showed no offense; a smile flickered in his eyes.

"You can aim for candidates who are experienced and used to riding high, whose biggest problems now are the degradation of their senses and . . ." I gestured at Grant's knee. ". . . the pain in their joints. Accomplished doctors, scientists, mathematicians, engineers—intellectuals whom everyone would consider too old and too weak to make the interstellar journey." I picked up the willdisc and held it like a gold nugget in front of a prospector's eyes. "What if you could offer them a chance to begin a new world where they can be young again—with all their memories of their Earthly lives intact, riding to the stars in curious little rings called willdiscs?"

Grant's gaze drifted to the side, as though frolicking in a theme park in his mind. But rather than easing it, my nervousness grew. There was one enormous question the doctor was now bound to ask. *How do we bring them back and give them new bodies?* Torula, though ill, was young and still capable of healing. What to do with aged astronauts? I was prepared to give a flurry of options, from clones to cyborgs and androids. None of these had solid-enough foundations on which to stand—but they were all I had for now.

The doctor took the willdisc and examined it. "I think crystal is far too fragile a keeper of one's memories. Do you have alternatives?"

I raised my brow. It wasn't at all the question I'd been expecting. "None, at the moment. We're aiming for something organic. I think." I cleared my throat. I wasn't about to mention pigs.

Grant nodded and handed back the willdisc. "Hmm . . ." He rose to his feet, this time more slowly, and walked towards his desk to access his computer. He glanced at what he had jotted down earlier, tapped on his keyboard, then focused his attention on his monitor.

After a long, tense moment, the doctor stroked his salt-and-pepper beard. "Why, exactly, did you come here today? Obviously, it's still not to give me an answer."

I walked over and stood across from him at his desk. "To ask for your help, sir. In exchange, Pangaea gets everything I learn in the process."

Grant pursed his lips and took a deep breath before posing his next question. "What kind of help?"

59

THIS WASN'T THE AFTERLIFE
(TORULA)

AM I DEAD? MY HOSPITAL ROOM HAD BEEN DECORATED IN AUTUMN shades, but now I opened my eyes to a brightly lit place of white and powder blue. *Would I recognize St. Peter if he walked by?*

A chuckle nearly made it out of me as I glanced around, but I barely had enough strength to even smile at the trick the room had tried to play on me. This wasn't the afterlife—it was the prelude to it. I'd been moved to the ICU, a somber place that borrowed what cheer it could from the color of a clear and sunny sky.

Mom was sitting in a chair next to my bed, her hands on her lap, back erect, eyes closed, earphones feeding her a private sound-track. Perhaps the lapping of waves on a shore. As I stared at her, something unusual at the center of her brow came into focus. It was a crease. Though a tiny one, it was enough to betray Mom's effort to maintain her calm.

In a span of one week, my mother had aged. My disease had knocked a dent in the decades she'd managed to defy.

Thanks to her and Bram, I had yet to wake up and find myself alone in the room. Even all my brothers fussed—Tromino through his worried scowl, Truth with his phone calls demanding to sleep over; even Treble, who was way across the ocean, sent a constant flow of video greetings. Everyone told me in their own way—*I am loved.*

A surge of tears came, and I closed my eyes to quell them. I knew how much each of them wanted to be there with me. To be near. So I would never feel alone. Was that how it would be afterwards? *Forever* afterwards?

I pictured Mom, stooped with age, wrinkled beyond redemption, meditating beside my soul encased in a digital time warp. I watched an older Truth, loading The Cellar with energy stores I needed before he rushed off to school. Then came an image of my eldest brother with his wife and children moving out of their home, Tromino having lost his license to practice. Then metal bars clanged shut, and I saw Bram in prison, broken and bent—a man chained to the Earth—paying the price for having killed a woman so she could remain blissfully undead.

My heart gave an anguished thud, and a soft sob escaped me. I didn't even know I was crying.

"Sweetheart, I'm here," came Mom's gentle voice along with a soothing touch.

I wept harder at the sound of those words, knowing that's how it would always be. They would risk it all for me, break every known code of laws—legal, biblical, medical—to save me. *I can't do this to them.*

"I want to go home." I gasped for breath and clasped my mother's hand. "Just . . . just let me go."

60

A DRAGON OF A DISEASE

Night had fallen, and I made my way through quiet hospital corridors heading towards the ICU. Turning a corner, I found myself in a bridgeway lined with windows where moonlight streamed through. It was like walking on stepping stones of light as I made my way back to Torula, ready to slay her dragon of a disease, with a laptop bag slung over my shoulder as if it were the only weapon I would ever need.

The fantasy of being her knight faded away as soon as I noticed a familiar figure, standing alone, head bowed, looking out a window.

"Triana, is everything all right?"

She turned slowly, as though afraid the very movement would cause things to go wrong. "Bram."

I waited for her to say something more, but words seemed to be beyond her now. I hurried closer. "What's the matter?"

She pulled her shawl tightly around her. "My baby wants to go home and die."

"What?" The hallway seemed to shudder. "What happened?"

"She's saying no to the willdisc. She's imagined the worst—for you. For me. For everyone who'd do anything to keep her alive.

She says saving her means breaking every known code of law, and now she believes fighting against death is just one big mistake."

"Why . . . why would she think that?" *She can't give up.* "What about the surgery?"

Triana shook her head. "She won't consent. She says surgery means a 97 percent chance she'll be dead before it's over. She'd rather live out the most of what she's got left. Bram . . ." She pulled her shawl even tighter. "Torula's accepted her fate. And people who believe it's all right to die while they're dying will give up the power of their decision not to die, rendering useless the will of the mind to overrule matter. Do you understand what I mean?"

Her words churned in my head. "I don't know. Maybe."

"I get psych consults like this all the time. Patients who make irrational decisions about treatments they refuse to have. If she were a patient, things would be crystal-clear to me." She looked at me with eyes that were like bottomless pits of sorrow. "I've lost all sight of what to do. I have no words."

"Just tell her . . ." I tightened my grip on my satchel's strap. "Tell her you agree to get her discharge forms processed."

She took a step back. "Have you lost your mind?"

"I have a plan, but I can't tell you about it."

"I'm her mother. There's no way I'd let you—"

I laid a soothing hand on her shoulder. "Torula's right. What we're going to try is testing every known law—maybe even unknown ones. If this explodes in our faces, you have to be in the clear. You've got Truth to think about. And Treble."

Triana's spirit seemed to go limp, her shawl falling off one shoulder.

"Just get her discharged." I smiled, even as my own heart pumped hard against the burden. "It's good news, Triana. Trust me."

Torula sat propped up on her hospital bed. Still standing by the doorway, I could already see the apology written all over her face.

I came to her bedside and kissed her on the forehead. Beneath the pungent odor of drugs, disinfectants, and antiseptics, I still detected the faint scent of lavender. It wasn't her perfume. It was her.

"What's this I hear?" I asked. "You're having second thoughts?"

"I didn't realize . . . how much was at stake for you. You could be imprisoned for this."

"Only if you don't come back to me. You promised we'd leave Earth together, remember?"

She gave a wan smile. "We both know you're the one meant for Pangaea."

"Hey, I can't leave without the only thing I have. It's not something I ever owned. But it's everything I ever wanted."

She reached out and held my hand. "Bram, you have to let me go."

"Go?" She'd just wrenched my heart out, but I acted as if it were still calmly beating. "Wait, are you backing out on me? You said you were going to help prove my Rembrance theorem. You volunteered."

She let out a breath for a chuckle. "You said so yourself. Rembrance isn't real."

"Of course I'd say that. I was trying to be humble." I forced out a grin.

"Slow coffee. Slash. Fast sugar. Slash. Stilettos. It's just an abstract thought scribbled in your sketchpad."

"But—" I clutched the thick strap of my satchel. "Every idea starts out abstract, right?" I slipped off the bag and slowly took out my paper-bound hobby, wishing I hadn't removed the sheet holding those random thoughts I'd scrawled down weeks ago. I flipped through the pages, skipping over doodles, discarded daydreams, and failed equations. "To be honest, I once doubted what your mother said about Mickey Mouse and Harry Potter. About how train rides can put people in the zone. Turns out . . ." I stopped at a page and showed it to her. ". . . some plane rides can have the same effect."

Her eyes widened at the sight of the formula I was toying with. "That isn't—" She stared at me. "Is it?"

"It's still a work in progress, so you're seeing it prematurely." I lowered the bed's side rail so I could explain the equation to her. "This product is the key: H_n. It needs to be greater than or equal to the value set by Rembrance for a hyperwill to be generated." I smiled with all the hope in the world bursting from inside of me. "And I can tell you— the product of your equation is far greater than the minimum we need." I pointed at a letter L. "This fellow over here is supposed to stand for the quantum of life—whatever that might be. It's with regard to your frequency, and I've tentatively given it this value in relation to Planck's constant. Maybe you can give it a name? You love making up words."

She just kept staring at me, dumbstruck, not even bothering to look at my notebook. I was worried she was having another seizure.

"Anyway," I shifted my finger to the next symbol, the letter S. "There's no escaping the effects of this: Entropy. But we also have this."

Her brow crinkled. "Is that . . . God?"

"What?" I glanced at my own writing, confused by her question.

"Isn't that a crucifix?"

"No, that's a T. It's my symbol for you."

"Me?"

"Your faith. One's unwavering belief in life after death. Or that there's a Heaven. Or reincarnation. Or a willdisc waiting somewhere."

She squinted at me. "Starr would condemn you to hell for reducing faith in Heaven to a factor in an equation."

"You'll be surprised. She gave me the idea."

"She'd never."

I chuckled. It did sound far-fetched. "Starr told me that belief in an afterlife is hardwired into the human psyche. That it's like a cross-cultural constant that evolution voted in favor of. Your mother, on the other hand, thinks it's like a Dawkins meme that helps keep humanity sane. Either way, it must be an important factor, and neurotheologists should be able to put a number to it—how much we believe that we can outlive death."

"And what's this last symbol?" she asked, tapping on the letter I.

"That's a Japanese term your mother learned from your father. *Ikigai.*"

She smiled. "A purpose."

"Yes. It's different things for different people. I imagine it to be the hyper force that drives the will to survive. A force so powerful, in fact, that even when one has a shortage on the other factors, a hyperwill can manage to survive with just enough of this one factor. Sort of like momentum—even if you don't have enough fuel, this can keep you going."

"So, in effect this 'I' is simply a reason to . . ."

"Live." My voice trembled over the single syllable I was begging her to do.

I put the sketchpad aside and composed myself before looking into her eyes to wait for the spark of hope to return. "So does that compute for you?"

"That depends. Will you still try for Pangaea, minus me?"

"Of course not. That equation doesn't exist."

She shook her head. "You made a promise to your parents."

"To chase the dream, no matter what?" I smiled. "I think I'm old enough to make up my own mind by now."

"I made a promise too, you know. That I would make sure you never gave up on that dream."

I looked at her askance. "That's not something I would have asked of you."

"You didn't. Your mother did."

"My mother?" I flashed back as far as I could but found no recollection.

"The morning of their flight." She reached out and laid her hand on mine. "She called me saying she'd woken up from a vivid dream, and it left her feeling something terribly bad was going to happen."

I leaned away and shook my head. "That doesn't sound like my mother. She didn't believe in anything like that."

Torula bit her lower lip. "She knew you'd say that. She also knew you'd be upset about many things."

"What things?"

"If you knew she'd called me instead of you. And that she was going on the plane anyway despite her reservations. And if the worst did happen, she'd be letting you down for not fulfilling her promise of helping you reach your dream. Which was why . . ." She shrugged. ". . . she made me promise too."

I pulled away slowly as I tried to process what she'd said. "Why would she? It's not like her at all."

"Maybe. But if you woke up believing you'd just had a prophetic dream of your own death, and you had a child, what would you do?"

"Go on with life as usual."

"Which was what she did. But only after making that call to me."

This was too surreal. Was she just making this up to convince me to join Pangaea? "Why didn't you tell me before?"

"Like I said, she thought it would upset you, regardless of when I told you. So why tell you?"

"But you're telling me now."

She reached out and touched my cheek. "Because you think you can let go of your promise to your parents. Because you believe they're no longer here. That it wouldn't matter. But I believe differently. Your mother's last act was to make sure you'd go the distance. Through me. So now, I need you to reaffirm that promise."

I took in a deep and ragged breath. "I promise. I'll apply for Pangaea—and you'll come with me, after I bring you back from the willdisc."

Sadness brimmed in her eyes. "Bram, the procedure you're planning is a crime. Even if you succeed, it will still be labeled a crime. There's no way NASA would take you back after that."

I smiled. "Not if they're on our side."

"What?"

I gently tilted her chin up so I could look in her eyes. "NASA has agreed to lend us technology for the procedure. I'm supposed to get you to the Ames Research Center by morning."

Her gaze faltered. "Have I gone delirious? What you're saying —it can't be true."

"It's all true."

"NASA . . . will break the law?"

"There's a term I got from their doctors. Deep hypothermic circulatory arrest. It's a legal medical technique that would stand up in the courts of law. You want to hear the plan?"

She nodded. Tentatively.

I drew closer, eager to tell her all I could. "They're letting us use a cryogenic chamber to work around the four-minute limit of brain cells. Liquid nitrogen can lower the temperature of the Faraday cage—up to 120 degrees below, but that's way more than what we need. They'll also employ antifreeze proteins—biological antifreeze found in all kinds of creatures that manage to survive in subzero conditions."

"Is this real?" Her gaze flicked from one eye to the other, as though trying to catch a lie. "You've convinced NASA to—"

"They're not exactly 'convinced.' But they're used to getting into things no one else would bother to try."

"Why would they do this?"

"Because we boldly go where no man has gone before." I tapped my finger on her nose. "Or woman."

"Oh, Bram. Don't you see?" Tears brimmed in her eyes. "I'll just be your burden. My mom's burden. My brothers'. And now, even NASA's? It's irrational. I'll be an immortal curse you won't be able to shake."

There was something about her words that triggered an inexplicable thrill. It was as though I'd been given an impossible mystery to solve, and I'd just spotted a clue that had been hiding in plain sight. Now all that jabber from Triana about "the power of her decision not to die" made sense. Suddenly, the equation in my head shifted, and it told me: This was going to work.

"The way you're talking . . ." A warm flush coursed through my body. "Spore, it's like you already *know* you're going to make it. You're already living through what it will be like afterwards."

"A living hell for you."

"What are you talking about? All we have to do is keep you safe in a willdisc in a cube. And when the time comes, I'll bring you back—the way you are." I gave a quick shrug. "Piece of cake."

She chuckled even as tears brimmed in her eyes. "You can't even take care of a potted plant. Now you want to be responsible for someone's soul?"

"Not just anyone's soul. It belongs to my queen."

Her tears fell.

I took out my handkerchief from my pocket. "If I could do this for you, I would. But I wouldn't have a chance at making it. You know why?" I wiped her tears away. "Because it all begins with belief. And your faith that life itself is immortal never wavered."

She took a shaky, labored breath, and I cupped her face in my hands, as though to grab hold of the spirit her disease was stealing away.

"There is a reason why you have to do this. A very meaningful and noble reason why you have to go to the other side and come back." I paused and steadied myself. "It's to give everyone hope. To convince even the stubborn ones like me that what seems impossible is real. That the end is really just an option, and that you can choose to stay. Do this, and you give humanity more than just faith in life that exists beyond what we can see. Show the world that happiness can last. And so can love. And so can we."

61

TRANSITION

DOCTORS AND TECHNICIANS SURROUNDED THE SURGICAL TABLE, A tense huddle in a cold and clinical room of wall-to-wall white. I gulped down the bitter taste of dread as I stood mere meters away —a reluctant witness to this new system designed to end a human life.

In a straightforward tone, the order to begin the procedure came crisp and clear.

"Transition, Stage One, commence."

Transition. It was the term Roy had given the procedure for Boner's changeover from a once running, playful, barking dog to captured memories in a disc. Now, at the Ames Research Center, scientists were applying the same term to Torula's last hope.

I crossed my arms and stepped back.

A robotic arm maneuvered a syringe into position and, with swift precision, delivered the injection straight into the ventricular chamber of the heart. A soft groan rumbled in my throat as monitors sounded their alarms, registering the medical emergency triggered by the lethal cocktail.

The black-haired mannequin, with the same build as Torula, lay with its eyes closed and mouth wide open, its drug recognition and response system giving everyone in the room a stark picture of what would happen to a real patient.

Dead in eighteen seconds.

I stared at the medical dummy, so lifelike in its portrayal of death. Christ. I forced myself to keep looking and listening. Maybe if I watched the dry-run enough times, I'd manage to hold myself together—through the real thing.

Medical jargon flew around as doctors discussed the results of this and earlier test runs. They seemed satisfied, perhaps even impressed.

"I'm glad it wasn't me who had to come up with the cocktail for this," said a woman amidst the huddle. "Whoever it was, I wonder how he dealt with the thought of what he had to do."

"What makes you so sure it wasn't a she?" asked one other doctor.

"Or a they," said another.

I walked away, not wanting to give them any hint I knew the answer. That it was the patient's brother who had finally agreed to his sister's pre-arranged death—and helped with it. But Tromino's identity had to remain concealed; he had a medical career to protect and a family to care for.

Same as Dr. Grant. Part of the agreement for us to proceed was for his involvement to be kept secret, which was perfectly understandable. The director of the Johnson Space Center was tasked to take humans farther out into space—not into the afterworld.

"Well, I'll be Jesus' ass enterin' Jerusalem."

Roy came strutting towards me, giving me an exaggerated once-over. From my gray slacks to my pullover in vanilla white. Smooth shave. Neat hair. I probably looked like a man about to ask for a woman's hand in marriage.

He took a deep, audible whiff of my cologne then raised his brows. "I think you've found your peace and coasted past nirvana."

I gave a lopsided grin. "Can't have her heading for the light instead of me."

"Good move. You were startin' to look and smell like the Devil 'imself. Where's Jackson?"

"On a holocall with Treble, her brother overseas."

"Bad idea."

I frowned. "Why?"

"No one should let 'er tie up loose ends. She's gonna *not* want to have closure. She's gonna *not* want to be ready for it all to end. She's gotta have every goddamn reason on the face o' this Earth to wanna come back and get on with 'er life."

I lost hold of one spasm of angst. "She can't possibly be ready. Can she?"

"Hey." Roy jabbed me on the arm, a lot lighter than how he usually did. I guessed he knew I was holding myself together by a thread. "O'course she can't. She knows you'd be a mess if she left you now."

Enrik, the project director, came walking towards us. Though he was dressed in white coveralls like everyone else in the team, he stood out because of his copper-colored hair cut like freshly mowed grass and bright blue eyes that always seemed to sparkle with "Eureka!"

"Bram, we're about ready. We've sent someone for Dr. Jackson."

I nodded as my stomach muscles tightened in reflex, and my gaze fell to the ground.

"C'mon, man." Roy had to nudge me to follow him out to the corridor and into a small anteroom where we were each handed a pile of sterile medical garments. I retreated to a corner and laid the items down on a bench. Surgical gown, a mask, gloves, shoe covers, and a scrub cap. The feather-light garments seemed made of lead as I sorted through them. These were meant to cover me from head to toe, except that one part of me I needed to hide from Torula: My eyes. If she took one look at them, they were bound to betray my fears.

More than anyone, she needed to believe that this would work. More than anyone, she needed to believe in me.

"You need a hand, bro?" Roy had donned his medical wear quickly and quietly and was done.

"No. I just need . . ." More time. Some answers. A drink. ". . . to just . . ." Find my courage that had suddenly gone missing. "I'm okay."

I walked towards the swinging doors that opened into the main room—*the* room where it would all happen. I peered through the view panels and folded my arms. The mere sight of the place made me shiver.

The area was about twice the size of where we had tested the mannequin, also a wash of white from floor to ceiling. I glanced around the room full of strangers. No friends or relatives of Torula around, just as she had insisted—but there had been no stopping Roy from coming. The equipment he'd designed was about to be used in an experiment that would involve ending a human life. We'd told him not to come so he could claim innocence. But he'd made a case about how, if it hadn't been for us, he would've lost his best friend, and that he knew more about this procedure than anyone else on the planet.

NASA agreed: He *had* to be here.

I had thanked him in some heartfelt, stilted, inadequate way. There was no expressing how grateful I was that he'd been so bull-headed about it.

A handful of people in surgical garb stood working behind the new Motown—a modified cryogenic chamber, which Roy had helped customize for Torula. It had been fitted with a fine wire-mesh coating and transparent mu-metal foil, turning it into a Faraday shield.

The Ames engineers had called the glass cylinder "a relic"—something they'd used in "bygone" studies on healing and pain management in case of injury during a space mission. But their so-called museum piece looked, in every way, space-age to me.

The see-through cylinder resembled the pressurized hyperbaric chambers used in hospitals, except this one was constructed to deliver liquid nitrogen instead of oxygen—and it was meant for outer space. Temperature control would be extremely precise. They would be able to program the exact degree at which the interior would be on any given second, allowing for slow and controlled-rate freezing. Suspended above where her chest would be was the iCube.

In my mind's eye, Torula materialized inside the glass cylinder, looking like Sleeping Beauty—her porcelain face framed by her shiny, coal-black hair—but dead. *Sweet Jesus.* I stepped away and sank down on the bench, the immensity of what I was about to do a heavy, teetering globe on my shoulders.

Enrik joined us in the anteroom. "Are we ready?"

I wasn't, but I said, "Yeah," and put on the surgical wear as quickly as I could, save for the mask.

"Just a final recap of what's ahead." Enrik flashed the uneasy smile of someone tasked to do an awkward thing at an awkward time. "We need to emphasize that there's no guarantee we'll take Dr. Jackson to a state of suspended animation. All the liquid nitrogen will do is buy her a few more minutes. After which, we will need to see a definite indication that a hyperwill transition is in progress. Only then will we have legal clearance to keep her clinically dead for several hours with machine-assisted circulation to finish the transition." He took a breath. "Otherwise, the doctors will be morally- and dutifully-bound to resuscitate her and abort the next stage of the procedure. Once stable, she will be discharged, and we will be released of obligations on any further medical procedures needed. That, in essence, is what's in the document that Dr. Jackson signed."

"I know. I understand." I turned away, my head throbbing with a secret I held with Dr. Grant and Torula. She had signed a DNR, a do-not-resuscitate order should she fail to activate the iCube in time. The decision had been made not to tell the rest of the team—because otherwise, no one would have agreed to take part in this mad plan. "Burn the ships," she'd said, in a feeble attempt at humor because she wanted to set her sights on nothing but the willdisc. Reviving her immediately after what we were about to do would only mean waiting for the end to come again before she could regain enough strength to go through surgery.

"I'll see you inside then," Enrik said with a sigh of relief, having no clue as to my anxiety.

I put on the surgical mask, my eyes fixed resolutely ahead.

"Yo, Morrison . . ." Roy looked like a man struggling to say something good when there was nothing good to say. "You're doin' the right thing."

I nodded, even though I wasn't sure I believed him. We walked into the main room together, and all eyes turned to me—the man who would give the signal to end Torula's life. I glanced around at everyone watching me, straining from a distance to gauge how I felt. Despite my doubts about what Roy had just said, with every step, I found it in me to *prove* I was doing the right thing. Everyone had to believe it: We were doing the right thing.

The mood shifted back to business when I got to my post by the Motown: The cryogenic Faraday chamber. It helped that the machinery had been intended for space travel. As far as everyone here was concerned, it was a space capsule, and Torula, the test pilot. It gave us all a rational way to deal with what was about to happen.

"Enrik, *ven aqui*," said a woman in a firm, commanding voice. It was Elena, the perfusionist—the clinical expert whom everyone referred to as "the Spanish dictator" in charge of the heart-lung machine, though with her plump physique and kind brown eyes, she made me think more of a doting mother. She was the key person whom everyone credited for having suggested using biological antifreeze to safely keep Torula in cardiac arrest for several hours to complete her transition. The doctors, after some deliberation, acknowledged she could be right.

I slipped the willdisc into the iCube. Somehow, my gloved hands remained steady, even though every part of me was shaken.

Then came the faint swoosh of doors swinging open, and a hush fell over the room. I froze, and after a strained heartbeat, turned to face Torula.

"Hey there." I smiled beneath my mask as I gazed at the woman who brought sunshine to my mornings and starlight to my nights. Here was the bravest person I knew—even though everyone else around me probably just saw a pale and fragile victim of a degenerative disease, sitting in a wheelchair, wan, weak, and sad.

Torula reached for my gloved hand. "How are you?"

"How am *I*? How are *you*?" My tone managed to stay light and casual like a straight line drawn by shaking hands. "You're the astronaut this time. You beat me to it."

She blinked in response, her quick wit now dulled by drugs and dread.

"Hi, Roy," she said. "Thanks for everything."

"Hell, what you thankin' me for? I'm gonna put all the work I did 'ere into your tab. With a rush fee to boot and overtime pay for m'boys. You owe me, y'hear?"

She smiled weakly. "You'll always be my favorite DJ."

Roy's expression shifted from flattered to flustered within a second. "You sayin' you like me now? Goddamn it! Who are you, and what've you done to Jackson?" He took a step closer. "Listen, yo. I want the real Torula Jackson in that willdisc. The same one who always confangled me with 'er vocab. The one who always stood up and fought to get to 'er goal." He pointed towards the iCube. "And that willdisc in there—that's your goal. You got fifteen minutes to find it. And with your smarts, I'm sure you can do it in fifteen *seconds*."

She gave his arm a feeble squeeze. "Thanks again, Roy. For everything."

I hated that she kept thanking him. It sounded so . . . final.

Roy sniffed. "Well, I ain't done givin' yet." Everyone was moving into position, and Roy's role, at this point, was to stay out of the way. He took a seat at a console table, next to three anonymous others in sterile garb.

Enrik handed me an earpiece, similar to the discreet device clipped on everyone else's ears.

I wheeled Torula towards the cryogenic Faraday chamber, each step bringing us closer to the executioner's block. My gait became slow and deliberate as I willed time to stop so the next moment wouldn't have to happen.

With the whoosh of a vacuum seal being released, the hatch at one end of the chamber was opened, and its bedframe holding a thin mattress slid out. My heart thudded, and I couldn't imagine how scared Torula must have been. I helped her to her feet, and the medical team enveloped us in a protective huddle. The woman averse to getting attention was now at the center of it, blindly trusting strangers with her life—and what would happen beyond it.

The preparations for the procedure would be uncomfortable, painful, and frightening. The stress could easily cause her to seize or have a stroke, so the doctors had asked her what might help keep her calm. Was there music she wanted to listen to? A video she could watch?

All she had asked for was that I stay by her side. I had smiled and squeezed her hand, grateful and relieved she had said so.

Torula eased herself onto the mattress, covered in a white sheet, as I took a seat next to her and held her hand. A mass of bodies surrounded us, inserting needles and attaching tubes and electrodes all over her bare limbs. I kept up a shallow stream of conversation, digging up silly memories from our childhood, teasing her about her little quirks. Every now and then, she would wince, bite her lip, or scrunch up her eyes as the doctors pierced and punctured her with their needles. I stroked her hair, taking care not to dislodge the electrodes that had been attached to her temples. All connections carefully snaked through the hatch that had been reengineered to accommodate all the medical tubes and cables attached to the equipment around us.

Torula squeezed my hand tight and closed her eyes. A tear coursed down her cheek—a tiny drop so potent, it tore a hole through my heart, and I went silent. When she opened her eyes, she gave me a reassuring smile, offering me comfort instead of the other way around.

"You're one amazing woman, you know that?"

"I don't really feel amazing at the moment," she said hoarsely.

"What are you talking about? You're about to wow the world as a pioneering hyperwill."

She crinkled her nose. "Now that I'm about to become one, the term doesn't sound so good. Hyper makes the afterlife seem like such a stressful state."

I bobbed my head in agreement. "Well, you'll be the best person to rename it."

When the medical team finally parted, Torula was hooked up to every contraption, monitor, and machine surrounding the chamber. Tubes had been attached to the arteries in her groin area, her lower limbs strapped down, slightly bent like frog's legs, exposing the inner thigh to keep the tubes from being dislodged or kinked. Beneath all the electrodes and wires that crisscrossed her body, she lay naked with two, slim pieces of hospital linen draped over her chest and pelvis, her feet and hands covered with dark socks and mittens as protection against the oncoming cold.

"Dr. Jackson?" Enrik said.

"Yes?"

"All systems checked. We're cleared to go. You all set?" He held two thumbs up.

No amount of congenial, business-like demeanor could dispel the finality that came with those words. The slightest trace of anxiety flickered in her eyes, and I had to fight to hide the anguish that flared inside of me.

With one deep inhale, she nodded.

"All right." Enrik's tone and manner remained hearty, but the furrows on his brow had become very much pronounced. "I just need to buckle up this arm . . ."

He needed me to release her hand, but instead, I clasped it tighter.

"Bram?" Enrik said. "It's time."

After a long and painful pause, I let go and took a step back.

"There we are," Enrik said, securing her arm. "You're all set. Good luck, Dr. Torula Jackson. You've got the best team around to help you take the next giant leap for humankind." He gave a slight bow. "Have a safe trip."

Technicians stepped forward, prepared to assist me in closing the hatch. The signal to begin the procedure would be when I reached out to push the bedframe in.

I couldn't move. Lifting my arm seemed beyond me now. It had taken all of my strength to keep from falling apart.

No one around us seemed to breathe.

Torula gave me a weak, reassuring smile. "This'll be worth it— if it finally makes you cry for me."

I answered in a voice surprisingly steady. "I'm never going to cry for you because I'm never letting go." I leaned in closer. "See you around, Spore."

I reached out and pushed the bedframe into the chamber. Enrik yanked me away and—like a Formula One pit crew—technicians and engineers swooped around the cryogenic Faraday chamber, securing connections and checking all the seals.

"Transition, Stage One, commence," said a matter-of-fact male voice even before the last latches clicked into place.

"Nuhh . . ." Torula groaned. Her vital sign monitors sent out piercing alarms.

I sucked in my breath. The robotic arm had delivered the injection so quickly, I didn't even see it happen.

"Get your bearings, Spore," I cried. "Find the willdisc." I tore my mask, cap, and gloves off; I had to make sure she could see my face.

The room filled with the din of her vital sign monitors, signaling her distress as the robotic arm continued with its series of tasks with cold precision.

A heart-wrenching groan issued from Torula. I expected her to be arching in agony but realized she couldn't even writhe through the suffering; her entire body had been strapped down.

"You've got to move out, now!" I shouted, my hands gripping the surface of the transparent cylinder.

The chamber filled with mist from a blast of liquid nitrogen, bringing the temperature inside below freezing in an instant, just like plunging Torula into an icy lake.

"Spore, I'm right here. Stay with me." I pictured her swimming madly in cold water, frantic and freezing, not knowing where she was going. "Keep going to the willdisc. Keep your focus on the willdisc." I had no idea if she could even see anything anymore.

Elena, the perfusionist, stationed behind the cage, issued updates in a clear and even tone, confirming that all connections to her equipment were secure and working.

"We're at ventricular tachycardia," said the impersonal annotator as the alarms continued their cacophony.

The haze inside the chamber settled.

"Look at me. You're not alone. I'm here."

Torula's head flopped to the side. I pushed my face close to the enclosure, looking into her eyes. She let out a long, drawn-out moan through a tightly clenched mouth.

"Focus on me. We're doing this together. Focus on me." I stared into her face as she struggled through her last, torturous breaths.

A guttural sound escaped her.

"Spore! Oh, Jesus."

Warning signals heightened in intensity, her EKG still running wild.

This is way more than eighteen seconds. My fingers scratched at the glass as I ached to find a way to ease her pain.

"We have ventricular fibrillation," came a sedate announcement.

"Is she still feeling all this?" I shouted over my shoulder to anyone who would answer me.

A woman's calm reply came through my earpiece. "She lost consciousness a few seconds ago."

"You can do this, Spore," I cried. "We're all watching over you. You'll be all right."

A gurgling, throaty murmur—it didn't even sound human—rippled from Torula. The alarms went silent, leaving behind a piercing, solitary tone.

Torula had flat-lined.

The room grew still. A sob escaped from someone behind me. And then I caught that instant when Torula's eyes told me . . . she was no longer there.

"No," I whispered, suddenly afraid I couldn't undo what had just happened. I fought to hold back the rising panic, but it gurgled up, and I grunted and gagged.

"Keep talkin' to 'er, Morrison," Roy called out. "She needs you."

"EEG continues to show signs of electrical brain activity," the voice from my headset confirmed. "In fact . . ."

"In fact what?" I asked.

". . . it's like there's conscious processing going on," the annotator said.

"What does that mean?" I asked.

"She's not conscious," Elena said. "It's a surge of, eh, electrical activity after clinical death. It differs for different people, but it's not, eh, unusual."

"C'mon, Morrison," Roy said. "Keep your focus on Jackson."

I swabbed my hands over my face—over sweat, tears, and saliva—and sucked in a ragged breath. "Okay, Spore. Find the willdisc. I'm right here. We're all waiting right here." Then, more softly, I said, "Don't go into the bloody wrong light."

The iCube remained dull. But the tiny nib, with its faint blue-violet glow, told me it was creating a conductive path for Torula to follow.

The annotator issued his next pronouncement. "All electrical brain activity has ceased. Dr. Jackson has reached clinical dormancy."

Clinical dormancy. A term they coined to keep from referring to her as dead. I couldn't think. Or move. Or breathe.

A sound escaped me. It wasn't a word. It wasn't a sob. It was a primitive growl I had to violently stifle.

The robotic arm inside the chamber swiveled and lifted a swaddle of thick, black cloth and laid it over her face, something I never saw happen during the test runs.

I bolted out of my seat. "Why are you covering her face? She isn't dead."

"No, she's not," Elena said, craning her neck so I could see her from behind the chamber. "It's insulation from, eh, frostbite in the intense cold of the next few minutes."

The answer gave me some comfort. It was something one would only consider for a living patient. But the grim, monotonous tone coming from the EKG kept declaring something else.

"Would someone turn off that blasted sound?" I called out into the room in general.

The next instant, it was switched off.

I sat back down and looked at Torula's face, now draped in morbid black. "It's okay, Spore. It's for your protection. Now, you just have to make that iCube light up. So get in there."

By now, I figured, I had no need to raise my voice for Torula to hear me, so I egged her on with whispers and mumbled words. My brain managed to reassure me with some explanation as to how that could be possible.

From somewhere behind me, I heard Roy's angry tone.

I glanced back right when Enrik pointed at his computer display—then mouthed the word "Nothing."

Roy glowered at him. "Whaddaya mean 'Nothin'?' All o' those monitors were goin' off the charts. Electrocardiogram, electrowhat-not, electrowhatthefuckever. What else do you fuckin' want? A pop-up sayin' 'soul in progress?' It ain't gonna happen. All that crazy fuckin' beepin' shit?" He waved his hands in an angry swirl. "All that, put together, spells 'soul gettin' the fuck outta there!'"

Roy stormed back towards his post tossing a glance at me, giving me a firm nod as if to say, "I got this." Before reaching his seat, he paused, with a frown, and looked back at Enrik, then strode towards me to stand by my side.

Having him there helped me breathe a little easier. I checked the wall clock that seemed to have been rigged to speed up; nearly ten minutes had gone by. I got up and surveyed the assemblage of experts, shaking their heads, arms folded, as they stared at their monitors. No one had any idea what would indicate the migration of a soul.

Before I knew it, the annotator's cold announcement came through the headsets. "Three minutes to Code Blue. Code Team, to your stations."

The medical team advanced, their crash cart at the ready. Enrik moved forward. "Please step aside, Bram."

I stood my ground, and the seconds ticked by in excruciating silence.

"Jesus H." Roy took on the stance of a boxer, dancing like a timid Muhammad Ali.

"Listen to me." Enrik raised his hand in a placating gesture. "We've given this our best shot. If we stop now, we can still bring Dr. Jackson back. We can still revive her and let conventional medicine have its chance."

I cracked my knuckles. "Medicine had its chance." I had set the system up so that at the last second of Torula's fifteen-minute window, the DNR would display on all their monitors.

"Not with all it's got to offer. Surgery can still work." Enrik gestured towards the doctors. "Let the team bring her back now." He took another step closer. The crash cart team inched forward.

I moved to block their path and glanced at the clock—a time bomb hung high that wasn't about to stop ticking.

One minute left.

My chest tightened. *Jesus, Spore. I've done everything I could. Everything.*

Suddenly, I heard a few faint staccato beeps.

All eyes shot to the iCube. But there was still no trace of the light that said Torula's soul had found its way.

"We have a . . . reading," the annotator said, not quite as impassively, and made the declaration sound more like a question.

I locked eyes with Elena standing right behind the glass chamber. "It's the EKG," she said. "It registered, eh, a—"

"Heartbeat?" I staggered forward and stared at Torula's chest.

"Holy shit," Roy said.

"No, it's not," Elena said with a knitted brow, then paused as her assistant spoke into her ear. "It's, eh, probably a stray electrical charge. Discharged earlier, but, eh, still running its course, and the EKG just caught it."

I cocked my head. A stray electrical charge? Or one last burst of electromagnetic energy that knew exactly where to go.

My blood rushed as I lay my hand on the glass chamber. "Come on, Spore. You can do it. It's time to change the world."

Absolute silence fell upon the room. And then, a bleep.

My breath caught, and I had to blink a couple of times to believe my eyes. A sliver of light shone at the iCube's base, then came the announcement: "iCube activation, confirmed. Transition, Stage Two, commence."

A subdued communal exhale of disbelief filled the room.

"That's my girl," I said, letting out my own monumental sigh, and collapsed back into my chair.

Roy slapped me on the shoulder and shook me heartily.

The perfusionist and her assistants went into action, and the heart-lung machine hummed to life. "Now, we restore, eh, circulation," Elena announced, looking at me, and I somehow saw her smile beneath her mask. "We have to make things colder, but we'll take good care of her."

"Stage Two in progress," said the annotator. "Cooling the chamber another three degrees."

I stared at Torula—her body crisscrossed by tubes, a unique combination of blood, biological antifreeze, and a drug cocktail being cycled through it, her face covered by a black cloth. She was cold. Without a heartbeat. With no trace of brain activity. But I knew—she was alive.

62

THE BLEAK AND BLACK CLOTH

FOR ITS MAIDEN VOYAGE INTO THE AFTERLIFE, NASA HAD A SOMBER room of doctors, engineers, technicians, and scientists on a vigil—waiting for the telltale glow of Torula's soul to light up a cube. Over nine hours had gone by since the procedure began, and she was still in clinical dormancy. The temperature in the Motown remained low and steady, a unique blood and chemical composition containing natural antifreeze and ketone bodies flowing through her arteries.

An arm's reach from Torula's glass-encased body, I sat in a daze, riven in three. I needed to think, and grieve, and hope. I ached but couldn't tell where. I had to do something but didn't know what.

"Transition at 95 percent," came the much-anticipated announcement.

Activity stirred in the room. It was past two in the morning. People who had dozed off in their seats were nudged awake; those slumped in their chairs sat up. Roy, who had wandered off, returned to his spot at the console table. Throats were cleared, garments straightened, and conversation, though subdued, came alive.

Only a slim fraction of the iCube remained unlit. I leaned forward and squinted at the nib—Torula's entryway into the willdisc—a ballpoint pen-like electrode that swiveled whenever necessary to keep the conductive path stable. Though it had but a pinprick of a glow in blue-violet, it was enough to remind me of her eyes.

You're doing good. I'd stopped speaking out loud to her hours ago, but I hadn't stopped talking. *I can't wait to see you again.*

I glanced at her face, still covered by the bleak and black cloth, and a vision of her flashed in my mind—of her eyes sparkling, her hair curling down one shoulder as she leaned closer to say, "We can make our own heaven here on Earth."

I laid my hand on the glass shield, in case it would help her hear my thoughts better. *You're doing it, Spore. You're doing it right now.*

"Transition at 99 percent."

I pulled myself up and cracked my neck. *We're at the home-stretch. Get ready.*

The iCube's glow crept up, about to touch the brim. In those final seconds, everything fell to a hush—as though all ears strained to hear an angel whisper.

The iCube issued its alert tone—a beautiful, harmonious, hope-filled hum that came with one brilliant pulse and settled down to a constant radiance.

"Transition complete."

Applause issued from all around, and a potent thrill shot through me.

Roy thrust his fist high in the air and shouted from across the room. "Fuck yeah!"

Others went for more sedate expressions of approval.

"Good going."

"Excellent work."

"Hear, hear."

The doctors and scientists expressed it to the floor in general. Perhaps, like me, they hoped—or believed—Torula could hear.

Enrik came to my side. "Maybe congratulations are premature but . . ." His eyes glowed their cry of eureka. "Congratulations. That was one mighty great liftoff. Now I can't wait for touchdown."

"Yes, it was," I said, smiling wide. This was one thing I loved about NASA. We saw hope in every launch without losing focus on the landing. "But I suggest you hold the congrats until a bit later. We're not done yet."

"Nope. We're definitely not." He nodded. "We're going to be here quite a bit longer. This is a real tricky part. It's in the warming up stage when irreparable damage to cells and tissues could occur. We have to take it slow."

The annotator continued with his updates as the temperature inside the chamber was raised in controlled increments. When Enrik had said slow, he'd meant *slow*. Time dragged on for nearly an hour before he instructed: "Phase Three Division, proceed to The Vault."

An entire console section, about half a dozen people, stood up and moved towards the exit. This first procedure had been conducted here because of the cryogenic setup and its liquid nitrogen supply. For the next stage, a special room in the basement proved more ideal. Completely encased in metal and steel-reinforced concrete, it would serve like a giant Faraday shield to keep Torula's hyperwill safe and secure in case of any willdisc or iCube malfunction.

Roy joined me and Enrik by the Motown. "The Vault. That's the room you told me about, right? In the basement."

"Right," Enrik said. "That's where we'll be taking the iCube. Five stories down."

Roy pursed his lips and squinted at nothing.

"Is it the distance?" Enrik asked. "You said the iCube has enough power to last two days, so—"

"Yeah, yeah. That's not the problem."

Enrik cocked his head. "Then what *is* the problem?"

Roy paused then smiled, though he didn't have a matching

sparkle in his eyes. "Nothin'. It's cool that Jackson gets extra protection until we can re-inspirit 'er."

I glanced at Torula's cloth-covered face and smiled to myself. Re-inspirit was the term she'd coined for the procedure she was about to pioneer. *You're so good at making up words. You still owe me on what I should call the quantum of life.*

An attendant handed us each a set of fresh sterile wear. I moved to one side to put them on; Roy sidled up to me.

"Yo, this Vault thing. Somethin's been buggin' me about it, and I didn't realize what it was until now."

I paused as I put my surgical cap on. "So there *is* a problem?"

"Your old friend, Franco. He's been seekin' you and Jackson out on 'is own. I was thinkin' if we can't find 'im, at least he can find you. But that's not gonna happen if the two o' you are shielded by some giant vault."

I strained to wrap my head around the issue, but my mind was too frazzled to handle more than one thought at a time. All I could think about now was seeing Torula's hyperwill, safe and intact inside a glass chamber. "We'll deal with it. Later."

Roy nodded and put on his fresh surgical wear; by the time we were ready, so was the rest of the team.

"Stand by for all systems check." After a long pause, Enrik gave a thumbs up. "All clear to open the Motown."

A fresh surge of adrenalin pumped through me. In mere seconds, technicians took charge of the cryogenic Faraday chamber. With a loud hiss, the seal of the cage was released, its hatch opened, and the bed frame eased out. Whatever cold was left inside cascaded to the floor in a curtain of mist that dissipated. The only thing keeping Torula's body temperature down now was the fluid being pumped through her arteries.

A pungent, earthy odor seeped through my surgical mask—an indefinable mixture of fear, drugs, and blood. A team of doctors moved in, blocking my view as they checked on Torula. I had to will myself to breathe as I waited.

"Go for iCube retrieval."

After a short but torturous while, the medical team parted and made room for me to take the iCube. I moved close and reached out to remove the shroud of black that smothered her. But just as my fingers touched the fabric, Roy grabbed me by the wrist, and shook his head.

"Let the doctors do that," he said. "You don't have to see 'er like this."

Enrik shivered and rubbed his arm briskly. "Man, that chamber's freezing up the whole room."

"You're imagining things," said an engineer. "The residual effect isn't enough to—"

I jerked when the black cloth flew off Torula's face and blew past us, as though yanked by an invisible thread. It landed at the foot of an attendant who jumped back and shrieked.

"What the fuck!" Roy cried.

I whipped around and looked at Torula on the white mattress, her eyes shut and sunken, skin ashen and tinged with a morbid blue, then I felt myself enveloped by the heady scent of lavender.

"Do you smell that?" Enrik's hand flew to his mask, as though to check if it was there.

Roy stared wide-eyed at me. "It's Jackson."

Goose bumps traveled from my scalp to my arms.

"*Madre mia de Dios.*" Elena made the sign of the cross. "Get the cube and take her away."

In a daze, I detached the iCube and held it close to me.

"Okay, she's ready to go," Enrik said. A technician pushed a trolley holding a metal case about two feet square and parked it next to the Motown.

I cast a parting look at Torula's lifeless body as the medical team surrounded her. *Where are you?*

"In here, please." Enrik rolled the trolley closer.

I stood, transfixed, clutching the iCube. Was she floating around? Or safe in the box?

"Bram, come on," Enrik said. "It'll be more secure this way."

The next thing I knew, I got a firm nudge against my shoulder, forcing me to take one step back from the trolley.

Roy's eyes flew wide open. "You shittin' me?"

"What's that about?" Enrik asked.

"I . . . don't know." I let out a baffled breath as I deposited the white box into the trolley. Enrik secured it with straps then shut the enclosure.

A faint, rhythmic beeping instantly issued from inside.

"Motherfrickin' meltdown." Roy looked at me in a panic. "That's the low power warning."

"You said it was good for two days," I said.

"Hell, I never figured she'd be doin' cartwheels."

The beeping quickened, and Enrik pushed the trolley out through the doors. The three of us dashed down the corridors until we came to a stop at the elevators.

The beeping intensified, and Roy hollered at the metal box. "Just try to relax, Jackson!"

"It's soundproof," Enrik said. "In fact, it's everything-proof. If this entire building blew up, she'd probably be the only one who—"

"Did you say 'everything-proof?'" I asked as fear gripped me.

He shrugged. "Theoretically, yeah. But no one can foresee—"

"Give me the cube." I tore off my surgical wear and lunged for the trolley.

Enrik raised his hand. "What are you doing?"

"It started beeping when you closed her in," I said. "Open the case."

Enrik shook his head.

Roy's eyes opened wide. "Shit, he's right. Jackson's claustrophobic. Let 'im take 'er."

The iCube's beeping intensified.

"She needs to sense us," I said. "Open the goddamned case."

Enrik hesitated, his lips moving as though he were gnawing on his own thoughts. At last, he tapped in the combination that opened the trolley door.

I expected the warning tone to subside, but it didn't.

"Damn it," Roy said checking the battery gauge. "Power's down to 3 percent."

"Goddamn it. I can't believe this. We're right back where we bloody started!" I grabbed the iCube.

Roy rushed to the stairwell entrance. "This way."

Enrik blocked my path. "We're five floors up. I'm not going to race down those stairs just holding that. And I won't let you either."

I glanced at an elevator. "Oh, well—that one's almost here."

Enrik turned to look at it. I dodged past him and into the stairwell entrance. Roy was waiting on the first landing down. "Let's go!"

Roy ran several paces ahead of me, Enrik behind me. I focused on the steps that zipped by below me. *Don't trip. Don't fall.* Flight after flight. *Don't trip. Don't fall.*

"Next landing, exit," Enrik said.

"Bro, stop!" Franco's voice exploded inside my head, and I froze on the steps.

Roy, just ahead of me, slipped and slid down to the landing. "Son of a bitch! Watch that step, it's wet."

Franco's here! I gripped the iCube tight. *Franco, tell me how to find you.*

The iCube escalated its already frantic beeping. "Let's go," Enrik said and ushered me past the wet zone. I glanced back, sending out an urgent thought that I hoped would make its way to Franco. *Help me find you.* Roy was already up on his feet as I ran ahead into the corridor.

Enrik sprinted past me and placed his finger on the scanner by the door then punched in his access code.

A red light and a sharp tone denied him entry. He put his finger back on the scanner and re-entered the code. Once again, rejected.

The iCube gave up on its warning and switched to one continuous, piercing tone that sounded painfully like a flat-line. Its glow began to pulsate slowly like a fading heartbeat.

"Holy fuck, man!" Roy grasped his own head with both hands.

I marched to the scanner, pulling out my handkerchief to wipe it clean, when suddenly—

The door flung wide open.

For a moment, we all gaped at the entrance, then a tall, imposing man emerged.

Enrik let out a huge sigh. "Thank God."

"No, it's just me, Dr. Grant."

I rushed through the open door, the iCube wailing its single, desperate note. *Please, please be all right.* I couldn't even pause to wait for my vision to adjust to the dimly lit interior and, half-blind, allowed myself to be guided to The Cellar and eased the iCube in. Roy was right beside me, plugging in the cables, and soon the iCube grew silent then glowed with renewed radiance.

A subliminal whoosh coursed through the air, and I blew out my cheeks.

"She's all right," Roy said. "We're good." He gave two thumbs up.

I turned around to survey the room. In the center stood a glass chamber the same size as what we had at the Green Manor. But this wasn't an empty shell. It was an airtight container of electrified plasma that Grant had requisitioned for Torula's 3D expression.

A handful of scientists—mere silhouettes in the darkened room —sat or stood behind a variety of equipment scattered around the glass enclosure that stood like an abandoned and empty display in a forgotten museum.

Then, from inside the chamber, radiating from its very top, came a faint blush of light. I ran both hands gruffly through my hair, hoping to fix some of the mess that I was, as I walked towards the chamber, throat dry, eyes misty, heart thudding madly.

With the faintest sound of a sizzle and swirl, a vortex of light appeared inside the glass enclosure, and from its apex, a shimmering orb descended.

"Spore," I whispered, recognizing her before I even saw her.

Two bright points of violet-blue twinkled and danced like butterflies. As though alighting on flowers, they stopped in midair and sparkled. The next instant, I was staring into Torula's eyes.

Subtle sounds of exclamation filled the room.

"Touchdown," Enrik said.

"Houston," Roy said, "you got yourself an astralnaut."

"Yes, indeed we do," Grant said.

Torula looked exactly as I had expected her to—skin like porcelain, dressed in rough low riders and a white tank top, her dark hair billowing in a nonexistent wind.

Barely breathing, I stepped closer to the chamber.

"Mist now light flowers," Torula said, in a voice that was undeniably hers. She looked so beautiful, glowing . . . and alive.

"Heaven on Earth." I pressed my palm against the glass as I stared into Torula's eyes. "Let's get started."

THERE'S MORE TO COME

A Ghost for a Clue is the first book in the *Immortology* series. If you enjoyed this book, please let others know. Your valuable feedback could take the story down new avenues, and you might even inspire spinoffs down the road!

Please leave a review at the site of your choice and invite others to join the conversation around *Immortology*.

To find out when the next book of C.L.R. Draeco will be released, sign up at:

clrdraeco.com

ACKNOWLEDGMENTS

My journey as a published author was long, bumpy and full of detours. The idea for *Immortology* formed in my head decades ago, but it had to vie for time and attention versus life in general. The draft made its first appearance, one rough chapter at a time, in the Online Writing Workshop (OWW) for Science Fiction, Fantasy and Horror—and languished there, unfinished, because part of me kept thinking maybe the story I was piecing together wasn't headed anywhere. Eventually, I did go back to OWW, where dozens of members took turns pointing out what I did wrong or right, until what started out a gnarl of nonsense came out stylized and sensible enough for the world to see. Most reviewers read only one chapter or two; several stuck around for a little more, and I am grateful to all of them. A few, however, became invaluable, and I give them special mention here—the reliable few who read this manuscript from start to finish (in slow-moving increments), giving me words of encouragement and making me believe I had a story lurking in those chapters. Profound thanks to B. Morris Allen, Steve Brady and Henry Szabranski who were there in the earlier years. And more recently, to Robyn Wescombe and Tony Valiulis. I owe you all my courage to write.

To Raphael, Yasmin, Brian, and Nadene, your critical eye in the final stretch gave this book the boost it needed to get to the finish line in its best shape.

Most of all, to my purpose, my loves, my life—A, N, and R. I thank you with every breath I take.

ABOUT THE AUTHOR

C.L.R. Draeco is a writer, university professor, and advertising executive whose childhood home burnt down from an electrical fire in the 1970s. After the house was rebuilt, visitors began to suggest that the house was haunted.

The Draeco family didn't believe it at first, until slowly, they began experiencing anomalies themselves. Those experiences were what inspired the author to explore scientific explanations for such phenomena. Non-fiction titles offered a wealth of ghostly anecdotes and either debunked them or left most questions unanswered. There was an absolute dearth of scientific explanations. Fiction, on the other hand, provided supreme escapes from reality —either in the genres of horror or paranormal fantasy. None, as far as Draeco could tell, looked at the supernatural through the perspective of level-headed, scientifically minded adults aiming to solve a mystery while keeping the story relatively grounded in reality.

Thus was born *Immortology*—a hard science-fiction book series that explores what might happen if a group of highly-intelligent, well-educated people of good repute worked together to give the afterlife a serious look. *A Ghost for a Clue*, the first book in the series, begins with the challenge of creating a scenario wherein characters that fit that mold end up getting involved in the bizarre.

Draeco is married to a photojournalist who travels the world. Their two "kids" are now a Doctor of Medicine while the other is studying to be a Doctor of Psychology. They share their home with two dogs, four cats, a few fish, a bearded dragon, and no ghosts.

Lightning Source UK Ltd.
Milton Keynes UK
UKHW040715290422
402257UK00002B/269

9 781648 263828